EXTREMIS

The first thing that crossed Tazendra's mind as she awoke was the reflection that she had been asleep for a long time. Then her memory began to return—walking into her home, the sudden explosions behind her, the feeling of a spell penetrating her defenses, and the sudden dizziness. And, as her memories came back to her, she realized that she was not alone, but, on the contrary, there were two individuals standing over her.

"We are together," said Illista, bowing. "Just as you will soon be, if I may use the expression, apart."

"Indeed?" said Tazendra, yawning. "You will forgive me if I am a little weary after my long sleep. Otherwise, you may be certain, I should display more emotion."

"Oh, we don't mind," said Illista. "No doubt, you will display more emotion presently."

"What am I to lose?" asked Tazendra.

"Everything," said Grita.

"All at once?" asked Tazendra in a tone of idle curiosity.

"No, we are beginning with your left ear."

"Ah, splendid. I have never liked that one. Indeed, I have often considered removing it myself."

"We are pleased to be able to perform this service for you."

"Well, why do you not begin?"

"Oh, we will in a moment, I assure you. We are only waiting for a guest."

BOOKS BY STEVEN BRUST

THE DRAGAERAN NOVELS

Brokedown Palace

THE KHAAVREN ROMANCES
The Phoenix Guards
Five Hundred Years After
The Viscount of Adrilankha,
which comprises *The Paths of the Dead*,
The Lord of Castle Black, and *Sethra Lavode*

THE VLAD TALTOS NOVELS
Jhereg
Yendi
Teckla
Taltos
Phoenix
Athyra
Orca
Dragon
Issola

OTHER NOVELS

To Reign in Hell
The Sun, the Moon, and the Stars
Cowboy Feng's Space Bar and Grille
The Gypsy (with Megan Lindholm)
Freedom and Necessity (with Emma Bull)

Sethra Lavode

BOOK THREE OF
THE VISCOUNT OF ADRILANKHA

STEVEN BRUST, P.J.F.

A TOM DOHERTY ASSOCIATES BOOK
NEW YORK

SETHRA LAVODE: BOOK THREE OF THE VISCOUNT OF ADRILANKHA

Edited by Teresa Nielsen Hayden

A Tor Book
Published by Tom Doherty Associates, LLC
175 Fifth Avenue
New York, NY 10010

www.tor.com

Tor® is a registered trademark of Tom Doherty Associates, LLC.

ISBN 0-812-53418-2
EAN 978-0812-53418-4
Library of Congress Catalog Card Number: 2003063454

First edition: April 2004
First mass market edition: March 2005

Printed in the United States of America

The Viscount of Adrilankha

BOOK THREE

Sethra Lavode

Describing Certain Events that Occurred
Between the 1st and 3rd Years
Of the Reign of Empress Zerika the Fourth

Submitted to the Imperial Library
By Springsign Manor
House of the Hawk
On this 3rd day of the Month of the Athyra
Of the Year of the Vallista
Of the Turn of the Jhereg
Of the Phase of the Phoenix
Of the Reign of the Dragon
In the Cycle of the Phoenix
In the Great Cycle of the Dragon;
Or, in the 179th Year
Of the Glorious Reign
Of the Empress Norathar the Second

By Sir Paarfi of Roundwood
House of the Hawk
(His Arms, Seal, Lineage Block)

Presented, as Always,
To Marchioness Poorborn
With Gratitude and Affection

Cast of Characters

Blackchapel and Castle Black

Morrolan—An Apprentice witch
Erik—A fool
Miska—A coachman
Arra—A Priestess
Teldra—An Issola
Fentor e'Mondaar—A Dragonlord
Fineol—A Vallista from Nacine
Oidwa—A Tsalmoth
Esteban—An Eastern witch

The Kanefthali Mountains

Skinter—A Count, afterward Duke
Marchioness of Habil—His cousin and strategist
Betraan e'Lanya—His tactician
Tsanaali—A lieutenant in Skinter's army
Izak—A general in Skinter's army
Brawre—A general in Skinter's army
Saakrew—An officer in Skinter's army
Udaar—An adviser and diplomatist
Hirtrinkneff—His assistant

The Society of the Porker Poker

Piro—The Viscount of Adrilankha
Lewchin—An Issola
Shant—A Dzurlord
Zivra—House unknown

Whitecrest and Environs

Daro—The Countess of Whitecrest
Khaavren—Her husband

Lar—A lackey
Cook—A cook
Maid—A maid

Dzur Mountain and Environs

Kytraan—The son of an old friend
Sethra Lavode—The Enchantress of Dzur Mountain
Tukko—Sethra's servant
Sethra the Younger—Sethra's apprentice
The Necromancer—A demon
Tazendra—A Dzurlord wizard
Mica—Her lackey
The Sorceress in Green—A sorceress
Berigner—A general serving Sethra Lavode
Taasra—A brigadier serving under Berigner
Karla e'Baritt—A military engineer

Arylle and Environs

Aerich Temma—Duke of Arylle
Fawnd—His servant
Steward—His other servant

On the Road

Orlaan/Grita—A sorceress in training
Wadre—A brigand leader
Mora—His lieutenant
Grassfog—A bandit
Iatha—A bandit
Thong—A bandit
Ritt—A bandit
Belly—A bandit
Ryunac e'Terics—A lieutenant in Skinter's army
Magra e'Lanya—Ryunac's sergeant
Brimford—An Easterner and Warlock
Tsani—Grassfog's sister
Tevna—A pyrologist

Elde Island

Corthina Fi Dalcalda—King of Elde
Tresh—An exile
Nywak—Her servant
Gardimma—Imperial Ambassador to Elde

The Halls of Judgment

Barlen
Verra
Moranthë
Kéurana
Ordwynac
Nyssa
Kelchor
Trout
Tri'nagore

Miscellaneous Others

Sennya—Dzur Heir
Ibronka—Her daughter
Clari—Ibronka's maid
Röaanac—A Tiassa
Malyapon—His wife
Röaana—Their daughter
Haro—Their servant
Prince Tiawall—Hawk Heir
Ritsak—Lyorn Heir
Jami—A Teckla in Mistyvale County
Marel—Proprietor of a general store

Preface

—∞—

Which Consists of a Succinct Summary Of All That Has Gone Before As Well as a Daring Literary Adventure Embarked Upon for the Benefit Of the Loyal Reader

Having, on the occasion of introducing the previous volume of this history, said all that needs to be said concerning the wisdom, or, rather, the lack of wisdom, of dividing a story into sections, we do not feel the need to repeat ourselves. That is, all of those who have read the previous volume understand our objections to making such necessarily arbitrary breaks in what was meant to be a single, unified text; and those who have not read the previous volumes will, without our having to say anything, quickly come to understand. However, in the course of preparing this summary, we came to the decision to do something that, so far as we know, has never been done in the history of letters—a daring step that we have chosen to take out of a sense of duty to the reader.

Instead of confining these few pages to an explication of the events which are already known to those of our readers who have done us the courtesy of remaining with us throughout the several volumes of this history, we have chosen to break with an iron-bound tradition for such summaries, and include, toward the end of this section, new information—that is to say, information which will be of value to all readers.

It is possible that we will come under attack for such a departure from tradition from our brothers in letters, as well as those who feed upon literature in the same way as certain insects feed upon deceased animals; but in our desire to be of service to the reader, we are willing and even happy to brave these attacks.

That noted, we will at once pass on to explain, as laconically as possible, the circumstances at the beginning of this volume of our history, and how those circumstances developed.

We have been following, first of all, two Dragonlords: Morrolan and Kâna. The latter of these has been attempting to expand his own holdings until they become, in effect, the Empire re-created. He achieved significant success, having started his projects around the fiftieth year after Adron's Disaster, so that, by the time two hundreds of years had passed, nearly half of the area that was once the Empire was either under his control or threatened by his forces.

The other, Morrolan, the Count of Southmoor, had been raised in the East in ignorance, not only of his heritage, but, indeed, even of his race. Early in our history, we saw how he migrated from the East along with several hundreds of practitioners of the Eastern heathen magical arts. He journied to Dzur Mountain under the impression that he was owed tribute, Dzur Mountain being part of his ancestral holdings. He received an immensely powerful artifact from the Enchantress, though we are inclined to believe this was less in the nature of tribute than it was a gift of friendship, or perhaps the product of inspired foresight on the part of the enigmatic Sethra.

Another figure whom we have been following with great attention is, in fact, Sethra Lavode herself, the Enchantress of Dzur Mountain. Seeing that the true Phoenix Heir, Zerika, had reached a sufficient age, Sethra revealed to this worthy Zerika's true name and destiny, and sent her, with the Viscount of Adrilankha, our old friend Tazendra, and a few others to the Paths of the Dead, where she managed to convince the Lords of Judgment to give her the Orb. She emerged from the Halls of Judgment, and so the Interregnum came to an end. This, the reader should understand, led directly to the Battle of Dzur Mountain, as this battle was, above all else, Kâna's attempt to take the Orb by force. He concentrated his two armies, together numbering over seventy thousand strong, on Dzur Mountain, which he knew was Zerika's destination. The attempt was defeated, largely thanks to Morrolan, as well as to assistance sent by Sethra Lavode, and a necromantic demon sent by the Lords of Judgment.

We should add that, after the battle, Morrolan caused to be built a floating castle, as was a tradition among his family, which had often lived in such structures before the Interregnum, either because of the ease of defending such a place, or else simply because they were able to.

With Kâna's army defeated and in retreat, Zerika marched from Dzur Mountain to Adrilankha and began construction of the Imperial Palace, unaware that the Pretender had other schemes working in case the military attack had failed. In particular, Grita, the daughter of our friends' old enemy, has offered her services to Kâna in exchange for help in achieving vengeance against Khaavren, Aerich, Pel, and Tazendra. She has been of no small help to the Pretender, in particular succeeding in finding Illista, an exiled Phoenix who has long nursed a hatred of our friends, and who, like Grita, is happy to assist Kâna in exchange for securing her revenge.

We have mentioned Piro, the Viscount of Adrilankha. It is also important for the reader to understand that he has fallen in love with the Dzurlord Ibronka, only daughter of Her Highness Sennya, the Dzur Heir. Khaavren, for his part, was outraged at Piro's wishes to marry outside of his House, and, after harsh words between them, Piro, Ibronka, and their friends, including the remnants of a certain band of brigands who had first been enemies and after soldiers of Her Majesty, have set up as highwaymen in a region some hundred miles northwest of Dzur Mountain.

With the reader's permission, we feel that, as we promised above, this is a good time to present new information: to wit, a general picture of what was occurring in the Empire during this crucial period, that is to say, what is usually considered the initial year of Zerika's Reign.

The reader should, first of all, understand that a confederation as strong and as large as that created by Kâna and Habil would not simply dissolve as the result of a military defeat or two. Though severely damaged, like a wounded toe-lizard, it thrashed around a bit, pulled its head in, retreated, hissed, and survived. By the time several months had passed, Kâna had pulled back so that he could reasonably claim to exercise his influence over the western third of the Empire, with the exception of the Fingers, which, except for its few ports, was of little importance anyway. Additionally, certain pockets above the Great Sea of Amorphia claimed allegiance to the Pretender, but this is generally considered to be a fluke, caused by age-old resentment against a previous Phoenix Emperor who took mining rights from various of the counts of the district.

While the geographical regions of support for the two supposed Emperors are clearly identifiable, the breakdown among the various strata of society is less clear. Zerika's support was strongest among the Lyorn, Tiassa, and Hawk nobles, a statistic that would seem irrational, as these Houses stood to gain the Orb sooner with a Dragon on the throne. Yet Lyorns have always held that the Orb was sacred, and, in such questions, the Tiassas have more often than not followed the Lyorns' lead. As for the Hawklords, many of them had interest in some of the iron-rich regions of the Southeast, and, as most of the smelters were near the Shallow Sea—that is to say, a region firmly under Zerika's control—they hesitated to offend her.

The House of the Dragon was, as the reader might expect, split, primarily according to family ties of those serving in the various armies, and secondarily according to other interests; but for the most part, they tended to support Kâna, because he was, after all, a Dragon himself. Most of the Dzurlords also sided with the Pretender, because so many of their holdings were near the Grand Canal and dependent upon it, and nearly the entire length of the Canal ran through the region firmly under his control.

We should note here that, as the reader may observe, it is, in fact, the influence of commerce, trade, and the practical considerations of day-to-day life that tended to exert the most influence on the loyalties and allegiances of the Houses, not high-sounding considerations of ideals, such as is believed by historians of the romantic school. Yet, to give credit to those historians, it is often those individuals who form exceptions to these tendencies who exert the most influence on the course of history, and are, in any case, the most pleasurable to study.

But to continue: Additional support for Zerika came from the Iorich, because most of them tend to live in cities, and, as a general rule, her support was stronger among those whose income depended upon the sort of manufacturing that was transported by sea, whereas Kâna had considerable sympathy among those who depended upon overland transportation, such as the Athyra (many of whom had logging interests in the region to the west of the Pushta) as well as the Chreotha and Vallista. Of the Orca, those involved directly in shipping firmly backed Zerika, who controlled the most important seaports (not the least of which was proud Adrilankha herself), but the rest—which is to say, the majority—favored Kâna for the same reason as the Chreotha and Vallista: because he controlled so much of the interior transportation.

In many ways, transportation, as the reader may see, was a key issue; at least, it seemed so to Her Majesty. She was never ashamed to say, later, that she had studied many of the improvements instituted by the Pretender and had learned from them. She immediately implemented and extended his system of posts, which included the delivery of mails and use of post horses by any peer, as well as those on Imperial business. While this was not tremendously successful as a means of garnering support among the more recalcitrant nobles, it quickly turned into a more general system for the delivery of mail, until we have the liberal, inexpensive, and efficient system that we enjoy to-day.

One of the more daring (and controversial) decisions of Zerika's early reign was that, while she maintained the army, she did not increase it, instead devoting what funds she was able to garner from those nobles who pledged loyalty to her as individuals (decisions on approval by the Houses and the Council of Princes still being some years in the future) to the improvement of roadways, hoping to lure in this fashion more of the merchants.

By the time fourteen or fifteen months had expired, this support was still not especially noticeable. Everyone knew that Kâna was still formidable. To be sure, Zerika had received a pledge of support—that is to say, a promise of future recognition—from the the House of the Tiassa, but none of the others (except, naturally, the House of the Phoenix, which consisted of Zerika herself) had yet even gone that far, all of them preferring an attitude of waiting to see how matters would play out after the inevitable clash.

This was insufficient for Zerika, who continued negotiating with the Heirs and the Delegates, and making such decrees as she thought would win them over. While these maneuvers were not met with a great deal of success, it is certainly the case that none of the Houses ever gave serious consideration to recognizing Kâna from the moment Zerika arrived in Adrilankha.

She also, we should add, entered into negotiations with Elde and Greenaere, as well as with certain of the Eastern kingdoms. And, while she wished to send an envoy to the Queen of Landsight, she did not, at this time, have access to a ship that was able to make this journey. These negotiations produced two results: The King of Greenaere did, indeed, officially recognize her as Empress, and an envoy arrived from one of the Eastern kingdoms, asking for (and receiving) certain guaranties about the safety of those from that kingdom who had emigrated to Adrilankha during the Interregnum. While this kingdom did not, during this period, actually recognize Zerika as Empress, this was due primarily to the length of time required for messengers to go back and forth from the East—teleportation not being possible for Easterners, and there being no human who knew the Eastern lands well enough to make the attempt.

Other than this, much of Her Majesty's time was, as we have indicated earlier, devoted to planning for the new Imperial Palace. The chief architect was the Vallista Baron Fernbrook, who, though old, being over twenty-one hundred years of age, nevertheless retained all of his wits and most of his memories. In addition, representatives of each House were consulted, so that Zerika could give some measure of control to each of the Houses as to its own Wing. It is significant that even the Teckla received such an invitation, although through their representative they delegated all such matters to a Vallista named Sandlewood.

The ground was broken on the new Imperial Palace at a ceremony held on the first day of summer: the fifth day of the month of the Hawk.

During the subsequent months, proud Adrilankha came to life once more. The grain exchange and the silver exchange were cleaned, refurbished, and officially opened. Several banking institutions were either begun or re-emerged from a long quietus. In a particularly daring and successful move, the Empress announced that the Empire would once more accept the filing of protection from debts. This was daring because, in fact, the Empire had nothing like the resources to carry this out on any sort of scale. But Zerika believed, and, in the end, was proven correct, that this announcement would give sufficient boost to businesses that it would not, in fact, ever be used. Moreover, it gave the impression of a return to a normally functioning Empire.

The slaughterhouses in South Adrilankha began to work once more, mostly using the labor of the Easterners who had settled there during the Interregnum, as kethna and cattle were driven in from the north. This was good news to everyone except those toward whom the winds blew from these slaughterhouses. Another effect this had was that more Easterners, who had been living to the north and east of the city and barely surviving as free farmers, gave up their nearly worthless plots and moved into South Adrilankha to work in these slaughterhouses. Although this concentration of Easterners (and, indeed, many human Teckla) would eventually lead to social unrest, this would not occur for hundreds of years, and so is beyond the scope of our history.

As a sort of footnote, we should add that certain aristocrats, including the Dzurlord Shant, whose holdings were north of the city, lost some number of Teckla to the employment available in South Adrilankha, which proves that, contrary to claims of those who operated the slaughterhouses, some Teckla did leave the land to which they were legally bound. This was followed up in a few cases, but the infant Dragaeran police force was mostly unable to cope with anything in South Adrilankha.

This, then, is the general state of the Empire. As we open this chapter of our history, our friends are not yet aware of Kâna's continuing machinations against the Orb.

Sethra Lavode

BOOK FIVE

In Which Matters of Great Historical Moment
Such as the Role of the Orb in Determining the Emperor
Are Brought to a Head

Chapter the Sixty-Ninth

How the Empress, Attempting to Work on the Design of the Imperial Palace, Manages Those Who Interrupt Her

On the ground floor of Whitecrest Manor was a wide enclosed terrace, the twin to the open terrace on the other side where the Count and Countess of Whitecrest were accustomed to take their morning klava and watch the ocean. The enclosed terrace, of course, was used during inclement weather and had been the place where the Countess was accustomed to carry on her work—except that now it was the room where the Empress was carrying on her official business. The room was reached by a hallway with two entrances, one leading down to the parlor, and the other to a flight of steps that went up to the second story of the Manor. This second entrance had been sealed off, and a guard was posted at the first, with instructions to admit no one without permission of either Her Majesty or the officer on duty.

The officer on duty, of course, was generally Khaavren, and it happened to be Khaavren on this day who entered the room, bowed to Zerika, and said, "A gentleman to see Your Majesty. It is Prince Tiwall, of the House of the Hawk."

"Ah!" said Zerika, looking up from the papers she had been studying, which papers were, in turn, a single entry in a seemingly endless list of details to be decided upon with regard to the design of the Imperial Palace. Before her were not only lists and diagrams, but several different models of the future structures, or portions there-of, one of which was a full five feet high and more than fifteen feet in length, and occupied most of the room.

This activity had taken up so much of Her Majesty's time and effort that she was often impatient with any interruptions. On hearing who was there, the Orb, which had been circling her head with a beige color of distraction, first turned to a faint red of irritation, then, after she had reflected, to a warm orange of pleasurable excitement. "Send him in at once," she said.

Khaavren bowed and, as he had been trained to do for so long, did as he was told.

"I greet Your Majesty," said Tiwall, a stern, forbidding gentleman of well over two thousand years, whose white hair, worn long and brushed back from his noble's point, made a stark contrast to his dark complexion.

"Come, Your Highness," said Zerika. "That isn't so bad. You greet me as Your Majesty. Does this mean that I have cause to hope the House of the Hawk looks with favor upon my claim?"

Tiwall bowed. "I use the title because of my own belief, madam, that the Orb is the Empire."

"Your own belief—what of your House?"

"Oh, as to my House—"

"Well?"

"They are considering the matter."

"Considering it?"

"Your Majesty must understand that these are difficult times, and no one wishes to be hasty."

"Yet, Your Highness has decided."

"I have, and I beg Your Majesty to believe that I am using all of my influence within the House on your behalf."

"I am glad to hear it. For my part, I shall be glad to use what influence I have on Your Highness's behalf."

"Oh, if Your Majesty means that—"

"Yes?" said Zerika, frowning.

"It could be of immeasurable help in that cause in which we are united."

"I do not understand what Your Highness does me the honor to tell me. Speak more plainly, I beg."

"I only wish to say that should Your Majesty act on my behalf, or, more precisely, on behalf of my House, it would be of great help to me in convincing them."

Zerika looked at him carefully. "Does the House of the Hawk wish to bargain with the Empire?"

"It is their contention—and believe me, I speak of them, not of me—that, not having been recognized by the Council of Princes, it is not yet the Empire."

"I see. So, then, the House of the Hawk wishes to bargain with a certain Phoenix who happens to have the Orb circling her head."

"Your Majesty has stated the situation admirably."

"I see. And what does the House of the Hawk feel this recognition is worth?"

"If Your Majesty will permit me, before I answer the question you have done me the honor to ask."

"Permit you to what, Highness?"

"To explain the situation as I see it. Perhaps there are aspects that I fail to understand."

"I doubt that," murmured Zerika. Then she said, "Very well, Prince. State the situation as you understand it."

Tiwall bowed and said, "Well, let us see. You already have approval of the Lyorn, have you not?"

"The Count of Flowerpot Hill and Environs came to Adrilankha within days of my arrival here, and at once pledged the support of his House."

"And of course, you have the support of the House of the Phoenix."

"As I am the only one in the House, yes, it is true that I gave myself my full support. And I even plan to continue doing so."

"But Your Majesty has not yet heard from the Dragon or the Athyra, which are, I should point out, the two most powerful Houses."

"Again, you are correct."

"It must be said that the indications of allegiance you have received from the Tiassa are important. They have influence."

"I received a letter only yester-day from Count Röaanac in which he informs me of the decision of his House and pledges his personal good-will. Your Highness is singularly well informed."

Tiwall bowed and said, "So then, will Your Majesty permit me to make an observation?"

"Certainly, Highness. Do so, by all means, especially if it brings us to the point of this political survey you have just made for my benefit."

Tiwall, after clearing his throat, said, "My House occupies an unusual middle ground. We have more influence than the Jhereg and the Teckla, but not so much as the Dragon and the Athyra. We have been consulted—informally, I should add—by parties from the Issola and the Iorich, as well as certain of the merchant Houses."

"Very well, go on."

"Should I manage to persuade my House to accept Your Majesty as the Empress that you are, well—"

"Yes, if you should convince them, as I know you are trying to do?"

"I am certain we would bring with us, as a matter of course, the Iorich, the Chreotha, and most probably the Orca as well."

"I see."

"Once that happens, I cannot imagine the Jhereg and the Teckla not falling into line."

"It seems as if Your Highness is doing my planning for me."

"Not in the least, Your Majesty. I'm attempting to explain—"

"Never mind, Highness. Go on."

"Yes, Your Majesty. I wish only to observe that, should my negotiations within my own House be successful, it may have the effect, by itself, of very nearly bringing the entire Council of Princes to Your Majesty's support."

Zerika remained silent, and the Orb, slowing down a trifle in response to this contemplation, took on a dark green shade as she considered, as well as flickering slightly when she consulted it for some detail on Tiwall's history or family. To be sure, this Hawklord was no one's fool, and he was, as Hawks always are, well informed. But how honest was he, within the lies he was telling that were meant to be seen through?

"Very well," said Zerika after a moment. "What might the Empire grant your House that could help you to convince them that I am the true Empress, representing their interests as well as everyone else's within the vast Empire that we once had and, with the Favor, will again?"

"Tolerably little, Majesty."

"We shall see."

"An estate."

"That is easy enough; there are many estates."

"A particular estate, Majesty."

"Then that is different. Who owns it now?"

"No one. That is to say, the Empire."

"So much the better. Is it valuable?"

"I will not deny to Your Majesty that it is."

"What is its value?"

"Nowhere else that I know of are iron ore, oil, and coal all to be found in the same, narrow region of a few small mountains and valleys. There are refining operations near-by where, before the disaster, kerosene was produced, and there is no shortage of waterways."

"And you say, these counties are not owned?"

"Not one of them. A few had a baron or two ruling part of them before the Disaster, but since then not even a younger son of any of them remain."

"How many counties are we speaking of?"

"Five."

"How much in area?"

"Perhaps twelve hundred square miles."

"That is not so much. Where are these counties, exactly?"

"Just south of the Collier Hills."

"Ah, ah!"

"Your Majesty knows them?"

"Nearly. I have just promised three of them to a certain Dragonlord who gave me some assistance against the Pretender. I had no idea they were so valuable."

"You have promised them? Ah, that is too bad!"

"Is there nothing else that will do?"

"I fear not, Your Majesty," said the Hawk, bowing deeply. "If I may be excused—"

"Your Highness may not," said Zerika coldly.

Tiwall bowed again, and waited in the perfect attitude of the courtier.

The Empress was discovering, as Morrolan had, that to govern others requires one to spend more time in consideration than one is used to—either that, or one must inevitably become a careless administrator, and history says nothing good about careless administrators. Therefore, Zerika considered, and, after considering, she said, "Very well, you may have your five counties."

The Hawklord bowed. "I believe I will be able to bring Your Majesty good news within a month."

"I depend upon it."

"Oh," he said, suddenly looking worried. "I hope Your Majesty did not interpret my words as a guarantee for any House other than my own."

"I hope," replied the Empress, "that Your Highness did not interpret my words as a guarantee of five counties to be given to your House."

"And yet—I understand, Your Majesty."

"That is good, Highness. It is important to understand one another."

Tiwall bowed to acknowledge this observation Her Majesty did him the honor to share, and inquired, "Will there be anything else?"

"No. You may go."

"Your Majesty will hear from me soon."

When he was gone, Zerika returned to her work, comparing certain figures on paper to some of the models and drumming her fingertips on the table, until the captain once again entered the room, and said, "Another gentleman begs to have a word with Your Majesty."

Zerika had been reflecting on what sort of passageway ought to connect the Imperial Wing with the Iorich Wing, which included certain philosophical issues about the relationship between the needs of the Empire and the abstraction of justice and therefore could not be easily delegated. She permitted a grimace to cross her countenance as she said, "Who is it this time?"

"It is I," said Khaavren.

"Yes, yes. But I mean, who wishes to see me?"

"The captain of your guard," said Khaavren coolly.

"But you are the captain of my guard."

"Then, it appears, it is I who wish to have a word with my Empress."

Her Majesty's eyes narrowed, and she said, "You must break yourself of this habit, Captain, of answering in tones that might be construed as deficient in respect for the Orb. Even when we are alone, I do not consider it in the best of taste, and I am surprised that an old soldier such as yourself, who has served the Empire for so many years, would permit himself such liberties."

"I beg Your Majesty's pardon," said Khaavren. "With age, we soldiers become brittle, and the least pressure upon us causes us to snap back quickly lest we break."

"I do not believe, Captain, that you are in any danger of breaking."

"I beg Your Majesty's pardon, but I must do myself the honor of disagreeing."

"You say, then, that you are in danger of breaking?"

"Your Majesty must know that I am old."

Zerika quickly consulted the Orb, and did some fast arithmetic, after which she said, "My dear Captain, you have not seen a thousand years."

"That is true, but Your Majesty ought to understand that each year of Interregnum, now thankfully passed—"

"As to that, we shall see, with the Favor."

"—must count as ten years when calculating my age."

"So many?"

"At the very least."

"Well, perhaps the Tiassa do not reckon figures as others do."

"That may be; but I swear it is the truth."

"Very well, then, Captain, I accept that you are old. What of it? Your service is still valuable."

"Oh, it is good of Your Majesty to say so."

"Not at all. I hope, at least, you do not dispute me on this as well?"

"Alas—"

"What, you say that you are no longer useful to me?"

"I am old, Your Majesty, and tired. I feel that, in having the honor to have served Your Majesty in so far as arriving to Adrilankha, I have done my duty."

"So then? What are you saying, Captain. Speak plainly."

"Your Majesty, I wish to offer you my resignation."

"What? I cannot believe it! You? Resign?"

"It is my fondest wish, Majesty."

"You offer your resignation."

"Exactly."

"And if I do not accept it?"

"Then I must find a way to convince Your Majesty to do so." He placed a paper on the table in front of her. "Here are a list of certain of my officers in whom I have great confidence; some of them were with me before the Disaster. Any of them can easily step into my boots."

"But why, Captain? Come, speak frankly."

"I have already had the honor to do so."

Zerika looked at the soldier carefully, noting his unbent posture, the attitude of humble respect that can only come from one who is secure of his own place, the lines of sorrow and joy on his face. At length, she said, "My lord, you are not being entirely honest with me."

"Your Majesty?"

"Do you require me to repeat myself?"

"I heard, but I do not understand."

"What could be plainer? I believe that you wish to resign, but I do not believe you have told me the true reason."

"I can only do myself the honor of repeating myself to Your Majesty, and, as that might be considered disrespectful, I must refrain from doing so, wherefore I stand mute."

"Permit me to observe, Captain, that you require more words to stand mute than you should have required to answer my question. So now I do myself the honor of asking again. Why do you wish to leave my service? Does it have something to do with your son, with whom you have quarreled?"

At these words, Khaavren stiffened almost imperceptibly, but he looked the Empress fully in the face and said, "No."

"Well then, what is the reason?"

Khaavren bowed his head and stood mute, this time without accompanying explanations.

The Orb turned to a dark, forbidding red, and Zerika slapped her palm upon the table. "Very well, then, Captain. You have tendered your resignation; I accept it. Farewell."

Khaavren bowed low to Her Majesty, and turning crisply on his heel, left the Empress's presence at a good, martial pace, which carried him, after two steps, to the Countess's apartment. The door being open, he passed within. Daro—whom we confess to our shame has been unfairly neglected by this history—had been, since giving the Manor over to Her Majesty, using the small secretary to carry out the business of the county. She looked up from this work as Khaavren entered, and stood up, smiling. Khaavren at once approached her and tenderly kissed her hand.

"It is such a pleasure, Countess, to be home, because I am able to see you every day."

"I give you my word, sir, that I share fully in this pleasure. But come, do not stand there so. Sit and speak with me."

"Nothing would give me greater pleasure, I assure you," said Khaavren, accordingly sitting down next to the countess.

"Well," said she, "what have you to communicate to me?"

"Communicate, madam?"

"Certainly. Can you conceive that I might live with you for hundreds of years without knowing when you have something to tell me, and are at a loss for how to begin? And so, sir, I beg you to simply tell me, whether it be good, ill, or merely amusing."

"As to which it is, in all honesty, I do not know. It could be any of them. But to say it—for you know you are correct on all counts—it is this: I have resigned my commission."

"Resigned?"

"Exactly."

"When?"

"Two minutes ago."

"So that—"

"Yes, I am completely at liberty."

The Countess looked at him carefully. "It seems a hasty action."

"Perhaps."

"Is it because of—"

"No," said Khaavren shortly, before she could pronounce the name of their son. This was a sore subject between them, and had caused a certain amount of strain; although the bonds of affection between them had not frayed, nevertheless Khaavren had no wish for them to become tied up on such a discussion now, when it could only lead to the issue being entangled with more tension.

"What then?" she said. "For I know there must be a reason."

Khaavren frowned. "The truth is—"

"Well?"

"I am not pleased with this little Phoenix."

"How, you are not?"

"You perceive, I remained loyal to Tortaalik, with all of his changing moods, and indecision, and impotence; but I was a younger man then."

"My dear Count, you are not as old as you pretend."

"Perhaps not. And yet, I find I have no patience for this young Phoenix."

"What has she done?"

"She has given away, to the House of the Hawk, certain counties that were promised to the Lord Morrolan, whom I consider to be a gentleman of the first order; indeed, he made such a strong impression on me that, were it not for the differences in our age, I could think of him as a friend. He reminded me of—"

"Yes? Of—"

"Well, if truth be told, of Lord Adron."

"Oh!"

Khaavren shrugged. "I know that to speak his name is to conjure an evil, both to the Empire and to myself, for he could, indeed, be called the author of all of my misfortune. And yet, I always liked him, and thought him an honorable gentleman, if headstrong and misguided. And Aerich feels the same way, which seems to me to prove the case."

"Oh, my dear Count, I do not dispute with you on Adron's character."

"As I have said, Morrolan reminds me of him. And, even if he did not, it was wrong of her to take back what she had given him."

"And so you have given her your resignation?"

"And she has accepted it, yes."

"And did you tell her why?"

"I told her that I was old and tired."

"And did she believe you?"

"No, but I wore her down with repetition. I did not presume to tell Her Majesty that I judged her actions."

"And you were right not to, only—"

"Yes?"

"My lord husband, I do not think that is what is disturbing your peace of mind. Or, at least, that is not all of it."

Khaavren started to speak, stopped, then shrugged. "Perhaps not all of it."

"It has not been easy for you, since the Disaster, my lord."

"Nor has it for you, madam wife."

"Oh, as for me, you know I am always cheerful. But I worry about you. And now this latest blow—"

"With Her Majesty?"

"You know that is not the matter to which I refer."

Khaavren lowered his eyes. "I know," he said. "But let us not discuss it."

"On the contrary, my lord. I think we should discuss nothing else."

"Very well, let us discuss it. What else could I have done?"

"What if it had been you?"

"Me? How could it be me? Would I have wanted to marry outside of my House?"

"Nearly."

"What do you tell me?"

"My lord husband, do you remember our first conversation?"

"The Gods! I think so! Your gown showed most of your back. It was red, with gold lace about the collar and the sleeves."

Daro smiled. "Your memory is excellent. What else do you remember?"

"I remember that you thought I was arresting you."

"Yes. And you thought I was a Lyorn."

"That is true, I did."

"And it seems to me that, even believing I was a Lyorn, you spoke with tolerable freedom."

"Was it displeasing to you?"

"Oh, not in the least; and the proof is that I am here. But, nevertheless, if I *had* been a Lyorn—"

"Were you a Lyorn, you would hardly be who you are, and I should not have felt as I did, and as I do."

"These ifs are useless."

"With this I agree."

"But you were too hard with our son, too inflexible. That is my belief."

Khaavren bowed his head once more, at last saying, "I do not know."

"Well, then?"

"Madam, what do you suggest I do?"

"What do you always do when you are troubled in your mind?"

"I do not know. It seems that I have been troubled in my mind for these last two and a half hundred years, and I do not know what I should have done were it not for you."

"Well, in the old days, were you never disturbed in your mind?"

"Why, yes, I think I was, at times."

"And what did you do on those occasions?"

"In the old days, I would speak with Aerich, who always seemed able to ease my heart."

"And then?"

"You think I should visit Aerich?"

"Why not?"

"You ask a good question," admitted Khaavren. "Perhaps I should indeed."

The Countess smiled, and, after a moment, Khaavren was forced to smile back. "Well, madam? What is it you have not yet told me?"

"I have spoken with him."

"You? You have spoken with Aerich?"

"I sent him a message by the post some days ago."

"A message? What message did you send him?"

"I merely explained that—"

"Yes?"

"That you would very much wish to see him."

"Astonishing," murmured Khaavren. "Madam, you are adorable."

Daro smiled and lowered her eyes.

Chapter the Seventieth

How the King of Elde Met with Certain Ambassadors And Practiced Diplomacy

Corthina Fi Dalcalda had been born some thirteen hundred years before as the youngest son of the Dalcalda family, which was, without question, one of the wealthiest on Elde, and, by their own reckoning, the house with the greatest claim on the royal throne after its then occupants, the family of Fintarre. By the time three hundreds of years had passed since his birth he was, instead, the only eligible son of the Dalcalda family; and the Fintarre family, except for Her Majesty Queen Legranthë, were no more.

The rumors spreading from this sudden blossoming of position are boundless, as must inevitably happen when an obscure individual in a powerful family suddenly becomes more powerful—there are stories of rare poisons, curses, assassination, and slow, carefully contrived plots. The truth, in fact, is far more prosaic: Most of the Fintarre family were destroyed, as, indeed, were so many others of the court of Elde, by a most shockingly virulent strain of the Innuthra Plague that visited the royal city and took thousands of lives before an effective quarantine could be placed, and Her Majesty was saved only by great exertions, and the work of the Imperial Physicker, Rendra, sent by courtesy of His Imperial Majesty Tortaalik. As for the Dalcalda family, there is even less mystery: his sister, the eldest, was drowned when the *Heartshope* was lost at sea with all hands; another brother had said all of his life that he had no interest in government, or the exercise of power, but wished instead to follow his vocation as a natural philosopher, for which reason, as expected, he swore his Oath of Renunciation at the age of two hundred and took ship to Greenaere, where he and several companions embarked on a course of categorizing and comparing the indigenous plant life along the coast; the author has no doubt that it will not be long before an interesting monograph appears in Elde's library, and we can only hope a copy is sent to the Imperial library as well. This left only one brother, who was disqualified for the simple reason that he was younger then Corthina. For this reason, then, upon the eventual death of Queen Legranthë, Corthina became one of the three or four leading contenders for the throne in the most natural way; and he took the throne upon the disappearance of the other claimants during the two weeks that followed the Queen's death. (The exact reason for the disappearance we cannot know for certain, as His Majesty Corthina decided that public funds ought not be squandered in an investigation into the causes.)

As a king, Corthina was far from the worst ruler one can imagine. He at once secured his relationship with the Empire through an exchange of gifts, including the famous Black Pearl of Diorath (which was, alas, like so many other treasures, lost in Adron's Disaster), instituted certain measures of sanitation to reduce the plagues, and caused various roads to be improved, thus making trade within his kingdom easier and more productive. Once informed of the Disaster, he gave tacit permission to reavers to raid the Dragaeran shore, but made it clear that these reavers had no official sanction, which insured that, should the Empire unexpectedly emerge again, he could not be blamed; for this service he charged the reavers a tax that was little more than token. He also, with the threat of the Empire gone, reduced the size of Elde's standing army for the first time in recorded history.

Physically, he was one of the more imposing of Elde's rulers—an extraordinarily tall, broad-shouldered man, with masses of dark, curling hair on a great head, distinguished by flashing dark eyes and wide mouth; it has been suggested by many reputable authorities that his success—and no one questions his success—was caused as much by his physical appearance as by his undoubted skills as a ruler, administrator, and diplomatist.

It is in the last of these capacities that we may observe him now, seated at a table of the finest white marble veined with silver. Across from him is a certain Countess Gardimma—her face wrinkled, her grey eyes bright beneath eyebrows that trail off to her temples like the wings of a daythief—of the House of the Athyra.

"Your Majesty," said Gardimma, "I cannot dispute you. Everything Your Majesty does me the honor to point out to me is true. That is to say, the Empress has only a skeletal army, and few of the Houses have as yet given her their declarations of loyalty, and she has not even a completed palace in which to live. Nevertheless—"

"Well?" said the king. "Nevertheless?"

"She has the Orb."

"Ah, yes. That is true. I do not question you on that."

"And we contend that, with the Orb, everything else must inevitably fall into place."

"Inevitably?"

"That is our contention, yes."

"And yet, I will tell you in all honesty—for out of respect for the Orb, if for no other reason, I will be honest—it is better for us if there is no Empire. You perceive, you are large, and we are small, and the Empire has always been hungry for land. And so we are forced to maintain an army that numbers a terribly large proportion of our population, just to keep from being swallowed up. Without the Empire so hungrily looking at us from across the channel, why, I have been able to reduce the army, and we are able to go on with our peaceful lives. And by giving you recognition, it would seem to me that I am aiding in the restoration of the Empire. Do you understand my position, madam?"

"Another might observe, Your Majesty, that your peaceful

lives include raids upon our shores, but I say nothing like this, because I understand this happens against Your Majesty's strict decrees."

The king bowed his head in acquiescence.

"I understand Your Majesty's position," continued Gardimma. "However, permit me to observe that everything will be much more agreeable, after the Empire is fully restored, if Her Majesty feels that you aided her now. And we, all of us, desire nothing more than that relations between the two nations be agreeable; is that not so?"

"Oh, of a certainty madam. You make a strong argument, and I promise you I will consider it carefully."

"And then?"

"Very well. Give me thirty hours to consider all that you have said. Return to-morrow, and we will speak more."

Gardimma bowed low, and said, "I thank Your Majesty for taking the time to listen to me. Until to-morrow."

"Until to-morrow, Countess."

His Majesty pulled upon a rope, whereupon a guard came in to escort the Countess out of the room. The King remained there for some few minutes, then, pulling the bell again, addressed the guard who entered with the words "If the Countess is out of the palace, bring in the next visitor."

The guard bowed and went off to do so, with the result that, a few minutes later, Lord Udaar was announced. This Dragonlord, whom we hope the reader remembers from his duty of escorting Illista to the mainland, bowed to the King and said, "I thank Your Majesty for being so good as to see me."

"My friend," said Corthina, "for so I hope I may call you—"

"Your Majesty does me too much honor."

"Not at all, not at all. My friend, the ambassador from Her Imperial Majesty, Zerika the Fourth, has just left." The reader may observe here the art of negotiation, as Corthina, by using this title for Zerika, at once put the ambassador on the defensive, as it were.

Udaar, for his part, ignored this thrust, recognizing it for the tool of negotiation that it was. He merely said, "Ah, has she?"

Corthina nodded. "She wishes me to recognize Zerika as the Empress of Dragaera."

"Well, I am not startled by this."

"But, you perceive, that is much the same as your own request."

"Oh, Your Majesty. I wish a great deal more than that!"

"Well, what do you wish? Come, let us see."

"I wish for troops to attack the mainland."

"Well, but you are aware that the army has been much reduced, and I am only now rebuilding it?"

"There will be time."

"Oh, as for time, yes. But consider the risk I run."

"Your Majesty, consider what you have to gain."

"Let us see, then. What have I to gain?"

"In the first place, there will be no danger of invasion."

"How, will there not? But what is to prevent you from turning on us as soon as you have your Empire secure?"

"We are prepared to give you guarantees in the form of treaties."

"Well, that is something, to be sure. What next?"

"Of course, this has no effect on the Crown, but it will please some of your subjects, no doubt, that, during the inevitable confusion, it will be possible for them to continue the coastal raids they have been enjoying for the last two hundreds of years—although we should ask that Adrilankha be exempted from these raids, as that is where we should like to establish the new palace."

"Very well, sir. Go on. What next?"

"Shipping, Your Majesty."

"Shipping! Now there is a subject that touches me very closely."

"Then let us speak of it, Your Majesty."

"Yes, indeed, let us speak of it. What do you say of shipping?"

"That we will give up our monopoly on trade with Greenaere."

"You will give up trade with Greenaere?"

"Oh, no, Your Majesty. Only the monopoly."

"Ah, so then, we will compete?"

"Exactly. Ships from Elde to Greenaere will no longer be interfered with in any way."

"I do not deny that what you offer is a powerful inducement."

"And so?"

"But there is a matter that still requires the utmost consideration."

"If Your Majesty would condescend to tell me what this matter is, well, I will address it if I can. And, if I cannot—"

"Yes, if you cannot?"

"I will send back to His Majesty Kâna for instructions."

"That seems reasonable enough. I will tell you."

"Your Majesty perceives that you have my entire attention."

"If I send you this army, what is to prevent it from being handled as easily as your own army was handled? I am not without eyes; I know what happened near Dzur Mountain."

"Ah, Your Majesty is aware of this?"

"I am tolerably well informed."

"So much the better. Then you know that we faced a necromancer who raised the dead and sent them against us?"

"I do."

"And Eastern witches who summoned animals to attack us?"

"Yes."

"Well, we have a way of neutralizing these forces."

"How, you do?"

"Entirely. And even a way to neutralize the Imperial Orb. And, moreover—"

"Yes?"

"Your army has never experienced the Orb, and so, fighting against it would not impair your army's morale. Many in our army are old enough to remember the Orb, and they are not pleased to be fighting it."

"Yes, I understand that."

"And, even after all that happened, we still have more than twenty thousands of troops, and they will be there, as well."

"A tolerably round number."

"Yes, Majesty."

"Very well. Let me consider the matter. Is there anything else?"

"There is, Majesty. A small matter, but which, nevertheless, I am required to raise."

"Go on, then."

"It concerns a certain Lady Illista."

"Illista? Why yes, I know the lady of whom you speak. She came here some hundreds of years ago. What of her?"

"This is a difficult matter for me to bring up, Your Majesty."

"Do your best."

"I shall."

"Well?"

"It concerns her treatment by Your Majesty's court."

"Her treatment?"

"Exactly."

"But, we did exactly what the Emperor, Tortaalik, wished of us. That is, she was permitted to live in peace, provided with the small pension supplied by the Empire, and not permitted at court. In fact, we did more, because after the Disaster, we continued the pension out of our own public funds."

"This was the request of His Majesty Tortaalik?"

"Exactly. It was so recorded by my illustrious predecessor, Queen Legranthë, and I have seen no reason to change it. Is there now a reason?"

"Well, after a fashion."

"Explain your meaning, sir."

"In the first place, Illista is no longer on Elde, but has returned to the mainland."

"How, she has? By whose authority was this done?"

"His Majesty Kâna's."

"Very well, what else?"

"We should like—that is to say, we would hope—"

"Come, come, my young friend. Say what you mean."

"His Majesty Kâna should like an apology, from Your Majesty, regarding the way the Lady Illista was treated."

"An apology?"

Udaar bowed his head.

The King frowned and considered for some few moments. "I am not accustomed," he said at last, "to apologize for my actions. Moreover, I do not understand why this concerns your Kâna in any way."

"If Your Majesty wishes, I will explain."

"Do so."

"We require Illista's aid in our endeavors, because she is very nearly the only remaining Phoenix, and the other is so far from aiding us that it is useless to ask."

"And she will not aid you without this apology from us?"

"It is not that, Your Majesty."

"Well?"

"It is that, with the apology, her aid would be more meaningful. To receive public aid from a noble of the House of Phoenix would have great influence with the other Houses. But if it came from a Phoenix who was disgraced—"

"Ah. I understand. You are working your own intrigues, and you wish for my aid to second them."

"That is exactly the case, Your Majesty. In addition—"

"There is more?"

"Your Majesty will see. In addition, we offer to Elde, as a token of good-will, Spaire Island, which has been in dispute between Elde and the Empire for thousands of years."

Corthina considered. "I confess," he said, "that it would be good to end these arguments over Spaire Island. The wood there is of immense value in building ships, and we all know the value of watering rights."

Udaar bowed.

"Concerning other matters," continued the King, "the supposed insult, if you will, was given by my predecessor, not by me."

"And so?"

"And so, this is my decision: If—I say, *if* I choose to aid you in your military endeavors, I will accompany this aid with the apology you request, in language that will be all you could wish. If I do not give you the other aid, then neither will I give you the apology."

Udaar bowed. "I do myself the honor of saying that Your Majesty's decision is full of sense."

"And," continued Corthina, "as to the question of giving you the assistance you request, I will give you my answer to-morrow."

"Very good, Your Majesty."

"Is there anything more?"

"That is everything on my part. But is there anything Your Majesty wishes to know of me?"

"No, my dear sir. I believe I comprehend the situation tolerably well."

"Then I eagerly await hearing from Your Majesty to-morrow."

Corthina nodded, and signed that the interview was now at an end. When Udaar had gone, the King retired to a more private chamber, there to consult with certain of his advisers, eat a meal he had long delayed and which included immense quantities of seafood and even more immense quantities of drawn butter, as well as dried fruit (the fruit being now out of season) and a mince pie of prodigious size. By the time he had finished eating and talking (Corthina was notorious for consulting with his advisers while eating) he had made his decision.

Gardimma was sent home the next day.

The following day the King spread the word that the army was to be rebuilt: For the first time in recorded history, Elde was preparing to invade the mainland.

Chapter the Seventy-First

How the Viscount of Adrilankha Took to the Life of a Road Agent

It was early in the morning on a Marketday near the end of winter of the first year of the Empress Zerika the Fourth's reign that Piro, the Viscount of Adrilankha, rode away from the public market in the village of Nearby in Mistyvale County, along with his friends and a pack mule which contained no small number of goods purchased at this market. Many of the items in the market had gotten there by trade from traveling merchants; there were also some items drawn from smokehouses to sell, as the approaching summer indicated how much extra was available. The market, while it could not be described as crowded, had at least provided them with what they required.

As they rode, Piro's lover and good friend Ibronka observed, "I believe we were recognized."

"Do you think so?" asked Piro, with apparent unconcern.

"It seems likely."

"Well, let us hear then: Why do you hold this opinion?"

"At the far end of the market was the fish-stall."

"Yes, I do not dispute this; at the far end was a fish-stall. I saw it. Not only that, but I believe that I smelled it."

"Well, I asked the gentleman in this stall to tell me about his fish."

"Well, and?"

"He said they were called kalpa."

"And then?"

"That is all."

"I beg your pardon, my dear Ibronka, but I do not understand what you do me the honor to tell me."

"He named the fish, and said no more."

"Well?"

"My love, have you ever known a fisherman, or an innkeeper, or a fishmonger, to be content with such a statement? It is impossible. It violates the laws of nature. He is required to explain that kalpa is like, well, a trout only less bony. Or like a longfish but more succulent. Or like a swordfish but not so tough. Or that it has a flavor unlike any other. Or that it is famous throughout the land, but is best from here, or, well, something of the kind."

"Yes, I take your point. The fishmonger behaved most unnaturally."

"Precisely. For this reason, I believe we were recognized."

"Of course, he might recognize us without betraying us."

"Yes, that is true."

"How much are our heads worth at this moment?"

"Five hundred imperials for the 'Blue Fox' and four hundred for each of his band."

"A tolerably round number."

"Yes, my lord."

Piro nodded, and, after a moment, said, "Kytraan, Ibronka believes we were recognized."

"Indeed? So does Röaana."

"Ah. For what reason?"

"I didn't ask," said Kytraan, shrugging.

"Röaana, why do you believe we were recognized?"

"The fishmonger failed to boast," said Röaana laconically.

"Well," said Piro, "so we were recognized. Does it matter?"

"No," said Ibronka.

"No," said Röaana.

"I think it does not," ventured Kytraan.

"Nevertheless," said Piro, draping his blue half-cloak over his shoulders, and fastening it with with its pearl clip. "It cannot hurt to move on; to find a new place to make our encampment."

"With this I agree," said Ibronka.

A few more turnings brought them to a particular row of stunted evergreen trees, where they left the road, traveling in a straight line for a little over a mile, after which they crossed a brook, climbed over a low hill, and so came to a place where several tents had been raised and a fire was burning.

The first one to greet them was Lar, who cried out, "Did you find coriander?"

"We did indeed, brave Lar; we have an entire pound of it, all fresh."

"Oh, my lord! A whole pound? I am beside myself with joy! But I cannot use so much; we must find a way to preserve it."

"We will consider the matter," said Ibronka. "I should imagine a means may be found."

Grassfog emerged from a tent, rubbing sleep from his eyes and wearing only breeches. "Was the market successful, my friends?" he said.

"Yes, except we were recognized."

Grassfog shrugged. "We will move south a little. I know some good places."

"Splendid," said Piro.

Lar took the coriander in its heavy pot and, with Clari's inexpert but enthusiastic assistance, at once set to cooking, which aroma presently brought Iatha, Ritt, and Belly from their respective tents, stretching and yawning.

"Well," said Iatha. "What are you cooking?"

"In fact," said Lar, "I cannot entirely answer that question, as I will not know until it is done. But I know that it will involve coriander and several jointed fouls, as well as certain other items that were secured at the market."

"And," said Piro, "while the food is being prepared, let us prepare to strike camp."

"Ah," said Belly, "we are moving?"

"We believe we were identified at the market."

"That is too bad," observed Iatha. "But, no matter. How are our funds?"

"After this last trip to the market, they are distressed," said

Röaana, who functioned as the treasurer for the firm. "That is to say, thin."

"And yet," said Kytraan, "it has seemed to me that we have been doing tolerably well in our investments."

"Indeed we have," said Piro. "And we should all be wealthy, if—"

"Yes?" said Iatha. "If?"

"If we did not all continually go into villages and buy drinks for everyone in sight all night and into the morning."

"Well," said Kytraan, shrugging.

Grassfog sighed. "I believe," he said, "that we must soon either begin conserving our assets as we acquire them, or else find a new enterprise."

"How, you think so?" said Piro.

"I am convinced of it. In a hundred years, or perhaps less, it will be useless to attempt to work the roads."

"Oh," said Ibronka. "A hundred years. Well, you perceive, a hundred years does not go by abruptly."

"It will when you are older," said Grassfog, shrugging.

"But tell me," said Piro, "why you say that in a hundred years or less we will be unable to continue?"

"Oh, I know that," said Ibronka.

"Well?" said the others. "Tell us."

"Teleportation," said Ibronka.

"Exactly," said Grassfog. "Soon, all merchants will either be able to teleport, or, perhaps, to hire it done. Indeed, had I a disposition to enter into a business, which I must confess I do not, why, I should become a sorcerer, and learn to teleport, and make a living by hiring myself to merchants with fat purses, teleporting them to safety for a small part of those purses, and warning them of the dangers of fierce road agents."

Kytraan said, "Do you truly believe teleportation will become so common?"

"I do," said Grassfog.

"And I agree," said Ibronka.

"Well, that settles it," said Piro. "Never will I be so foolish as to dispute with both of you. But then, if we have a hundred years—"

"Maybe twenty years," said Grassfog, shrugging again. "Who knows? These things happen quickly. And consider that if this region becomes known as dangerous for travelers, well, it will be even quicker here, so that we may be forced to find another place to operate."

"That would not be so bad," said Kytraan. "This region is pleasant enough, especially now that winter seems to be over, but to be sure there are others."

"Do you know," said Ritt, "it seems to me that one of us ought to learn to teleport."

"In fact," said Ibronka, "I had considered that."

"How, had you?" said Piro.

"Well," said Ritt, "consider that we could transact business with a fat merchant here in Mistyvale, and then teleport to, for example, Candletown."

"Indeed," said Kytraan. "Why, that would be a splendid idea! I do not mind living out of doors, at least when the weather is warm, but to have a pleasant room in a comfortable inn, with plumbing, and—"

"Alas," said Ibronka. "It would not work."

"How, it would not?" said Röaana.

"It is impossible."

"You had already thought of this means of operating, hadn't you?" said Piro, admiringly.

"Well," said Ibronka, "I had never intended to be a road agent, but it seems to me that, if I am to be one after all, I may as well be a good one."

"You are adorable," said Piro.

"And yet," said Iatha, "I wish to hear why this would not work."

"My lords and my ladies," said Lar, "I beg to be permitted to observe that your breakfast is now ready."

Each took his messkit and formed a queue: Piro being served first, then Ibronka, followed by Röaana, Kytraan, Grassfog, Iatha, Ritt, and Belly. They presented their empty plates to Lar and Clari, who served out the breakfast with great solemnity and even a certain touch of ceremony, after which service the Teckla retired to wait for whatever might be left.

After receiving the food, our friends sat down on the ground and ate, all of them in turn giving Lar a thousand compliments on the food and its preparation, compliments to which Lar responded first with a bow, and then with the murmured word "coriander."

As they ate, Iatha said, "I continue to be curious, Ibronka, about why you say that we cannot use teleportation, should we learn it, in order to assist our efforts."

"I beg your pardon, good Iatha," said Piro. "But you know the rule: there will be no business conversations during meals. We must, after all, maintain a certain degree of civilization, don't you think?"

"Oh, certainly," said Röaana. "Indeed, in my opinion, the more time we spend in the wilderness, the more important is civilization."

"This is only barely the wilderness," observed Ritt.

"Well, but it is living out-of-doors," said Röaana, "which is tolerably close."

"I could not agree more, my dear Röaana," said Kytraan. "Lar, more klava."

"Coming, my lord."

"But do you know," said Grassfog contemplatively. "It is inherent in our line of work that it is sometimes difficult to say what is business and what is not."

"That is true," said Belly.

"He speaks!" cried Röaana, laughing.

Belly graced the Tiassa with a look that we must identify as a friendly glare, if the reader can imagine such a thing, after which he went on to say, "For example, should I wish to discuss those three merchants of yester-day, one who became ill upon his own shoes, well, would this be business, or merely amusement?"

"Why, I think that might be considered amusement," said Grassfog.

"Although unsuitable for dinner conversation for other reasons," said Ibronka.

Belly flushed slightly, which led Röaana to say, "Ibronka, my dear, we must wait a week between each comment of our good Belly, and then, when he does venture to speak, you chastise him. The Gods, it will now be a year before he dares open his mouth again. For shame."

"You are right, my dear, and good Belly, I tender my apologies."

"Besides," said Röaana, "I like hearing him speak. Every time he pronounces an ahr it sounds as if his tongue is turning upside down, and when he makes the el he does so with his whole body and soul, as if committing to it fully. It amuses me."

"Röaana, you are embarrassing him," chided Ibronka.

Indeed, Belly was now extremely flushed, but was doing his best to devote himself to his food. Piro caught Kytraan's eye and said, "They are cruel, aren't they?"

"Exceedingly," said Kytraan.

"Well," said Röaana, "how else am I to get Belly's attention? I have been looking at him from beneath my eyelashes for a year, and it is as if I addressed a wall."

"Bah," said Grassfog, shrugging. "Enter his tent some night. I promise you will get his attention."

"Ah, sir, you are rude," said Röaana.

"I am without artifice," said Grassfog.

"It comes to much the same thing," observed Iatha, who was, for her part, doing everything possible to keep from breaking up into peals of laughter at poor Belly's expense.

"Well then," said Röaana, "how should I induce him to speak to me?"

Piro said, "As to that, ask him about—"

"Oh, oh! You are hardly the one to explain," teased Ibronka affectionately.

"Well," said Piro, turning slightly red in his turn, "there is something in what you say."

"Pah," said Kytraan. "It is easy enough. Ask him how he became a highwayman."

"Well, in fact," said Röaana, "I confess that I have a certain curiosity about this. Come, Belly, if you can manage to bring your head up long enough to say two words, tell me how you happened to fall into your profession."

Belly did manage to raise his head, and, with some difficulty, he said, "Oh, it was a girl."

"How, a girl?" said Röaana, leaning forward.

"Certainly."

"Then, she rejected you?"

"Well, yes, but not immediately. That is, the rejection came well after I had turned bandit."

"Well now, you perceive, you must certainly tell me this story," said Röaana, "because I declare to you that I will die if you stop now."

"There is little to tell," said Belly. "I was born into the House of the Iorich, to a family of some property. This was, you perceive, a hundred and forty-three years before the Disaster. When I reached the age of one hundred and twenty, I became apprenticed to my uncle, and read law under his tutelage. At a certain time, he was engaged to defend a young lady of the House of the Tsalmoth. She was a lovely girl, with black, piercing eyes, and she carried her head like a Dzurlord."

"Ah, well, go on," said Röaana. "You must believe this conversations interests me exceedingly."

"I will be laconic. She was accused of stealing money from her employer. I fell in love with her, and when she was found guilty and sentenced to the galleys, I bribed one guard and struck another a good knock on the head to help her escape from the justicers; you must understand that being apprenticed to her advocate, I was permitted to see her, which not only helped in no small measure, but meant that I was unable to conceal my own rôle. And so, after I helped her to escape, there was nothing either of us could do except to leave the city and set up as bandits."

"Well, but were you good at it?"

"I think so. She had something of a knack, and I, well, I must say that I took to it rather well."

"I understand. And then?"

"We gradually drifted west, and, shortly after the Disaster, we met with Wadre, who convinced us to join his band. The Disaster drove us even further west, and well, here I am." He punctuated this tale with an eloquent shrug.

"Well, but you perceive you have not finished."

"How, what have I left out?"

"My dear, have you no romance in you?"

"Tolerably little."

"Well, what became of the girl?"

"Oh, we remained together for nearly a hundred years, which is not so short a time. But then, she is a Tsalmoth, and they are sufficiently changeable. She became weary of me at last."

"How, did she?"

"She claimed I had no romance in me."

"Ah, that is sad."

"Not too sad," said Belly. "You perceive, she and I are still friends—are we not, Iatha?"

"Oh, certainly we are, my good friend."

"How," cried Röaana, "it was you?"

"Indeed it was," said Iatha.

"And was his tale true and complete?"

"So much so, my dear Tiassa, that I have no need to tell you my own history."

"Well, but—"

"Yes?"

"There is one thing I must know."

"What is it? If I know, I will tell you."

"Had you, in fact, stolen from your employer?"

"No, I had not. He kept his savings in a tin box hidden in a secret compartment in the floor of his shop. And, well, I would have stolen it, only someone else got there first; I don't know who." She shrugged.

"A delightful tale, upon my honor," said Piro.

"And," added Kytraan, "I am now done eating."

"As am I," said the others.

This announcement was greeted with no small joy on the part of Lar and Clari, whose empty stomachs had been performing a duet ever since they had finished serving the repast—they now accordingly set in to devour what was left with an urgency in direct proportion to the delay; filling up the lack with good toast when the fowls had been quite picked clean.

"Do you know," remarked Clari in a low voice, "you ought

not to cook so well. If you were not so skilled with the skillet, why, there would be more left over for us."

Lar did not reply, being too engrossed in using a piece of toast to gather every drop of sauce he could scavenge.

In the meantime, Iatha raised her black eyes to Ibronka and said, "And now, my dear, as we have finished our repast and so it is no longer forbidden to touch on matters of business, I hope you will be so good as to explain to us why this plan of teleporting away from the scene of our activity is not a good one. For my part, I confess I find the idea entrancing, and so I warn you, if your explanation is not a good one, well, I will argue with it."

"Oh, I assure you my logic is tolerably sound—so much so that I venture to guarantee that, once you have heard it, you will never again raise the suggestion."

"If it is that good, it must be a powerful argument indeed."

"You will judge for yourself."

"Very good. Let us hear it, then."

Ibronka reached out her hand. Piro placed his own in it, and they exchanged the tenderest of looks as she said, "Do you remember when we first came to Dzur Mountain?"

"Nearly," said Kytraan. "Röaana and I were biting our lips until they bled trying to find ways to bring the two of you together."

"And we are more than a little grateful that you succeeded, my friend," said Piro, smiling.

"Bah, we should have gone mad otherwise," said Röaana.

"That is true," said Kytraan. "The Viscount never raised his eyes off the floor."

"And," added Röaana, "Ibronka would vanish for hours at a time, to be found in some corner with her eyes red."

"Ah," said Ibronka, "but you do not know what I was doing during those hours I was gone. I give you my word, it was not all spent in tears."

"How, it was not?" said Ibronka.

"Not in the least. You must understand, I was nearly out of my senses, not knowing if I dared to speak to the Viscount, and so—"

"Well? And so?"

"I thought to distract myself. After all," she added, with a significant look at Röaana, "I could not remain in your company for more than a minute without you beginning to practice upon me."

"Ah, my love," said Röaana, "it was with the best of intentions, I assure you."

"Oh, I give you my word, I do not doubt that in the least, my dear."

"But," said Piro, still looking at her in the fondest way, "what did you do to distract yourself? Because, as for me, I had Kytraan who nagged like a fishwife, and being vexed at him was sufficient distraction for me."

"Ah, Piro!" cried Kytraan.

"Well, but what is the answer?" said Röaana.

"I made a friend of—"

"Of whom?" cried Piro, prepared to be jealous.

"Of the Sorceress in Green."

"Of her?"

"Certainly."

"But, why?"

"Because, my dear, she pretends to have not the least interest in love, and therefore her conversation was a comfort to me."

"Well, I understand that," said Piro.

"As do I," said Röaana, "only what did you talk about?"

"Sorcery," said Ibronka. "I considered devoting myself to its study. And, indeed, I would have, only—"

"Yes?"

"Shortly thereafter I became diverted."

"Well," said Piro, now blushing.

"To be precise, then, the Sorceress in Green and I carried on a conversation about teleportation, which she pretended was the most remarkable thing to come from the improvement of the Orb."

"Do you think she is wrong?" said Röaana.

"Oh, I do not feel qualified to have an opinion on this matter. But she and Sethra the Younger had been studying it, and, indeed, had branched off into different aspects of the art. To be precise—"

"Oh yes," murmured Iatha. "By all means let us be precise."

"Sethra the Younger concerned herself with how to *prevent* a teleport—that is, with finding ways to be certain no one could enter or leave a certain place."

"My House of the Iorich will be much interested in that," observed Belly.

"Whereas the Sorceress in Green had become interested in the thaumaturgic marks left by a teleport."

"Thaumaturgic marks?" said Piro. "But, what is meant by this term? I give you my word, I have never heard of such things before."

"It refers, my true love, to traces that linger in the ether after a teleport has taken place, and other traces that appear along with the individual or object that has been teleported."

"Are there such?" asked Kytraan.

"Indeed there are. And they linger," added Ibronka.

"How long?"

"When I spoke to the Sorceress, she had not yet determined this, but she had found traces that were more than two days old. And—"

"Well, and?"

"And she was able to use these to determine the destination of the teleport."

"Ah, ah!"

"But," said Piro, "is there no way to teleport without leaving these marks."

"Oh, as to that," said Ibronka, "no means has been discovered yet. You perceive, if one is found, well, that will change everything."

"Yes," said Röaana, "well, I understand. If we should attempt to escape by teleporting, well, we will lead the agents of the law directly to us. It will be worse than attempting to outrun them on good horses and hide among the hills and forests."

"That is my opinion."

"Oh, I am in complete agreement," said Röaana.

"And my argument, is it convincing?"

"Perfectly," said Iatha, bowing.

"So then," said Piro, "we have only a few years left of living this life that I, for one, find so excellent, before it is taken away from us by the teleport."

"Exactly," said Ibronka.

"And, moreover, we cannot, ourselves, use this means for own purposes, in order to escape those who would interfere with our delightful life."

"You have understood exactly, Viscount."

Piro frowned. "I believe I should like to discover who perfected this spell, and kick him."

"If I am not mistaken, that would be Sethra Lavode," observed Kytraan.

"Ah, well, perhaps I shall modify this determination."

"That would be wise," agreed Röaana.

"Do you know," said Grassfog, speaking for the first time, "I should like to make an observation."

"Well, and that is?" said Piro.

"As we have decided that teleportation is impractical—"

"Yes?"

"And, moreover, as none of us have the skill to perform it anyway—"

"That is also true," said Piro, struck by the extreme justice of this observation.

"I would suggest that we finish striking these tents and move on. You say that we were recognized, well, it may be that this good peasant will say nothing—you know that many are in sympathy with us. But then, there are rewards on all of our heads, so let us not count overmuch on the good feelings of the Teckla."

"An admirable suggestion," said Piro, "and one to which I subscribe with all my heart."

In a very short time, then, the tents were struck and loaded onto the mules with their other supplies. This being done, they mounted and made their way down to the road, and began riding slowly south.

As they rode, Piro said, "Ibronka, my love?"

"Yes, my lord the fox?"

"Are you happy?"

She gave him a puzzled look, and said, "I do not understand the question you do me the honor to ask."

"Well, but consider: Your mother is a princess, and you, well, you were certainly destined for higher things than to sleep under the skies and ply your sword on the road."

"And it is this reflection that has caused you to ask this remarkable question?"

"Exactly."

"Are you not happy with me, my lord?"

"The Gods, Ibronka! If you were there, I should be happy in a hovel is South Adrilankha earning my bread by sweeping refuse in the streets!"

"And can you imagine, my lord, that I feel any differently? Besides—"

"Well?"

"I must admit, I rather enjoy this way of living. It is as if the adventure we set off on never ended. And, moreover, sometimes they send soldiers against us, and so I am able to play a little. What more could I ask?"

"You heard Grassfog; it must end, sooner or later."

"Then let it be later."

"And when it ends?"

"If you are there, I will be happy."

"Ibronka, I may be the happiest man in the world."

"You know I adore you, Viscount Blue Fox."

"I am delighted afresh each time you say it."

"Then I will say it often."

"We have come a good distance, have we not?"

"Yes, a good distance."

"In another hour, we will begin to consider our next camp. Where do you think we should sleep tonight?"

"Together, my lord."

"You are right, my lady; that is all that matters."

Chapter the Seventy-Second

How Khaavren Received a Message From a Teckla Who Dressed in a Particularly Unusual Fashion, And, as a Result, Determined To Attend an Entertainment

It was on a Skyday in the early spring toward the end of the first year of Zerika's Reign that Khaavren happened to be passing the time with the Countess in her apartment, which pleasant activity occupied much of his time after leaving the Imperial service, when the subject was introduced of an entertainment to be given the next day at Castle Black.

"We can attend if you wish," said Khaavren. "I have received an invitation; and, I should add, an invitation written on silk in gold lettering."

"Well, and how have you replied?"

"Replied? I was to have replied?"

"It is the custom, my lord."

"Ah, well, you see, if there are customs to how to set the guard, or even how to salute a gentleman into whose skin one is about to poke a certain number of holes, I know these. But, as to customs for entertainments, I confess to a lamentable ignorance."

"So then, you have not replied?"

"Exactly. And, as I have not replied, well, I should imagine we can do as we please."

"Well then, my lord, how do we please? That is to say, what is your pleasure in this regard?"

"For my part," said Khaavren, shrugging, "I confess that I have little enough interest in such pastimes. Yet, should you wish to attend, why, I give you my word it would be no hardship."

Daro smiled softly. "Oh, I am a most complaisant wife, my lord, you know that. If you do not wish to go—but what is this?"

"My lady," said the maid, whose entrance had occasioned this interruption, "there is a Teckla who pretends he has business with my lord."

"A Teckla who has business with me?" said Khaavren. "Cha! I am no longer in the Imperial service, which is the capacity in which I was accustomed to receive messages. Is he not aware that it is my lady the Countess who handles all matters concerning Whitecrest?"

"As to that, I do not know, my lord. But it was your name he gave."

"Was it? That is strange. More than strange, it is unusual."

"And then?" said Daro.

"Well then, I will go and see this Teckla, and it will be unusual, or at least strange, if I do not succeed in learning what his business with me is."

According to this decision, he at once made his way down the stairs and to the front hallway, where he was approached by a Teckla who said, "My lord the Count?"

Before answering this question, Khaavren took a moment to study his interlocutor. He was a Teckla, which was not remarkable; his livery, on the other hand, was: he wore a bright orange shirt, white pantaloons, absurd orange boots with silver buckles, and a sort of black and white headband. Notwithstanding his outrageous dress, the bow he presented was entirely regular, and he took a properly obeisant attitude while waiting to hear whether Khaavren should admit to his identity.

"Well," said Khaavren when he had completed his inspection. "I am Khaavren, and Count of Whitecrest by courtesy. And you are—?"

"I?" said the Teckla. "Oh, I am merely a messenger."

"Indeed? I confess to more than little curiosity about who it is who dresses his lackeys in such a manner."

"Oh, my lord, may I do myself the honor of disputing with you? I am not a lackey, merely a messenger."

"You are a messenger, but not a lackey?"

The Teckla bowed.

"Then, if you would be so good as to explain? For I admit that I am now puzzled."

"My lord the Count, I have the honor to be employed by Goodrow and Niece."

"Goodrow and Niece?"

The Teckla bowed.

"I'm afraid I have never had the honor of meeting either of them."

"My lord, Goodrow and Niece is a telepathic messenger service."

"A telepathic messenger service?"

The Teckla bowed.

"But," said Khaavren, "you must see that this intelligence tells me nothing. What is a telepathic messenger service?"

"Why, it is the simplest thing."

"So much the better; then it will easy for you to explain."

"Yes, that is true," replied the Teckla, struck by the extreme justice of this observation.

"So then?"

"Do you wish me to explain?"

"I confess that I would like nothing better."

"Shall I do so now?"

"Blood of the Horse! I think it is an hour since I've wished for anything else!"

"This is it, then: Imagine that a certain gentleman desires to get a message to another, who lives far away."

"That is not difficult to imagine. And then?"

"Imagine, moreover, he does not wish to wait for the post."

"He must be in a great hurry indeed in that case, because, through the posts, I can get a message anywhere in the Empire in three or four days, if it is sufficiently urgent."

"Well, but we can get this message in three or four *hours,* my lord."

"Impossible!"

"I must do myself the honor of disagreeing, my lord. Indeed, this message which I am prepared to deliver to you left the hand of him who wrote it less than an hour ago."

"The Gods!"

"It is as I have the honor to tell you, my lord the Count."

"How is this possible?"

"Sorcery, my lord."

"Sorcery?"

"Certainly. Goodrow and Niece employ sorcerers—indeed, the niece referred to in the name is a sorceress herself—and they pay sorcerers from other parts of the Empire at a certain rate for each page of a message. These sorcerers all know each other sufficiently well that this communication presents no difficulties, and they are always happy to have a few extra orbs."

"And so?"

"Why, all you need to do is come to our offices, and your message will be sent to the agent nearest to the person with whom you wish to communicate, and then delivered by an errand runner such as I." The Teckla punctuated this speech with a bow.

"It is astonishing," said Khaavren. "And, as an errand runner, you must wear that . . . that . . . clothing?"

"My lord Goodrow pretends that, if his errand runners attract attention, people will ask questions, and we will answer them, and then more people will know of us, and so come to us when they wish messages sent."

"As far that goes," said Khaavren, "I have no doubt he is right. Only—"

"Well?"

"For my part, I should not think the increase in custom worth the indignity of having my name associated with such . . . clothing."

"My lord, may I do myself the honor of agreeing with Your Lordship?"

"Oh, I don't mind that," said Khaavren magnanimously.

"That is kind of you, my lord."

"Only—"

"Yes, my lord?"

"Who is it who wishes to reach me so urgently?"

"As to that, permit me to look."

"Oh, I don't mind you looking."

The Teckla drew forth a moderately heavy sealed paper and, not without a certain amount of display, studied the name upon it.

"I perceive that you know your symbols," said Khaavren, who never objected to gratifying anyone's self-love, as long as it didn't conflict with his own.

"Oh, yes, certainly; Your Lordship must understand, it is an absolute requirement for an errand runner in the employ of Goodrow and Niece."

"That is very well, then. But, as to the name—"

"Oh, you wish to know that?"

"Obstinate fool, I asked!"

"That is true!"

"Well?"

"It is from," said the Teckla, slowly and carefully pronouncing each word, "His Venerance, Temma, the Duke of Arylle, Count of—"

"Aerich!" cried Khaavren. "You have a message for me from Aerich! Quick, hand it over, you idiot."

"Here it is, my lord."

Khaavren grabbed the message from the Teckla's hand, ripped it open, and greedily devoured the words. What exactly these words were, we will discover to the reader in due course. For now, however, we will only observe that, upon finishing it, Khaavren turned on his heel and returned to Daro's apartment, where, after greeting her affectionately, he addressed these words to her: "Madam, I have had cause to change my mind, and, in fact, I should like, of all things, to attend to-morrow's entertainment at Castle Black."

Daro smiled. "I am delighted to learn this, my lord, as I have not been to an entertainment since leaving the court. But, if I may ask a question—"

"Madam, you may ask ten."

"Well, to what shall I attribute this sudden change?"

"Oh, as to that, you may see for yourself," he said, showing her the message.

This message read as follows: "My dear friend, I am entirely at your service regarding whatever undertaking you may require. If you wish to confer with me, I have been prevailed upon to be to-morrow at Castle Black, where Morrolan is giving an entertainment, and where I know you have been invited. If you wish, I shall be glad to consult with you at your convenience. Please convey my humble respects to the Countess. I remain, as always, your friend, Aerich."

"Well," said Daro, "that is clear enough. Only—"

"Yes?"

"How are we to get there? You perceive, my lord, that not only is this entertainment to be held seventy leagues away, but it is also a mile in the air."

"My understanding is that the Lord Morrolan is prepared to levitate his guests up to the castle, so then, we need not worry about the vertical mile."

"Well, but there are still the horizontal seventy leagues."

"That is true."

"So then?"

"It seems we must teleport."

Daro frowned. "Yes, I know that teleports are now simplicity itself for a skilled sorcerer. But, do we know anyone capable of such a thing?"

Khaavren reflected upon this question, which proved that it was a good one. "I will attempt to discover this," he said.

Taking his leave of the Countess, Khaavren returned once more to the front hallway, where to his surprise he found that the Teckla was still waiting. "Well?" he said. "Did you wish for something?"

"Only to know if there is a reply, my lord."

"No, there is no reply."

"Then, will there be anything else?"

"What else could there be?"

"Oh, as to that, I don't know, my lord, only that I am to ask."

"Well, no, there is nothing else."

"Very good, my lord," said the Teckla, who then bowed respectfully and left for the servants' entrance with an obscurely disappointed expression on his countenance.

Khaavren put on his sword, hat, and cloak, and left through the front door, where, the instant he was outside, he found his old comrade, the current ensign of the Imperial Guard, on duty. He said, "Sergeant," this being that gentleman's name, he being the son of an old comrade of Khaavren from the days before the Interregnum.

"Yes, Captain?" said Sergeant.

"I am required to be in the duchies. What is the fastest way to get there?"

"Why, by teleporting, Captain."

"Yes, but, alas, I do not know how."

"The court wizard is adept at this."

"This is personal, Ensign, and I am, as you know, no longer in the Imperial service."

"Then the fastest method would involve finding a sorcerer who has set out his public mark and who specializes in teleportation."

"There are such?"

"Oh, certainly."

"I had begun to suspect this might be case."

"Several of them, to my certain knowledge."

"Recommend one, then."

"I shall be glad to do so, Captain."

"Well?"

"There is a sorcerer who works on the Street of the Candlemakers who is, I'm told, acquainted with many places around the Empire. You perceive, what determines the value of such a sorcerer is how many places he knows."

"Why should this be?"

"I am not a sorcerer, my lord, but I am told that it requires a good knowledge of the landscape in order to safely teleport."

"Well, I am no sorcerer either, but that seems reasonable."

"Therefore, the more places a sorcerer knows, the closer he is likely to be able to place you near to your destination."

"Yes, I understand. Where on the Street of the Candlemakers?"

"Facing directly on the market circle near Ash Street. Number thirty-three or thirty-four, I believe. I know that it is next to a hatter, because I went there to get my hat blocked."

"And permit me to say, Ensign, that the hatter did a good job of work. I shall have to keep him in mind, as my own hat is soon going to require the same treatment."

"He uses boiling water, Captain."

"Boiling water?"

"To make steam, and the steam softens the hat, and this permits him to reshape it. And then he slides a certain amount of wire inside the fabric around the brim, so that it holds its shape, and then stitches the fabric together over the wire."

"Wire? Inside the fabric?"

"As I have had the honor to tell you, Captain."

Khaavren removed his hat and studied it for a moment, then shrugged and clapped it down firmly on his head. "I believe I will stay with what I know," he said. "But, certainly, I thank you for the information."

"You are most welcome, Captain. And may I permit myself to wish you a pleasant and successful journey?"

"Thank you, Sergeant."

Khaavren then made his way to the stables, where he called upon his stable-boy to have a horse saddled, which task was performed promptly (the confusion over Imperial horses being stabled with Khaavren's and Daro's personal horses having been settled some weeks before). This being done, the stable-boy assisted him to mount, after which he set out through the manor gates and so onto the street.

After the inevitable delay required to ride across the city, he found himself outside of the thin wooden door, painted green, of a shop next to a hatter's. Upon entering, he was greeted by a gentleman who appeared to be a Jhegaala. On the floor was a large circle crisscrossed with many lines, and on the walls were several maps of different parts of the Empire with dozens of small red circles drawn on them. The opposite wall was filled with a single map of the entire Empire—or, to be precise, the area that had been the entire Empire before the Disaster.

The Jhegaala was dressed in simple breeches, with a sort of thin singlet over a plain shirt with thin sleeves. He had rings on two of his fingers, a necklace containing a small pendant or amulet, and shoes without buckles. When Khaavren entered, he had been reading a book (Khaavren, always the curious Tiassa, looked for the title but failed to see it), which he now put down as he rose and bowed. "I wish you a good day, my lord, and I bid you welcome. Did you wish to arrange a teleport?"

Khaavren returned the salute and said, "You are exactly right, sir. I require a teleport for myself and my lady, for tomorrow evening."

The other bowed. "Very good, my lord. Where would you like to go?"

"Are you familiar with the county of Southmoor?"

The Jhegaala frowned. "If Your Lordship would do me the kindness to point it out on the map."

"I will do so at once."

"So much the better."

Khaavren did so, and at once the Jhegaala said, "Ah! Yes! So, then, you are going to Castle Black?"

"Why, yes. How did you know?"

"I have several requests for such, although the others did not identify the county, or else I should have recognized it at once."

"I see. And so, can you do it?"

"I believe I can bring Your Lordship tolerably close."

"How close is tolerably. You perceive, I wish to arrive at a particular hour, and so I must regulate the time of the teleport according to the distance to be traveled to the destination."

"My lord, I can bring you to the village of Nacine, which is, in fact, within the county of Southmoor, and, from what you indicated, only two hours' ride by carriage to your destination."

"So much the better."

"Now, as to the fee—" said the Jhegaala, with a slightly embarrassed bow.

"Oh, yes. I had not considered this. What is required?"

"For two of you, it will be six orbs."

"Very well. Do you wish it now?"

"Oh, no, my lord. When you arrive, there will be time."

"I should prefer to pay you now, so that the Countess need not be witness to such matters."

"Very well, my lord."

Khaavren counted out the coins (observing by accident that two of them had been stamped with Zerika's face, proving that the mints, at least, had accepted her as Empress), which the Jhegaala accepted with a bow.

"Then," said Khaavren, "I will return, with my wife, at the seventh hour after noon."

"I shall do myself the honor of expecting you, my lord."

In this way, Khaavren arranged to be at Castle Black on the following day.

Chapter the Seventy-Third

How History Was Changed By the Flight of a Pen Across a Room

It was very nearly the sixth hour after noon when Her Majesty, with no ceremony whatsoever, took the pen she held in her hand and flung it across the room so that it struck the opposite wall, leaving a black stain to mark its point of impact. She accompanied this action with a soft curse barely vocalized, and an exhalation of breath in the form of a sigh.

Insofar as they understood, matters were coming together splendidly for Kâna and his cousin Habil until Her Majesty's pen struck the wall of the chamber in Whitecrest Manor that was reserved for Imperial use.

The reader might wonder how there can be a relationship between the schemes and plans of Kâna and the action of Her Majesty. We consider this question not only reasonable, but even insightful, and we extend our compliments to the reader for having thought to ask it. More than our compliments, however, we propose to give to the reader an answer, and without delay.

In order to do so, however, there are a few details with which the reader must become acquainted.

Khaavren rarely saw Her Majesty during this period—that is, during the hours and days that had expired since his resignation. Although they shared a roof, as it were, the Empress kept very much to the covered terrace, or to her apartments, which could be reached without passing through any part of the Manor in which Khaavren could be found. In point of fact, we should say that he rarely saw anyone, spending much of his time on the uncovered terrace with Daro when the weather was kind. The only exception was Pel, who, though he remained near Her Majesty, did, from time time, pay visits to Khaavren—visits which the Tiassa enjoyed immensely.

As we have brought up the enigmatic Pel, we should say that, whatever his plans and schemes might have been, no signs of them were apparent during this period: he went about his business as Her Majesty's Discreet, and if he continued, as was his wont, to collect information, he kept it to himself and did nothing with it that can be identified even at this stage.

Lord Brimford—that is to say, the Warlock—was rarely seen around Whitecrest Manor, which is a tribute to his abilities if nothing else is, although, to be sure, from time to time the muddy prints of a dog had to be cleaned up in the hallway outside of Zerika's apartment.

The reader must also understand that the Empress had, for the last year, been engaged, without a break, in a sort of work that was particularly irksome to her, as it required cajoling of persons and shuffling of papers, and as, moreover, she wasn't used to it. To judge by the color of the Orb, she spent most of her day in a state of constant annoyance, with occasional moments of melancholy.

All this was known, by some means, by Kâna and his cousin, and, in particular, the resignation of the annoying Tiassa was exactly on schedule, according to their plan. The trap for Tazendra had been laid and was ready to be sprung on an instant, which trap would also, as a secondary result, make certain of the troublesome Lyorn Aerich. The plans for the invasion by the islanders was progressing, a means had been found to neutralize the Necromancer (and, even more important, the Orb), a stratagem had been found that would render useless the foul Eastern magic that had been so effectually employed against them, and, now, the necessary break had been made between Her Majesty and Khaavren. All was going well, as far as they knew.

And, even had they somehow been able to observe Her

Majesty at the critical moment, they would not have been able to guess that her precipitate action might threaten their carefully laid schemes—that, indeed, this simple action, by itself, provided the knife that would cut the snarls and knots of the intricate tapestry they had woven.

And the beginning of this unraveling, that is the first loosening of joints that permitted a seepage of water into the carefully constructed vessel (if the reader will permit us to mix metaphors in mid-stream before the tapestry is even hung), was accompanied by the harsh metallic sound caused by the pen striking the wall at the sixth hour after noon.

The pen had begun life some forty years ago as one of the interior wing feathers of a stunted lichbird, or that kind which is called a wader in some part of the Empire. The owner of this feather was a young boy who sometimes cut purses on Lower Kieron Road, sometimes begged on the Twisty Way, and sometimes ran errands for Lessor & Daughters, Bronze- and Tin-smiths, on Cliffside Street. He had found the feather, discarded, from the pluckings of the bird, which had been intended for a meal served by a local wine-merchant, and at once recognized its usefulness, wherefore he solemnly presented it to Lessor, who, with equal solemnity, presented him with a bright copper penny.

Lessor also recognized the perfect splendor of this feather, and at once took it back into his shop, where he made a pen of it, had it covered in bronze, and then prominently displayed it, with a small plaque indicating its price. There it remained for many years, along with whistles, touch-it glass housings, knockers, and other samples of his wares. When the Empress entered the city, in a rare burst of loyalty, he inscribed upon it, "To Her Majesty, From Her Devoted Servant Lessor & Daughters, Number 4 Cliffside Street, Adrilankha," and had it sent to her, for which he received a polite note written by one of Her Majesty's scriveners.

It was, to be sure, an eminently successful pen, rarely splotching, fitting her fingers splendidly, and capable of holding sufficient ink for nearly a full line of Her Majesty's fine, elegant hand. Indeed, Zerika's decision to throw the pen across the room as if it were a dart and the wall an enemy had nothing whatever to do with the characteristics of the pen itself, but, rather, with the amount of time she had spent using it, which was, in her Imperial opinion, far too much of late.

The construction of the Palace had begun, and, indeed, progressed to the point where she expected to be able to live and work there within only a few years, but there was still a great deal left to decide upon it, and she was frequently interrupted by designers and architects who would ply her with questions that they could not take it upon their heads to answer. The more weighty question of securing the Empire—which meant securing the agreement of all the Houses that she was, in fact, the Empress—required even more effort. It seemed that a hundred emissaries a day would enter, to be bullied, cajoled, or entertained; and a thousand letters had to be written, many of them signed with her own hand—that is to say, her own pen. Indeed, it seemed to her that she had been working, without a pause, for something like a hundred years, although a hundred days was, in fact, closer to the mark.

But, for whatever reason, or combination of reasons, Zerika, on that day, at that hour, came to the realization that she could no longer concentrate on her work; that she (as does everyone, whether engaged in physical labor, mental calculation, or emotional turmoil) needed to rest herself. This may appear to be a small matter—an accident, no more; yet, what is history except the arrangement of accidents, combined with the activity of human will operating on those accidents? To put it another way, one might say that man, who sets out to make history according to his wishes (although, to be sure, he is usually unaware that he is doing so) must perpetually weave his way in and out of happenstance and chance incidents; some far-reaching in their effect, some so trivial as to be lost, receding in the ocean of events before their occurrence, like a speck of sand upon the beach, can even be noted.

The reader may ask: Is it the actions, more or less deliberate, of men striving to make the world as they wish that determine the eventual course of history, or is it the preponderance of accidents? One must admit that if the answer were simple, the Imperial library would not be packed full of books purporting to answer this very question; the entire discipline of historiology would not exist. But for our purposes, the answer is this: Both factors weave in and out of each other, men doing the best they can with circumstances that might have been determined by caprice or chance, and then, in attempting to shape events, generating, as an icehouse generates steam, a fresh outpouring of accidents; a process that continues forever.

And, in this case, the accident was that it was on this day, rather than the day before or the day after, that Zerika happened to decide, to the extent of throwing her pen across the room, that she had had enough work, and must give herself something of a holiday or else she would, as she put it to herself, "either dissolve into the Orb, or explode like my predecessor."

Having come to this decision, then, Zerika called out, "Captain! Sergeant! Ensign!" We should explain that it was not, in fact, three soldiers for whom Her Majesty called, but, in fact, only one: in such circumstances, she had been accustomed to summon the captain, and so had made the first call. She then, however, remembered that the captain was no longer on duty, and, instead, recalled to her mind his replacement, the first name on the list with which Khaavren had presented her, that being an experienced guardsman whose name happened to be Sergeant. On reflection, however, after asking for him, she thought she ought to address him by his rank, which a moment's reflection brought to her mind; it being, of course, Ensign.

Whether three or one, this worthy appeared quickly enough in answer to her call and made a respectful bow.

"Your Majesty desired something?"

"Yes, Ensign. I desire to be entertained."

The worthy soldier frowned. "I beg Your Majesty's pardon, but, while I know a few barracks songs well enough to sing them when there are enough other voices so that mine is lost—"

"No, you idiot. I am not asking you to entertain me."

"Ah. Well, I tell Your Majesty in all honesty that I am just as glad."

"I wish to know," said Zerika, speaking slowly and carefully, as one might speak to an outlander or a small child, "what entertainments are available this evening—entertainments that it would not compromise the dignity of the Orb for me to be at. I require distraction, life, noise."

"Your Majesty, how am I to tell?"

"How? Well, there is a stack of invitations on that table in the corner; go and see if any of them are dated this evening."

"Yes, Majesty."

Sergeant crossed to the indicated table, picked up the topmost of the rather large pile of letters, and, after glancing at it, announced, "Today the Count of Southmoor celebrates the completion of his home, Castle Black."

"What do you tell me?"

Sergeant repeated what he had said.

"Southmoor, do you say? Morrolan?"

"Yes, Your Majesty."

"But, it has been less than a year!"

"It seems, Your Majesty, that he has an astonishing number of Vallista at his disposal."

"Well, but, why wasn't I informed of this?"

"But Your Majesty was informed—the invitation is here, on thin black paper with gold lettering, addressed to: 'Her Imperial Majesty, Zerika the Fourth, House of the Phoenix, Empress of Dragaera, at Whitecrest Manor, Adrilankha.'"

"Bring it here."

Sergeant handed the invitation to Her Majesty with a bow. Zerika looked at it carefully, and noted that, in fact, it was not written on thin paper, but, rather, on silk; and, moreover, the lettering itself was, in fact, gold.

"Well, that is certainly addressed to me. And the proof is, the invitation is here. And, moreover, it does not lack for style."

"Then shall I make arrangements?"

"Yes, do so."

"Very well. But—"

"Yes?"

"What arrangements am I to make? That is to say, how will you get there?"

"Do you remember a certain Athyra named Bebbyn?"

"I do."

"He is the Imperial Sorcerer. He will arrange transportation."

"Very well. What else?"

"Do you know Lord Brimford?"

"The—that is to say, the Easterner?"

"Exactly."

"I have seen him."

"Inform him that I will be at—what is the name? Castle Black. That I will be at Castle Black this evening."

"Yes, Majesty."

"And find my maid," said Zerika, standing up. "Send her to me in my apartment. I go now to dress."

The Empress was going to the ball.

Chapter the Seventy-Fourth

How the Entertainment at Castle Black Took Place

It was on a Skyday in the winter of the first year of the reign of the Empress Zerika the Fourth that Morrolan opened the doors of Castle Black. Lady Teldra was there to greet the guests, who included, among others, Sethra Lavode, Sethra the Younger, the Sorceress in Green, the Necromancer, Viscount Lászlo of Brimford (that is, the Warlock), Khaavren, Aerich, Tazendra, and three score or so of nobles of various Houses, mostly Dragon, who were either teleported in by Morrolan himself, who had fairly mastered the art, or were levitated up to the courtyard after arriving below it by some other means.

It is worth mentioning that this event, quite aside from its effect on the history we have taken it upon ourselves to relate, marks the first time an entertainment was given to which any of the guests (not to mention most of them) arrived by teleportation, and, as such, is significant to those who make a study of the social customs of such affairs. While no doubt interesting, such a study is beyond the scope of this history, wherefore we will content ourselves with the mere observation of the fact.

Morrolan himself was kept busy answering questions, most of them having to do with the problems unique to construction carried on far off the ground. Even endless repetitions of the remark "Well, it is certainly a defensible position" or near variations did nothing to depress his spirits—he smiled and laughed and greeted his guests through the night, at one time remarking to Teldra, "This is very nearly as enjoyable a pastime as battle."

Morrolan had arranged for confections from Nacine, where there were two quite respectable bakers. In addition, he had imported creepers from the Shallow Sea, squabs from the Southern Coast, beef and kethna from the surrounding peasants (prepared by chefs discovered and recommended by Teldra), and wines from as far away as Aerethia. For entertainment, he had raided both Hartre and Adrilankha for instrumentalists, singers, and jongleurs, as well as bringing in several of the local peasant orchestras, with their traditional instrumentation of violin, bagpipe, fretted demkor, and slim-whistle. There were, as well, a number of cittern players, some of them quite skilled, others only providing accompaniment for their voices, which in these cases was never less than pleasant.

The ball-room, which had nearly been a temple, and before that had been a room of some unknown purpose, served its function quite well: there was not only easy access to the kitchens and storage lockers, but, in the event, the small alcoves connecting to it were perfect places for those who desired a few minutes of private conversation, and were thus in nearly constant use.

Khaavren, dressed in a pure white shirt with ruffled collar and sleeves, an azure doublet, blue leggings, and black boots, accompanied the Countess of Whitecrest, who had made, it must be admitted, a spectacular toilet. Her dark hair was swirled up, held in place by a golden pin set with four pearls. Her gown was bright red, cut low enough to attract interest, and it fell quite simply to her trim ankles—its only shape was Daro's shape, which was certainly sufficient. The gown featured tall wings of lace upon the shoulders creating a sort of frame for her lightly powdered face. Around her neck hung another string of pearls, this one so long that it fell nearly to her waist. A sort of sash or baldric of bright, shimmering blue ran loosely from her left shoulder to her right hip, and on it were three small rubies. Her shoes were white, buckled, and adorned with a sapphire upon the toe. She had rings on each hand, one a pearl, the other a ruby. Upon seeing her complete ensemble as they prepared to leave Whitecrest Manor, Khaavren had observed, "Madam, it would appear that, today, I am an accessory."

Khaavren met Morrolan in the ballroom, and, bowing deeply, said, "My lord Morrolan, Count of Southmoor, permit me to present my wife, Daro, Countess of Whitecrest."

For the sake of completeness, we ought to mention that, by advice from Teldra, Morrolan had dressed very simply, in an elegant black and silver warrior's costume—Teldra pretended that, as the host, he ought not to wear anything that might make any guest feel he had paid insufficient attention to his toilet.

"But," said Morrolan, "is it not as bad if someone feels he has gone to too much trouble?"

"No one will feel that way on this occasion," said Teldra. "Your invitation will insure that."

"How, it will?"

"You will see."

Having made this necessary interruption, we return to the introduction of Daro and Morrolan. The Dragonlord made a courtly bow (Teldra had gone to some pains to show him how this was properly done) and kissed her hand. Daro, for her part, made a thousand compliments on his castle, not forgetting to observe the sweeping marble stairway, the elegance of the gold banisters, the fountain in the central hallway, and the three quite remarkable chandeliers, each with over two hundred candles, that graced the ballroom itself.

"You are too kind, madam," said Morrolan. "May I show you and my good friend Khaavren where we have hidden the wine?"

"A splendid idea, sir; we should like nothing better."

"But," observed Khaavren, "Cha! Who is this I see guarding the wine?"

"Not guarding it in the least, my dear Khaavren," said Aerich. "Rather, standing in what I knew would be the best position to intercept you."

"You are right once more, my friend." He turned to Morrolan, saying, "I hope, sir, that I may trust you with the Countess for some few minutes while my friend and I have conversation."

"Sir," said Morrolan, "I promise that she will be entertained, but not excessively."

"That is exactly right," said Khaavren, while Daro said, "You are charming, sir."

"Your arm, Countess?"

"Here it is, Count."

"Come, I will introduce you to the Sorceress in Green."

"Ah, permit me to guess: She is the one wearing green?"

"How did you know?"

As Morrolan led Daro in one direction, Khaavren took his friend Aerich in the other, finding one of the private rooms that was, by chance, unoccupied. They took chairs, and silently toasted each other, after which Khaavren, looking carefully at Aerich, said, "If you were Pel, rather than yourself, I should say, 'my conscience pierces me.'"

"'Stabs' is the formula, my friend."

"Well, stabs then. It doesn't matter, as you are not Pel."

"No, I am not. And yet—he has become the Discreet. I am happy for him."

"Yes, his ambition is realized. Or, at least, one of his ambitions. Who knows how many he has?"

"That is true, dear Khaavren. And Tazendra has realized her ambition—Tazendra Lavode. For myself, I should never have guessed it."

"Nor I, and yet we should have. You remember how well she and the Enchantress seemed to understand one another."

"That is true, and she has always had an abiding love for sorcery."

"And what of your ambitions, my dear Aerich?"

"Mine? They are all fulfilled. I grow grapes, I watch them turn into wine, I drink the wine. What more could I want?"

"And that is enough for you?"

"More than enough, my dear friend."

"Family?"

"Perhaps, someday. It would be good to be able to pass on my estate to an heir, but I am in no hurry."

"That is good."

"Moreover—"

"Yes?"

"I very nearly have a son."

"How, you do? You, Aerich?"

"I said nearly, Khaavren. I was speaking of the young Viscount. He—but what is it, my dear friend?"

"What is it? Why, you wrote to me."

"That is true, but then, you know that the Countess wrote to me."

"Well that is true."

"She indicated that you would be pleased to speak to me."

Khaavren smiled. "I do not deny it. But she said nothing of the subject upon which I desired speech with you?"

"Not the least in the world. Does it concern your son, my friend?"

"Aerich, how did you know?"

"Because of the expression that crossed your countenance when I mentioned his name."

"It is impossible to deceive you."

"Well then, it does concern the Viscount?"

"It does, Aerich."

"Is he well?"

"I don't know. That is to say, I do not know where he is."

"How, he has vanished?"

"He has run off."

"But, he must have had a reason."

"Oh, yes. I think he had a reason."

"Well, relate the entire history to me."

"I will do so."

Khaavren described his conversation with Piro. Aerich shook his head upon learning that the young Tiassa had wished to marry outside of his House, and looked sad upon hearing of the Viscount's embittered departure.

"My poor friend," murmured Aerich.

"Tell me frankly," said Khaavren. "Have I done wrong?"

"To drive away one's own son is wicked; to permit him to marry improperly is infamous."

"Had I a third choice?"

"I don't know, my friend. I am only glad, now, that I was never faced with the challenge of raising a child during a time when there was no Empire. The Empire is all we know of right and wrong; without it, we are lost, as a ship is lost when out of sight of land, with no record of its direction and rate of sail."

Khaavren emitted a short, barking laugh—the laugh one gives out of bitterness, rather than amusement—and said, "If the Empire is all we know of right and wrong, then I am surely wrong, for I have left the Empress's service."

"Have you, Khaavren? That astonishes me."

"Well, it is good that I can still astonish you on occasion."

"Would you care to tell me why you resigned, Khaavren? You needn't if you don't wish to."

"Bah. This Phoenix annoys me."

"Does she?" said Aerich, with something of a smile. "More than the last one did?"

"Oh, the last one couldn't help it, so I didn't mind."

"You have unusual standards."

"Perhaps I do."

"So then, what will you do now?"

"I wish I knew. Aerich—"

"Well?"

"Do you think I ought to search for him?"

The Lyorn nodded slowly. "If you wish my opinion—"

"I always wish your opinion, Aerich."

"Well then, yes, I think you ought to at least speak to him."

"Ah, well!"

"Yes?"

"I must tell you, first, that I do not know how to find him."

"Yes, and after that?"

"After that? Well, if I did find him, I do not know what to say."

"As to what you will say, well, I cannot tell you. It may be there is nothing to say that will do any good. But you must try. And, as to finding him—"

"Well?"

"Perhaps, working together, we will discover a way."

"You will help me?"

"Khaavren! How can you doubt it?"

"You are a good friend, Aerich."

"Well," said the Lyorn, shrugging and permitting a smile to touch his lips.

At this moment, there was a clap outside of the door.

"Who is there?" asked Khaavren.

Someone whose voice he did not recognize said, "If that is the Lord Khaavren, late of Her Majesty's Guard, then I would beg a moment of your time."

"It is I," said Khaavren, rising and opening the door. "And I believe I have a moment to spare."

The woman on the other side of the door, who seemed rather old, with lines of care on her forehead and marks of worry beneath her eyes, was dressed as a warrior, entirely in black with not the least speck of color, and had the distinctive ears and eyes of the House of the Dzur. She bowed to Khaavren and said, "My lord, I am called Sennya."

Khaavren's eyes widened, and he said, "Your Highness? I remember you from the days before the Disaster, though you perhaps never noticed me."

"Indeed, I remember you very well, the Captain of Tortaalik's Guard. And yes, I am the Dzur Heir, but it is not as Dzur Heir that I wish to exchange thoughts with you."

"Nevertheless, madam, please accept my respectful salute, and permit me to name my friend the Duke of Arylle."

Aerich, who had also risen to his feet, bowed. Sennya, for her part, returned the courtesy and, addressing Khaavren once more, said, "Perhaps we ought to speak in private, my lord."

Aerich bowed again and made a motion as if he would leave, but Khaavren said, "Not at all. Indeed, I believe I know the matter about which you would address me, and it is exactly what my friend Aerich and I have been discussing."

The Lyorn turned an inquiring look upon Khaavren, who

said, "Her Highness Princess Sennya is, in addition to being Dzur Heir, also the mother of Ibronka."

"Ah. I comprehend," said Aerich.

The Lyorn pulled up a chair for the Princess, then waited. After a moment, as if she had to make up her mind, she sat; Khaavren and Aerich did the same.

"I have been deciding," said Sennya, "whether to begin by saying, 'You are the man whose son has corrupted my daughter.'"

"The reverse," observed Khaavren, "would be equally valid."

"Certainly. And, whichever way it were put, there can only be one result of such a statement, and I would welcome it."

"You wish, then, to fight?"

"I am in no condition to fight. It would be a slaughter, and that is why I would welcome it."

Khaavren bowed his head. "I hope Your Highness will not think it too familiar of me to say that I understand."

"What happened?"

"I have not the least idea in the world, Highness. I gave her permission to accompany me when I left on an errand in the service of the Empire. I feared what I would say to you if she were killed—"

"Oh, I nearly wish she had been!"

"But this, I never expected this. Do you know, she had a friend?"

"No, I know nothing of any friend."

"And the friend was as pretty a Tiassa as you could imagine. This Tiassa and your daughter traveled together. How could I have thought that, when my son and your daughter met—"

"I do not blame you, my lord."

Khaavren bowed his head.

After a moment, he said, "My friend and I are going to look for my son. I imagine that, when we find him—"

"Yes. You will, no doubt, also find Ibronka."

"Yes."

Sennya considered. "Do you know the Hotel of the Tides in Adrilankha?"

"I do."

"That is where I will be."

"You do not wish to accompany us?"

"I am not ready to see my daughter yet. I do not trust what I might say."

"Your Highness is wiser than I am."

Sennya gave him a glance of inquiry, but he chose not to expand on his response. She said, "Very well. I will await word."

She rose, as did Khaavren and Aerich; they both bowed to her respectfully, and followed her out into the ball-room, where Khaavren, upon seeing a familiar face, cried, "Tazendra!"

"Khaavren! Aerich!"

The three of them embraced warmly, and were soon joined by Daro.

"My dear Countess," said Khaavren. "I fear—"

"You are leaving again."

"How, you knew?"

"It would be beyond my comprehension if you did not go to look for Piro, my lord."

Khaavren smiled. "Aerich will help me look."

"How," said Tazendra. "Your son is missing?"

"Yes," said Khaavren.

"Then I will help you find him as well."

"And do not leave me out," said another.

"Pel!" cried the others. "Or," continued Khaavren, "should I say, Your Discretion."

"Ah," said the Yendi, smiling. "It is all the same, it is all me. But what is this I hear, Khaavren. Your son is missing?"

"It is a tolerably long story, and one that is painful."

"You know," said Pel, "that it makes me only too happy to be of service to you."

"You are too good," said Khaavren.

"Not in the least."

"But your duties—"

"Oh, as to that. The Empress can spare me for a while; she has a tolerably clear conscience."

"Indeed?" said Khaavren.

Pel gave him a quick glance, but Khaavren only shrugged and said, "Well, perhaps she does at that. It is more than I can say of myself."

Daro, who had been holding his arm, pressed it gently.

"So then," said Khaavren. "You are with me? We go to find my son?"

"We are with you," said Aerich. "I must only take a short time to arrange matters with my steward, which cannot take more than a day."

"Indeed," said Pel. "For my part, I am ready as soon as I have packed a few belongings, and dusted off my sword."

"Certainly," said Tazendra. "A day or so to prepare a few spells that may be useful on the road, and I am at your service."

As Tazendra finished speaking, Lady Teldra entered and cried in a voice that carried throughout the room, "The Empress, Zerika the Fourth."

Her Majesty, resplendent in a high-necked gold gown, shimmering with opals and diamonds, also wore trim gold slippers, her yellow hair flowing entirely free behind her. Everyone bowed, which courtesy Her Majesty returned with a nod of her head and a wave of her hand. It was easy to see, from her countenance, that she was in the best of spirits: her lips and eyes smiled, and each movement was animated; she laughed as she was introduced to certain of the guests, and, although Khaavren could not hear what was said, it seemed that she was amused by everything that was said to her, and everything she said. Even when her path took her near Khaavren, whose courtesy to her was not without a certain stiffness, her spirits gave no hint of failing, but she gave him a cheerful greeting as if there had never been the thought of ill-feelings between them.

Needless to say, she was equally delighted to see the Countess, whose path she rarely crossed, though they lived for the moment under the same roof; the Countess smiled happily to Pel, and gave Tazendra and Aerich each a friendly smile.

By chance, at the moment the Empress had made her entrance, Morrolan had been involved in a conversation with the Necromancer in the far end of the ball-room. Breaking this off, he arrived to greet Her Majesty at just the moment that Pel and Tazendra were giving her their respectful courtesies.

"Your Majesty!" cried Morrolan. "You honor my poor house."

"Not at all," said Zerika, laughing. "A splendid place. You must do me the honor of visiting my own, when it is done. It should only be another five or ten years, I believe, now that all the best artisans are free, having finished yours."

"Oh, Majesty, if I have—"

She waved him to silence. "It is nothing, my friend. But come, we are in a public place, so, very publicly, I will tell you that I have broken my word to you, and I am sorry."

"How, broken your word to me?"

"There are three counties to the north that I promised you. Well, for reasons of state, I have been forced to give them elsewhere. I am very sorry, Southmoor, and I swear that I will find a way to make it up to you."

As it happened, Morrolan, though enjoying his reception in the event, had not expected to; that is, so much of his effort was directed at his study of the sorcerous arts that he had resented the interruption, though, indeed, he had agreed to it some months before when Teldra had proposed the idea. The result was that, with most of his attention absorbed by the ball, and the remainder still running the combinations for certain spells through his mind ("draw, twist, spread; draw, twist, send"), he had no attention left for matters of politics or economy—he had not given those three counties a single thought from the day they had been promised him. Accordingly, his only response was to wave his hand and say, "I beg Your Majesty will think nothing of it," with such obvious sincerity that Khaavren, for one, was astonished.

"You are generous, my lord," said Zerika, "and I shall not forget it."

"Oh, Your Majesty is free to remember or forget what you wish."

"Yes, Count, and it pleases me to remember this. And it

pleases me, as well, to pay you a thousand compliments on your lavish entertainment. You are giving me a lesson from which I hope to profit once there is an Imperial Palace again."

"Your Majesty is kind."

"Sethra Lavode," announced Lady Teldra.

The Enchantress of Dzur Mountain—powerful, enigmatic, moody—had been looked upon by many Emperors in many different ways. There had been times when she had been sought and courted, other times when she had been banished and threatened with arrest; but, so far as this historian has been able to discover, this was the first time the Empress of Dragaera had thrown herself into the arms of Sethra Lavode, embracing her as a dear friend, to the silent astonishment of those present who were old enough to have known the ways of court. She dressed, as was her custom, in the ancient Lavode uniform of loose-fitting trousers and shirt of black, with only the flair of the former and the collar of the latter giving any hint of style.

As for Zerika, she cared not all for what anyone thought, nor for the Enchantress's garb, but was merely glad to see her friend. "Ah, Sethra! I had not known you would be here!"

"Nor had I planned to attend, until I learned that Your Majesty was coming. As it is, alas, I cannot remain long."

"Well, I understand, but I cannot express my joy to see you."

"And I am equally delighted to see Your Majesty."

And so the evening passed—indeed, the evening, the night, and much of the next morning, until at length Lady Teldra observed to Morrolan that they ought to consider sending around the bottle of parting.

"Indeed? Why is that?"

"Well, my lord, the entertainment cannot continue forever, after all."

"But why can it not? You perceive, we sent out hundreds of invitations, and it seems that every time someone arrives, he must speak with a friend and inform him that the entertainment is entertaining, and so someone else appears. Indeed, I have had a full score of our guests approach me and beg to be permitted to extend an invitation to a friend who was not included in our list."

"Well, and?"

"And so, I see no reason to ask my guests to leave. Some, indeed, have already departed, although this has seemed to me to be from an excess of wine rather than from an onset of sleepiness. So, some leave, some arrive; let it continue."

"My lord—"

"Well?"

"You cannot remain awake forever."

"Nor do I need to. We have plenty of servants to continue supplying wine and food, and enough musicians. Should I require sleep, well, I will turn the matter over to you. Should you wish to sleep, no doubt Sethra the Younger will manage. If she becomes tired, she may ask the Sorceress in Green. And, by the time the Sorceress is weary, well, I shall be awake once more."

"My lord, you wish this entertainment to run forever?"

"Why not?"

Teldra frowned. "In fact, I must consider this question."

"Very well. While you consider, I—"

"Yes, my lord?"

"I will order more wine from the cellar."

The wine-cellars of Castle Black were not as famous then as they would become, but were tolerably well filled with casks, barrels, and bottles. At this moment, however, they held something else, that being a pair of Teckla, who sat against one of the walls, each holding a large wooden goblet, which he refilled from the nearest cask as the need arose. The reader will hardly be surprised to learn that one of these is our old friend Mica, the other being none other than Aerich's servant, Fawnd.

"So then," said Fawnd in a clear voice, as, it must be admitted, he held his wine remarkably well for a Teckla, "how is your dear Srahi?"

"Oh, splendid," said Mica. "After a hard day's work, if she has exerted herself, I bring her pilsner and rub her back.

Whereas, if it is I who have been working hard, why, she brings me ale and rubs my foot."

"Your foot, my friend? Not your feet?"

"Well, you perceive it would be useless to rub the wooden stump that replaced my foot when I lost it, so long ago."

"Ah, yes. I had forgotten this circumstance. Well, you must remember me to her."

"I shall certainly do so, dear Fawnd."

"Well, we have seen some adventures, you and I, have we not?"

"Of a certainty we have. And, moreover—ah, my cup is empty."

"Here, permit me."

"You are kind."

"There. What were you saying?"

"I no longer recall."

"Adventure."

"Ah. Yes. Well, I see no reason for it to stop."

"You do not? Even with the Empire restored?"

"Oh, I do not believe that is settled, you know."

"How, you do not think it is?"

"No, nothing is certain."

"And yet, there is now an Empress, is there not?"

"The Houses have yet to agree on that."

"Well, that is true, good Mica. But I have overheard my master speak of this, and he sounds sufficiently sanguine."

"Does he? But what of this Kâna?"

"It is true, he has not yet been found, arrested, and starred, as he certainly deserves to be. But, if he has done nothing for this last half year and more, he cannot be overly strong."

"You think not? And yet—"

"Well?"

"A peculiar thing happened yester-day."

"Would you care to tell me of it?"

"Tell you of what?"

"Do you need more wine?"

"Not yet."

"Then tell me of the peculiar thing that happened yesterday."

"Oh, yes. That. I was serving my mistress at Dzur Mountain, and I chanced to be in the kitchen with Tukko—"

"Who?"

"Sethra's servant. A very strange fellow. I shall introduce you. His name is Chaz."

"I thought his name . . . but never mind that. He is friendly?"

"Well, not as you would say friendly."

"But a good companion?"

"Well, no."

"Then never mind introducing us."

"Very well."

"But what were you saying?"

"I was telling you about Tukko."

"No, before that."

"I do not recall."

"You were in the kitchen."

"Yes, with Chaz."

"And—?"

"Ah, yes. Well, as I was in the kitchen bringing out biscuits after having selected the best wine—because you know my mistress has a fine palate—"

"Oh, yes. I have remarked upon it many times."

"And, as I emerged, I heard what I took to be a child's voice."

"A child? In Dzur Mountain?"

"So it seemed."

"Did you go out and look?"

"Certainly. I had to bring out the biscuits, did I not?"

"Naturally."

"Well, and what did you see, Mica?"

"As pretty a little Dragonlord as I have ever seen, speaking to Sethra Lavode—to the Enchantress, you understand—as if she had known her all her life."

"Do you truly tell me so?"

"I even insist up on it."

"A Dragonlord, you say?"

"Without question. There is no mistaking the cheekbones, even in a child, and she was already growing her noble's point."

"Well, so the Enchantress knows this child. It does make one wonder, does it not?"

"It certainly made me wonder."

"What was she saying."

"Well, in fact, it was something arcane and mystical."

"How, this child was saying something arcane and mystical?"

"I think so. At least, I didn't understand it."

"But, what did she say?"

"She said, 'Tri'nagore has been missing from the Halls of Judgment.'"

"Well, I agree."

"You agree that Tri'nagore has been missing?"

"No, I agree that it is arcane and mystical."

"Oh. Yes, tolerably."

"What did the Enchantress say upon learning this arcane and mystical thing?"

"She said nothing, but—"

"Yes?"

"She appeared to be anxious."

"Did she?"

"Without doubt. In fact, more than anxious, she seemed concerned."

"Well, that is certainly interesting. I wonder what it means."

"And then—"

"There is more?"

"Yes, I have not yet told you the most remarkable part."

"Well then, tell me."

"The child vanished."

"How, vanished?"

"Yes, as if she turned into a—"

"Yes?"

"Into a thousand flecks of gold, which then turned into nothing at all."

"Do you know, I have heard that gods appear and vanish in that way."

"Could she be a goddess?"

"Who knows? But I wonder about what she told the Enchantress. That is, I wonder what it means."

"It means—may I trouble you for more wine?"

"You spilled most of your last cup."

"And if I did?"

"Nothing. Here it is."

"You are a splendid fellow."

"Still, I am curious about what it means."

"Oh, as for what it means, that I can tell you."

"Well, I should be most happy to learn."

Mica looked into the wine of his cup, such a dark red that it was nearly purple, and he said, "There is a great deal more to do."

Chapter the Seventy-Fifth

How Khaavren Began His Search For Piro in the Heart of Adrilankha

It was in the morning on a Farmday near the beginning of the second year of the reign of the Empress Zerika the Fourth that Khaavren began, in earnest, the search for his son. He wore a white shirt with his second-best blue singlet, a heavy cloak of light blue, and his favorite rapier, which had served him well for more than seven hundred years, although, in point of fact, he had twice had to have the blade replaced.

He required the stable-boy to bring him his favorite horse, a nine-year-old roan gelding of the breed called Táncoslábú, a horse with a fine, proud gait, as well as one capable of running at truly astonishing speeds for two full miles; beyond this, he would respond to the least pressure of Khaavren's knees; indeed, at times it seemed that Khaavren had only to formulate his wish and the horse, whom he called Stepper, would obey. So, then, with his best horse, his best sword, and his second best singlet, our Tiassa set out on that morning, with a bitter wind coming off the sea. It took him over an hour to negotiate the twisting roads leading to the north bank of the river, a delay increased by the construction that was blocking off many of the major roads, as not only was the district where the Palace was being built blocked off, but several other roads were taken up by over-sized wagons negotiating narrow streets with construction materials. At length, however, he arrived at a certain manor house distinguished by several large boulders in front and an iron gate surrounding it. As the gate happened to be open, he rode through it, and leaving his horse tied to a convenient hitching post (there not being a stable-boy in sight), he approached the door and pulled upon the clapper.

A pretty little maid at once opened the door, inquiring as to what His Lordship might wish.

"I am Khaavren of Castle Rock, Count of Whitecrest by courtesy, and, if it is convenient, I should wish to wait upon your master, your mistress, or both. If it is not convenient, then I should desire an appointment."

"Yes, my lord. If you will do us the honor to step into the waiting room, I will convey your message at once."

After only a short wait, Khaavren was led into a comfortable sitting room, or perhaps a library, as there was no shortage of books on shelves along the walls, these books being the only decoration save for a sword of indifferent quality that was hung by a pair of wires. And in this room were both the master and the mistress of the house, both dressed casually; the one in Dzur black, the other in green and white. They bowed to Khaavren respectfully, although with a hint of coldness, and asked if he would care to sit.

With a certain aspect of ceremony, Khaavren unbuckled his sword belt and leaned it against a wall before returning to the middle of the room, bowing carefully to each of his hosts, and saying, "I believe I shall stand."

"As you wish," said Shant, the Dzurlord.

"May I offer you wine?" asked Lewchin. "I have some of your esteemed namesake, and it is a tolerably old date. Or we may have klava brought to us; here we brew it exceptionally strong, and have plenty of honey."

"Thank you for you kindness, madam, but I require no refreshment, only conversation, if you would be so agreeable."

"Certainly, sir," said Shant. "We are entirely at your service."

"Upon what subject, sir," inquired Lewchin, "does Your Lordship wish conversation?"

The words "you know perfectly well" reached almost to Khaavren's lips, where they were stopped, pushed back, and swallowed, perhaps in part by the elegance of the courtesy with which he had been addressed. Instead he said, with a certain abruptness, "Where is my son?"

There was a silence—hardly less awkward for being brief—at the end of which, Lewchin said, "My lord, are you entirely certain you would not care to sit?"

Khaavren clenched his jaw. His position, to be sure, was difficult; while he had never forbidden his son to see these two, and had known they were close, he had never approved of their arrangement: Dzur and Issola living together as husband and wife. Indeed, it seemed likely to Khaavren that it was their example, more than any other factor, that had led Piro to not only fall in love with a girl of another House, but believe that he might marry her. All of this was true, and yet, it was also true that he was here as a guest.

In the end, he compromised: sitting on the edge of his chair, his back upright. Shant and Lewchin, on the other hand, sat fully in their own chairs—quite comfortable leather padded with some resilient material on the arms as well as the seat—in a way that struck Khaavren as just on the right side of insolence. It flashed through his mind how he would treat these two if they were guardsmen under his command; after which he brought his attention back to the present moment.

"Very well," said Khaavren. "I am sitting. May I do myself the honor of putting my question a second time?"

"Instead," said Lewchin, "perhaps you would do us the honor of permitting us to put a question to you?"

Unspoken at the end of this remark was the observation "as you are in our home." Khaavren heard it, and, though far from delighted, found himself unable to offer a good reason to decline, wherefore he nodded. "Very well, then. That is but just. What is your question?"

"It is simply this: Why ought we to tell you?"

"What is that?" said Khaavren, turning pale and his voice sounding rather hoarse in his own ears.

"My lord," said Shant, "you perceive that we do not deny that our friend Piro has communicated with us. Indeed, he has, and on more than one occasion. And it is obvious from the very fact that you ask your question that he has not told you where he is. It therefore seems plain that he does not want you to know. Why, then, ought we to break a confidence with which he did us the honor to trust us?"

"He is, then, alive?"

Lewchin, whose manner, as we have said, had been somewhat cold—indeed, remarkably cold for an Issola—softened her expression and said, "Yes, my lord. There is no harm in telling you that he is alive, and in good health when last he wrote to us, which was this Marketday week."

Khaavren bowed his head in thanks for this intelligence, then, raising it once more, said, "To answer the question you did me the honor to ask: In the first place, I should point out that I am his father."

Shant and Lewchin nodded—which nod gave very nearly the impression of a shrug.

"Moreover," continued Khaavren, "well, I wish to speak to him."

"It is possible," said Shant, "that he has less interest in speaking to you. I say this only because he has not done so. It is true that, hitherto, neither have you; yet surely you must see that I cannot take it upon myself to make this decision for him. It would not be the act of a friend. You must, sir, see how impossible your request is." It occurred to Khaavren that somewhere during the course of the conversation he had lost the moral advantage—if, indeed, he had ever held it. "I should very much like," he said, after reflecting for a moment, "to learn from him if what you say is true."

"And if it is," said Shant. "Will you respect his wishes in this matter?"

"No," said Khaavren.

"Well," said Shant, and this time he did shrug.

Khaavren felt himself trembling with anger, so that he had to fight to master it.

"He is my son!" cried Khaavren.

"He is our friend," said Shant coolly.

"Come sir," said Lewchin. "Would you not do as much for a friend of yours, should he ask?"

"A friend of mine would not—" He broke off, aware that, should he bring the sentence to its conclusion, he could do his cause no good.

"Do what?" said Shant, a light growing in his eye.

Khaavren matched his glare. "Do not seek to provoke me, young Dzur. I promise you that nothing good could come of any games played between us."

"And why not? I have not fought in—how long?"

"Twelve weeks," said Lewchin. "And you should not fight now."

"And yet—"

"How do you suppose," continued Lewchin, "Piro would feel to know that you and his father had slaughtered one another? Can you explain to me what good would come of such a course?"

Khaavren bowed his head. "Exactly my own thoughts, madam."

"Well," said Lewchin.

"You are right," said Shant, sighing as with regret.

"So then, sir," continued Lewchin, "if there is no more to say—"

"Please," said Khaavren.

Lewchin looked down. "I am sorry. In all conscience, I cannot. He has trusted us. To do as you ask would be nothing less than a betrayal."

Khaavren frowned. "Well, can you at least tell him that I wish to speak to him?"

Lewchin nodded slowly. "Very well. That, at least, I can do."

"At the earliest moment," added Shant.

Khaavren rose to his feet, bowed stiffly to each of them, and picked up his sword belt, although he did not strap it on until he was outside of the house. There he mounted his horse once more, and slowly rode through Adrilankha, pulling his heavy woolen cloak more tightly about himself.

Instead of returning to Whitecrest Manor, however, he turned onto Canal Road, and so came, after a short ride, to the Canal Inn, where he found a quiet table and ordered klava. The host explained that his establishment did not serve this most estimable brew, but a few coins convinced him to send a boy down the street and return quickly with a steaming glass, embellished exactly to the Tiassa's specifications—which was done the more readily as Khaavren was the only nobleman there, and the first to pass its doors in more than a year, wherefore the host hoped to encourage such custom.

Khaavren sat in a corner and drank his klava, and, when it was done, ordered another, which was supplied with, if anything, even greater promptness and precision than the first. By the time Khaavren had finished his second glass, he was ready to order a lunch, which he did, partaking of a bowl of the inn's lamb stew accompanied by thick-crusted bread and a glass of wine. He ate his lunch slowly, not so much in order to savor it (although, in fact, it was a most respectable stew, as such stews go) as to make the time pass.

In this way he was rewarded, because the inn's servant had hardly cleared away the bowl and received the order for a second glass of wine before Khaavren was joined at his table.

"I wish you a pleasant morning, Pel."

"Morning? It is after noon, my friend."

"Is it? Well, so much the worse; there is half a day wasted."

Pel gave him the smile that only Pel, or perhaps another Yendi, was capable of giving. "I would not say it was wasted, my friend."

Khaavren looked up. "You have put the day to good use?"

"Certainly. Even very good use."

"Then you have—"

"Made a discovery."

"How, so soon?"

"Why else do you imagine I am here?"

"I had no idea. For my part, my errand failed entirely."

"I think not entirely."

"No, that is true; it occurred to me to request of them to ask Piro if he would consent to let me know his whereabouts."

"Would you consider it boastful, my friend, if I were to say I had guessed it would come to that?"

"Not in the least, Pel. You know me, perhaps, better than I know myself."

"Exactly. I not only guessed it would come to that, but—"

"Well, what else?"

"I thought to use that knowledge."

"But, in what way did you use it?"

"In a way that you would not have approved if I had told you ahead of time I planned to."

"You must understand, Pel, that I do not at all understand what you do me the honor to tell me."

"Then permit me to simply relate my history, and then, well, you will understand everything."

"Very good, I will be as mute as an Ekrasanite."

"That is best, believe me. So then, you had not been gone half an hour before the maid-servant left, evidently on an errand. Apropos, did you notice that she is a very pretty girl?"

"How, you were there?"

"Outside of the house, yes, while you had your interview."

"But . . . well, go on, my friend, go on. Where did this maid-servant go?"

"Where else, but to the posting house on Settled Way, near Nine Stones."

"Ah, ah! She was posting a letter!"

"Certainly. And the proof was, it was in her hand as she walked."

"Posting it for her master or her mistress?"

"So we can assume."

"To Piro!" cried Khaavren, understanding of Pel's ploy coming to him at last.

"That is very nearly a certainty."

"So then, what did you do?"

"What did I do? Well, I followed the girl."

"Yes, and?"

"And then I became lost."

"You, lost?"

"Certainly. You know that I have only lived in Adrilankha this last year, and have never been in this part of the city."

"Well, but what did you do?"

"What anyone would do when lost: I asked for help."

"Of whom?"

"Of Macska, of course."

"Macska?"

"The pretty maid-servant."

"Ah, ah! And was she able to help you out of your plight?"

"Oh, she had not the least difficulty. She pointed out exactly the turns I needed to make in order to get to my destination."

"And what destination was that?"

"Why, this charming little inn where we now find ourselves."

"Of course. Well, so she was able to direct you?"

"It required a certain amount of gesturing and pointing."

"And, during this gesturing and pointing?"

"Why I just happened to get a glimpse of the address."

"Ah, you are remarkable."

"And I got more than that."

"What, more?"

"Yes. I got a promise from Macska to permit me to show her an evening's entertainment."

"What? You, Pel, with a Teckla?"

"I give you my word, I have no intention of marrying her."

"Nevertheless—"

"But do you wish to hear the address?"

"Indeed, I wish it more than anything else."

"The letter was addressed to a certain Kékróka, in care of the Deepwell Inn, Mistyvale County."

"So then, it wasn't to Piro!" cried Khaavren."

"Ah, my friend. Do not be naïve. Do you think it probable that your son is having letters sent to him in his own name?"

"Ah, that is true!"

"And then?"

"Pel, you continue to astonish me. I tell you so. And you are right, had you told me what you were planning, well, I should certainly not have approved."

"But now that it is done?"

"Well, I do not know about approving, nor do I know what our friend Aerich would say, but I cannot help but use the information you have provided. And, moreover—"

"Yes?"

"Now I understand why you had such confidence we would learn where he was by to-morrow."

"And so?"

"I am in your debt once more."

The Yendi bowed and said, "Well, it now but remains to collect our friends, and to learn where Mistyvale County is, and, well, we are on our way."

"Our friends did not anticipate our setting out before to-morrow at the earliest."

"Perhaps, but I believe they will be ready in any case."

"So then?"

"Are you packed, my good Khaavren?"

"I have everything I need with me. And you?"

"Oh, you know that I am always ready to travel on short notice, or no notice whatsoever."

"Then I will pay the shot, and we will be on our way."

"Will you finish your wine first?"

Khaavren shrugged and, still holding his wine, signaled the host, who scrupulously calculated what was owed him. Khaavren paid it and thanked the host for the service he had received, which was both prompt and cheerful. The host was delighted, and assured Khaavren that, should he ever grace his house again, there would be klava.

Khaavren tipped his hat, his host, and his wine-glass, after which he followed Pel out the door.

Chapter the Seventy-Sixth

How Matters Transpired at the Deepwell Inn

Mistyvale County—that is to say, the Mistyvale County between Adrilankha and the Shallow Sea, as opposed to one of the other three—took its name less from any romantic notions engendered by this name (though no doubt the name is, indeed, tolerably romantic) than from simple observation. It is one of the handful of counties nestled between Southmoor and Bra-Moor, south of the Collier Hills, and twenty-five or thirty leagues west and north of Aerich's home of Brachington's Moor. The entire region is hills and valleys, with the Adrilankha River cutting through them like an orange ribbon; most of the hills being grass-covered, but some showing only bare rock. The hills and valleys are all modest, even compared to the Collier Hills, but, perhaps because of the ubiquitous river, or perhaps because of some strange effect generated by its hills, the valleys are filled with a thick carpet of fog nearly every morning. Perhaps the most striking effect of this fog is that the district has nearly as many stories about it as the Kanefthali Mountains or the desert of Suntra; indeed, Dewers's famous *Tales of the Landlocked Harbor* are set there, and many of the landmarks referred to in his tales of supernatural wonder are in fact real (although, to be sure, the events he described seem to come from his own fertile imagination).

Numerous roads crisscross Mistyvale County: from Riverwall to Steps, from Brambles to Crossway, from Nacine to

Gridley, from Hillcrest to Ripples, from Lottstown to Gorge. Moreover, these roads have not been carefully named; to be sure there is the Gridley Road, and the Lottstown Road, but there are three distinct roads called Hillcrest Pike and two that are known generally as the Brambles Road, so traveling in the region was problematical for a stranger, especially since the Disaster, as the various signs and markers had fallen apart and not been repaired; yet, even during the height of the Interregnum these roads had been used, as there continued to be a certain amount of trade in coal and ore even with the refineries long closed and abandoned.

Inns and taverns were built, flourished, and died with a brutal regularity along these roads, the average lifespan before the Disaster being only a few hundred years, and during the Interregnum perhaps a few score. Of course, there were exceptions: the Feathers, in Brambles, has been in existence for at least six thousands of years, and the Pins, between Crossway and Hillcrest, has been in existence for so long that this historian cannot learn its origins (and does not care to accept the word of its present owners). Another exception, to be found on the Hillcrest Pike not far from Deepwell, is the Deepwell Inn, which claims its date of origin as the Fifteenth Tsalmoth Reign—certainly long enough ago to be respectable by any standards.

The Deepwell was a narrow, two-story building—indeed, it had been built to have three stories, but it had been constructed so well, of stone reinforced with iron braces driven into the stone, that, over the millennia, it sank into the ground rather than falling apart, and several hundreds of years ago the owners had been obliged to tear out the bed-rooms and create a jug-room from them. As a result, it had one upper story of bed-rooms to let; the main floor which held the jug-room; kitchen, pantry, and storage below; and additional storage yet further below, in what had been the original basement and wine-cellar. The main floor had two windows looking out from the jug-room, one looking west and the other north, and two doors, one opening to the west and the other to the east. In addition, it had a third door, which opened from the kitchen, below the ground, and into a tunnel that went south and emerged in the stables.

According to what sources we can find, the Deepwell had been a welcoming home to highwaymen since its erection, and no matter how many times its owner was taken by the Count, or occasionally the Duke (Mistyvale had been part of Arylle, Luatha, and even Hampers at various times), and fined, imprisoned, or even starred for aiding road agents, the new owner would continue the practice without the least hesitation. In the words of the owner at the time of which we have the honor to write, a certain Dunnclay, "I can help my friends, and I am assured of as much custom as I could wish as well as not infrequent gifts; or I can turn them in to the authorities, in which case I will petition for Protection of Debts in a month and be dead in a year. I know which end of my cup has the hole."

At the time of which we write, Dunnclay did, indeed, have as much custom as he could wish: the over-sized jug-room was tolerably crowded, nearly all of them Teckla, though there were one or two Chreotha or Tsalmoth merchants. One of these, a Tsalmoth, was engaged in an earnest conversation with one of the Teckla.

"But my friend," said the Tsalmoth, "for so I hope I may call you—"

"Oh, certainly. Why, if you buy me another cup of this excellent stout, you may call me anything that comes to mind!"

"So much the better," said the Tsalmoth. "Then, you will answer a question?"

"For this splendid stout, I will answer ten."

"Then, if you please, tell me of these road agents I hear so much about."

"Well, what do you hear?"

"That for one such as I, travel can be dangerous."

"One such as you? You are, then, a wealthy man?"

"Oh, by no means. I would not say *wealthy*. It is true that I own a small, that is, a modest iron mine that employs some two hundred miners, and another twenty smelters, and brings me an income of three thousand imperials—"

"Three thousand imperials a year?"

"Please, not so loud."

"But, that is riches beyond belief! In the old days, Count Mistyvale, I am told, only received an income of two hundred imperials, although, to be sure, this was augmented by a certain amount of livestock, and the odd bushel of rye."

"That is a good income," said the Tsalmoth complacently. "I think you are rich."

"Well, but my brother's wife, who owns three mines, well, her income is at least ten thousand imperials."

"I cannot conceive of that much."

"I have a good imagination."

"Well, that is reasonable, my lord."

"To return to my question—"

"Well?"

"Are the roads safe?"

"Oh, yes. The roads are entirely safe."

"So the much the better."

"Unless you are wealthy."

"Oh!"

"Then you must be careful of the Blue Fox."

"Who?"

"The Blue Fox. A most fearsome bandit."

"Oh, I don't like to hear that!"

"When he robs someone, he likes to make sure he takes every penny, and so—"

"Yes, and so?"

"If he thinks you have not given him everything, he will hang you upside down from a tree, and cut you to pieces."

"Oh! Oh! Oh! But, what if you give him everything?"

"Oh, then that is different. If he thinks you may be worth something in ransom, he will keep you safe and sound, treating you like a prince until the ransom is paid."

"And if the ransom is not paid?"

"Why, then he will begin sending you back to those he thinks should pay. First a finger, then a toe—"

"Say no more, I beg you! What if the ransom is paid?"

"Why, then it will be just the same as if you were never

held for ransom in the first place—that is, he will simply cut your throat in the neatest and most efficient possible way. He is not a cruel man."

The merchant shuddered. "Does no one go free?"

"Oh, never. He pretends that dead men are unable to identify him."

"You terrify me!"

"Bah. There is nothing to fear. Why, nearly half of the wealthy men who travel upon this road at night never even meet him, and arrive safely at their destination."

"What about those who travel in the day?"

"Oh, that is much safer. Nearly two out of three wealthy men reach their destination with no trouble."

"But what of the Empire? Does it do nothing?"

"Oh, yes. From time to time soldiers are sent in to look for the Blue Fox."

"Well, and do they find him?"

"You perceive, soldiers are not wealthy."

"And so?"

"And so he lets them pass, if they do not attempt to take him."

"And if they do?"

"Why, then he sends them back a little more battered, that is all. I believe three or four soldiers have been killed, but no more; usually they are only wounded, even if they persist in attacking. I have never heard of him setting out to attack soldiers, which is kind of him."

"He must be a demon!"

"Oh, not in the least. His band can be demonic, you perceive, but he is kindness itself."

"His band? Then he does not work alone?"

"To be sure he has a band. There are perhaps a score of them, all told, who serve the Blue Fox, and would permit themselves to be roasted over a spit for him."

"The trey! What are they like?"

"They are not like the Blue Fox."

"In what way?"

"They are vicious and cruel, and only kept in check by their loyalty to their leader. Why, if it weren't for the Blue Fox, the roads hereabout would be unsafe for an honest man!"

"The Gods! From what you tell me, they are sufficiently unsafe now!"

"Oh no, my lord. They are perfectly safe for an honest man."

"But you said that if you are wealthy, you are likely to be robbed, hung upside down, cut to ribbons, held for hostage, carved into pieces, and have your throat cut!"

"Yes, you have understood exactly."

"My friend—"

"Well?"

"It is possible, you know, to be wealthy and yet to be honest."

"How, is it? You perceive, I had not been aware of this circumstance. But then, I am a poor peasant, and so, naturally, ignorant of many things."

"Oh, it is true, I give you my word."

"Well—"

"Yes?"

"Perhaps someone ought to inform the Blue Fox of this. He does not seem to comprehend it either."

"What does he do with all of his money?"

"Oh, he and his band spend it freely."

"Where?"

"All over the county. They purchase food and wine and pic-nic in the glades, or else they will come into an inn and buy out all the supplies for everyone present, and command that music be played. I have had the honor to be present at one of these, and I assure you it was a wonderfully gay time."

"Perhaps I should post a reward for their capture."

"Oh, there is already a reward for their capture. Five hundred gold imperials for the Blue Fox, and four hundred for each of his band."

"Why, that is a tolerably round number."

"I think so."

"And has no one endeavored to get it?"

"Some have, yes."

"Well, what has become of them."

"Why, three of them are buried behind this very inn. Others are buried elsewhere."

"Oh, oh! I shall never arrive in Adrilankha!"

"Adrilankha?"

"Why, yes. I have bank-drafts on the house of my lord Kentra, who is my second cousin, and has a very sound institution—his assets are over a hundred thousand imperials."

"Impossible!" cried the Teckla. "There isn't so much money in the world!"

"It is the simple truth. And I have two drafts, one for five hundred gold, and the other for three hundred, and I must present them. But, if I am robbed and my throat is cut, well, you perceive it would be utterly impossible."

"Well, yes, only—"

"Well?"

"What is a bank-draft?"

"It is very much like note-of-hand, only with a guarantee of gold behind it."

"Oh, my lord, you perceive I do not comprehend at all what you do me the honor to tell me."

"Have you never had anyone give you a note in which he admitted that he was indebted to you?"

"Why, my neighbor once had use of my prize boar, and I received a note saying that, in exchange, I should have my choice of shoats—at least, I believe that is what it said; you perceive I do not know my symbols."

"Well, but did you receive the shoat?"

"Oh, certainly—and a fine thumping sow she was, too!"

"Well, you see, the same thing can be done with money."

"How, can it? I had never known. And then, you get the choice of imperials when they have bred?"

"No, no. That is not what I meant. Well, in a way it is. But a draft on a bank is promise to pay gold, you see, just as you received a promise to pay you a shoat."

The Teckla clapped his hands. "I comprehend!"

"It is good that you do, only—"

"Yes?"

"How am I ever to reach Adrilankha with my drafts?"

"Oh. You must avoid the main roads, that is all, and travel by back roads only until you reach Covered Springs. From there it is safe, or else, if you are still worried, there are barges that go down the river until you reach Adrilankha as easy as picking berries."

"Well, but—"

"Yes?"

"I do not know these back roads. I should become lost."

"Ah, ah. I had not considered this possibility."

"What shall I do?"

"If you become lost, ask someone."

"Is it safe to do so?"

"Certainly, as long as you are not wealthy."

"Well, and if you are?"

"Then it may be that you will be asking someone in league with the Blue Fox. I am reliably informed that there are many such on the back roads."

"I am lost!" moaned the traveler.

"Certainly, it is difficult," said the Teckla, who seemed to be moved by the Tsalmoth's distress.

"But what do others do in this circumstance?"

The Teckla considered for a moment, then said, "Some of them pay some local as a guide to show them safe paths."

"And does this work?"

"Oh certainly. It is the safest way."

"And what sort of compensation is expected for this service?"

"I beg Your Lordship's pardon?"

"How much does it cost?"

"Oh. Three or four silver orbs will usually answer."

"Very well. I will pay you four silver orbs to guide me safely to Covered Springs."

"Me?"

"Certainly, and why not you? You know the paths, do you not?"

"Well, that is true."

"And then, you can use the silver?"

"Oh, certainly. I could buy my adored wife an entire bolt of fine linen with it."

"Then, there you are. An evening's work, and you have a bolt of fine linen for your esteemed wife."

"Adored wife."

"Yes, pardon me. Adored wife."

"It is a tempting offer."

"Well, have we a bargain?"

The Teckla frowned, began to shake his head, appeared to reflect, and at last said, "Why not? Very well, I agree. When would Your Lordship wish to leave?"

"At once!"

"Oh, but—"

"Well?"

"I have half a cup of stout before me."

"Very well, then. After you have finished your drink."

"I thank Your Lordship exceedingly for his courtesy."

"After you, my friend."

"No, my lord. After you. I insist upon it."

"Very well."

The Tsalmoth led the way out of the inn and recovered his horse, which was saddled and ready. He mounted it, and the Teckla mounted upon a pretty little mule.

"Now, my friend, you must lead, as I do not know the way."

"Yes, my lord. I am leading."

"And I am following." They set off through the night. There was little conversation as the Teckla picked his way among roads that were little more than the ruts of wagon wheels, sometimes little more than animal tracks, but, as he appeared to know where he was going, the Tsalmoth gave no signs of worry, until the Teckla suddenly stopped, and held up a single finger in the universal gesture for silence, a finger the Tsalmoth was able to observe by the light of the single lantern that provided the illumination for the journey.

After a moment, the Teckla said, or rather, whispered, "I hear something."

"What do you hear?" asked the Tsalmoth, also in a whisper.

"I believe—I fear we are being followed."

"You think so?"

"I hear horses behind us."

"You seem to be worried."

"Well, my lord, aren't you?"

"Not in the least. Let us go on."

"How, you are not worried?"

"So long as they are behind us, and not before us, I wish to continue. Besides, I think it likely you are mistaken."

"You think so?" said the Teckla doubtfully.

"I heard nothing."

"And yet—"

"Lead the way, my friend."

"As Your Lordship wishes."

The continued on for perhaps another mile before the Teckla stopped again.

"What is it?" said the merchant.

"My lord, I am convinced that we are being followed."

"You think it is this Blue Fox?"

"No . . . that is to say, I don't know."

"But, if it were, why have they not waylaid us?"

"As to that, I cannot say. And yet—"

"Well?"

"I am frightened."

"And yet, didn't you say that an honest man has nothing to fear?"

"That is true."

"And are you not an honest man?"

"Oh, as to that—"

"Well?"

"I once cheated at cards."

"That is not so bad."

"You think it isn't?"

"Not unless you make a habit of it."

"Nevertheless, I am worried."

"Well, if they are behind us, we cannot go back."

"That is true."

"And remaining here, well, we should not make any appreciable progress."

"I cannot dispute with Your Lordship."

"Then let us go on."

"And yet—"

"Go!"

"Yes, my lord."

From that point, they had not gone half a mile before they halted again, only this time it was not from the Teckla's orders, but, rather, from the orders that came from behind a particularly thick tree—one that would have easily concealed a man even without the additional aid of the heavy darkness. Upon hearing the imperious command, the Teckla and the Tsalmoth both drew rein, the Tsalmoth saying quite coolly, "The Blue Fox, I presume."

"So I am sometimes called, sir," said the other, stepping out from behind the tree, and showing, in the dim light of the lantern, that he held a naked sword. Moreover, other figures now appeared, behind them, and the glint of steel came from their hands as well.

The merchant, however, said, "Address me as Your Venerance," in a tone that assumed respect would be given—indeed, in a tone far different from what the Teckla had yet heard him use.

"Very well," said the Blue Fox. "I have no objection to courtesy."

"So much the better."

"Now, if Your Venerance will be good enough to hand over his purse, why, he may be on his way without delay."

"I'm afraid," said the other, "that there must be a delay in any case."

"Oh, indeed? I sincerely hope Your Venerance does not contemplate resisting us. There are, after all, several of us, and we are all armed, and know what to do with steel, and, I give you my word, if you force us to pierce you, we will have your purse in any case, leaving you poorer than you would otherwise be, being reduced by not only whatever coins you may carry, but also by some quantity of blood, and perhaps even your life, upon which Your Venerance may place some value."

"Some," said the other.

"Well then—"

"But you mistake, I am not alone."

"Oh, Your Venerance refers to Jami, your friend on the mule."

"You know him?"

"Well enough; he has been of service to us before."

The Teckla, Jami, bowed at this, while the merchant said, "It is good to have friends."

"You think so?"

"I am convinced of it."

"Then we are in agreement."

"I have friends of my own, in fact."

"Do you?"

"Assuredly. In fact, it was my own friends to whom I referred just now. I have three, as it happens." And, even as he spoke, there was the sound of horses, and, indeed, three more drew up.

"Make light," said the Blue Fox, and two of the bandits behind him lit lanterns, illuminating the face of the merchant.

The Blue Fox stared at the merchant in the growing light, and suddenly cried out, "Pel!"

The Yendi dressed as a Tsalmoth bowed from his horse, even as the three riders behind him drew up into the light.

"Hello, my son," said Khaavren in a grim tone. "Well met."

Chapter the Seventy-Seventh

How Father and Son Spoke After a Separation of Some Length

"Well met, my father," said Piro in a shaky voice. "You perceive, I had not expected you."

"Am I less welcome for that?"

"Did you expect to be welcomed?"

"I had, perhaps, hoped."

"As to your welcome, I cannot say. But at least you may dismount your horse—or, rather, follow us a short distance, and we will give you what hospitality we have in our camp."

"Very well. I thank you for the hospitality."

Piro bowed from his saddle, turned his horse's head, and led the way.

"If the rumors are true, then I understand you are no longer in the service of the Empire, my lord."

"The rumors are true, Viscount."

"So much the better, as you are not, then, required to arrest me, and I am not required to decide if I am to resist you."

"Would you have resisted me, Viscount?"

Piro shrugged. "I am pleased, my lord, that the question has not arisen."

As promised, the bandit's encampment was very close, and so, in a short time, they had arrived there, where Lar, who had been cooking, was more than a little astonished to see that he had additional guests for dinner.

"My lord Khaavren!" he cried. "And Your Venerance! And . . . oh my goodness!" After this outburst, and observing that Mica was not there, he retreated in confusion back to his work, which, at this moment, was to be certain each horse that had returned was safely tied up and well groomed, which task he carried out with his usual precision before beginning on either a very late supper or a very early breakfast, a distinction the Blue Fox was in the habit of neither making nor requiring, wherefore the good Lar meticulously followed this example.

While the horses were thus being tended, the others sat down around the fire, except for Piro and Khaavren, who set off walking through the darkness together.

For a time, neither of them spoke, Khaavren because he could not think of what to say—or, at any rate how to say it; and Piro because, as he was the one who had been hunted down, he did not feel it was his responsibility to begin. This train of thought, however, led him to eventually break the silence with the words "How did you find me?"

"Ah, you wish to know that?" said Khaavren.

"You must understand my curiosity. I had thought I was sufficiently well hidden."

"You must recall we had Pel searching for us."

"Ah yes, that is true. You have told me no few stories about him."

Khaavren nodded. "He tricked your friends, Shant and Lewchin. It is true that he also tricked me, but I will not play the hypocrite and claim that I object to this."

"I understand. So it was from them that you learned where I might be found?"

"Yes, after spending some time with a map and determining which Mistyvale County was most likely. Of course, it was Tazendra who observed that this Mistyvale County was where the Blue Fox could be found."

"The Blue Fox? But, how were able to determine that I was the Blue Fox?"

"From Aerich."

"Aerich?"

"He speaks more languages than I knew existed. The ancient tongues of the Dragon and of the Lyorn, and even some of the Yendi. He can squeak like a Serioli, yowl like a cat-centaur, and grunt or trill some ten or twenty of the Eastern languages, in one of which the name that you used to Shant and Lewchin translated to Blue Fox."

"Ah. I comprehend."

"After that, it was Pel once more, as you saw."

"Yes, and, permit me to say, a well-played stroke."

"Pel will, I am certain, be pleased to hear you say so."

"Then tell him, if you please."

"I will not fail to do so."

"Well, now I know how you found me."

"Yes."

"It remains for me to know why."

"Can you ask?"

"The Horse! I not only can, it seems to me that I did!"

"Well, that is true. You know that your mother misses you."

"I miss her."

"It is wrong of you to be away from her."

"It was wrong of you to make me choose between romantic and filial love."

"Then you feel some filial love?"

"You know that I do."

"I had hoped."

"Well?"

"You perceive, it was not I that forced this choice upon you, it is the world that forces this choice."

"Ah, Father, you are wrong to hide behind such a claim; it smacks of the sycophant."

"You would use such a word with me?"

"It was you who taught me that there is a time to state unpleasant truths. Can you deny that this is such a time?"

"You believe, then, there is no justification for my claim that it is the world itself that is to blame?"

"There is some, I do not deny that."

"Well?"

"But it was you who made me to know that I could not love the woman I love, and still retain your affection."

"How, you believe that?"

"It seems to me that you were adamant on the subject."

"It is true that I felt strongly."

"Well?"

Khaavren looked down. "Let us speak of this."

"Cha! I thought we were doing exactly that!"

"Let us continue to do so."

"Very well, with this I agree."

In spite of the comment he had just made, Khaavren found that he was unable to say anything—or, at any rate, that his next words ought not to be uttered without at least a certain amount of thought. He felt, in fact, as if he were walking on a tension-wire; it seemed to him that a single wrong word, and he might lose forever his son. And yet, an answer was required. Piro, for his part, remained silent and permitted him to think, either out of courtesy, or for lack of anything to say.

At length, Khaavren said, "Did you give any thought to this marriage before suggesting it?"

"No," said Piro.

"Well, do you not think that marriage—that is, the agreement to remain together for a lifetime, which is tolerably long—ought to be given some thought?"

"No," said Piro.

"How, you do not?"

"I love her. I cannot conceive of life without her. You perceive, such a life would be meaningless to me. Therefore, well, what is there to think about?"

"And what of your children?"

"Perhaps we shall have none."

"That would be a pity, to have no children."

"It would be a pity to spend my life alone."

"Well, that is true."

"Moreover, it would be a pity to have children with a woman I did not love."

"That is true as well," admitted Khaavren.

"Or to spend my life with someone toward whom I am indifferent."

"Well, of course, not all marriages last for-ever—"

"Father, do you hear what you are saying?"

Khaavren sighed. "Yes. Will you permit me to withdraw my last observation?"

"Certainly."

"Thank you."

They continued walking for some time, just within sight of the fire, which was always to their left.

As they spoke, indifferent to the smells of the food, Lar took a heavy cook-pot and, with Clari's help, began dishing out a sort of stew made of norska, tubers, and onions, along with various seasonings. Lar having added a certain quantity of water to the stew, as well as a few extra tubers, there was plenty for all. Lar served portions of this stew to everyone except for Aerich, who declined, pretending he was not hungry. When everyone had food, Lar passed around the wine, which, significantly, was a Khaav'n, and one that Lar said was of a very nice year. Lar, Clari, and Jami served it out to everyone except Aerich, who again declined, saying he wasn't thirsty.

If anyone was disturbed by Aerich's lack of interest in food or drink, the Lyorn was not: he sat placidly on the ground, leaning against his saddle, his legs stretched out in front of him, and a calm smile on his noble countenance as a being perfectly happy within himself, unconcerned for the rest of the world, which world was presently eating and drinking with great energy, the only conversation being praise of the food or demands for more wine. Jami, still humiliated by having been taken in by the Yendi, remained in the background, saying nothing and doing his best not to be seen; Lar, for his part, responded to both praise and demand in the same manner: that is, by bowing. Clari served the wine as needed.

Tazendra, who always ate quickly, was the first to begin the general conversation, which she did by saying, "It is good to see you again, my dear Kytraan."

"Why, it is a great pleasure to me as well, and permit me to offer you my wish for good fortune in the upcoming battle."

"Ah!" said Tazendra. "There is to be a battle, then?"

"I think so," said Kytraan.

"With whom?"

"With the Pretender. You perceive, it is nearly all anyone talks about."

"What do they say?"

"That the tyrant must be defeated."

"Tyrant?" said Pel, now listening to the exchange.

"The Pretender," explained Kytraan.

"Ah. I had not known he was a tyrant."

"Well," said Kytraan, shrugging. "Anyone who attempts to take the Orb and fails is a tyrant. At least, that is the general opinion."

"So then, if he succeeds he will not be a tyrant?"

"Exactly. If he succeeds, then Zerika will become the tyrant."

Pel shrugged. "I do not pay especial attention to general opinions."

"Nor does Piro," put in Ibronka. "You perceive, that is what he and his father are now discussing, I think."

"That," said Pel, "or specific opinions, which are another matter entirely."

"Yes. And while we are talking of specific opinions—"

"Well?"

"Has anyone," asked Ibronka, "heard from Her Highness, Sennya?"

"I only know that she has been to court," said Pel.

"But she said nothing about me?"

"She spoke of you to Her Majesty," said Pel, "desiring you to be found, and using terms that left no doubt about her continued affection for you. But, as I heard this conversation as part of my official duties, you perceive that I cannot relay it to you."

"Well, I understand."

Clari addressed Aerich, saying, "Would Your Venerance care for wine now?"

Aerich declined with a gesture of his hand and returned to his contemplations.

Pel said, "Offer him water."

"Would Your Venerance care for water?" said Clari obediently. "It is fresh from a clear spring not twenty steps away; we made our camp around it, and I can testify as to its purity."

"Very well," said Aerich.

While Clari went to fetch the Lyorn a cup of water, Röaana said softly to Pel, "Has His Venerance giving up the drinking of wine?"

"No," said Pel. "But, if I were to guess—"

"Well?"

"I believe he does not wish to partake of anything that was purchased with money from robbery."

"Ah," said Röaana, "I had not considered this circumstance."

"And you," said Kytraan, "You have no such compunctions?"

"Oh, it is different for me," said Pel. "You perceive, I eat from Her Majesty's table."

"Well, and then?"

"Her Majesty's table is filled from tithes given by the Great Houses, and these tithes are collected from taxes on homes, and on grains, and on trade."

"So that?"

Pel shrugged. "So that, one might say, all I partake of is purchased with money from robbery."

Tazendra said, "You see no distinction between taxes and robbery?"

"Oh, no doubt there are differences, but I do not bother with them."

"That seems odd," said Ibronka, "for an official of government."

Pel shrugged.

"There is a difference," said Aerich quietly. "It is the difference of law."

"Oh, law," said Pel, shrugging again.

"You disdain the law, my friend?" said Aerich, smiling a little.

"Nearly."

"So then, you have nothing to say against our friends here,

who waylay travelers to relieve them of their purses, filled with coins earned by more or less of hard work?"

"More or less," repeated Pel. "I wonder which it is?"

"As to that, who can say?"

"Exactly. Who can say?"

"But then, my dear Pel, you should prefer to live in a society without laws?"

"Such a thing is impossible," he said. "If there are no laws, then, you perceive, there is no society."

"I beg your pardon, my friend," said Aerich, "but it appears to me you contradict yourself."

"Not in the least," said Pel.

"I do not comprehend."

"Then I shall explain."

"Very well, I am listening."

"There are laws, laws, and laws, my dear Aerich."

"Three sorts?"

"More than that, but let us simplify."

"I am in favor of simplifying, if nothing of consequence is lost."

"We will see."

"Very well."

"First, there are laws of nature."

"I understand those."

"Then there laws of man."

"That is clear enough. And the third?"

"Laws of honor."

"Are these not laws of nature?"

"Not in the least."

"Then, they are laws of men?"

"Only of a particular kind."

"Go on, then."

"We all obey the laws of nature."

"Well, how can we not?"

"Exactly. And then there laws of man, which some obey, and some do not, and most of us—"

"Yes, most of us?"

"Why, most of us walk a sort of line, choosing which of these to obey, and which to ignore as inconvenient."

"You think so?"

"Well, those with whom we are sharing a meal—except for you, of course—have chosen to ignore the laws that say if a man buys a pound of bacon for ten pennies and sells it for twelve, he is entitled to the two extra."

"That seems a good law to me."

Pel shrugged. "Perhaps it is. To be sure, if there were no such law, it would be more difficult to find someone willing to sell a pound of bacon."

"That is my opinion as well. And then?"

"Why, you remember when we were in the Guards, and we met those charming fellows who believed they could ignore the laws that required taxing of all games of chance."

"I remember."

"And our fellow guardsman who so much agreed with them that they felt they, in turn, could ignore the laws that said a guardsman must not turn his head from violations of the law, and certainly must not accept money to turn his head."

"You remember that I took no such money."

"You are above normal men, Aerich."

"Well."

"Yet those who took the money, they were good guardsmen, good Dragonlords, and often good citizens."

"I see where you are going."

"It is clear enough is it not?"

"It is a matter of honor."

"Precisely, Aerich. The laws of honor speak of duty, and love, and friendship, and loyalty, and place them in a nice order. The laws of honor are how we make choices among them, and choices of which of the laws of men we obey."

"You make a powerful argument, Pel. Don't you agree, Tazendra?"

"Oh, well, yes, certainly. I had been remarking upon this. Duty, that is Aerich. Love, that is Khaavren. I am friendship, and Pel is loyalty. There, you see? That is why we get along so well."

"No doubt you are right," said Pel.

"So then," continued Aerich, "each man has his own laws of honor?"

"Certainly," said Pel. "Inherited from his family, his friends, and everyone and everything he meets every day of his life. Except for you, of course, my dear Aerich."

"I am the exception?" said the Lyorn with a smile.

"Certainly. You were born with the laws of honor intact, and they have never varied a day in your life. That is why you cannot understand them. You can no more understand your own sense of honor than you can tell the flavor of your tongue."

"I do not know if you give me too much credit, or too little."

"Well."

"But, you believe, this gives you license to break the laws of men, if you follow those of honor?"

"Certainly. Not everyone, Aerich, can always follow both. Sometimes you must break one or the other. Were you confronted with such a choice, I know which direction you would go, and so do you."

"My dear Pel, to be confronted with such a choice means that either there is something wrong with your code of honor—"

"Yes, or?"

"Or something is wrong with the laws."

"With this, I agree."

"Ah. Well, you see, I am wrong; I had not thought we would agree on anything."

"How could we not, Aerich, when, for an inflexible, supercilious termagant, well, you are most agreeable. I should clink my cup with yours, if you had anything in it but water."

"How, that prevents you?"

"Nearly. I should not like to dishonor the sentiment."

Aerich chuckled. "Well then, in my heart I drink with you. But tell me—"

"Yes?"

"Was it your sense of honor that led you to abandon the service of the Pretender? Or was it perspicacity, knowing that Zerika would ultimately triumph?"

"Neither. Either of those would have led me to support Kâna; in the first place because I had committed myself, and in the second because I thought he would win."

"Well then, what was it?"

"You know that very well, Aerich. It was friendship, of course, which is not unlike love."

"So then, friendship and love can conflict with honor?"

"Friendship and love are part of honor. Friendship and love, however, can conflict with each other, and both can conflict with duty. Witness our poor friend Khaavren at this moment, not to mention his son."

Aerich sighed. "I believe you are right. How do you think it will end?"

Pel shook his head. "The fact is—"

"Well?"

"I have not the least idea in the world."

Aerich and Pel (and occasionally Tazendra) carried on this conversation as if they were alone in the world or back in the old house they had lived in in Dragaera City, instead of sitting among a number of highwaymen keeping a respectful silence. Ibronka, for her part, stared at them and listened, as if she had been permitted to eavesdrop on conversations of the gods—something only the reader has been permitted to do in fact. And as this conversation went on, Khaavren and his son continued their long, slow walk.

"So then," said Khaavren. "Tell me something, Viscount."

"I will answer any question you ask."

"What do you wish?"

"What do I wish?"

"Yes, Viscount. What would you like to happen?"

"Why, I should like you and the Countess my mother to embrace Ibronka, and for her mother to embrace me, and then I should like to return to Adrilankha."

"Do you think this can happen?"

"It seems unlikely."

"You ask a great deal of me, Piro."

"On the contrary, my lord. I ask nothing of you at all. You did me the honor to ask what I wished, that is all."

"In some ways," said Khaavren, speaking slowly, "I should prefer that I was able to disregard—that is to say, completely ignore—the rules and the laws of society, and the way I was reared."

"In some ways only, my lord?"

"It seems simple to you, doesn't it? You love, and your love is pure, and so that which follows from your love must be pure as well, and that which interferes with your love must be evil."

"My lord the Count, I am not such a fool as that."

"Well then?"

"How much am I to sacrifice, my lord? And to whom or to what is this sacrifice to be made? Who gains, and how much?"

"You sound like a merchant."

"Then I am ahead of my time, that is all."

"How, you think we are all to become merchants?"

"In ten years, it will be impossible to survive as a highwayman in this region. In a hundred years, it will be impossible anywhere. And in a thousand years, no one will be able to speak the word 'honor' without a disagreeable smirk upon his countenance."

"Do you really think it will come to that, Viscount?"

"I fear that it might."

"If so, well, I pity Aerich."

"And I pity you as well, my lord."

"Well, and you?"

"Oh, I do not pity myself; that would be useless, and nearly infamous."

"I meant, what will you do if all of these dire predictions of yours come to pass?"

"I shall have to find a way to survive that is less satisfactory than this, that is all. I am still young; I can always change my name and take a career in arms. Didn't you tell me once that, when you joined the Phoenix Guards, half of your comrades had enlisted under assumed names?"

"I should not like you to have to change your name, Viscount."

"Well, but I did so already, didn't I?"

"Yes. The Blue Fox. Apropos—"

"Well?"

"Do you believe there is something noble and romantic about being a highwayman?"

"Oh, as to that—"

"Well?"

"I very nearly do."

Khaavren sighed. "I imagine that, at your age, well, I would have thought so, too."

Piro bowed. "That was a noble admission, my lord."

Khaavren chuckled. "Well, but you must promise not to let my friend Aerich learn that I said it. You perceive, it would shatter his inflated opinion of my attributes."

"I will not say a word."

Khaavren smiled and fell silent once more.

In a little while, Piro said, "You will give my love to the Countess?"

"Of course, but you make it sound as if I am about to leave."

"Is there a reason to continue, my lord? You will not accept the woman I love, and I—"

"Yes, and you?"

"I will never leave Ibronka."

"Are you sure of her?"

"Cha! Are you sure of my mother the Countess?"

"Some might consider the question impertinent, Viscount. But I will simply say yes. But—"

"But?"

"I have never asked her to live in the woods, and survive by robbing poor merchants."

"Rich merchants, my lord."

"Very well, then, rich merchants."

"No, you have never asked her to live in the woods and rob. But, if you had, what would she have said?"

Khaavren frowned. "Well, that is to say—bah! Why could this girl of yours not have been a Tiassa?"

"For much the same reason that I could not be a Dzur."

"And yet, Viscount, it is wrong, that which you wish to do. Each time I try to bring myself to your position, I cannot get past that."

"What makes it wrong?"

Khaavren sighed. "The world is what it is, my son; not what we wish it to be."

"Have you not always taught me that we should make it what we wish it to be? And, indeed, haven't you been so engaged for the last year? I hope so, because that is what I thought I was doing as well."

"You have an answer for everything."

"I am in love; love answers everything."

"No, it does not, Viscount."

"Well, for a nature such as mine, it thinks it does, and that is very nearly the same."

"It pains me to leave with matters unresolved between us, Viscount."

"You can always reach me in care of Kékróka, at the Deepwell Inn."

Khaavren nodded. "Viscount, I am going to take my friends and return to Adrilankha, where I must have a conversation with Princess Sennya that I look forward to not at all."

"Yes, my lord."

"Before I go—"

"Well?"

"I should like to embrace you, Viscount."

"My lord, I should like nothing better."

Chapter the Seventy-Eighth

How Aerich Discovered Certain Unsettling Things Near His Home, And Was Able to Draw Various Carefully Deduced Conclusions

It was on a Farmday in early winter—that is to say, more than half a year after the last chapter of our history—when Fawnd presented himself before his master, Aerich, Duke of Arylle.

Aerich was, at this time, sitting before the fire in his parlor reading poetry, which was a customary way for him to spend time when nothing more pressing was occurring, and he was not inclined to crochet. On this occasion, the book was an anthology of some of the Athyra poets of the early Ninth Cycle, which he was reading because it would naturally include Redgrew, to whom the Lyorn was especially partial. Fawnd, observing his master's activity, signaled his presence with a slight cough, and then waited, perfectly motionless, with complete confidence that Aerich would give him attention after he finished the present canto.

The Lyorn eventually turned his limpid eye from book to servant and raised an eyebrow, indicating, "What is it?"

"A messenger, Your Venerance."

"From whom, pray?"

"From the Enchantress of Dzur Mountain, Venerance."

"Indeed?" said Aerich, at once setting his book down. "Then let him be brought in at once."

In an instant, the messenger had presented himself before Aerich and bowed. "Your Venerance," he said, "I have a communication from Sethra Lavode."

"Very well, hand it over."

"I shall do so at once, Your Venerance."

As good as his word, he handed Aerich a neatly sealed letter, the seal of which Aerich at once broke, after which he unfolded the letter and read. It took him only an instant, as the message was tolerably short, after which he said, "Very well. There is no reply. Fawnd, give the messenger an orb for his troubles and see him out. Then return."

Fawnd bowed and escorted the messenger out of the room and the manor. Aerich, notwithstanding his excellent memory and comprehension, read the brief note a second time to be certain he understood it. The message was simplicity itself, and we will reproduce it at once: "My lord Temma," it said, "I have become worried about Tazendra, who left Dzur Mountain last spring to return to her home, as she said, 'for a while.' I have not heard from her since, nor am I able to touch her mind. I should be glad if you could make certain she is all right, and let me know what you discover. I declare myself, sir, your servant, Sethra Lavode."

By the time Aerich had completed his second reading, Fawnd had returned. Aerich addressed him with these words: "Send me Steward. Then find my vambraces, sword, and an appropriate costume to match and lay them out. Have Ranger saddled and ready, with a supply of food in the saddle-pockets sufficient for a week, and an equal of amount of grain."

Fawnd bowed, and permitted himself only six words, "Am I to accompany Your Venerance?"

"Not on this occasion."

Now knowing everything he needed to know, the worthy servant set off to perform his tasks, with the result that, in only minutes, Steward arrived and presented himself. Aerich spent some few moments with his steward, making certain that his various fiefs should continue functioning during his absence.

He then opened the bottom drawer of his secretary and removed from it a metal box, which he opened with a small, ornate key that he kept on a chain around his neck. He opened the box and removed from it a small sheaf of papers, which contained the disposition of his property to be made after his death. He reviewed this document carefully, made a few small corrections, then replaced it in the box. The box went into the drawer, but the key he left out in plain view on top of the secretary. He indicated the key with a gesture to Steward, who, without a word being required, only bowed to indicate that he understood.

When the Lyorn's arrangements were complete, he dismissed Steward and returned to his apartment, where Fawnd assisted him into his loose-fitting red blouse, vambraces, warrior's skirt, and darr-skin boots; after which he buckled on his old, beaten belt with sword and poniard. Then he simply walked out of his manor, mounted his horse, and turned its head toward the barony of Daavya, setting out at a good speed.

As the reader may recall from our previous works, Daavya not only was part of the duchy of Arylle, but, in addition, happened to directly abut Bra-Moor County, of which Aerich was, of course, count. And so, as he rode at a good, martial speed, on a good horse, it was not many hours before Aerich had crossed over the small brook (one of thousands of streams with the name Barony Brook, as it marked the limits of a barony) and was then within the confines of Daavya.

Within a mile or so after crossing this boundary, Aerich drew rein and looked around. "Blood of the Horse, as my friend Khaavren would say," he murmured to himself.

All around him were indications of some great catastrophe: that is to say, every tree in sight was a blackened stump with the exception of a few saplings that appeared to be very recent. Even certain of the rocks showed signs of having been through some sort of conflagration. Aerich took a second, more careful look, attempting to judge how long ago it had occurred, and came to the conclusion, from the health of the grasses and various other signs, that it had been some months since whatever had happened.

"But," he wondered, "how is it possible that such a thing could have happened without my awareness, only a few miles away? Someone ought to have seen the flames if it was night, or the smoke if it occurred during the day, and reported it to me in my capacity as Tazendra's liege."

He frowned and considered. "Sorcery," he decided at last, and urged his horse forward at an even greater speed.

Presently, he came to Castle Daavya, which was, indeed, a castle in the old sense, having been built over two thousand years before (on the site of the previous castle) and kept up continuously. There was the traditional courtyard, where livestock, fodder, and supplies could be kept, as well as the peasants protected, in time of siege or attack. The castle itself was tall, with battlements, towers, and walls from which javelins, stones, or sorcery could be hurled. As for sorcery, there were large staves permanently set in all corners of both the outer and inner walls, so that spells could be more easily placed.

But it was none of this that struck Aerich's eye; rather, it was the fact that there were no signs in the castle of whatever had devastated the surrounding landscape. It seemed as if the spell had not passed the outer wall, either because of some protection surrounding the castle, or because it had not been intended to. This was, however, an indication that it was not mischance—that is, that whatever had happened was not the result of one of Tazendra's experiments having gone awry.

He also observed, in the dust of the courtyard, footprints, indicating that there were still dwellers within, and for a while he felt hope.

He tied his horse to a hitching post near the great front doors, approached them, and pulled the clapper. Presently, the doors swung open and he found himself facing a servant he did not recognize.

"I am Temma, Duke of Arylle, here to see the Baroness," he said.

The Teckla gave him a bow, but not the bow of a Teckla, instead one that, very nearly, mocked the salutes of the courtiers, and he said, "I am master here. How may I be of assistance?"

"Don't be absurd," said Aerich disdainfully. "Where is the Baroness?"

The Teckla shrugged and turned his back on Aerich, as if to say, "I have given my answer." Aerich scowled and stepped forward, raising his hand to chastise the impudent peasant, but the Teckla, not running, but walking at a good rate, had already disappeared within.

Aerich scowled again, but the briefest reflection convinced him that he ought not to lower himself by pursuing a Teckla, and that the indignity of giving the chastisement the servant deserved was greater than that of accepting it; in other words, he decided that such an insult was beneath his dignity to give heed to, and so, without giving the matter another thought, he stepped into Castle Daavya.

The most notable feature about the Great Hall of Castle Daavya was the domed ceiling, some seventy or seventy-five feet above the floor. The dome itself had been built with the castle, but Tazendra had replaced it with one with alternate triangular sections of colored glass, so that red, blue, green, and yellow shone down on the floor during daylight. Moreover, she had hung upon the walls samples of her own artwork—most them oils or pastels on tapestry—some renderings of Tazendra's ancestors (in many cases of which resemblances to our Dzur friend could be seen, especially in the wide forehead and the arch of the eyebrows), others depicting such scenes as a dzur fighting a dragon, a tiassa about to land on the back of a darr, a man armed only with a poniard fighting a bear.

These depictions were, we should say, violent, yet they had also a certain grace to them, as if the artist strove less to show the violence of the encounter than the ennobling aspects of the struggle. For while many artists—and viewers of art—may enjoy only the prurient aspects of works that show us violent activity, it is nevertheless the case that it is in moments of violence, of danger, of the greatest threat to life, that human character can become its most base, or its most sublime. As to why the artist may focus on these matters, this is revealed, in painting, by the use of light, shading, emphasis, and texturing; and the sympathetic viewer will, even if unaware of these things, nevertheless find himself moved by them. Certainly, Aerich was not unmoved, the more-so as he had a nervous, sensitive nature, and had been, himself, in mortal danger frequently enough to understand something of the feelings engendered by such extremities, although we must say that to our Lyorn such events were occasioned only by a strict sense of duty and obligation, and so many of the loftier, more ennobling, or, if we may, more *Dzur-like* facets of struggle were an enigma to him.

But then, to the left, it is exactly here that art may play its most vital rôle: by opening the heart and mind to feelings, the particular expressions of feelings, of which it had been otherwise unaware. Indeed, the fact that the same work of art might touch the heart of beings as disparate as a Teckla and a Phoenix, or a Serioli and an Easterner, is, more than anything else, the proof both of the value of that work in particular, and of art in general.

And what greater proof of the power of art can exist than that these reflections are caused by the work of Tazendra, whose personality, as the reader must by now be aware, is defined by violent activity, strong passions, and a certain lack of sensitivity which must almost inevitably characterize someone who can, with sword and staff, make herself as feared as our Dzurlord?

Another aspect of the Great Hall which impressed itself on Aerich's mind was that there was, by Tazendra's design, no place in it to sit. To be sure, she wished all of her guests to see, admire, and be moved by the grandeur of the hall, but for conversation, she preferred a more comfortable and intimate setting, which she assured herself would happen by making certain that anyone wishing to engage in discourse with her for any length of time would have to find another place in the castle in which to do so.

Aerich, after a moment's study, passed on, and began a general tour of the castle, looking for Tazendra, or Mica, or

Srahi, or, indeed, anyone else he knew. In fact, he saw no one except the Teckla he had earlier encountered, and who made a point of keeping out of his way.

After assuring himself that Tazendra was not there, Aerich went back through the castle, all sixty-one rooms of it, a second time, on this occasion studying each room, each corner, each closet, each drawer, looking for something that might give him an idea of where she might be, or what might have happened to her.

It was, we should add, a mark of how serious Aerich considered the matter that he submitted to the need for this sort of intrusion. This careful, detailed inspection took him into the next day. When he was finally overcome with weariness, he slept for a while in one of Tazendra's guest rooms, then continued his work. He ate three times from the supplies Fawnd had packed for him, and was also required to stop a few times to care for his horse. Eventually, however, he had inspected the entire castle.

After finishing this survey, conducted with a care that Khaavren would have approved, he returned to a small room where Tazendra had been accustomed to carry out the business of her barony—a room little used at the best of times, as Tazendra's custom was to let things go as they would until some event forced her to pay attention to the normally dreary responsibilities of her position.

In this room there were two large maps: one of them showing her barony in great detail, and the other a map of the Empire drawn during the Seventeenth Cycle. What had caught Aerich's eye was a tiny red dot on the map of the Empire. It was significant for the simple reason that it was the only mark that had been added to either of the maps. Returning to this room, Aerich studied the maps once more, then opened up drawers of Tazendra's secretary until he located where she kept her other maps, of which she had a good supply, most of them drawn on paper, but some on leather, and one or two on cloth. He carried out a minute inspection of these maps, until he was able to determine that Tazendra was, indeed, one of those who did not care to make markings on maps, presumably because she considered it defacement.

"Yes," said Aerich to himself. "There is no question. The mark was put on the map by whoever has taken Tazendra. Moreover, it was put there for no purpose except to be found. And found by me, of course. This means that it is someone who knows me, which means that, not only is there a trap, but it will be a tolerably clever one, and thus all the harder from which to extricate both Tazendra and myself. But, to the left, a living Tazendra will be better bait than a dead Tazendra, because, if I am to go in after her, I shall require some proof that she is still alive. Therefore, there is hope.

"Next," he continued, "there is the question of who might have done this. Well, the answer to that is simple: Grita, who else? We know well enough that she is involved with the Pretender, who is probably even now preparing his attack on the Empire. So then, Grita has taken Tazendra. The question remains: What to do about it? She has, almost certainly, prepared for all of the most obvious means of attack, and prepared even more for the subtle ones."

He sat behind Tazendra's secretary, staring at the map of the Empire, and reflected for some time. After completing his reflections, he walked out of the now deserted castle (at least, he had seen no sign of the Teckla for some time), saddled and mounted his horse, and began riding west.

Chapter the Seventy-Ninth

How Piro Met Someone Who Proved to Be Skilled at Arithmetic, And Grassfog Discovered That He Was Something of a Prophet

Thirteen or fourteen months had passed after Khaavren spoke with his son: months that included great and sweeping changes in all of the cities, especially in Adrilankha, which changes gradually slowed down and diminished as one got further away from the great centers of commerce. In many ways, the nearly two years between Zerika's appearance with the Orb and the Battle of Adrilankha saw more changes more quickly than had ever occurred before, or ever would again.

It could also be said that the changes produced by the end of the Interregnum (the term coming to be used for the period of history ended either by Zerika's emergence with the Orb or her arrival in Adrilankha) had effect in direct proportion to the effect of the Interregnum itself—in other words, if a certain area had only slowly and gradually felt the effects of Adron's Disaster, then it only slowly and gradually felt the effects of the return of the Empire.

One of these regions where change was felt only slowly was, to be sure, Mistyvale County, where Piro, still under the name of the Blue Fox, inspired fear in the hearts of all travelers. To some extent, even in the short months to which we referred above, Grassfog's prediction had been proven correct:

Some travelers, indeed, preferred to pay a sorcerer to teleport them from one place of safety to another. But for those who had goods to deliver—and with the kerosene refineries and the smelters beginning to work again, there were plenty of these—the cost of having goods teleported would have been prohibitive, and so, instead, they used the time-honored system of caravans, hoping that large numbers of merchants traveling together, along with mercenary soldiers in good numbers, would give them a measure of protection against road agents in general and the Blue Fox in particular.

The caravan system met with some success, at least as far as Piro was concerned. While some of them were small enough to be taken, Piro had, regretfully, to let many of them pass by, as he did not choose to risk injury to his small band any more than was necessary.

On the occasion of which we write, the size of the caravan was barely respectable, consisting of five small carts, covered in heavy canvas, and pulled by mule or pony, and the escort was only three warriors in front and an equal number in back, commanded by a tired-looking captain on a tired-looking horse. As the caravan came around a turning of the Great Southern Road (it had once been at least relatively great, and certainly ran through the southernmost part of Mistyvale County) Piro, looking through a particularly fine touch-it glass (ebony with gold embossing, a recent gift from Ibronka), remarked, "I believe we can take them easily enough. Grassfog and I to stop them, first group take the flank, second group in reserve from behind."

"I have no quarrel with this plan," said Ibronka. "Come, let us act quickly before they reach a place where they can run, giving us that much more difficulty in chasing them down."

"With this I agree. You will take the first group?"

"Of course. And Kytraan the second?"

"Naturally."

"Then I will inform them."

"Do, and send Grassfog to me. But first—"

"Yes?"

"I should like to kiss your hand."

"Certainly. Here it is."

"You are precious."

"My brave bandit!"

"Quickly now!"

"I am already leaving."

It took only minutes to arrange everything: by this time, the Blue Fox and his band were well versed in such games. Grassfog returned with the word that everything was ready, and everyone understood his instructions. Piro nodded, and together they stepped out onto the road. Piro held up his hand, and the captain of the escort, who was riding in front, drew rein and looked down, saying, "Well, gentlemen? Is there something you wish? I beg you to speak quickly, because we are in something of a hurry, wishing to reach Covered Springs before night falls."

"Oh, I do not believe that will present any problem. In only a few more miles you will strike the road that runs directly to it; but I am certain you are already aware of your route."

"Entirely."

"Then all is well. It remains merely for us to transact our business, and you can be on your way."

"Business? I do not understand what you do me the honor to say. What business have we to transact?"

"Why, only that my friend and I," here Grassfog bowed elegantly, "are anxious to assist you by reducing your burden. That way your animals will not have so much weight to pull."

"Reduce our burden? Well, and by what do you wish to reduce our burden?"

"Well, let us see what you are carrying so that we may consider the matter."

The horseman frowned. "You want to see what we are carrying in order to consider how to reduce our burden?"

"You perceive, you have only repeated my statement, turning it into the form of a question."

"Well, but it very nearly sounds as if you are proposing to rob us."

"I admit it is something very like."

"I do not wish to insult you by laughing—"

"Ah, you are delicate. So much the better."

"But there are two of you, and seven of us, and, moreover, I am mounted, and you are not."

Piro, who had been closely following the other's arithmetic, nodded his agreement with these calculations and said, "I have no argument with what you say, only—"

"Well?"

"You may observe by looking behind you that, in fact, instead of two of us, there are five."

The captain of the escort dutifully looked back, as Ibronka emerged from the woods, and, next to her, stood Iatha and Ritt.

"Well, but you perceive, seven is still greater than five. And then, there is, in addition, the matter that, by spurring my horse forward, I could ride you down easily enough."

"As to the second, sir," said Piro, "that is, without question, true. But you must perceive that, should you be so precipitate as to spur your horse at me, my friend here would be obliged to run his sword through your body." As he finished this speech, Grassfog coolly drew his sword, which was nearly as heavy as the one Ibronka carried, and held it in the relaxed grip of one who knew its length.

"Well, that is true for the second, but what of the first?"

"Oh, as to that, if you would look again, you will see that our numbers are, in fact, eight." As he spoke, Kytraan, Röaana, and Belly emerged, swords drawn, and positioned themselves behind the caravan.

We should add that, during all of this, the merchants themselves had grown successively paler. As for the captain, he observed the new arrivals, and said, "Yes, the numbers do alter the case."

"That is my opinion, sir; I am glad that we are in agreement."

"Before we continue with our business—"

"Then," interrupted Piro, "you agree we have business?"

"Oh, certainly; you have convinced me completely."

"Very well then. But forgive me; you were saying?"

"Yes, before we continue with our business, will you permit me to put a question to you?"

"That is only just," said Piro. "What, then, is this question?"

"Are you not, in fact, the Blue Fox?"

Piro bowed. "You have named me, sir."

"And so, then, there is a reward, is there not, of a thousand imperials for your capture? And that, in case you should (may the Favor preserve us) be brought in dead, you are still worth five hundred imperials?" (The reader may observe that, in two years, the size of the reward has increased.)

"Sir, permit me to observe that, with regards to numbers, you reckon like a true arithmetist."

"Well, it is true that I have a tolerably long head. And, is it not also the case that there is a reward of eight hundred imperials for each of your companions if you are brought in alive?"

"Why, yes. And if these figures were all added together, why, it would be a good round number."

"Thanks, my lord. That is my opinion as well."

"But then, I hope you do not think of attempting to collect these funds?"

"I fear, my friend, that this was exactly my thought."

"I beg to observe that you will not be given this reward unless we are brought in."

"Of this statistic I am already aware."

"And that does not deter you?"

"Not in the least."

"You perceive, nothing good can come of such a rash intention."

"You think not?"

"Well, consider that we are all tolerably skillful players."

"Oh, of that I have no doubt. I hope you will be equally generous with regard to us?"

"Certainly, I have no doubt at all. But yet—"

"Well?"

"Eight against seven. Come, you must know that some of you will be killed if you make this effort. Is it worth it, just for a bit of gold?"

"I think so. And then, I must dispute with your numbers."

"How, my numbers are wrong?"

"You have said I was something of an arithmetist."

"That is true, I do not doubt your skills in this regard."

"Very good. Then attend."

"I am listening."

"It is true that your number is eight."

"Ah, I am glad of that, at least, because it proves that I am not given over to illusion."

"Oh, there is no question of that."

"And then?"

"It is in regard to *our* numbers that your estimate may be incorrect."

"Well, let us see then."

"Yes, we will count carefully, so that there can be no mistake."

"Very well, we will begin with you, as you are in command. That is one."

"One, yes. Go on."

"Then there are three who are directly behind you, and who are even now exchanging grimaces with my three friends."

"You are right again, which makes—?"

"Four."

"I agree. Four. Go on."

"There are another three in the back, who are facing three of my friends, all of whom have drawn weapons, and they but await the word to begin what promises to be a frightful—and, I should add, unnecessary—slaughter."

"So then?"

"Well, that makes seven."

"That is true."

"And so?"

"But then, you have not counted the carts."

"The carts?"

"Yes. The five carts."

"Well, but what about them?"

"Why, each cart has room for two soldiers."

"Oh, I agree that each has the room, but does each have the soldiers?"

"Certainly. Why else should they be covered? Gentlemen!" he called. "If you please, it is time."

The covers on the carts were thrown back, and, indeed, each cart held a pair of warriors, each of whom now stood up, leapt to the ground, drew, and placed himself on his guard.

"Now then," continued the officer. "If my reckoning is correct, twice five is ten."

"It is," said Piro, who was endeavoring to overcome his astonishment at the contents of carts which he had assumed carried only goods to be traded.

"Well, and ten and seven is, let us see, seventeen, is it not?"

"Oh, I have already said that I cannot dispute with you as to figures."

"So then, it appears, our numbers are seventeen to eight, and—"

"Yes, and?"

"Then there are those who appear to be merchants."

"Ah, you say, 'appear to be.'"

"Well, yes."

"So then, they are not in fact?"

"Not in the least."

As he said this, the five supposed merchants pushed aside their robes, revealing that each had a sword, which he now drew in good style.

"So then," continued the captain, who, we should add, no longer appeared to be as tired as he had, any more than the "merchants" appeared to be pale, "seventeen and five is twenty-two, is it not?"

"You calculate soldiers the way a merchant counts coins—that is to say, without a flaw."

"So then, it seems we have twenty-two against your eight, and so—"

"Yes, and so?"

"It only remains for me to beg you to surrender."

"Oh!"

"Well?"

"That word! 'Surrender'!"

"Is it not a perfectly good word?"

"I confess, I do not like how it sounds in my ears."

"And yet, consider that, to resist, well, I believe you, yourself, used the word 'slaughter.'"

"That is true."

"And so?"

"Will you permit me to put to you a question?"

"It seems to me that you were sufficiently complaisant to permit a question from me; how can I do any less? What, then, is this famous question?"

"Did you, in fact, set out to-day with the intention of setting a trap for me?"

"How, you don't know?"

"Oh, I suspect; nevertheless, I should like to hear if my suspicion is correct."

"Sir Blue Fox, you must know that you are not popular among the merchants."

"Well," said Piro, shrugging.

"To answer your question, yes. We set out to-day to capture you."

"I am honored."

"I am glad you take it that way, sir."

"How else?"

"Some might disdain us for our choice of industry."

"Perhaps, but I would not be one to do so. You are procuring your bread with your sword arm, as soldiers have always done, and, moreover, as we do ourselves."

"You are very gracious, sir."

"It is nothing. Only—"

"Well?"

"It is a shame that, from time to time, such gentlemen as ourselves must cross swords. But then, if we did not, why, what reason would we have to exist?"

"Do you truly mean to resist?"

"Cha! Can you doubt it?"

"But, what of your friends?"

"Well, if you will give me a moment, I will ask them."

"Take as much time as you need; the day is young, and contrary to an earlier remark I may have made, we have nowhere we need to be."

"You are very kind. Well, my friends? Do any of you wish to surrender?"

This produced an immediate, emphatic, and unanimous denial, followed by Ibronka saying, "My dear Blue Fox, are we to begin the dance soon? I am beginning to feel a certain ennui."

Piro returned his attention to the captain and shrugged. "You see how it is?"

"Then, there is nothing that remains but to play it out."

"One thing first, sir."

"And that is?"

"I believe that, in an instant, I am going to do my very best to pass my sword through your body; I anticipate you attempting to be just as polite with regard to me. Therefore, I should very much like to know your name."

"That is only just, but—"

"Well?"

"I only know you as the Blue Fox, which I am certain is not your real name."

"So then?"

"If you give me your actual name, well, then I shall give you mine."

"But consider, sir, that, as I live outside the law, well, I have good reason for not wishing my name to be known."

"Oh, I do not dispute your reasons."

"So that, if I were to tell you my name, it would follow that I would have to kill you in order to keep my secret."

"That is but natural."

"You are sanguine about this?"

"Perfectly."

"Very well, then." And dropping his voice, he said, "I am called Piro, the Viscount of Adrilankha."

The other bowed and said, "I am Noarwa e'Tennith."

"Honored."

"The same."

"Would you prefer to give the charge, or receive it?"

"Oh, on that subject, I am utterly indifferent."

"Very well then," said Piro, at last drawing his sword, "we are about to have the honor of charging you."

"Very well."

"Charge!" cried Piro, and lunged up at the one called Noarwa. The Dragonlord parried the attack, using his knees to direct his horse to the side; but that is exactly where Grassfog was, and the latter, also striking upward, caught Noarwa with a thrust that entered under his rib cage and penetrated very nearly as far as his right shoulder. It is probable that this would have killed him in any case, but Piro, wishing to take no chances with his identity, made certain by severing the Dragonlord's throat as he slid off his horse.

Ibronka took the word "charge" in its most literal sense, and, wielding her longsword in both hands, she stepped forward, striking down from right to left; then, without ever stopping the motion, from left to right, after which she took another step forward and executed a two-handed lunge. The most likely explanation for the results of the first instant of battle is that the warriors had not truly expected to receive a charge; or, if they had, they had not considered that it would occur so quickly. But the fact remains that Ibronka's first three strokes had removed three of them from combat, one with a slash across his chest and stomach, a second who was missing her sword hand, and a third who had received two feet of steel fully in her chest. Before the others around these three had quite recovered, Ritt and Iatha were next to Ibronka, and furiously dueling—indeed, so furiously that Iatha gave one a cut on his wrist that caused him to drop his weapon from a nerveless hand.

Kytraan, notwithstanding the order to charge, had something of a grasp of tactics in such combat, and so he quickly arranged his small force—that is, himself, Röaana, and Belly—in a sort of triangle facing out, where they endeavored to keep their blades moving continually to avoid any injury to any of them, while simultaneously looking for any openings their enemies might give them. This method was so effective that, although they did not inflict any wounds, neither did they receive any, although they were, in point of fact, holding off nine opponents.

In the meantime, Piro and Grassfog had not been idle. Stepping past Noarwa's horse, they saw three warriors facing them, and at once charged into them, attempting to attack them before they could separate. In this they were at least partially successful, in that Grassfog struck one through the throat almost at once. Unfortunately, while Piro dueled with another, the third managed to step over the body of his fallen comrade so that Grassfog's back was, for a moment, exposed to him. He did not waste this opportunity, but, on the contrary, cut viciously, striking Piro's friend and comrade in the middle of his back with a horizontal stroke.

Grassfog arched his back and moaned, and at the same time thrust his sword blindly behind him, by luck striking his enemy just above the hip. Piro, upon hearing the soft moan, understood what it meant, and, suddenly feeling a terrible fear—for his friend, be it firmly understood—sent his blade flashing around his enemy's eyes and ears so quickly that the other was bewildered, and Piro then put her down with a good thrust through the shoulder, following it, almost as an afterthought, with a slash across the face so that she did not get any foolish notions about continuing the contest.

Piro turned to Grassfog, who gasped, "Never mind me. The others!" Piro nodded, and stepped forward three steps to where Ibronka, Iatha, and Ritt were dueling with five of the enemy. Piro did not even consider such niceties as whether it was proper to strike from behind; we beg leave to doubt if, under the circumstances, even Aerich would have, so that, in an instant, instead of five of the enemy, there were four; and just as quickly Ibronka found the blade of her enemy and twisted, sending his weapon flying, and Ritt made a sudden stop-cut, striking under his enemy's shoulder and causing him to stumble backward and fall, after which he quit the contest. The remaining warrior, suddenly realizing that, in this part of the battle, it had suddenly become four against one, decided that the money he had hoped to earn was not worth dying for, especially as he would be unlikely to be able to collect the reward if he were dead and his enemies escaped; so he begged off the remainder of the fight by the simple expedient of taking to his heels.

Then, without another word being spoken, Piro, Ibronka, Iatha, and Ritt charged the nine enemies who had surrounded Kytraan, Röaana, and Belly. None of our friends had been wounded, and the only damage they had yet done to their enemies was a scratch Röaana had inflicted on a forearm that had gone too high and delayed too long before striking.

Ibronka was about to engage, but Piro held up his hand for her to wait. Then he cleared his throat and said, "Gentlemen, may I invite you to retire?"

While some might consider it absurd for seven warriors to make such an offer to nine, the fact that shortly before it had been eight against twenty-two made it appear less preposterous. And, considering that, with such odds, it seemed unlikely that they would be able to bring back enough of the bandits to justify the risk, the question was far more reasonable than it might at first seem. Certainly, that was the opinion of the nine remaining warriors.

"Will you permit us to take our wounded and dead comrades?" said one of them.

"Certainly," said Piro.

"And our horses and carts?"

"We shall not quarrel over such trifles."

"Then we will withdraw."

"Well, but one thing—"

"And that is?"

"Your purses, gentlemen."

"That is but fair. Here they are."

"Very good, then."

"And we bid you a good day."

As the warriors collected their wounded and dead and loaded them onto the carts, Piro rushed over to Grassfog.

"My friend, are you all right?"

"Ah, Piro. Is it over?"

"Oh, yes. And you are the only casualty."

"Well, that is good. Twenty-two of them, were there?"

"That, or something close. I did not check his arithmetic."

"A pretty little victory."

"But you, are you all right?"

"I confess, there have been times I have felt better."

"We must find a physicker for you."

"Useless," said Grassfog, wincing suddenly.

"What do you tell me?"

"I have no feeling below my waist; I am tolerably certain of what that means. Moreover, my kidneys have been laid open. It was a good stroke."

"Blood of the Horse! Ah, I led us into a trap! It is my fault!"

"Not in the least. Never worry your heart about it, Blue Fox. Such things are part of the game. Do you imagine I didn't know how I would end? And, twenty-two against eight, well, that is worth a song."

"I think so!"

"Piro, you must do something for me."

"Name it."

"There is a chain around my neck."

"I see it."

"Can you see that my sister gains possession of it? It is a family heirloom of sorts."

"Of course I will. But, how do I find her?"

"Her name is Tsira."

"Very well."

"She lives not far from a village called Six Horses, on the northern slopes of South Mountain."

"Not far from it?"

"She lives in the mountains, hunting, fishing, and trapping. You may—" Here he stopped and coughed for some period of time, his face growing more pale by the second. At length he continued, "You may have to look for her."

"Very well. I will do it."

"Take my hand."

"Here it is."

He looked up the others, all of whom were kneeling next to him, and gave them a smile. "Never trouble yourselves, my friends." He pressed Piro's hand and the Viscount returned the pressure. Grassfog closed his eyes then, and his breath became more and more shallow. Presently he gave a sort of sigh and his breathing stopped altogether.

Piro, and, indeed, all of them remained there for some few minutes, until at last Piro disengaged his hand, then reached forward and removed the chain from around Grassfog's neck, putting it around his own. Then he stood up. Ibronka placed her hand in his.

After a moment he looked at the others. "We will burn his body before doing anything else; let us speed him to his next life."

There were murmurs of agreement with this plan; Grassfog had not been the least liked of the band.

"Come then," said Piro. "Let us pick him up and hasten to break camp. We must see to his body, and then I wish to be on our way to South Mountain before nightfall."

Chapter the Eightieth

How Sethra Lavode Attempted To Relax with a Good Book

One day near the end of winter, as Piro and his band were approaching South Mountain, where they hoped to find Grassfog's sister, Sethra Lavode emerged from the depths of Dzur Mountain and said, "Find me my apprentice." She spoke in an even, conversational tone, with no special emphasis; nor was this order at all unusual, as she often had reason to consult with Sethra the Younger; the only thing about her request that is worthy of note is that, to all appearances, there was no one anywhere near her. She added, "Have her meet me in the library," to the emptiness around her, and continued through narrow hallways, up narrow stairs, to wider hallways and stairs—the latter showing less sign of having been carved out of the stone of the mountain.

This steady, leisurely walk presently brought her to her library, where, after a short time of looking around and considering what she wished to read, she was joined by Sethra the Younger, who said, "Tukko says you wished to see me."

"Tukko is right."

"Well, madam?"

"You have studied the gods, have you not?"

"I think so, Enchantress! I seem to remember a good number of years where, at your insistence, I did little else!"

"Yes, only—"

"Well?"

"It seems you have continued your studies beyond what I suggested."

"Suggested!"

"Well, required then."

"Yes, I confess, I have become fascinated by what it means, metaphysically, to be a god, and by the duties and responsibilities of the Lords of Judgment, and by the characteristics of some of them. But why do you ask me?"

"Because not long ago I received a piece of intelligence."

"Concerning the gods?"

"Exactly."

"And this intelligence, it has been preying on your mind?"

"Your comprehension is perfect. I find myself disturbed and anxious, and, at length, I came to the decision that perhaps there was something to be concerned about."

The apprentice bowed. "If there is any knowledge I have that is useful, madam, you must know it is at your disposal."

"That is good of you, madam."

"But then, what is this intelligence?"

"I have been told that Tri'nagore has been entirely absent from the Halls of Judgment for some time."

"Time? And yet, you know as well as I—that is to say, better than I—that time means little enough in the Halls of Judgment."

"That is true, but there is, necessarily, some relationship."

"How, is there?"

"Certainly. The gods have an interest—more than an interest—in the Empire. They sent us that demon."

"The Necromancer."

"Yes. As you know, she was of great aid in delaying the Jenoine, so that they still have made no effort against us. And she was even of some assistance against the Pretender."

"This is all true. And then?"

"It proves that there must be a connection, of some kind, between time in the Halls of Judgment, and time as it flows here."

"Very well, I accept that there is a connection."

"And so, if Tri'nagore is absenting himself from the Halls, it may mean something."

"That is possible."

"And, so, I wish to know what it means."

"I can tell you what I know of this god, but—"

"That is exactly what I wish."

"Truly?"

"My dear apprentice, am I in the habit of being jocular?"

"I beg your pardon, Enchantress."

"Well, go on then."

"Tri'nagore was one of the servants of the Jenoine, as was Verra, and so he goes back to the beginning. He has, however, always been independent—has rarely had anything to say to the other gods. He dislikes all of them, they dislike him, although, to be sure, he has never failed to do his share against the Jenoine."

"Well, go on."

"No one of any consequence has ever made a pact with him, at least, so far as my knowledge extends, and this is probably because he has no especial talents, save some skills in the Eastern magical arts."

"So he is worshiped in the East?"

"Not so much; they believe he wishes human sacrifice of them, and they are not fond of this practice."

"And yet, do they not believe that Verra desires this, as well?"

"Yes, but Verra is happy with the sacrifice of an enemy; Tri'nagore is reputed to be happy only with the sacrifice of his own worshipers."

"That would seem self-defeating."

"I do not know how this belief came about. But then, I do not know how any of the Easterners' beliefs have come about."

"You should, however."

"How, I should?"

"Assuredly."

"But, why is this important, Enchantress?"

"Because, my dear apprentice, you are so very determined to go eastward and conquer."

Sethra the Younger nodded. "I take your point, Enchantress. But, as for Tri'nagore, or—forgive me, I cannot say his full name—"

"Tristangrascalaticrunagore."

"Yes, as to him, I'm afraid I know no more. Shall I attempt to learn what I can?"

"Yes, I believe that would be wise, if there is time."

"Time, madam?"

"Time before whatever happens, happens."

"You believe something is going to happen?"

"I am convinced of it. I spoke with Arra—"

"Who?"

"Arra. Morrolan's high priestess. You met her at Castle Black."

"Ah, the little Eastern girl."

"Yes."

"Well, you spoke with her?"

"She has the Sight, you know."

Sethra the Younger looked scornful. "Do you believe in that?"

"Certainly."

"Pah. If there were such a thing, they would never lose a battle."

"No, it is not prescience."

"Then what is it?"

"It is the ability to observe some thing that is happening at the moment of the Seeing, not, as is commonly thought, the ability to see the future. Sometimes, indeed, a Seer may get a glimpse into the future, but these are invariably only possibilities, and they are, furthermore, notoriously inaccurate. A true Seeing is invariably truthful, within the limits I have outlined."

"That does not seem so much."

"That is because, my love, you do not understand what is implied."

"Well, and that is?"

"If one Sees a certain event, then, along with the Seeing, one has the knowledge that this certain event matters, and this fact makes it invaluable."

The apprentice frowned, and considered this.

"It is also," added the Enchantress, "one of very few magical arts that can be called a gift—that is, that are inherent in the person, rather than being a skill one learns. The ability to create amorphia, as you know, is another, and there are certain others."

"Is that important?"

"It is important, my dear, only in this way: Skills that are inherent in a person are very difficult to interfere with."

"Very well, I accept that."

"I spoke with Arra."

"I believe that I remember you saying something about that an hour ago."

"I asked her to do a Seeing."

"Well, and?"

"She said that, for the past month, she has been unable."

"How, unable?"

"Exactly. To be more precise, she says she is being prevented."

"And yet, you have said that it is difficult to interfere with this gift."

"Exactly."

"Tri'nagore?"

"It is, at least, possible."

"And if it is the case?"

"Then certain matters are coming to a head, that is all."

"The Jenoine."

"It is possible."

"Kâna?"

"It is likely."

"You think Kâna made a pact with Tri'nagore?"

"It is not unthinkable."

"For what reason?"

"Ah. There I cannot answer you."

"Well, I will discover what I can."

"Very good."

When she had left, the Enchantress observed to the air, "I should like to see the Sorceress in Green."

After some few minutes, this lady, in turn, arrived and gave her respectful greetings to the Enchantress.

"And how are you, my friend?"

"I thank you for asking, Enchantress. And I am, in a word, enchanted."

"Oh?"

"You cannot fail to be aware of how much more powerful the Orb is now."

"Yes, there can be no doubt that the gods did something to it while it was in their possession."

"Well, and so I have been delighted in the new powers."

"I perceive you have not yet destroyed any appreciable landmasses."

The Sorceress laughed. "No, I have not done that. But, indeed, I nearly could, if I could contain such power long enough to shape it; because I swear to you that is all that is missing."

"It is true that Orb has changed; the Mountain is aware of it." As Sethra said this, she touched the blue-hilted dagger she always carried at her side.

"I beg your pardon, madam, but—"

"Yes?"

"You seem worried."

"Not worried, my love; but concerned."

"You make a nice distinction."

"Well, and are not nice distinctions better than coarse ones?"

"Oh, certainly; where would we be without nice distinctions?"

"I am glad we agree."

"But tell me—"

"Yes?"

"What concerns you?"

"Two things."

"Well, let us see what they are."

"First, I do not believe that Kâna has given up; it is not in his nature to do so while he yet lives."

"Very well. And next?"

"I do not know what he is doing."

"I comprehend your dis-ease, Enchantress. And yet—"

"Well?"

"With the Orb so much more powerful even than it was, what can he do?"

"I wish I knew the answer to that question. Which, in fact, is why I asked you here."

"There is something you wish me to do?"

"You have understood me exactly."

"You know you have but to name it."

"I will accept your offer with all the frankness with which it was made."

"So much the better."

"I would like you to see if you can find out where Kâna's troops are. I think you know how to perform such a search. I know that, a thousand years ago, it would have been prohibitive, but, with the increased powers of the Orb, I think it worth the effort to search."

"Then, Kâna still has troops?"

"At any rate, he did. And, in the confusion of the march to Adrilankha, and finding a place for the Court to sit, and advising Her Majesty on the Imperial Palace, I lost sight of them."

"I collect you are still acting Warlord?"

"Precisely."

"Then I shall search until either I find them, or—"

"Well?"

"Or until I can convince you that they no longer exist."

"That is exactly right."

"I will begin at once."

"You are charming."

"Until next time, Enchantress."

"Until next time, Sorceress."

These tasks having been accomplished, the Enchantress

took herself back down to the lower chambers of Dzur Mountain, visiting several, one after the other, with the attitude of a general inspecting his troops, or the captain of a ship studying the arrangement of ropes and sheets, and then, evidently satisfied, she returned once more to her library, where, selecting a volume called *Sketches of the Early Eleventh Cycle,* by Early of Alban, she began reading. Shortly thereafter, Tukko appeared, and gave her a very small glass of dark red wine.

"I believe, madam, that you have read that book before," observed Tukko.

"Not above a hundred times, I believe. But then, it is the mark of a good book that it rewards many readings, is it not? And I find Lord Early to be a delightful writer; his sketches of the people of the time are amusing and insightful. Moreover, I believe they are accurate, insofar as I recall. Of course, it is the case that my memory of this work is now stronger than my memory of any of those people, so perhaps the words have replaced the reality in my mind. Nevertheless, it helps to take my mind away from my troubles for a time."

"I had thought you preferred novels for relaxation."

"Sometimes. But then, I judge a novel more harshly."

"Do you? Why is that?"

"Because history is able to rely upon the truth, of course. A novel, in which all is created by the author's whim, must strike a more profound level of truth, or it is worthless."

"And yet, I have heard you say that any novel that relieves your ennui for an hour has proved its usefulness."

"You have a good memory. It must have been ten thousands of years ago that I uttered those words."

"And if it was?"

"In another ten thousand, perhaps I will agree with them again."

"In my opinion, the proper way to judge a novel is this: Does it give one an accurate reflection of the moods and characteristics of a particular group of people in a particular place at a particular time? If so, it has value. Otherwise, it has none."

"You do not find this rather narrow?"

"Madam—"

"Well?"

"I was quoting you."

"Were you? It must have been an eon ago."

"Tolerably long, yes."

"Well, now I find those standards too narrow."

"You are changeable."

"Is that a bad thing?"

"Perhaps it is."

"How so?"

"It makes one unpredictable."

"Is, then, predictability, by itself, a virtue?"

"It is not sufficient, Enchantress, but I believe it is necessary. Am I not predictable? When you sit down in the library, does the wine not appear directly? When you receive an Imperial summons, is not your Lavode costume laid out directly? When the klaxon tells us that the Makers are stirring, is not your Pendant of Felicity found waiting near the Six Rods?"

"I have never complained of your service, my dear Tukko."

The servant bowed. "I was not speaking for self-aggrandizement, Enchantress, but to make an observation about predictability and virtue."

"You are unusually loquacious today."

"Well?"

"I had not predicted that."

"Perhaps you ought to have."

"Indeed?"

"With the Makers only kept out by a hair's breadth, and an Empress who is complacently sitting upon a trembling throne as if it were immovable, and a gifted Seeress finding herself blind, and a god missing from the Halls of Judgment, and you discovered reading light entertainments, well, you ought to have predicted that I would have something to say."

"I am not, then, permitted an hour of relaxation?"

"An hour? Oh, yes, certainly an hour. But—"

"Well?"

"I have never known you to open a book and then close it again in an hour."

The Enchantress sighed. "What would you have me do?"

Tukko moved over to the shelves, selected another volume, and, with a bow, placed it on the small, grey, stone table next to Sethra's right hand. She glanced at it. "*The Book of the Seven Wizards?* I have attempted it a hundred times, and I still understand nothing of it."

"Well," said Tukko shrugging.

"The author appears to enjoy obscurantism for its own sake."

"But the author is, at least, a good servant, and predictable."

The Enchantress condescended to let a chuckle escape her lips, after which she said, "Come, Tukko. What are you trying to tell me?"

"Enchantress, like the author of this book—" here he tapped the volume on the table, "—if there was a way to say it more plainly without introducing errors of tremendous magnitude, well, I would say it that way."

The Enchantress gave Tukko a look impossible to describe, and then, taking the book into her hands, opened it to a random page, glanced down, and read aloud: "'Each wizard is a coachman. It is true that the destinations may vary, and the horses, and the style of driving; yet it must be observed that few indeed are those who notice anything beyond the difference in the color of the coach.'" She closed the book with a thump and said, "I trust you will permit me to remain skeptical upon that point."

"And yet, I swear that it is true."

"Well, if you swear to it, I cannot doubt you."

Tukko bowed.

"Very well," said Sethra, opening her book again. "Give me an hour. After that, you may return once more, and I promise you I will endeavor to do something more useful."

Tukko bowed again.

"Sometimes," said the Enchantress, "I become very weary."

Tukko bowed yet a third time, and departed, while Sethra began reading. Some few minutes before the expiration of the agreed-upon hour, however, Tukko returned, saying, "The Sorceress in Green."

The Enchantress sighed and put her book down. "Very well," she said.

The Sorceress entered and said, "I have found them."

"Who?"

"Why, the troops. What had you sent me to look for?"

"I am astonished, madam. That took you no time at all."

"That is because they were in, if not the first place that I looked, then the second or third."

"Well, and that is?"

"There are some twenty or twenty-one thousand troops two days' march west of Adrilankha, and moving east."

"Two days?" cried Sethra.

"No more than that."

"Twenty thousand, you say?"

"At least."

Sethra stared at her, as if expecting her to announce that, in fact, she was only jesting, and she had really returned because she desired a glass of wine. At length, the Enchantress rose and, addressing Tukko, said, "My Lavode costume and my best cloak. I must go see the Empress at once."

She retired to her apartments where, in two minutes, Tukko had returned with the costume, the cloak, and *Sketches of the Early Eleventh Cycle*. In response to her look of inquiry, Tukko observed, "You may be required to wait before seeing Her Majesty."

A teleport—once an astonishing feat of thaumaturgical genius, but now, reflected Sethra, hardly more difficult than stepping into a carriage—perhaps a moving carriage, but still no great effort once one had practiced the skill sufficiently—a teleport, we say, brought the Enchantress to a place just outside of Whitecrest Manor, where she was admitted at once, and asked to wait until the Empress was able to see her. The waiting room contained seven or eight courtiers, emissaries, or envoys, but no one with whom Sethra wished to carry on a conversation at that moment, for which reason she seated herself on a bench along with the others (that is, five of the others; the rest were pacing).

She had, in fact, just opened her book when Sergeant called her name, and, ignoring certain looks from the others in the waiting room, some of these looks directed at her from those who knew who she was, and others from those who didn't, she closed her book and, following the guardsman, came at once before Her Majesty.

Chapter the Eighty-First

How Her Majesty Considered Maps While Sethra Formulated A Plan of Battle

Sethra Lavode, upon entering the room in which Her Majesty conducted Imperial business, found there not only Her Majesty, but also an Issola she did not recognize, but who was introduced to her as the Lord of the Chimes—given the title Lord Brudik by tradition. Sethra greeted them both respectfully, after which Brudik, who had just taken his post, went about his duties.

Once the Lord of the Chimes had left the room, Sethra turned back to the Empress, who was studying certain papers that were arrayed—or, rather, disarrayed—upon the table that was serving as her work area. Before Sethra could speak, the Empress, holding one of them aloft, said, "Tell me, Warlord, have you ever heard of the Blue Fox?"

"The Blue Fox? I must admit to Your Majesty that this name, or title, is completely new to me."

"A highwayman, operating in the west, in the area between Bra-Moor and Southmoor. It seems that it is beyond the ability of the local barons to catch him, and Imperial aid has been requested."

"A new brigand? Just when we have the resources to deal with them? How foolish."

"Yes. But clever enough to work in a region with plenty of travelers, no count, and no duke. Damned few barons, even, although you know how effective they are at the best of times."

"Does he work alone?"

"He has a band of some size; a score or so, according to this note."

"I will send a detachment of cavalry, when we can spare one."

"When we can spare one, Warlord? Is there, then, some demand upon our forces?"

"Nearly."

"You must explain to me what this demand is. But first, did you observe a gentleman out there dressed in a very rich blue?"

"Yes, Majesty. He was sitting next to me on the bench, his eyes closed, and he seemed to be either thinking deeply or sleeping lightly."

"That is the emissary from Elde. I am hoping to find a way to heal the rift with them. You know our last emissary was sent home."

"Yes, I remember."

"The last time I met with that gentleman who now awaits my pleasure, he demanded that their ships be permitted full trading rights with Greenaere."

"Indeed?"

"I need hardly tell you how the Orca and the Tsalmoth would feel about that."

"Well, and, if I may ask, how did Your Majesty respond?"

"I said that we should be most happy to, if they would give us full access to water and provision our ships in Redsky Harbor."

Sethra chuckled. "I should imagine that this was not entirely satisfactory to Elde?"

"He didn't even waste the time to send for instructions; he merely declared it to be impossible. I had the honor to point out to him that it was not at all impossible, as we had taken this harbor from them less than three hundred years ago, and would be most happy to do so again."

"Ah. Well, no doubt this was a popular remark."

"Indeed. He stormed out without so much as a farewell, turning his back upon me, and committing, oh, I don't know how many separate breaches of etiquette. I lost count after nine or ten."

"Splendid. So that now, whatever his orders might be, he must either return to apologize, or be disgraced, which certainly will do him no good at home."

"Exactly."

"And you, of course, can apologize as well, and offer more reasonable terms."

"Yes, which he will be nearly obligated to accept. And if he doesn't—"

"Yes, we will know where Elde stands without any room for doubt or confusion."

The Empress nodded.

"Your Majesty is a formidable diplomatist, I perceive."

"I am learning, I hope. The House of the Hawk has done as they said, at least in part."

"Indeed?"

"They have publicly declared that I am Empress, and have called for a Meeting of the Principalities."

"Have they, then? Well, that is good, because I do not believe we can continue feeding the army much longer, although, to be sure, the subscriptions from certain Lyorn and Dragons have done wonders."

"I am glad to hear it, Warlord. At all events, it is progress."

"Without question."

"So, then, is that all?"

"Your Majesty—"

"Well?"

"I beg to remind Your Majesty that it was I who asked for this interview."

"Shards! That is true! And, in addition, there is the matter of your insistence that a detachment of cavalry will be difficult to come by in the near future. I imagine these matters are connected?"

"Your Majesty is perspicacious."

"Well, let us hear, then. Upon what subject would you address me, Warlord?"

"Oh, on war, as a matter of course."

"Naturally. But, if you please, be precise."

"Oh, Your Majesty knows I desire precision in all things."

"Well then?"

"Your Majesty, I refer to the Pretender."

"Ah, yes. Come, permit me to show you a map."

"Your Majesty knows that I adore maps."

"Then look at this one."

"Is it Your Majesty's work?"

"It is."

"A splendid map, Your Majesty. What does the blue represent?"

"That is the area in which, a year ago, the Pretender had a reasonable claim to control."

"It is tolerably large."

"Oh, yes."

"If I had seen this then, I should have been more worried."

"Warlord, you were not worried?"

"Not as you would say, worried. Perhaps concerned. But what is the area marked in pink?"

"Ah! You noticed that?"

"Well, it would have been difficult not to see it—Your Majesty observes that it is, after all, pink."

"Yes. The pink is the region that, according to our best intelligence, he controls as of to-day."

"Your Majesty, how good is our best intelligence?"

"It could be better," admitted the Empress.

"And then?"

"Still, I believe this is close."

"Well, so we have made considerable gains, there is no denying that."

"I am pleased you see it, madam."

"However, it is my respectful opinion that the map is slightly, well, out of date."

"Indeed? You have more recent intelligence?"

"Exactly. And it was to share this intelligence that I did myself the honor of coming to see Your Majesty in person."

"Well then, let us hear. If it was sufficiently important for you to leave your sanctuary, I will listen to it."

"And Your Majesty will be right to."

"So then, what is this famous intelligence?"

"I should say that the Pretender now controls an additional area approximately . . ." She put her finger in the map. "Here."

The Empress turned pale. "What do you tell me?"

"The Pretender has an army here. Our best guess is that they are two days from the city."

"How is it possible for them to get so close without our knowing?"

"Oh, as to that, I would guess they moved only small units until they reached somewhere near Hartre, and then marched just inland from the coast, following it."

"Nevertheless, it doesn't seem possible."

"We think they may have divine or demonic aid, Your Majesty."

"Humph. Of the two, I would think demonic is more likely."

"Your Majesty may be right."

The Empress sighed. "Well, Warlord? What shall we do?"

"Majesty, I would suggest that we fight."

"Fight. Good. Yes, I agree. Let us fight. Instead of meekly surrendering to the Pretender, I think fighting is a good plan. The more-so because I lived in this very city, and so, should I abdicate, well, I should have nowhere to go. So then, having settled that, exactly how should we fight?"

"Have you a map of Adrilankha to hand? If not, I can easily procure one."

"Certainly. There was one upon the wall of this very room. It is a map of all of Whitecrest, most of which is the city, because it was from this room that the Countess was accustomed to transact her business. It is now in that corner, behind the book-shelf."

"Very good," said Sethra, fetching the object in question. With Her Majesty's permission, she laid it on top of the table (covering most of the papers there), and studied it from this position.

"I should cover these three roads, each with a division stationed a quarter mile outside of the city, so that, in case the line is broken, we can retreat into the city, and there defend it, if need be, house by house."

The Empress nodded. "Continue, then."

"I will give this division to my apprentice, this one to Morrolan who is the least experienced, and this one I will command myself, wearing two badges, as we say. A fourth division will remain in reserve, and a fifth division will guard the harbor, in case they attempt to land boats. The Lord Khaavren will be perfect for that duty. Apropos, I should speak with him as soon as practicable."

"Alas, the Lord Khaavren is no longer the Captain of my Guard."

"What then is his rank?"

"None."

"None? Have you dismissed him?"

"Not the least in the world. He tendered his resignation."

"For what reason?"

"None that he would give me. He pretended he was old and tired. I believe you know as well as I how much truth there is in such a remark."

"Well, I will speak with him. If he is not to command the harbor defenses, then, at least, I should like to see him here, guarding Your Majesty. And then I will require Brimford, as well. Does Your Majesty know where he is to be found?"

The Empress flushed at this question, and the Orb turned a faint pink, but Her Majesty said, "He will be produced."

Sethra, feigning not to notice Her Majesty's confusion, said, "I will, in addition, speak with the Necromancer to see if we can repeat the games we played with such effect at South Mountain."

"Will not the Pretender have prepared against this?"

"Perhaps, although I cannot think of how. You perceive, I know of few forces that can counteract a necromancer except a more skilled necromancer, and I take my oath that nowhere on the world is there a more skilled necromancer."

"Very well, Warlord. But I am nevertheless concerned."

"As far as that goes, Majesty, so am I."

"What do you think of this battle? Come, give me your honest opinion."

"Your Majesty, I don't know. In numbers, they have the smallest edge, but, as we are defending, that means that, even if we set ten companies to guard the harbor, tactically, we have a pronounced advantage; it takes far fewer to hold a position than to take it."

"Well come, that sounds good."

"Moreover, we have Lord Brimford and the Necromancer, and, with more time to prepare, I believe they ought to be able to be give a good account of themselves. And, above all, we have the Orb. I have not yet put together a sorcerers' corps, but there are several of us who will be more than able to do our share as part of the regular army. This is an advantage they do not have, and no small advantage it is."

"You fill me with hope."

"Well—"

"Yes?"

"As Your Majesty has indicated, the Pretender knows these statistics as well as I do. It is possible he is counting on surprise, but, well, it is possible he isn't."

"Well, what is he depending upon, then?"

"Your Majesty, I should give anything to know."

The Empress frowned, then shrugged. "Very well," she said. "What next?"

"I will go to speak with Khaavren, and to summon the Necromancer and my apprentice. And I must at once put together something of a staff, at least sufficient to handle logistics, communications, intelligence, and engineering. If I may make a suggestion to Your Majesty—"

"You may."

"I believe Your Majesty should summon Brimford, and then command the Countess regarding bringing food and supplies where they will be needed for the army. Once my staff is in place, I will send a list of what is needed, and the material required for building such fortifications and defenses as we can construct in two days."

"Very well. I shall also inform Brudik to tell those who wait that I will be seeing no one to-day."

Sethra frowned and reflected for a moment. "I would suggest, in fact, that Your Majesty not do so."

"But, how will I have time to see them?"

"Your Majesty almost certainly must attempt to make time; business ought to go on as much as possible. Should Your Majesty do as you have suggested, and suspend business, word of this might reach our enemies, and they might conclude that they have been discovered. You perceive, this would cost us a certain amount of our advantage."

Her Majesty bowed her head and said, "It will be so. This will be better, in some ways."

"Yes?"

"I believe that, while you set about your errands, I will have at least time to meet with our emissary from Elde. That is one matter I should like to have settled."

"Your Majesty is full of wisdom."

Sethra at once set off about her errands, leaving Her Majesty to, first, call for Brudik to have the emissary announced, and, while waiting, to contemplate her maps.

Upon leaving Her Majesty's presence, Sethra at once went past the waiting room (exchanging the briefest and friendliest nods with Brudik) and, by means of certain hallways and passages, soon entered the area of the Manor which was still reserved for the use of the Countess. It took only moments to find a servant, who seemed to be both maid and cook. Having found this worthy Teckla, she addressed her, saying, "I am called Sethra Lavode. I desire to know if it would be possible to have two words with your master the Count."

Now this maid, we should say, had gradually become accustomed, over the last two years, to the notion that the Empress was sharing a roof with her; and having powerful nobles and occasional sorcerers coming and going was no longer a trial to her—the more-so because, remaining on her side of the Manor, she never encountered them personally. Yet, to find herself suddenly face-to-face with the Enchantress of Dzur Mountain was rather more than the girl could have been expected to manage. What tales she had been told as a child in which the Enchantress was featured as the ultimate evil, we cannot say, any more than we can know precisely how much she believed them. Her reaction, however, was unmistakable: She turned pale, then she flushed, then she turned pale again, as if unable to decide if all of her blood or none of it should be in her head. After several of these transformations of her countenance were completed without a decision being reached, she ultimately managed to solve the dilemma by the simple expedient of fainting dead away.

Sethra, who had, perhaps, predicted such a denouement, caught her before she had entirely hit the floor, and carried her to a couch. There being no other servants present, the Enchantress, with something like an amused expression on her face, went into the kitchen and herself procured water, which she applied to the girl's forehead and lips. Presently the maid's eyes fluttered open, she looked up at the Enchantress, who was staring down at her not unkindly, and opened her mouth with the obvious intention of emitting a scream.

"Hush, child," said Sethra.

The maid, whose instinct to obey was stronger than her fear, closed her mouth.

"Come, stand up, my dear. No one is going to hurt you. Just you run along and find out if the Lord Khaavren is available."

The maid attempted to regain her feet. Sethra offered to help, an offer from which the Teckla at first shrank, which reaction was followed by another flush. Sethra feigned not to notice this reaction, and, eventually, the maid suffered herself to be assisted to her feet. She then managed a trembling curtsy, and said, "Yes—" stopping because she appeared unable to decide exactly which honorific would be appropriate. The Enchantress, for her part, never lost her kindly smile, and it was this, as much as anything else, that permitted the maid to walk off—unsteadily it is true, but under her own power—to carry out her errand.

Sethra paced slowly, regretting her book, which she had left on Her Majesty's desk, but soon enough she heard foot-falls too heavy to be the maid's, and, indeed, Khaavren appeared at the doorway.

Chapter the Eighty-Second

How Khaavren and the Empress Came to Something of an Understanding

Khaavren had been involved in keeping Daro company, while she considered county business in her apartments. Daro, in between reviewing, amending, and signing papers, would engage in various conversational gambits with him, speaking amiably; from time to time he would kiss her hand, smiling into her eyes.

It was in the middle of these activities that the maid appeared.

"My lord the Count," she said.

"What is it?" he asked mildly, and then, observing her countenance, he said, "Come, girl, it seems you are distraught. Has the Manor been invaded? Because if it concerns the part of the Manor which is our own, you must speak at once, whereas if it is an attack on the Orb, I must decide if I wish to concern myself."

"My lord husband," said Daro, "you know that, in such a case, you would take an interest."

"You think so, madam?"

"I am convinced of it."

"Well, but let us see. Is the house under attack?"

"No, my lord."

"Well, then we shall not find out, at least on this occasion. But then, what is it that has so upset you, my dear? For it is clear, to judge by your pallor and trembling, that something most unsettling has occurred."

"My lord, you have a visitor."

"How, that is all?"

The maid signified with a nod of her head that this was, indeed, the case.

"Well then, it but remains for you to tell me who this famous visitor is."

"My lord, it is—"

"Well?"

"It is . . ."

"Say it!"

"Sethra Lavode!" she burst out, then immediately ducked her head, as if to avoid a supernatural blow that, having uttered this name, must necessarily follow.

Instead of a blow, natural or supernatural, however, what followed was, in its way, even more disturbing. Khaavren shrugged and said, "Well, is that all? What does Sethra Lavode wish?"

The maid's eyes widened. "What does Seth—that is, what does she wish?"

"Yes, exactly."

"Why, to see you, my lord!" Having said this, she took a deep breath, drew herself up to her full height, and said, "My lord, if you wish, well, I will go and delay her while you make your escape."

Khaavren's eyes widened, and he turned to Daro. "My love."

"Yes, my dearest?"

"We must double this girl's salary."

"I had come to that same conclusion, my lord."

Khaavren gave the maid a smile that was not unkind, patted her on the head, and said, "Well, I believe that I can exchange two words with the Enchantress of Dzur Mountain without losing my soul directly. But, did she indicate what she wished of me?"

"My lord, I—that is, she didn't say."

"Very well."

Khaavren frowned, shrugged, realized that he was incapable of guessing, and, taking an affectionate leave of the

Countess, took himself at once to the aforementioned parlor, where, indeed, Sethra Lavode awaited him.

"Enchantress," he said, bowing low. "You do my house honor."

"It is a pleasure to see you, sir. May I beg two minutes of your time?"

"Certainly. I am in no hurry."

"So much the better."

"Upon what subject do you wish to converse?"

"Her Majesty has been studying maps."

"Has she?" said Khaavren, shrugging as if what Her Majesty did was of no concern to him.

"She has been studying maps, I say," repeated Sethra, "for a particular purpose."

Khaavren, by now aware that the Enchantress was in the process of telling him something important, looked at her closely. "A purpose, you say?"

"Yes, and a most serious purpose."

"And does this purpose in some way concern me?"

"It might."

"Then, if you would care to tell me this purpose, well, I promise that you will have my entire attention."

"It is for the purpose of planning her battle."

"Her battle?"

"Exactly."

"What battle would this be, if I may ask?"

"Most certainly you may ask, my dear Count. Indeed, I have been doing nothing else for an hour but attempting to convince you to ask."

"Very well, then, I am asking. What battle?"

"Against the Pretender. He will be attacking the city within two days."

"What do you tell me?" cried Khaavren.

"It is as I have had the honor to say. The Pretender has an army to the southwest, two days' march from where we stand."

"The Horse! It is impossible."

"I would not go so far as to say impossible," said Sethra.

"That is, anything that actually happens ought not to be considered impossible. To use the word 'impossible' to discuss something that happens, you perceive, would be to weaken the sense of a perfectly good word."

"Well, the Lords of Judgment keep us from weakening the sense of a good word," said Khaavren. "But then, the Pretender will attack the city, you say?"

"I have said so, and I even repeat it."

"Well," said Khaavren. And, as if that were not sufficient for such a revelation, he added, "Well, well, well."

"Indeed," said the Enchantress fervently. Then she said, "It is my understanding that you have given Her Majesty your resignation."

"I have, madam. I am a free man. Or, at least, as free as it is possible to be in this world of ours."

"May I ask why?"

"Madam, I am—"

"Bide, my lord."

"Well?"

"I simply wish to observe that if the word 'old' is about to escape your lips, I will be forced to remind you to whom you are speaking."

"An excellent observation, madam. I should, above all, not care to weaken the sense of a perfectly good word."

"And then?"

Khaavren reflected for a moment, for being unable to use the word "old" caused him to re-evaluate what he ought to say. At length he said, "Considering everything, I cannot believe that it would be proper for me to answer your question. That is, without lying; and I do not choose to lie to you, madam."

"I am glad of that; for my part, I do not choose to be lied to."

"So much the better; we are in agreement then."

"Nearly."

"Well?"

"If Her Majesty did something of which you do not approve, then I beg you to reflect."

"I have been reflecting, madam. More, I spoke with

Aerich, who caused me to reflect even more. And, if that were not enough, I happened to encounter—well, it is of no moment. I learned that the action with which I have been reproaching Her Majesty may have been less of an offense than I had thought, and this, too, has caused me to reflect. So, you perceive, I have been spending more than a little time in reflection. Indeed, I am becoming somewhat weary of the whole business."

"Ah, you learned something that may have changed your mind?" asked the Enchantress, extracting the one significant fact from Khaavren's uncharacteristically effusive speech.

"Something overheard a year ago at Morrolan's entertainment at Castle Black."

"Just so," she said, as if she expected that answer and no other. "And so, what is there now to prevent you from serving Her Majesty once more?"

Khaavren frowned, rubbed his fist over his lips, and said, "Self-love."

"Ah. Well, I comprehend."

Khaavren bowed, pleased that he was not required to explain that, having resigned, he could not easily beg Her Majesty for his commission to be restored.

"But then," continued Sethra, "suppose Her Majesty were to ask you to take up your position again? And suppose that I were to do the same?"

"Madam, I cannot imagine Her Majesty doing so."

"I have a better imagination than you, my dear sir."

"Nevertheless—"

Sethra said, "My lord—"

"Well?"

"If you will excuse me for a moment, I will return directly."

After some few minutes, Sethra returned, saying, "My dear Khaavren."

"Yes, madam?"

"If you can spare two minutes—"

"Are these the same two minutes you desired from me before, or are they an additional two minutes?"

"Oh, these are entirely separate."

"Well, if all of these two minutes are combined, I shall soon be required to spare two years. Nevertheless, my dear Sethra, for you, well, I would spare two years were it required."

"So much the better."

"But then, to what purpose are these two minutes to be dedicated?"

"Her Majesty would like to see you."

Khaavren stiffened—this information, while, we are certain, entirely expected by the reader, was sufficiently astonishing to our brave Tiassa. Without another word, then, he bowed in Sethra's direction, and took himself to the enclosed terrace—which is, as the reader may recall, the room given over to Her Majesty's use. Here he encountered the Lord of the Chimes, who, after two words, agreed to bring him to Her Majesty at once.

Brudik led the way past several others in the waiting room, all of whom—that is to say, all of those who had been waiting patiently for Her Majesty's time, only to see first the Warlord and now the Tiassa precede them—gave Khaavren looks more or less eloquent.

Upon entering the terrace, the Lord of the Chimes announced, "The Count of Whitecrest," and took himself back out of the room, leaving Khaavren alone with Her Majesty.

"My lord Khaavren."

"Your Majesty," he said, bowing respectfully.

"Are you at liberty, Lord Khaavren?"

"At liberty? I do not understand the question Your Majesty does me the honor to ask."

"Have you made commitments to anyone, or are you at liberty?"

"Ah! I comprehend. I am perfectly at liberty, Your Majesty."

"Then, having thought over all of the available candidates as fully and carefully as possible, I have come to the decision that you are the most qualified individual for the position of Captain of the Imperial Guard."

She stopped here, and waited. Khaavren, taking the hint, bowed and said, "Your Majesty is too kind."

"Not at all," said she. "Dare I hope you will accept? I have already written out your commission, and but await your word before signing it."

"I accept happily, Your Majesty."

Zerika nodded and, with a stroke of the pen (a particularly fine instrument, as we suspect the reader may remember), Khaavren was once more Captain of the Imperial Guard. His first words upon receiving his commission were "I am at Your Majesty's service."

"You know of Sethra Lavode's plan?"

"Our conversation did not extend to include her plans."

"Then go and speak with her; the Warlord is, naturally enough, in charge."

"Very good, Majesty," said Khaavren. "I look forward to a rewarding association in the service of the Empire." Then, saluting her most respectfully, he left the room.

When he passed the waiting room, Sergeant, on duty outside of it, could not prevent a certain smile from touching his lips, as he pronounced the word, "Captain."

Khaavren gave him an answering smile, though an even more minuscule one, and returned to where Sethra awaited him.

"Well, Captain?" said the Enchantress.

"Yes, Warlord?"

"I took the liberty," continued Sethra, "of having your maid bring this for you." With this, she held out the gold-colored half-cloak, with captain's badge, that he had put away when he had resigned.

"Well," said Khaavren, donning the cloak once more. "This is rather much of ceremony for a year's absence."

"What ceremony?" asked Sethra.

Khaavren smiled and bowed.

"And now, Captain," continued the Enchantress. "You understand that there is to be a battle?"

"So I am informed, and I give you my word, I have no inclination to disagree with you and Her Majesty."

"So much the better. And how have you considered your own rôle in this?"

"That is a simple enough question to answer."

"Well?"

"You know that the last time an Emperor was threatened, I was away from my post, making an arrest, and His Majesty died. This time, that will not happen."

"So then, you wish to remain with Her Majesty?"

"I not only wish to, but I must insist upon it."

Sethra nodded. "Very well, I understand. And now, if you will excuse me, Captain, I must prepare the defenses of the city. Apropos, have you any comments on the harbor?"

"What of it?"

"Its defense."

"Ah, that is simple enough. It falls into two categories: that which does not require defense, and that which is indefensible."

"How, indefensible?"

Khaavren shrugged. "I overstate the case. That district which we refer to as 'the harbor' may sometimes refer to the harbor itself—that is, the body of water upon which ships are anchored for loading and unloading—but more often refers to the area bordered on the south by the water, on the east by the mouth of the Adrilankha River, and on the north and west by the cliffs."

"Very well, what of it?"

"There is no need to defend this area, for the simple reason that twenty soldiers, stationed at the top of each of the staircases that climb the cliffs, can hold it against any numbers you should care to bring against it."

"Very well, I understand that. Next?"

"There is also the district of the city that we call the East Harbor, that is, east of the mouth of the Adrilankha River. Here, instead of cliffs, there are only hills, and these become easier the further east you go. Here it would be possible for an enemy to make landings, and even to approach the city through South Adrilankha."

"And, you say, it is indefensible?"

"In fact, perhaps not. It depends on the number of troops available, and the numbers attempting the landing. I should wish for at least ten troops for each boat landing."

"Regardless of how many are in each boat?"

"Yes, exactly. But—"

"Well?"

"If they once effect a landing, then it is a different matter entirely."

"And then?"

"I would suggest that, should an enemy establish a landing—"

"Yes, in that case?"

"That you let him have the East Harbor, and South Adrilankha, and guard the bridges over the river and the canal. This can be done with a few thousand well-placed troops."

"And will you be willing to consult with us as to their placement?"

"Gladly."

"Very good. I will look at some maps and consider your advice. Although, in point of fact, we do not believe they have sufficient troops at their disposal that they would allocate a sizable number for such an attack. But then, to the left, it best to have considered even unlikely possibilities."

"So I have always believed, Warlord."

"That is it, then."

Khaavren bowed. "Would you care to join us for dinner, madam?"

"Alas, I must begin my preparations for the defense of the city. Apropos, there will a meeting of the staff at Dzur Mountain. I will arrange a teleport for you."

"I will be there."

"I will expect you."

"In that case, if you are leaving at once, it only leaves me to thank you, Warlord."

"Thank me? But for what, Captain?"

Khaavren smiled in answer and bid the Enchantress a farewell. Then, before taking his dinner, he took himself around the Manor, both inside and out, in order to carry on an inspection of the guard posts, which was a task he did not care to leave to another, now that it was his responsibility once more.

In fact, this inspection, seemingly so trivial, turned out to be another small but critical element in the unraveling of a complex tapestry whose first thread had come loose when, nearly a year before, Her Majesty had thrown her pen at the wall.

Exactly how this inspection served to tug at these threads is not something about which the reader must wonder for long; on the contrary, we propose to discover it to the reader directly.

Chapter the Eighty-Third

How the Discreet Was Accused
Of a Great Indiscretion,
And the Empress Received a Lesson

As Khaavren was beginning his inspection, Pel, who had been in a small room of the Manor set aside for his use, heard his name spoken. Looking up, he perceived one of the guardsmen, who, doing duty as messenger, begged a moment of his time.

"Well, what is it?" said Pel.

"It is Her Majesty."

"She wishes to see me, then?"

"Exactly. She wishes to see Your Discretion, and that directly. I am bidden to inform you—"

"Well?"

"That an instant's delay would be, in her words, highly inappropriate."

Pel shrugged. "The gods save me from being inappropriate."

"So then?"

"So then, I am going to her at once. So much so that, without waiting an instant, you may accompany me, and it will then be seen that you have done your duty in exemplary fashion."

"So much the better," said the guardsman, not without a certain satisfaction, because, now that Khaavren was back, he knew that, while no dereliction would be overlooked, zeal would also be noted, appreciated, and rewarded.

True to his word, Pel accompanied the guardsman, which brought him, in two steps, to the covered terrace. When he entered Her Majesty's presence, he bowed, and, before he was again upright, he understood that something was amiss—there was a fire in Zerika's eye that he had never seen before; indeed, he felt himself under a sort of scrutiny that he hadn't experienced since his interview with the Institute of Discretion—the memory of which was sufficient, even now, to cause perspiration to come to the brow of the Yendi, whose nerves were normally as cool as ice. Moreover, the Orb was the purest, angriest red that Pel had ever seen. He felt rather as a sailor might feel in the instant between his ship's broaching to, and its going down before the next swell.

That memory of his interview with the Masters of Discretion came back even more strongly while he waited for the Empress to speak. His interviewers on that occasion, requiring of him details of his life, history, thoughts, and feelings that he had never before revealed even to himself, had been the most terrifying during the seemingly interminable pauses between questions; and now, aware that, whatever was on the mind of Her Majesty, there was no question of joking, and that he, himself, was the object of her scrutiny, those same feelings returned—feelings that, nevertheless, he succeeded in concealing entirely.

At length she said, "I had thought I could trust you, Duke."

Such words as these are, without question, the worst disaster that can befall anyone who has committed himself to the study of discretion. It took, indeed, all of his reserves to meet Zerika's eyes and reply with coolness that would have done credit to Aerich, "And so Your Majesty can."

She glared at him again, her eyes narrowed, and the red of the Orb became, if it were possible, even brighter.

"Do not compound your crime with dissimulation, Duke."

"Your Majesty is invited to put me under the Orb."

She brushed this aside with a wave of her hand. "I know something of the discipline you have studied, Duke. I am prepared to believe you can fool the Orb as easily as you fooled me."

"Would Your Majesty condescend to tell me with what I am accused?"

"I should prefer you to admit to it without that formality; it sickens me to think of it."

"Alas, I have nothing with which to reproach myself, and so I cannot imagine with what I could be charged."

"Would it make matters any more clear, Yendi, if I were to tell you that I have just given the honor of an audience to His Highness Prince Ritsak, the Count of Flowerpot Hill and Environs?"

Pel bowed. "I regret that this tells me nothing."

"The Prince, the Lyorn Heir, had the misfortune to be forced to tell me that his House, that is, the House of the Lyorn, the House to which others look for moral guidance and political leadership, could not support my pretensions—that was his word, 'pretensions,' at which he had at least the grace to blush while uttering—to the Orb. The Orb, I might add, that circled my head as he spoke."

"That is, indeed, a great misfortune, Majesty."

"That is my opinion, Duke."

"I do myself the honor of telling my Empress, with all sincerity, that I cannot imagine how I could be responsible for this misfortune."

"You lie, Duke."

Pel's eyes flashed as did Her Majesty's, and he said, "Your Majesty may well give me the lie, knowing that I cannot demand satisfaction of my sovereign."

"Save your casuistries, Duke."

Pel continued to glare, and made no response. At length, Zerika grunted and said, "Very well, your point is well taken. I ought not to calumniate you when you cannot respond. I withdraw the word."

Pel bowed stiffly, and Zerika continued, speaking in carefully controlled tones, "I was reproached, by the House of the Lyorn, with what he did me the honor to call 'inappropriate relations.'"

Pel frowned. "Inappropriate relations, Your Majesty? I cannot imagine what this might mean."

"It means, Duke, that the House of the Lyorn reproached me with my lover."

Pel felt his eyes widen as understanding came to him. After an instant's reflection, he said, "I consider that an impertinence, Majesty."

"As do I, and I said so."

"And may I do myself the honor of asking Your Majesty what reply His Highness made?"

"He replied that it would be an impertinence if I were the Empress."

In spite of all that had happened, Pel could not prevent the ghost of a smile from creasing his lips as he said, "There is Your Majesty's casuistry."

"Perhaps," said Zerika. "But the fact remains, Duke, that no one knows about this matter except for you, and me, and my lover. And I give you my word that neither of us have spoken of it."

"I have, in no way, by word, act, or implication, violated in the least part my Oath of Discretion, nor Your Majesty's trust. To put it in the simplest terms, Your Majesty, I have told no one, nor have I so much as hinted to anyone of this matter by the least clue, word, or gesture."

"That is a tolerably exhaustive denial, Duke."

Pel bowed.

"However, I do not believe it."

Pel bowed once more, there being nothing more to say.

"Unfortunately," continued the furious Zerika, "I have no means of proof."

Pel waited quietly, meeting Her Majesty's gaze.

After a moment she said, "You are dismissed from your post, and my presence. You are to leave this house at once. I never wish to see you again. Go."

Pel bowed, backed up three steps, turned on his heel, and, without another word, left Her Majesty's presence. Two steps took him to the front doors of the Manor, where, by chance, he happened to meet Khaavren, who was making certain the guards were posted correctly outside of these doors. We must observe that here, in fact, is another link in that chain of destiny: had Her Majesty not, a year before, thrown her pen against the wall, then Khaavren would not have been on duty, and, therefore, would not have been inspecting the guard posts at that moment, and, in conclusion, would not have encountered Pel as he left the Palace.

However, in the event, Her Majesty *did* throw her pen, and so Khaavren saw Pel as he was descending the wide, shallow stairway in front of Whitecrest Manor.

"Ah, my dear Pel," said Khaavren.

"Khaavren! You are wearing your cloak!"

"Well," said Khaavren, shrugging.

"You are, then, re-instated?"

"As you see."

"How droll," observed Pel.

"Droll?"

"That you should return to the Imperial service on the same day as I—but never mind, it is of no matter, my good friend."

Khaavren, who knew that the last way to get any information from the Yendi was to ask it, changed the subject (as he thought) by saying, "I perceive you are on your way to some destination."

"Oh, as far as that goes, I am setting out, yes."

"Has Her Majesty done you the honor the give you an errand?"

"In a manner of speaking, my good Khaavren."

"Well, I will walk with you for a while. In what manner of speaking? Or is it, perhaps, something you are forbidden to discuss?"

"On the contrary, I have received no order not to discuss it; but there is, in fact, tolerably little to say."

"So much the better, then you needn't delay your mission to tell me."

"You wish to hear it then?"

"Why, unless there is a reason not to tell me, I should be delighted to learn what you are about."

"Then I will tell you without delay."

"You have my complete attention."

"This is it, then: I am leaving."

"You perceive, that I can see for myself. But, where are you going?"

"As to that, I don't know."

"You don't know?"

"No, something will, no doubt, occur to me."

"But, when will you be back?"

"Alas, I will not be back."

"Pel!"

"Yes?"

"What does this mean?"

"Ah, let us not speak of it."

"On the contrary, let us speak of nothing else! What has happened?"

Pel shrugged. "If you insist upon knowing—"

"I give you my word, I do."

"Well, Her Majesty has done me the honor to require me to leave."

"You are exiled?" cried Khaavren.

"Oh, not in the least. Merely required to leave Whitecrest Manor."

"The Trey! Pel, what have you done?"

"I give you my word, Khaavren: I have done nothing at all in the world."

"How, you were dismissed from Her Majesty's service and required to leave over nothing?"

"In fact, Her Majesty believes that I have done something."

"What does Her Majesty believe you have done?"

"Been indiscreet."

"You? Impossible!"

Pel smiled. "I am glad that you say so, my dear friend; it is good to know one's friends have faith."

"Cha! It requires no faith to say that if someone has seen a winneasourus fly, that person is deluded."

"You are good to insist upon it. But now—"

"Yes, now?"

"May I suggest that it will do your career no good to be seen with me?"

"Seen with you? I will be more than seen with you, my dear friend. Come with me at once. I insist upon it."

"Come with you? Where?"

"Back to the Manor."

"And yet, I have been ordered to leave the Manor."

"Well, now you are ordered back—or, if not ordered, at least requested strongly."

"Alas, it was the Empress who gave the order."

"Well, it is I who make the request."

"You perceive, the order of an Empress is stronger than the request of a friend."

"Cha! That is true!"

"And so?"

"Well, in that case—"

"Yes?"

Khaavren put his hand on Pel's shoulder. "I arrest you."

"How, you arrest me? But, on what charge? Even Her Majesty, knowing she could not prove her allegations, did not go that far."

"Oh, the charge, well, I arrest you on the charge of leaving a friend who does not want you to leave."

"And is that a crime?"

"If not, it should be; in my opinion, someone who refuses a friend's request is more culpable than someone who wishes to play a friendly game without informing the Imperial tax collectors, don't you think?"

"There is something in what you say," admitted Pel.

"I am pleased that you agree. And now I'm afraid you must come along."

"Am I truly arrested?"

"Truly and officially, my dear friend."

"Then, it appears, I have no choice."

"None."

"Would you like my sword?"

"How you go on! What would I do with your sword?"

"Yet, if I am arrested—"

"Oh, it will be a mild sort of captivity, I assure you. Now, let us return to the Manor."

"Very well, it seems that, being arrested, I must comply."

"Precisely."

"Shall I precede you?"

"Not in the least. Arm in arm."

"Very well; but this is a peculiar sort of arrest you carry out."

"Oh, I set my own standards for such matters; you perceive, it is a perquisite of my position."

"If you continue using such perquisites, you will not long have your position."

"My dear Pel, do you imagine that I care so much for my position? I assure you, I became tolerably weary in the old days of salutes, and ceremonies, and the making of schedules, and the false smiles of the courtiers, and the giggling of the coquettes."

"If that is true, why did you accept Her Majesty's offer to return you your commission?"

"Do you truly wish to know?"

"Yes, in fact, I do."

"Because this Phoenix still needs help, and she—"

"Yes."

"She is a friend of my son."

"Ah!"

"After all that has happened, well, it seemed like the least I could do."

"I had not understood this circumstance," said Pel, pressing his friend's hand.

"Now you know."

"Well, but is that the only reason?"

"I give you my word, Pel, that is most of it. But here we are at last. Come in. Let us adjourn to the dining room, and see if there is any food set out. If there is, you shall eat, and I will join you in an instant."

"Since I am arrested, I must comply. But it is good to know that, at least, you do not starve your prisoners."

"Oh, you know I would never do that."

By chance, Daro had come down to the dining room, where she had anticipated being joined by Khaavren. "Here, madam," he said. "I turn this miscreant over to your care.

Have an extra plate set to dinner, and I shall return to claim it in a moment. Pel has been arrested, you know, and therefore may not leave. I can depend upon you?"

"Arrested!" cried the Countess. "My lord, are you jesting?"

"Oh, as to that, Countess, I do not insist that I am entirely in earnest. Yet, neither am I entirely in jest. But Pel will explain if he wishes."

"But what about you? Where are you going?"

"Oh, I? I have an errand with Her Majesty that will not wait. I shall return directly. Have a care for our tricky Yendi, and be certain he does not escape."

"Oh, I promise," said Pel, "I shall be the most compliant of prisoners."

"Excellent. I depend upon you."

"But Khaavren, I think you should re-consider—"

"Not another word, Pel. You are my prisoner, and, as such, I conjure you to silence."

Pel bowed his head.

With this, Khaavren took his leave of Daro and Pel, and himself back to the covered terrace, which room he entered immediately, as was his right as Captain of the Phoenix Guards, and, seeing Her Majesty speaking with the emissary from Elde, he took himself to a far corner of the room until this audience was complete. Though he made no effort to either listen to or watch this audience, he could not help but notice that at the expiration of the interview the emissary appeared humbled.

"So much the better," observed Khaavren to himself. "Whatever humbles Elde must be good for the Empire."

When this worthy had left, punctiliously giving Her Majesty every courtesy, the Empress sat down behind the paper-covered table and turned her attention to Khaavren, who placed himself before her and bowed.

"Well, Captain?" she said, acknowledging his salute.

"If I may beg for two minutes of Your Majesty's time—"

"You may. What is it?"

"A trifling matter of jurisdiction, that is all, yet one that cannot wait."

"Jurisdiction?"

Khaavren bowed.

"Explain yourself, for you perceive I have not the least idea in the world of what you are speaking."

"Then I shall do myself the honor to explain it in terms that can leave no room for doubt."

"That will be best, believe me."

"Your Majesty, in practice, controls territory stretching from somewhere west of the city to Methni's Channel, and from the coast to very nearly South Mountain."

"I am aware of this, Captain."

"And, in theory, which we hope to make true in practice soon, Your Majesty controls considerably more."

"Well?"

"And, more than this, Your Majesty even has control of the comings and goings of a portion of this Manor, which Your Majesty has done us the honor—the great honor—of using to conduct Imperial business."

"Come to the point, Captain."

"I am about to, Majesty."

"Well?"

"Your Majesty, as I have observed, has control of a portion of this manor."

"Yes."

"But not the rest of it."

Zerika frowned and said, "You are speaking in riddles, sir."

"Then does Your Majesty wish me to speak more plainly?"

"I have been wishing for nothing else for an hour, Captain."

"Then here it is, as plainly as I can state it: Your Majesty has no right to decide who is and is not welcome in my home."

The Orb darkened with anger—as, indeed, did Zerika's face. "You presume to speak so your Empress?"

"Evidently," said Khaavren, bowing.

Zerika fairly glared. "This is an impertinence."

"Well."

"How long have you been back in my service, Captain? An hour? Two? And now, it seems, you wish to be dismissed again?"

"That is as Your Majesty wishes; for myself, I care very little about it."

"This is insupportable."

"Not in the least."

"I believe you are doing yourself the honor of disputing with me, Captain."

"Your Majesty has accused my friend of an action that is manifestly impossible for him to have committed, and, moreover, have expelled him from beneath my roof. Does Your Majesty truly believe that a gentleman can be expected to countenance such behavior? If so, I fear for the Empire under Your Majesty's hand, because it will be a poor sort of court and a poor sort of Empire that it governs."

In an instant, the Empress was on her feet. "Captain! How *dare* you!"

Khaavren bowed but said nothing.

"And did Galstan, then, give you all of the details of his crime?"

"He told me nothing except that he was leaving. When I questioned him, he explained that he had been dismissed from your service for having revealed a communication which Your Majesty did him the honor to confide in him as part of his office."

"Well, and so he did."

"Impossible."

"Now you give me the lie?" cried Zerika, quite nearly hysterical.

"Not in the least; Your Majesty is mistaken, that is all."

Zerika took two deep breaths in a failed effort to overcome her wrath, and said, "Tell me, Sir Khaavren; did you speak to your last master in this fashion?"

"His Majesty Tortaalik? No, Your Majesty. Never."

"And why do I receive such treatment when he did not?"

"Because he was weak, and small, and mean. I do him honor for having done his best, but he could never become more than he was, so it was useless to treat him with respect."

"You call this treating me with respect?"

"I do, in the only way a plain soldier is capable of."

Zerika stared at him. "Let me understand you, Captain. You do yourself the honor to scold—*to scold*—your Empress, and you call this respect?"

Khaavren bowed his assent.

"And to my predecessor you were the soul of courtesy, because he was weak, and small, and mean?"

Khaavren bowed once more.

"Cracks and shards! If I were my illustrious ancestor, Zerika the First, who founded the Empire, why, what would you do then? Pull your ear at me?"

"I should have treated her with the same respect I show Your Majesty, and for the same reason."

"What reason is that?"

"Because Your Majesty has the potential for greatness—for real greatness. I have seen it in your managing of diplomacies, and in your conversations with subordinates, and, even now, when Your Majesty feels she has been treated in a way no person, much less an Empress, ought to be treated, Your Majesty attempts to control her temper and be just and fair, looking past the extraordinary provocation.

"Your Majesty," he continued, "why could not you have done as much with my friend Pel? I have known him for more nearly nine hundreds of years. It is impossible for him to have committed the crime with which he is accused."

"You think so."

"I insist upon it."

"You dispute with me to my face and call it respect?"

"Yes."

"If you respect me so much, why did you leave my service before, Captain?"

"Because I was in too much pain over a personal matter to see things as clearly as I do now, Majesty. But now that I see it, I know that I was wrong; I was wrong for failing to give Your Majesty the opportunity to act as an Empress."

"Do you presume now to instruct me, Captain?"

"Not in the least, Your Majesty."

Khaavren, in one of those unfeigned outbursts that is irresistible to anyone of heart, walked around the table so that he was very nearly touching Her Majesty's garments, removed his hat, and knelt, looking up her. "Your Majesty, I am a soldier who failed, or Tortaalik would not be dead. And I am also a father who failed, or my son would be under this roof. But let no one question my loyalty to either my Empress or to my friends—that loyalty, along with the love of my wife, is all I have left.

"I do not presume to teach my Empress how to behave. But I have been around the court, and on the field of battle, and in the dueling circle, often enough to recognize a great heart; and a great heart cannot be lied to. Your Majesty, my only wish is to serve you—to somehow do some small thing to in part atone for my failures. How could I, then, live with myself if I permitted my friend to be dishonored, and, in so doing, permitted my Empress to dishonor herself, when I might prevent it? Or, for that matter, even if I could not, when I could see the way clear to try? That a task is impossible is no excuse for not attempting it, not when my heart tells me it must be done."

Khaavren fell silent and bowed his head after this remarkable speech. Her Majesty, after a moment's thought, sat down once more and put her head into her hands for some few minutes. At length she said, "Do you truly believe, Captain, that it was impossible for your friend to have betrayed a confidence?"

"It is more likely, Majesty, for the Orb to betray a confidence than for Pel to do so."

"But then, how could it have happened?"

"Your Majesty, I do not know what confidence was betrayed, or how it could have happened; I only know that Pel cannot have been responsible, any more than the point of my sword could pierce the hand that holds it, and for the same reason: It cannot bend that far without breaking."

For some time Her Majesty made no sound—it seemed to Khaavren as if the Manor itself was holding its breath; he did not dare to raise his eyes to see what color the Orb held, but merely waited.

At length, Her Majesty spoke. "And yet," she said in a

quiet voice, as if speaking to herself, "it is hard to admit to a mistake when one has been so angry, and so . . ."

"Sanctimonious, Majesty?"

A pale smile crossed Her Majesty's countenance. "Exactly."

"Oh, Your Majesty! It is yet another mark of greatness to be able to do so. I know, because of how far beyond my powers it is."

"How, you? I cannot imagine you being sanctimonious, Captain."

"You did not hear how I spoke to my son, Majesty."

The Empress nodded. "Then it would appear that, as your Empress, I must provide a good example. Rise, Captain. Go and send your friend to me; I wish to speak to him."

"Your Majesty, before I go, dare I make one last impertinent request?"

"What is it, Captain?"

"May I kiss Your Majesty's hand?"

Zerika smiled slightly and held out her perfect, white arm. "Here it is, Captain. Now go and bring me your friend."

Khaavren reverently touched his lips to the proffered hand, then rose, bowed, backed away, and left the room without ever raising his eyes to meet Her Majesty's. Outside of the door he put his hat on his head once more and, coming to the dining room, said, "Pel, I believe that Her Majesty wishes to say two words to you."

Pel glanced at Khaavren, reading something of the ordeal through which he had just passed in the expression on his countenance, and pressed the Tiassa's hand.

"My friend—" he began.

"No, no. See Her Majesty. And Pel: there is goodness in her, and I believe greatness as well."

"I know that, Khaavren; I have seen it myself."

Without another word, then, Pel took himself to the waiting room, where he was at once admitted by Brudik. He approached Her Majesty and bowed.

"Your Discretion," she said. "My conscience stabs me; I have been unjust to a loyal servant."

"I will bind the wounds, Sire," said Pel, bowing once more, as if nothing out of the ordinary had happened.

And it was in this way that the Duke of Galstan, in spite of the plans and enmity of Kâna, Grita, Habil, and Illista, remained at Whitecrest Manor as Kâna's troops approached the capital.

Chapter the Eighty-Fourth

How the Warlord Prepared The Defense of Adrilankha, And Morrolan Acquired a Mission

We have not hitherto mentioned Kiraamoni e'Baritt, nor, in point of fact, do we intend to spend any considerable time with her; but it is only fair, after having previously mentioned the emergency fortifications created by Fentor around what would become Castle Black, to note that it was this worthy, one of the truly great military engineers of the age, who directed the construction of the fortifications around Adrilankha. While Kiraamoni had, it is true, both more manpower and material with which to work, it is also undeniable that she had considerably less time.

Her work was nothing short of astonishing, the more-so in that it was conducted without the awareness on the part of the citizens of Adrilankha that the purpose of this sudden construction was either military or immediate—the Countess of Whitecrest and the Empress were both very much aware of the danger of a panic in the city, and the degree to which such a panic would do Kâna's work for him—indeed, there is some reason to believe that the instigation of confusion and social unrest was a part of his plan.

It is sad that so many of those who study military history (and shameful that so many of those who write it) give insufficient weight to *efficiency*. If every battle that had ever been lost because of clumsy staff work, slow communications, and sloppy logistics had been won, we should be living in such a different world that we could scarcely recognize the very hills and rivers. But if aficionados of military history are unaware of this, we can be grateful that Sethra Lavode, for one, was not, and it was, without fail, a quality she looked for in staff officers: Kiraamoni arranged for supplies, manpower, and subsidiary design work with such a cool efficiency that within three hours of receiving her instructions, wagons had been gathered, horses rounded up, shovels, hammers, nails, and lumber requisitioned, plans laid, and the wagonloads of supplies were rolling briskly to the points designated, while construction battalions, shovels in hand, were beginning to work.

The three roads that Sethra considered the most likely to face attack were the Old West Road (also called the Hartre Pike), Lower Kieron Road, and the Northgate Ferry Way. Along each of these roads, within the astonishing time of fifty-two hours from when the order was given by the Warlord, there appeared two small, low, wooden, but perfectly serviceable fortresses. Each of these fortresses was well supplied with javelins and troops who knew how to use them, as well as food, water, latrines, and stabling and fodder for the horses of the (admittedly scanty) cavalry corps of the Empire. It is worthwhile to note in passing that one of these fortresses is, in a substantially modified form, it is true, still standing: and should anyone visit the Fortress Inn on the Old West Road he will now understand something of why it has the peculiar form that it has.

In addition to fortifications, then, communications had been established in a new and efficient manner: next to each brigade-level officer was a specially trained sorcerer who could speak, mind to mind, with at least one other sorcerer, the second belonging to the support unit for the Warlord's staff. In other words, every brigadier was able to instantly—*instantly*—send and receive messages to and from the Warlord. To be sure, there were still errand runners at the ready; the Warlord, while happy and even eager to adopt any new method that promised to give an edge in battle, was not willing yet to utterly abandon the systems that had proven reliable for thousands of years.

In retrospect, now that hundreds of battles, large and small, have been fought using this communication system or close variants, it may confound the reader to know that many of the middle-level commanders (by which we mean those between division level and company level) were so resistant to what appears to us as an advancement in military science without drawback; to this, we can only say that stubbornness, obstinacy, and resistance to change are no more unknown in the House of the Dragon than is a tendency toward redundancy, repetition, and reiteration among historians.

This communication system proved its efficacy at once: The Warlord maintained herself at Dzur Mountain, and was not even seen in person during these critical days except by her division commanders and staff officers; at least until the fortifications were complete, at which time, using the ability to teleport, she was able to carry out lightning-fast inspections. We need hardly add that, upon completing these inspections, she had nothing but praise for the worthy Kiraamoni—an important but, sadly, almost forgotten personage in the Battle of Adrilankha.

It was while this construction was occurring that Sethra Lavode paid a visit to Castle Black, where a celebration of the completion of this remarkable structure had been in progress for nearly a year. Morrolan, for his part, was not participating at this moment, having secluded himself in the room he had set aside for a library (mostly consisting of comfortable chairs and empty shelves) in order to continue his study of the sorcerous arts, which had become a passion for him. Upon learning that the Enchantress wished to have a conversation with him, he desired her to be brought to him at once.

Morrolan set his book down and rose to his feet when the Enchantress entered, but, instead of welcoming her to his home, or even saying how happy he was to see her, the words that came from his lips were "Is it true that all matter consists mostly of energy, and that to alter the form of this energy is to change the nature of the matter?"

"I perceive you have been reading Yebro."

"Exactly."

"I applaud your decision."

"You should, madam; you recommended him."

"Ah. Yes, well, then I applaud your decision to follow my advice."

"But is what he says true?"

"All matter is mostly empty space, with particles held in certain relationships by bonds of energy, this has been proven beyond all possibility of doubt. To alter those bonds, is, indeed, to change the nature of that matter."

"But then—anything can be transformed into anything!"

"In theory, yes."

"In theory?"

"In practice it is not so simple."

"But, why is that?"

"Because every detail of each transformation must be held in the mind of the sorcerer, which is nearly impossible; and then the precise amount of energy must be applied in precisely the right way, which can rarely be done at the same time as one is holding all of this information in one's mind. I hesitate to guess at the number of sorcerers who have destroyed themselves in the attempt to cast or create spells using such methods."

"Ah. So, it is useless."

"Nearly, as a practical matter. Although, in fact, there have recently been some very promising experiments in terms of removing salinity from sea-water. But the understanding of the foundation of sorcery, which is Yebro's actual point, is of inestimable value."

"Well."

"Ah, do not look so disappointed, my friend. While you cannot turn a piece of basalt into a dinner for two, well, it was the use of these principles that resulted in the first flash-stones, which were tolerably useful at one time. And there are sufficient other uses to prove the importance of the theoretical in the practical. And, indeed, there are certain methods of making dinner for two appear from nothing, or seem to, so even that is not lost."

"Yes, I understand."

"I am glad that you do."

"But come, my dear Sethra—I do not believe you have come to see me in order to be questioned about aspects of magical philosophy, however interesting."

"Well, that is true, though you know that I am happy to give you what help I can in your pursuit."

"I know that you have been kindness itself. But in what way may I be of service to you?"

"May I sit down, Lord Morrolan?"

"Oh, my dear Sethra! You perceive, I am most distracted. Of course, please sit. And would you care for wine?"

"Not at all, but I thank you."

"Come, then. You have my full attention, for I know you could not have come here without some purpose in mind."

"Oh, you are entirely correct; I did not arrive without a purpose."

"And then?"

"In a word, the Pretender is preparing an assault on Adrilankha, which we have only discovered at the last moment. That is, the very last moment. We expect his banners to be in sight to-morrow."

"To-morrow!"

"Exactly."

"Verra! What is to be done?"

"I wish you to command your division once more."

"My division?"

"Certainly."

"But when did I have a division?"

"Why, during Zerika's march to Adrilankha."

"Ah, yes! That is right. I had forgotten. You perceive, Fentor did most of the work."

"Well, but now I wish you to take active command, although, to be sure, you may have him on your staff, or in any other position you choose."

"My dear Sethra, I should be honored, to be sure. Only—"

"Well?"

"Why?"

"You ask why?"

"Yes. That is to say, why am I chosen for this honor?"

"Oh, I did not select you for the honor, my friend, but rather for the duty. Such honor as there may be falls naturally with it, but, I assure you, had there been no honor at all, I should have chosen you just the same."

"You perceive, my dear Sethra, that this answer, gratifying as it is, merely begs the question to be asked again, wherefore I do so. That is to say, why have you chosen me? You must know a score, a hundred, a thousand officers with more experience and knowledge of the military arts and sciences."

"As to that, a thousand may be over-stating the case."

"Well."

"But the simple fact is, my friend, that, while there is truth in what you say, there are other aspects to the matter. I will be precise, because I know you value precision."

"Yes, that is true."

"If you were to be called upon to make a complex attack—a double envelopment, for example, or a grand flanking maneuver such as we used so effectively in the campaign that culminated at Brownstone Creek, I should wish for a commander with experience. If the intention was to have an independent campaign to coincide with my own, then I should require a general with great knowledge of how to maintain lines of communication and retreat. But you are to hold a position, or, at most, lead a countercharge at some point. And I have no commanders whose troops look at them, and speak about them, in the same that way the yours do."

Morrolan frowned. "Madam, I confess that I do not understand what you do me the honor of telling me."

"That does not startle me, good Morrolan. It may be because of your sword, or it may be an accident of manner that is inherent in your character, or it may have to do with your history. Perhaps it is something of all of these. But, although you may not be aware of it, you are the sort of commander that a soldier would follow over Deathgate Falls, or for whom he would defend a line against an army made up of the demons of Se'haganthú."

"How, I am?"

"You are, I promise you."

"I had not been aware of this fact."

"Perhaps I have erred in informing you of it. The knowledge may be of help to you, or it may hinder you. I believe it will do no harm, however, or I should not have told you."

Morrolan shook his head, still endeavoring to comprehend what Sethra had done him the honor to explain. At length he said, "Well, I must consider this."

"Assuredly. But, will you agree?"

"Agree to what, madam?"

"Why to command the division, as I have asked you to?"

"Oh, yes. I had forgotten that matter."

"And yet, it is rather too important to forget, don't you think?"

"Oh, assuredly."

"And then?"

"Why, now I recall."

"Certainly, but do you agree?"

"Oh, that is your question?"

"Indeed, my lord; it seems I have now done myself the honor of putting it to you several times."

"But of course I agree, my dear Sethra. How, had you ever doubted it?"

"In point of fact, my lord, I had not. May I depend on seeing you, in two hours' time, at Dzur Mountain?"

"If you wish me to be there, madam, then I will be there."

"I do indeed. There I will outline the general plans for the defense."

"You may depend upon me, Warlord."

After the Warlord had taken her leave of him, Morrolan took himself out of doors to the courtyard of his castle, where there were some thirty or thirty-five guardsmen on duty in various towers. This time he was aware of certain subtle changes that came over these worthies, Dragonlords all, when he appeared. He remained there for some few moments, reflecting on this, before turning and going back to his castle. However, instead of returning to the library, he brought himself to his apartment, where he took down his sword from where it hung by its sheath on his wall from a single hook. He drew it, letting the peculiar and powerful sensations fill his thoughts, suffusing, if we may be poetic, his very soul with its energy and personality. "Is it you," he asked it, holding the blade up before his eyes. "Is it you, or is it I? If it is both of us, my black wand, then, where do you leave off, and where do I begin? Do you miss the excitement of battle, my friend? Well, so do I."

He studied its length carefully, the dull grey-black metal giving off no hint of reflection, as if, instead, it were absorbing the light that struck it. "Well," he continued, "if there is to be an attack, then we shall both see action, and be all the happier for it. Indeed, perhaps I shall endeavor in this battle to use some of the sorcerous skill I have been studying with such diligence that, I fear, I have neglected you. Will you mind if I kill with sorcery instead of letting you feast, as you so much desire, on the blood of an enemy? If, perhaps, I draw a certain amount of energy from the Orb and then send it out in some direction, spewing destruct—"

He broke off, at this point, because even as the thought had formed in his mind, a sort of black light (if the reader can imagine such a thing) had left the tip of his weapon and, traveling upwards, carved a narrow hole through the ceiling, the rock of the next story, its roof, and so out into the sky. This event, as might well be imagined, so startled the Dragonlord that for some few moments he was unable to formulate a thought.

"Remarkable," he murmured at last. Then, after reflecting for a while, "I must directly find some workmen to repair the damage; it would not do at all to have a hole running right through the middle of my home." And then, "I do hope no one was in the way."

Morrolan had just time to communicate the need for repairs before the time indicated by Sethra had been reached, and so, walking out to the middle of his courtyard (for reasons we will explain on another occasion) he, with great care, not wishing to embed himself into a solid piece of rock, nor to scatter himself to the six winds, bethought himself of an image of the door leading into Dzur Mountain that he had first seen, closing his eyes until he was convinced he could see with all the clarity that he would have if he had been standing in front of it; then, drawing exactly enough energy, he executed the teleport, becoming, in effect, non-existent for some few seconds while he was in two places at once, and then, casting loose of his now tenuous grip on his position at Castle Black, permitted himself, not without a certain disorienting shift, to exist in the place he had seen with his mind's eye; he emerged, therefore, outside of a particular door into Dzur Mountain. The teleport was complete.

He adjusted his cloak (Morrolan, even then, favored the full, flowing, ankle-length black cloak in which he is usually pictured today), ran a hand through his hair, made certain the ties on his doublet were in a neat and ordered line, and stepped up to the door. He was just considering whether he ought to clap, when it opened before him. On observing that there was no one there to open it, he reflected, "I must have one of those doors," and stepped into Dzur Mountain.

Alas, having once set foot into the dim corridors of the mountain, he lost not only his way, but his exact punctuality (the latter being a direct consequence of the former), it taking him some fifteen or twenty minutes of making the exact wrong turnings and so avoiding both the correct corridor, and the industrious Tukko who had been sent to look for him.

Eventually, however, he was found and escorted to the room where were seated Sethra Lavode, Sethra the Younger, the Sorceress in Green, Khaavren, the Necromancer, Lord Brimford—that is, the Warlock—and a few Dragonlords he did not then recognize. Morrolan mumbled an apology which was politely brushed aside, and he took his place at the long, smooth, brightly polished table made of stone that looked as if it, like much of the rest of Sethra's home, had once been part of the mountain.

"We had not gotten very far," said Sethra. She pointed to a large map of Adrilankha that hung on the nearest wall, and said, "I was merely pointing out the positions from which I intend to defend the city."

"Very good," said Morrolan. "I shall give you my whole attention, I promise."

Sethra took a moment to introduce Morrolan to those of her staff officers whom he had not yet had the honor of meeting, after which she outlined her plans for engaging the enemy. "Once we know for certain where he intends the attack," she said, "we will, of course, move forces there as quickly as possible. If you study the thin lines on the map, you will observe that they indicate the best routes from one position to another. You must memorize those roads, and even journey along them once or twice, so that there will be no mistakes if you need to move your divisions. I have already arranged with Khaavren, Captain of the Phoenix Guards, for small patrols to keep those routes empty. For my part, I will make my headquarters in the field, where-ever I feel I am most needed. But I caution you all to be prepared for the unexpected."

"Do you know," observed Khaavren, "I have often heard that one ought to be prepared for the unexpected, but I am not entirely certain of how to do so."

"Well, sir," said the Warlord at once, "that is because there is no good way to accomplish this. But the caution must nevertheless be given, for the simple reason that if is not, and something unexpected happens, I should not look nearly so wise had I not made the remark."

There were a few chuckles over this display of wit, and Khaavren, for his part, nodded to show that he held himself answered.

"However," continued the Enchantress, looking carefully at everyone present in turn, so that each should realize that, in what she was about to say, there would be no question of joking, "however much I may, and, indeed, do insist upon a regular military plan in order to fight off this invasion, I cannot help but believe that there will be a great deal more to this battle than we expect. That is why the warlock Brimford," here she indicated the Easterner, "is preparing, as he did before, to see that the enemy is attacked by whatever wildlife can be pulled from the surrounding jungles and forests. It is why the Necromancer—" here she nodded to the pale demon, "—intends to re-animate any of the enemy who should be killed in the battle. It is why I intend to make as great a use of sorcery as ever we can manage. There will be much that must necessarily be left to decisions made in the moment, because of how little we know; we ought, therefore, to be as certain as we can about what is ours to control, and that, above all, includes our military forces."

"For all the good they will do," observed Sethra the Younger, shrugging.

Morrolan looked at her, then at the Warlord.

"My apprentice," explained the Enchantress in answer to Morrolan's look, "is convinced that the battle will be decided entirely by how we respond to whatever schemes our enemy may have concocted. In this I believe she may well be right but, as I have said, that is no reason to ignore the direct, simple forces that are about to attack us."

"How," said Morrolan, "you agree with her?"

"I have believed for some time that Kâna has certain plans and stratagems with which he hopes and expects to overcome our advantages. I have had no reason to change my mind—indeed, I have reason now to think so more than ever."

"Well, but—" He stopped then, and a certain flush rose to his face as he looked at the others at the table.

"No, go on, my friend," said the Warlord. "Now is the time to speak freely. To-morrow morning, unless I am much mistaken, it will be time for you to follow orders without question."

"Well then, I was merely about to express my curiosity about what these new reasons are."

"Oh, as to that. Well, I have some small indication that Kâna may have enlisted the aid of a certain Tri'nagore, one of the Lords of—"

"Tri'nagore!" cried Morrolan.

"How, you know of him?"

"Nearly."

"Well, come then. Tell us what you know."

"You wish to hear about Tri'nagore?" asked Morrolan, obviously agitated to a greater degree than any of them had seen before.

"Certainly," said Sethra Lavode. "And at once, if you please."

"He is worshiped by barbarians near Blackchapel—that is, near the village where I lived before coming here. Near, but not too near—a day's ride, perhaps."

"Barbarians?" said Sethra Lavode, as if unsure how he was using the term.

"Barbarians?" echoed Sethra the Younger, as if wondering how this could be true of some Easterners more than others.

Morrolan continued speaking, with barely contained fury. "They attacked my village for no reason, except, perhaps, to appease this fetid-breathed evil-eyed cat-eating mucklord of a god they worship as who should say kethna worship the filth of the farmyard. Not for gold, nor food, nor wine, nor even desperation for congress, but only for blood did they fall upon us, while I was meditating, and unaware until it was over and saw what had been done by the hand of this . . . Tri'nagore."

He uttered this last name as if it were a stronger curse than any he had used leading up to it, after which he fell silent, as did everyone else at the table, until, after some period of time, the Warlord said, "My goodness."

Morrolan shrugged and glowered at the table in front of him.

"And yet," ventured Sethra the Younger after another moment, "I had thought that Tri'nagore desired sacrifices from his own followers, not those of others."

"Bah. He doesn't care. He desires blood, that is all. These barbarians live in villages that always run with blood—human, animal, they don't care. In one of the villages is an altar where they raise his presence—they drench it with blood to appease him. They raid and plunder because their god tells them to, and so they worship a god who tells them to plunder instead of raising food as man was intended to do."

"I thought you said," remarked someone, "that they didn't steal food."

"No, I did not," said Morrolan coldly. "I said that was not why they raided. That doesn't mean they do not carry off what they can."

"But then," said the Dragonlord, "if it were not for the plunder, well, I do not understand." He fell silent.

Morrolan said, "Well, if truth be known, I do not understand myself. Nor even does Arra, who knows them better than I do."

"Who is Arra," asked another Dragonlord.

"My high priestess, and the head of my Circle of Witches."

"Ah, witches," said the Sorceress in Green contemptuously.

"And there you have your answer," said the Warlock, speaking for the first time.

Suddenly all eyes were upon him.

"Explain yourself, sir," said the Warlord, and if anyone objected to her referring to the Easterner as *sir*, at least no one thought to correct Sethra Lavode.

"Tri'nagore," said Brimford, "is a god of witches. If, indeed, Kâna has a made a pact with him, and if, moreover, he has been manifested by these barbarians of whom the Lord Morrolan has done us the honor to speak, well, then we might guess that my arts will be ineffective."

The Enchantress nodded slowly. "That, then, must be part of the Pretender's plan. Can he also interfere with the Necromancer?"

The Warlock shrugged. "I would think not, but I know little of the gods, and less of necromancy."

"What can be done?" asked Khaavren from the far end of the table.

"Ah, that is easy to answer," said Brimford.

"Well?"

"The god must be banished."

"Very well," said the Sorceress in Green. "I accept that he must be banished."

"And you are right to," said Brimford.

"But, how can this be done?"

"That is not easy to answer," said Brimford.

Morrolan suddenly rose to his feet and, flipping back his

cloak, drew his sword. We need hardly explain the effect on all of those present when this weapon was brought forth—there was a sound as everyone drew in his breath at the same moment, and everyone except Sethra Lavode flinched. And, lest there be any mistake, Morrolan set it upon the table, where it echoed harsh and loud on meeting the stone, so they could all look upon it, and he said, "As to that—I will banish him."

"You?" cried the others.

"I have said so, and I even repeat it. I will banish him."

Sethra Lavode nodded slowly. "What help do you require?"

"None," said Morrolan. "Everything that concerns this god I take upon myself."

"And yet," said the Sorceress in Green, "we expect the dance to begin to-morrow at dawn."

"In that case," said Morrolan, picking up his sword and sheathing it, "I will nominate Fentor to take my place, and, moreover—"

"Well?"

"I should be on my way. Warlord, do I have your leave to attend to this matter?"

Sethra Lavode studied the young Dragonlord, and appeared to be reflecting. Then she said, "Very well. Your lieutenant will command your troops. You have my leave, and my blessing on your mission."

Morrolan bowed, and, without another word, walked out of the room.

Chapter the Eighty-Fifth

How Morrolan Returned to the East In Order to Settle an Old Score

Morrolan made no particular arrangements before setting off on his mission; indeed, he made no arrangements at all. He walked out of Dzur Mountain and took in great lungfuls of the clear mountain air in order to settle his mind—he was just calm enough to know that he ought not to attempt a teleport while so furious that he could not focus his thoughts. Bringing himself to a state where he might safely perform this exacting spell took, in fact, rather a long time: as he stood there, doing nothing, he would remember again the attack on Blackchapel, and again he would work himself into a passion. He paced and kicked at stones, sometimes even bending down to pick one up and throw it, hearing the clatter down the slope. Sometimes he would slap his hand onto the smooth, black pommel of his sword. Sometimes he would stand, his arms folded over his chest, and simply fume, letting his rage carry him as it would.

Eventually, his thoughts drifted to his home—still new enough to give delight—and these thoughts gave him a certain degree of satisfaction. He had not the traditional nobleman's mistrust of anything new, first because he was young, and second because he had been raised far away from the Empire and its traditions, and so had not had the opportunity to learn that older is invariably better. And so he reflected with sincere pleasure on his home, recalling its marble and obsidian, and thinking about improvements he might make.

Next, he mentally went through the convolutions of certain

spells that had been his most recent study, and he thought about the upcoming battle, and the compliment he had been paid by Sethra Lavode—from whom a compliment had meaning if it had meaning from anyone.

After that, he thought about his Circle of Witches, now strong enough so that keeping the castle in the air was routine, automatic, and required only the least supervision from Arra, who instead could devote the energies to her two interests: studying the nature of witchcraft, and continuing prayers to the Demon Goddess. Neither of these, we realize, are of much practical use, but if we indicated that Arra was of a pragmatical character, we have been wrong to do so, and so we therefore tender our apologies.

Presently, he realized that he could safely manage a teleport.

His focus on Blackchapel was remarkably easy—he had only begun, and instantly it brought itself to his mind, so that the accomplishment of the teleport was, in fact, carried off without difficulty. The first thing that he noticed was the abrupt change in temperature: whereas Dzur Mountain had been chilly, even cold, here it was rather warm, although a certain refreshing breeze came off the Thundering Lake, with the freshwater smell that he had been unaware of missing until it reached him once more. In appearance, the inside of the chapel, which was unoccupied when he appeared there, was little changed from when he had last seen it. That it was still in use could be seen by the lack of cobwebs and dust, and there were, perhaps, a few more cracks in some of the benches and other woodwork, but for all of that it looked very much the same.

Morrolan stepped out of the chapel and onto the street that, although it had no official name (that is, there were no signposts, and, indeed, nowhere in the world was there a map of the village), was known as Chapel Road, and he at once had to use his hand to shade his eyes against the terrible luminescence that he had all but forgotten in the few years since he had been in the East. He remained there, blinking in the light, until, in a matter of a few seconds or minutes, his eyes had made an adjustment to the brightness and he felt that he could safely negotiate the street.

Two steps brought him to a place between the dry goods store and the silk merchant's, both of which, he was pleased to see, had been rebuilt since he left. Once there, we should add, he was at once recognized. Indeed, in only a few moments, he was surrounded by townsfolk and facing a barrage of questions: How was Arra? Had the elfs killed everyone but him? Was he under a curse yet? Had he learned to speak foreign? Was he coming home? And countless questions about certain of his Circle, usually from someone who had strong feelings for this or that witch. But above all, he was aware that they were glad to see him, and so glad that, in spite of the cold venom that filled his heart, he found himself touched by their expressions of friendship, not unmixed with a certain reverence. And, in spite of his hurry, he could not but take a moment to speak with some of those he had known. Everyone was well—indeed, flourishing. There had been no curse, and no, he was not coming home. What was he doing in the land of the elfs? As to that, he did not choose to say except that he was learning many things, but—was there a horse he might purchase? A fast horse, as fast as can be.

A horse? But why did he wish a horse?

Because, he explained, there were certain heathen barbarians who required to be taught a lesson, and to-day was the day upon which it would happen.

This announcement, which he made with tolerable coolness, was greeted by stunned silence.

"You cannot mean it," said someone.

"I assure you," he replied. "I have never been more serious in my life. Indeed, leaving without having finished that little affair was more difficult than I can say. You remember that, when I left, they had just razed the entire village."

"And they came back," he was told, "just a few days after you left."

"How, they came back?"

"Nearly," said someone else. "And they burned down everything we had started to rebuild. And a score of us were killed, and I don't know how many injured. I, myself," added the speaker, "received such a cut across my back that I still bear the scar."

"And since then?" said Morrolan.

"Oh, they learned that you had left, and they have not been back since."

"Well," said the Dragonlord, "they will have no need to search for me; on the contrary, I will be easy enough to find."

"But, have you an army?"

"Yes," said Morrolan. "Here, at my side." With this, he touched the hilt of his sword.

The villagers looked at the sword, and even through its sheath seemed to feel it—there was, therefore, no answer to Morrolan's observation.

"Now," he said, "who can tell me how to find them?"

"Oh, that is easy enough. They live in four villages, forty miles away following the shore of the Thundering Lake. The first of these villages can be identified by a double row of sycamore trees lining its main street as you enter. It is, to be sure, something of a ride."

"Something of a ride? Then, as I said, I need a good horse. Forty miles is a tolerably long distance, and I need to be there to-morrow."

He was brought—very nearly forced by the press of the crowd, which now numbered some thirty or thirty-five—to the livery stable, where an argument was promptly begun. Whatever differences there may be between human and Easterner—and the reader knows very well how numerous and profound these differences are—in one way at least we are similar: the Easterner is as little inclined as the human to admit to anyone that his horse is second-best to another.

"Fast? Why, yes, you have a fast horse, but His Lordship wishes to travel more than half a league, by which time your horse will have run himself to death."

"How can you stand there and lie in that fashion? Moreover, what horse would you recommend? That half-mule of yours? Bah, you would give His Lordship a horse with such a mouth, a horse that will twist and throw him on a whim, and will need to be fought every step to merely go in the right direction?"

"Then mine, here! Take mine. Why, he can run all day and night and be ready for a day's work to-morrow."

"That horse? Oh, you cannot insult him by offering His Lordship that nag with his head below his knees and tail ever drooping; why, she will die of old age before leaving the village—it is a wonder that she has not died in her stall."

"Here, then: simply look. Come, have you seen a finer animal in your life?"

"No, no, can't you see that His Lordship is *tall?* Why, on that little pony his feet will drag."

"No no, milord, do not even consider Juno's walking glue-factory; why, she is barely suitable for pulling a trap! Here, look at my good friend Dan. Such shoulders . . ."

"Too young." "Too old." "No speed." "No endurance. "Untrained." And so on, and so on.

The argument became heated and moved to jostling and pushing as well as raised voices. A few blows were exchanged, and some of the participants began looking for sticks to reinforce some subtle aspect of an argument that was insufficiently clear. At this point, one of the more reasonable individuals, in fact an elder of the village, and one who had no horse to offer in any case (knowing full well that his own elderly mare had most of the faults the others were accused of), suggested a race, the winner to have the honor of giving His Lordship the horse. This was greeted with great approbation, and would have been carried by acclaim except that Morrolan was obliged to observe that a horse which had just completed a race would hardly be suitable for bearing him to his destination with the alacrity that, he must insist, he absolutely required.

In the end, four horses were put forward, and lots were drawn, and in this way a horse was selected (a dappled three-year-old Nemeslelklú stallion named Huzay), saddled, and, after considerable argument, its owner, a wealthy freeholder named Peitro, agreed to accept a piece of gold, with which he promised to buy drinks for the entire town and spend the rest on offerings to the Demon Goddess.

Morrolan mounted upon the horse, who was, to be sure, rather jittery, and not used to carrying a rider of Morrolan's size, but Morrolan spoke softly into his ear, patted his neck, and displayed that gentle firmness so salutary in gaining the enthusiastic cooperation of horses and servants, and the animal settled down quickly. With a wave of his hand and a flash of his cloak, he turned the horse's head northeastward and set off at a gallop, which, by the time he was outside of Blackchapel, had become a run.

He had not been misled: where there were roads, they were good, and where there were no roads, it was because none were needed. He stayed within half a mile of the shore of the Thundering Lake, its song constantly in his ears. As night fell, he used the simplest of sorceries to create around himself a moving sphere of luminescence, which upset the horse considerably for some moments until he became used to it, after which he was willing to continue.

Morrolan stopped twice to rest his legs (which had become slightly cramped in the high stirrups) and the horse, but neither stop was long. During one of them, Morrolan stared out into the lake and said, "Goddess? Are you with me? I will say now that all I do is for you, and all of these deaths—for I promise, there will be many—will be dedicated to you." As he stood in the dark and the stillness, he imagined he felt a soothing touch on his brow, and, whether he had been graced by Verra or not, he believed that he had been. He opened his eyes, remounted his horse, cast his light-spell again, and set off.

Morrolan had the rider's instinct—that is, he knew just how much he could push the animal so as to gain every bit of speed without killing it. This, and the fact that the horse really was of the first quality, brought him, by the first light of morning, to the first of the four villages of which he had been told, which he recognized by the row of sycamore trees, leaves hissing in the light breeze.

He drew rein and patted his horse's neck. "Well done," he told it. "I am informed that dawn is a good time to launch an attack. So, then, let us be about it."

BOOK SIX

In Which Our History
Is Brought to a Satisfying
And Elegant Conclusion

Chapter the Eighty-Sixth

How Some Feel Apprehensive Before the Battle While Others Feel Apprehensive After It Has Begun

Some five miles west of the city on Lower Kieron Road, there is a place called Barlen's Pavilion, where the road was widened to permit carriages to turn around and where, moreover, there is a park, with, as the name implies, a pavilion over a portion of it. In this place, under the pavilion, before the first hour of morning had quite run its course, the Duke of Kâna, mounted upon a fine grey gelding and surrounded by some number of his staff officers, as well as, we might add, his entire army, turned to his cousin and said, "Is all in readiness?"

It was as good a day for a battle as anyone could wish: a strong wind blowing in from the sea gave all the banners a snap, and might present some problem for those whose duty included the throwing of javelins, and there was, perhaps, a very slight chill in the air, but it promised to warm up later (and, as one of the waiting infantryman remarked to his friend, it would become tolerably hot before it cooled down). The Enclouding was high up, and of a faint orange tinge with little red; skies of this color being considered a good omen for sailors. The smell of the sea was strong and invigorating, and even the horses of Kâna's staff officers and errand riders seemed fully alive and anxious for the day's festivities to begin.

Habil, who was mounted upon a horse very similar to her cousin's, said, "Your Majesty, it is now six times that you have asked me this question."

"Well, and then?"

"It is only that I might nearly begin to believe that you are unnerved."

"I, unnerved?"

"I could almost believe it."

"Not in the least."

"If you insist that you are not."

"My dear cousin, you know very well that, when the time comes for action, I shall be cool enough. It is these moments of waiting. I mislike waiting."

"You always have."

"That is true."

"Well, I comprehend."

"Moreover, since we have learned that there are unexpected defenses upon both of the roads we mean to use for the attack, so that we have had to change the timing of our attack, well, I think I have some reason for concern."

"Ah, we had not anticipated that we would be able to keep our army concealed for the entire distance and into the city itself."

"No, that is true. But our scouts have spoken of fortifications, which causes me to wonder how much warning the enemy have had."

"Well, and if they had considerable warning? If they have had days to prepare? What then?"

"Then they may have found ways to counter our advantages. We both know that, with their sorcery, their necromancy, and their use of the heathen arts, we cannot defeat them with pure military force—even though we outnumber them."

"Believe me, cousin; you tell me nothing of which I am unaware. But—"

"Well?"

"What ways could they have found?"

"I can think of nothing."

"Nor can I."

"Nevertheless, you may understand why I may appear, as you put it, unnerved at this moment."

"The time for action is near at hand, my good cousin, and, as you say, when it arrives at last you will be perfectly sound. We but await the final report of the scouts, and there will be no reason why you should give the command to advance."

"What of our Athyra?"

"He is ready."

"And Tsanaali's band, within the city?"

"We have exchanged signals, and they are anxious for the right moment to arrive."

"I hope so. You perceive, everything else is merely a feint for that attack."

"I am aware of this, my cousin."

"If it should fail—"

"There is no reason for it to fail. Tsanaali is ideally suited for such ventures, and has time to train his forces. And, you observe, they have been safely within the city for weeks now, and no one the wiser."

"But consider the complexities of the timing. The ground attack, the sea attack, our necromancy, the response to our necromancy—now there is an area of some concern."

"How so? Have we not the assurance of the god?"

"Well, but may we rely upon a god?"

"I believe so."

"And, not only that, but consider that we are opening the door to dangerous forces."

"And we can close the door."

"Well, that is true."

"So, then."

"What of the Islanders?"

"They are just over the horizon. We have received word from them by means of signal-boats that indicate that they shall not have to row; the wind is serving most admirably for them—do you not perceive that there is a strong wind even now blowing from the southeast, or even a trifle south? It could not have fallen out better. Perhaps the Tri'nagore has had a hand in setting the wind for us; you know that this is within his powers."

"It is good if they do not have to row; they will be here sooner, and in better condition to fight."

"Exactly."

"Then all is in readiness?"

"That is now seven times."

"Well, but you perceive, you did not answer the last time."

"That is true."

"So, then?"

"Yes, all is in readiness. For my part—"

"Well?"

"I should long to see the faces of our enemies when they learn that all of their sorcery, and necromancy, and their strange magics, are of no effect."

"Indeed."

"Then you are satisfied?"

"Nearly. I must admit that up until now, we have had matters our own way. If it continues thus for only a few more hours, why, we shall have won."

"Indeed, everything has gone perfectly. And, moreover, you have made a name for yourself in military history."

"You think so?"

"I am convinced of it. Consider what you have done, cousin: An army of more than twenty thousands of troops, assembled by tens and twenties to a spot within four days' march of its target, supplied, equipped, and fed, and all without detection by the enemy. Such a thing has never been done."

"There was some divine help in that."

"And if there was? Does that make it any less remarkable?"

"I admit, Habil, that this part of the plan did proceed without a flaw."

"It is a triumph."

"I beg to disagree."

"How, you think it was not?"

"Certainly it was not, because we have not yet won. If we win, then, perhaps, you may use such words as 'triumph.'"

"I take your point. But will you accept that it was a magnificent feat?"

"Do you positively insist upon it?"

"I do."

"Then I will accept it."

At this moment, Izak rode up next to them and said, "Your Majesty, I beg leave to report."

"Well, General?"

"The last two scouts have returned, and nothing is changed. There are fortifications, and, indeed, troops drawn up, but they are not advancing."

"Numbers?"

"On this road, perhaps five thousands. No cavalry. A like number on the Hartre Pike. We have not been able to make a determination about their reserves."

"As to that," said Kâna, "I know from my spies in the city. There is park near the canal where there are some ten thousands of the enemy waiting."

"As many in reserve as they have on the roads?"

"So it seems."

Izak shrugged. "Very well. What of the harbor?"

"Only a few scattered soldiers, less than a hundred. It is possible they are not even stationed there, but merely walking along the pier looking for the sorts of entertainments a soldier can often find in such districts."

"Good. What are we facing first along this road?"

"Three spear phalanxes."

"And along the Pike?"

"The same."

"Well, the enemy is consistent, at least. Do we know who is in charge of the enemy defenses?"

"We do not, Majesty. We can be certain it is not Khaavren, however."

"Why is that?"

"Why, you know very well that he has resigned the Imperial service."

Kâna and Habil exchanged a glance and a smile. "Ah yes, that is true," said Kâna.

"So, then, orders?"

"On both roads, begin the attack with a unit of light cavalry, and two of lancers. Once they are well engaged, bring up two more units of cavalry to flank them, on both sides. Once the cavalry is engaged, you may order the javelin throwers to attack, after which the infantry may charge. Is all of this clear?"

"You will judge, Majesty: light cavalry, two lancers. Then two more cavalry, javelins, then infantry."

"That is it."

"I understand, Your Majesty, but—"

"Yes?"

"Suppose that, when we reach them, they have changed dispositions?"

"In that case, General, you are to alter your own dispositions as you think best."

"Very good."

"Have a messenger sent to Brawre with these same orders."

"Yes, Majesty."

"And, of course, do not advance until you receive orders from me."

"I will await your word."

Kâna nodded, took a deep breath, and said, "Signal the Islanders to launch their attack."

"Yes, Your Majesty. And, if I may make an observation?"

"Yes, what is it, Izak?"

"For my part, I want nothing more than to atone for my failure in the last battle."

"Well, General, you will have your chance, and I trust you will make the most of it."

"Yes Your Majesty. I will now order the the signal given."

"Good. And I am to be informed the instant the ships are over the horizon."

"Yes, Majesty."

Izak rode off, Kâna anxiously following him with his eyes.

He then began pacing, his hands behind his back, and twice more asked his cousin if all was in readiness. He seemed about to ask a third time, when Habil remarked, "I have been thinking about something, cousin."

"What is that, Habil?"

"You should consider marriage."

"How, marriage?"

"Certainly. It is always a good thing for the Emperor to have an heir."

"Well, but, whom shall I marry?"

"I would recommend a Dragonlord, Sire."

"Well, yes, but you perceive, there are many Dragonlords."

"Then I should recommend one who is presently unmarried. That way, you perceive, she will not have to become a widow before becoming Consort."

"You must understand that this still leaves a good number to choose from."

"Well, is it not good to have a large number out of which to make a choice? It increases the likelihood of finding one who is suitable."

"On the contrary, cousin. It makes it more difficult."

"How, you think so?"

"Certainly. If there were only one, why, the decision would be the easiest thing in the world. But with so many I hardly know where to begin looking."

"If you like, I will attempt to select one for you."

"If I must marry—"

"I believe it would be a good idea, Your Majesty."

"Then you select someone."

"Very well, if you are certain you have no one in mind."

"I have no one in mind. In fact—"

"Well?"

"In fact, if truth be told, I have no interest in marriage at this time."

"Nevertheless, it would be a good idea."

"Oh, I do not doubt that, only—"

"Yes?"

"Why are you bringing it up now?"

"Why am I bringing it up now? Why, in order to distract you, of course."

"You believe I require distraction?"

"It is possible. And even if you don't—"

"Well?"

"I require you to be distracted, otherwise, I fear I may commit regicide."

"My dear cousin—"

At this moment, a messenger rode up to them, and said, "Your Majesty, I beg to report that the boats are on the horizon."

"In that case," observed Kâna, "if I am correct about this wind, they should reach the harbor in a little less than an hour."

"Well?" said Habil.

Kâna dismissed the errand runner and summoned a young subaltern who served on his staff. This subaltern, a Dragonlord of good standing, brought her horse up to His Majesty by careful movements of her knees and gestures with her reins until she was quite close, at which time she made a graceful bow from the back of her horse.

"Yes, Majesty?" she said.

"My compliments to General Brawre, and he may advance and engage. After delivering this message—*after* delivering this message, you will find Izak and give him the same orders. And then, after this message is delivered, you will present my compliments to the Baron of Loraan, and tell him he may begin. Then the signal sorcerer is to communicate with Lieutenant Tsanaali, telling him that he may commence his operation. Do you understand?"

"I believe so."

"Let us see, then."

"Brawre first: compliments, attack and engage, and then the same to Izak after Brawre has received his orders, then Loraan is to begin. Then message to Tsanaali, he may commence."

"That is it."

The subaltern saluted and rode off.

"Cousin—?"

"Yes, Habil?"

"You are right."

"Well?"

"You are noticeably cooler now."

"After all of these years and all of these campaigns, did you doubt me?"

"Not in the least."

"This one is, perhaps, larger than any of the others, and for grander stakes—that is, we are now staking everything on a single throw. Nevertheless, it is another campaign, another battle, that is all."

"That is well, and I agree with everything you have done me the honor to tell me."

After a moment, Habil sighed. Kâna said, "Well? Why do you sigh?"

"I have been thinking."

"Well, share these thoughts then."

"We ought to have told the Islanders to attack at first light, so the enemy could not see the boats until they were in the very act of landing, and then we could have timed our own attack for the same moment."

"That was, indeed, the plan, Habil, and it was a good one until we observed the fortifications, which let us know that we should not, in fact, surprise them. At that moment, I decided it would be best to wait until we had a chance to make a close observation, and so I had the Islanders wait."

"Yes, I know that."

"Moreover, thirty hours ago you agreed with this plan."

"Yes, yes. That is true."

"Do you have a reason now for regretting this decision?"

"Well, that is to say, no."

"Then you still think it a good one?"

"I think so. That is to say, I hope so."

"We are well matched, my dear cousin. While I become unnerved before the battle has begun, that is when you do your best planning and have the coolest head. Whereas, once the action starts, why, nothing disturbs my coolness. I am an animal."

"I do not deny what you say."

"Ah, it is a shame, is it not, that—"

"There, the vanguard is in motion."

"So it is. I will ride forward, in a position just to the rear of the vanguard, while you remain here. We have no shortage of errand runners, so be certain I am kept well informed."

"I will not fail to do so."

"Once the battle is fully engaged, if there is no disaster, I will return here, so that messages may reach me more efficiently."

"Yes, that is a good plan."

"But, before that, well, I wish to see the opening of the ball."

"I understand."

"Until later, then, my dear cousin."

"I will see you in the city, with the Orb revolving around your head."

"Let us hope so," said Kâna, and put the spurs to his horse.

Much can be said (and, to be sure, *has* been said) about the Pretender, the Duke of Kâna, as a military commander, and much of it, we regret to say, has been sheer nonsense; but no one has ever questioned his ability to create a trained and disciplined army, and this skill was nowhere displayed better than in the opening moments of the assault on Adrilankha.

Consider that at that moment there were two armies, eight brigades, fifty-seven regiments, two hundred and thirty-four battalions, four hundred and seventy-one companies, more than twenty-one thousand troops, all of them marching steadily, guided by capable officers, ready for action.

The spirit of the army, considering how soundly it had been defeated at Dzur Mountain, was astonishingly good. It may be that, although the troops had been told nothing officially, they had come to understand, in the mysterious way soldiers have of gathering up and interpreting subtle clues, that a means had been found to overcome the artifices that had caused their defeat in the previous battle.

But for whatever reason, there is no question that their spirits were high, and they were eager for the battle—many of them were only Teckla, it is true, but they were guided by young Dragonlords and in some cases young Dzurlords, and even a few of other Houses, unfamiliar with the Orb, mistrusting the House of the Phoenix, and eager for glory.

It was fifteen minutes after the second hour after noon when Brawre's leading units—two platoons of lancers and a company of light cavalry—came around the corner of Lower Kieron Road where lies the abandoned building that was once the posting house of the Running Chicken. Once around this corner, they were, quite suddenly, five hundred meters in a straight line from where three spear phalanxes, part of the division commanded by the Warlord, waited, blocking the road.

Brawre's units continued forward as if the road were empty. Two minutes later, there was the clash of arms.

The Battle of Adrilankha had begun.

Chapter the Eighty-Seventh

How Morrolan, Attempting to Find a God, Found Instead What His Sword Could Do

The village at which Morrolan arrived that morning was, to be sure, a very small village: only half a dozen diminutive houses and something in the nature of an inn, as well as a sort of general store. Morrolan pulled up and looked around. At first, he thought the place entirely deserted, but on a second look, he saw that in front of this store was an old man (or, rather, Easterner) with a magnificent belly, a scrawny beard, and very little hair. This unknown frowned as Morrolan dismounted and said, "Is there something that you desire?"

"Certainly," said Morrolan, and, drawing his sword, he said, "My goddess has as much a taste for blood as your own, therefore you may go to her and give her my warmest regards." Before the old man had time to consider what these words might mean, or even to understand the sensations that must have flooded through him as the Dragonlord drew his weapon, Morrolan had cut him from right shoulder to left hip and left him in his own blood.

The old Easterner had no time even to cry out—Morrolan's sword had taken both his life and his soul even before his body struck the ground. For anyone in the least familiar with the effect of sword-cuts, such a result is, to say the least, unnatural.

But then, there is nothing *natural* about Morrolan's weapon.

What became of this soul—this insubstantial part of humanity, that provides the life-spark of any being and contains the essence of personality? We cannot answer this question—whether the sword utterly destroyed it, as is the case with those foul weapons called *morganti,* or whether, as Morrolan had said, this soul, in some way, was taken to be consumed, destroyed, or preserved by Verra, or whether something else entirely became of it, we cannot know. But, whatever our own opinion of the Lord Morrolan, we must face the truth: This crime, the crime of taking the essence of a living being and ripping it from his body, denying it the right of rebirth, is on Morrolan's head.

For his part, he gave not a moment's thought to this circumstance. His heart was filled with what had been done to his own people, and if there was any room left in this organ, it was taken by his mission. Once this old Easterner's body was stretched out upon the ground, Morrolan gave him no more thought than he'd have given an insect upon whom he happened to tread as we walked. He stood there, his sword dripping blood, and looked around, waiting to see if he would be challenged.

The only response was a scream, coming from within one of the buildings. Without being exactly certain of what he was doing, or why, Morrolan raised his sword, pointing it at the small wood-frame house. The house did not so much explode as dissolve and collapse into flame.

"And that," said Morrolan in a voice of a clarity and power that could be heard over the cracking of timbers, "is for my goddess as well."

When his words elicited no response, he methodically repeated this performance with each structure in the small village, mounted his horse, and left the nameless hamlet ruined and burning behind him.

Now he brought his horse over the pathway to the next village, which was sufficiently close that the smoke from the villiage he had just left in ruins scould clearly be seen. When he came there, which took only a few minutes, he found that it was in appearance very much like the first, the biggest differences being the lack of sycamores, and that here there was something of a crowd gathered, staring up at the smoke, pointing to it, and speaking in low tones. They all looked at Morrolan: men, women, and, it must be confessed, however much we may deplore it, even children.

Morrolan, for his part, was in no mood for conversation. He dismounted from his horse, drew his sword, took two steps forward, and began to cut, his face drawn into a furious grimace. How many of them he killed, we do not know. He was not resisted—on the contrary, the gathered crowd instantly scattered. Morrolan did not pursue them, but instead, as he had before, made certain that every structure in the village was in flames and burning.

In ten minutes, he was mounted once more and following the only road worthy of the name; a road that continued through the village, and which he correctly deduced must lead to the next one.

This third village, at which he arrived in good time, was the one that, in fact, he had been looking for. In size and appearance it was very like the others, but, to Morrolan's delight—insofar, that is, as he was, at this moment, capable of experiencing such an emotion—the streets were full of armed men, perhaps fifty in all. And, moreover, all of them appeared to be gathered around an icon in the form of a four-foot-tall piece of basalt, carved into a sort of horned head, intended to represent in some symbolic way the god Tri'nagore.

Exactly why they had gathered—whether they were about to make a raid, or had just returned from one, or were engaged in one of their heathen rituals—we cannot say; but gathered there they were, staring first at the smoke, then, afterwards, at the tall stranger who rode coolly into their midst and said, "I am Morrolan. Some years ago you came to Blackchapel looking for me."

He jumped from his horse, smacked its rump to encourage it to get out of the way, drew his sword, and calmly announced, "Well, I am here."

As for what happened next, we can only say that any Dzurlord who had been able to witness the events would have been filled with envy not unmixed, we should imagine, with a certain grudging respect. How much of what followed was Morrolan, and how much was his weapon? This is a question that, we must say, Morrolan asked himself afterwards on more than one occasion.

At the very least, a good measure of it was the sword, and it was doing far, far more than Morrolan had ever suspected it could. It seemed to leap in his hand, and, moreover, each time it struck, it seemed to Morrolan that its next blow came faster. From this, it may sound as if the sword was making its own decisions; yet it was not, from Morrolan's perspective, so clear and straightforward. While many swordsmen have spoken of the feeling that the sword was merely an extension of the arm, to Morrolan, it seemed as if the weapon was an extension of his *mind*. That is to say, he might observe someone making a head-cut at him, think that it would be best to remove this individual's head from his shoulders before the blow could land—and this was done. Then he might observe that, from the position and angle of the sword, a sorcerous blast from it might strike another in the chest, and thought was no sooner formed than acted upon. How much was Morrolan and how much the weapon? He did not, then or ever, truly answer this question.

For our purpose, however, it does not signify. Morrolan felt not even the beginings of exhaustion; it felt as if he could continue forever—again, whether by some property of his "black wand" or because of help of the goddess to whom he was dedicating each kill, or because of some aspect of himself, cannot be known.

In some ways, it was like his first taste of battle, but this time, instead of the fierce heat of joy, his heart was filled with a cold rage. In the first few seconds he made his way through the enemy as one might walk through a crowd on a narrow street during a parade, never touched himself, but leaving seven or eight of the enemy stretched out upon the ground.

"Your god likes blood, does he?" said Morrolan, speaking in a low, controlled voice which, nevertheless, could be clearly heard in the stillness of the moment. "Let him have his fill, then."

When they made a move as if to attack him in a mass, he held out his left hand, all of his fingers stretched out, and, just barely aware of what he was doing, cast a spell which sent from each finger a furious red light, faster than a yendi's strike, and far more deadly; there was a loud cry, and six or seven more of the enemy dropped, each straight down where he stood, not falling backward or to the side, to lie utterly still, with not so much as a quiver coming from them, as if they had already been dead for some minutes when they fell.

Whether this would have been sufficient to cause these barbarians (for we must, in our admitted ignorance of this people, use Morrolan's description) to have run we do not know, but they did not have the chance: Morrolan took his sword in both hands and swept into the largest group, spinning as he did so, his weapon striking high, striking low, thrusting, cutting; stopping only when he had run out of enemies—for the survivors, indeed, were now running in all directions as quickly as they could.

Instead of chasing them, Morrolan cried, "For my Demon Goddess!," and, as he had done earlier, with no apparent effort caused every building in this hamlet to collapse in on itself, burning—screams coming from within them to prove that at least some of them had been inhabited.

All of which left Morrolan apparently alone in the middle of the village—alone, that is, except for the icon of Tri'nagore. He turned his attention to it and advanced slowly and deliberately, his sword held comfortably in his hand, still dripping blood upon the dirt street.

Chapter the Eighty-Eighth

How Lord Brimford Attempted To Enter the Battle While the Warlord Received Disturbing Intelligence

The opening of the Battle of Adrilankha went very much according to plan—that is to say, Kâna's plan. The Warlord was very accommodating: she permitted her spear phalanxes to be driven back, and very nearly permitted her forward units to be outflanked before ordering a fighting retreat toward the fortifications—this same thing occurring, be it understood, on both the Hartre Pike and on Lower Kieron Road. She instructed her sorcerers to hold back—performing a minor spell now and then, but nothing devastating. Her reason for this strange order was twofold: For one, she hoped to achieve a sufficient concentration of enemy forces so that, with luck, an entire regiment, or more, could be devastated by sorcerous attacks. For another, she was convinced (and, as it turned out, she was right) that Kâna had something "under his cloak," and she did not wish to have her sorcerers mentally exhausted before learning what this was, in the event that it could be countered with sorcery (although, as it turned out, it could not).

The joining of the battle on Lower Kieron Road occurred perhaps a quarter of a mile west of the newly constructed fortresses; on the Old West Road it was closer to half a mile. In both cases, the Imperial forces were forced into a slow, grudging retreat by the ferocity of Kâna's onslaught, as well as the skillful deployment which it cannot be argued his generals, Izak and Brawre, made of their forces.

Sethra Lavode did not herself view either of the battles, rather staying in touch with all of her forces by using her corps of adepts, from whom came a constant stream of information. In this way, she monitored the unfolding of the battle, considered, reflected, and waited.

This continued for some twenty or twenty-five minutes, which, while it may sound like a short space of time, is, in fact, a very, *very* long time to be engaged in a pitched battle, with its furious activity, its strange sights sometimes so clear as to be more than real, other times so confusing as to be merely blurs. And, above all, with its sounds. A reader who has never been in the vicinity of a battle (and, in the opinion of this author, there is a great deal to be said for avoiding the vicinity of a battle!) cannot imagine the volume produced. Between the clash of steel on steel, and the cries from mouths of those either inspiriting themselves with war-fury or screaming in agony from wounds, the din can be heard from a far, far greater distance than one might imagine.

The peculiar and interesting Easterner whom we have come to know as Lord Brimford was alerted to the commencement of the battle first by these sounds—clearly discernible more than a mile behind the front lines and then almost at once by his dog, Awtlá, who, from lying down, rose to an alert sitting position, perked up his droopy ears as much as he could, and gave the Warlock a look of inquiry, as if to say, "Master, is this something that concerns you?"

Brimford rose to his feet and stepped out of the pavilion tent where he had been taking his ease.

"My dear Awtlá," he said, "I think it nearly does. I should imagine we shall be officially informed in an instant, and then we shall be asked to do our part, and then we shall have the honor of informing the Enchantress of Dzur Mountain that her request is impossible, and then, why, we shall return here to sit uselessly and await the outcome of a battle upon which rests the future of my belovèd, my own happiness, and certain less important matters, such as the existence of this Empire on which the elfs place so much value."

The dog twitched his ears in a manner quite nearly intelligent; the cat, Sireng, merely yawned.

As the Warlock stepped out of his pavilion, a messenger wearing a badge which claimed him as belonging to the Warlord's suite approached, bowed, and said, "My lord—" these words appeared to come from the messenger only with a certain amount of effort, "the battle has begun, and you may initiate your enchantment at any time."

"Very well. Where is Sethra Lavode?"

The messenger hesitated. He was, we should say, uncertain as to whether it was proper for him to answer this question. After all, he had been told only to run errands, not provide intelligence. For another thing, this was an Easterner. For yet another, the Easterner was not even in uniform (the uniform of the Imperial forces involved a badge with the Phoenix emblem worn over the left breast, and a gold beret worn on the head—even Sethra Lavode herself affected this costume for the engagement).

Brimford waited patiently, and at length the messenger decided that, as her headquarters was clearly marked with a flag that could be seen for half a league in any direction, it would not be a terrible breach of security if he were to part with this information, he therefore pointed out this flag and explained that the general was to be found near it, surrounded by messengers and adepts, and could be identified, first, by her pale skin, and, second, by the three swords, indicating her rank, that were embroidered on her beret.

Brimford saluted the errand runner and followed these unnecessary directions (that is, had the messenger simply replied, "she is at her headquarters pavilion," it would have served admirably) and so quickly found the Enchantress, who was sitting calmly and, evidently, quite at her ease on a low, light chair, her legs stretched out in front of her. Awtlá at once put his nose into her hand; Sireng, for her part, jumped onto Sethra's lap.

The Warlock bowed and said, "General, for so I believe I ought to address you—"

The Enchantress shrugged, as if to say that any of a number of ways of addressing her were equally satisfactory.

"—I hope the battle goes well."

"Greetings, sir. It is, of course, too soon to say. The battle is fully joined on the Old West Road, and equally so on Lower Kieron. If there is to be an attack on Northgate Road, well, at least it has not yet been launched. I believe you were told that you may now begin—that is to say, you may now bring us what aid you can, in the way that you have so admirable done before."

"And yet, as I had the honor to tell you yester-day, something is preventing any of my efforts from yielding results."

"That was yester-day, my dear sir. Have you made the attempt
to-day?"

"I have, in fact."

"Well then, keep trying. I have reason to hope that, sooner or later—and I hope sooner—you will be able to perform your function."

"Very good, General."

"So you will continue to make tests?"

"I will make one this very instant. You perceive, General, that I should like nothing better than to be of service. And I will not delay in letting you know if I fail."

"Well, that is good, if you fail. But, you perceive, I should also wish to know if you succeed, because I may then adjust my tactics accordingly."

"Oh, if I succeed, I do myself the honor to believe you will be aware of it very soon. Indeed, I beg leave to insist that, in that case, there will be no possible room for doubt."

"Then the results will be sufficiently dramatic?"

"I give you my word upon it."

"Very well. I depend upon you, sir."

"You may, General."

Brimford then gave a silent command to Awtlá and Sireng, letting them know what he wished of them, at which time these strange, enigmatic animals ran through the camp, onto the road, and so into the forests to the northwest of Adrilankha. The warlock, for his part, was preparing to test once more his particular species of enchantment when a messenger appeared out of the pavilion tent behind the Enchantress.

As we have said before, this was the battle where the powers of *telepathy,* as it is called, that is, the ability for an individual to converse with another without physical proximity, was first used. Having said so, we will say two words about how this was done.

Sethra Lavode had recognized at once the degree to which such communication might help to contrive a favorable outcome to a battle—indeed, it is reported that she observed to Her Majesty that the ability to instantly send and receive messages could be of more importance in a battle than the destructive powers of sorcery in all of their fury. She had, therefore, well before she knew that Kâna would be making an assault against which she would be forced to arrange a defense, begun the work to provide such communication. For this reason, the Enchantress had, beginning months before, instituted the training of what she called a "communication corps" numbering some fifty or fifty-five sorcerers under the tutelage of a certain Hawklord called Paarfi of Hovaal (no relation, we should add, to the author of these words). By time of the battle, then, there were several pairs of "mutual adepts" as the Enchantress called them, or "adepts" as they were informally called—sorcerers who could bespeak each other as easily as you are I might hold a conversation face-to-face (indeed, easier, if this conversation were to be attempted in a crowded jug-room).

With the battle at hand she made arrangements for a special sort of messenger to be posted near her. Each of these messengers had at least a certain skill in sorcery—which, while not strictly necessary for psychic communication, does significantly aid it, as was proven as far back as the Ninth Cycle by the Athyra Marquis of Trigaar. Some twenty of these sorcerers remained at all times with the Enchantress, sitting in the pavilion tent playing quoins-of-four while the battle raged on the road not a mile away. From time to time, one would receive a communication from a fellow adept, and would at once leave the game to speak with the Enchantress. It was just such a sorcerer, or "adept" as we have called him, who appeared at that moment, approached the commanding general, and waited to be recognized.

"Speak," she said.

"I have a report from the harbor."

"Very well."

"Enemy boats have been sighted, apparently to attempt a landing, numbering some six hundred and fifty or seven hundred. They are expected to land in ten minutes. The reserves have been called up and are marching toward the harbor."

Sethra stared at the messenger for a moment, then said, "May I beg you to repeat the number."

"Six hundred and fifty or seven hundred, General."

"Is that seven hundred troops, or seven hundred boats?"

"Why, that is to say, boats, General. Or so I understood the message."

"Be so kind as to confirm that."

"At once, General."

Lord Brimford, who had not yet left to begin his work, turned to Sethra and said, "Is it possible?"

"In all honesty, I do not see how. Unless—"

"Yes? Unless?"

"Unless the Pretender has formed an alliance with Elde."

"Could he have made such an alliance?"

"If he has, well, he must have made more than a few concessions. I shudder to think of what he must have promised, and I shudder again to think of what will happen to the Empire if these promises are fulfilled."

The messenger said, "It is confirmed, General. The observers do not yet know how many warriors are in each boat, though they say it seems to be more than twenty."

"The Gods!" cried the Warlock. "What shall we do?"

"We shall depend upon Lord Khaavren's advice," said Sethra coolly. "And you shall begin your enchantment." To the adept, she said, "They are making for the East Harbor, I presume?"

After the instant it took to relay messages, the adept said, "Yes, General."

"Very well," said Sethra.

Brimford recovered from his momentary astonishment, bowed, and took two steps away, going behind the pavilion in which the sorcerers continued their game. Here he simply sat upon the ground, closed his eyes, and bowed his head. The dog and the cat had already run off, in different directions, in order to infiltrate the jungles and wooded areas, and to be his eyes and ears. He began to attempt his spell once more, and, though his contact with his familiars was unbroken, he had no better results than he had achieved previously.

The Enchantress, however, had told him that he ought to keep trying, and so that is what he did. As Kâna caused his signal to be given to set in motion a certain prepared plan from which he hoped to achieve great results, and as the Imperial forces were gradually driven backward toward the fortifications, Brimford patiently attempted to exert his influence upon the tiassa, dzur, bear, wolverines, darr, greensnakes, and other animals who would be able to fall upon the enemy with such effect.

And still he could do nothing.

It lacked an hour of noon, and the assault from Elde Island would land at any instant, and the full degree of Kâna's treachery had yet to be revealed. And, perhaps more significant, the raid by which Kâna hoped to achieve his ultimate result was only now about to begin.

Sethra Lavode, and Her Majesty, and the Imperial forces in general, were not in the least aware of what was about to be unleashed against them.

Chapter the Eighty-Ninth

How the Direct Attack On the Orb Was Organized

We hope the reader has not forgotten Lieutenant Tsanaali, with whom Pel had exchanged such words that neither of them could doubt the other's opinion of him, and, moreover, the individual in whose mission Kâna and Habil had expressed such hope.

At this instant, as battle raged around Adrilankha and slaughter raged in the East, Tsanaali's thoughts were on neither Pel nor Kâna, but, purely and simply, on his mission.

We have shamefully misled the reader if we have failed to establish that this Dragonlord was not only as courageous as that species invariably is, but also thorough and methodical in his planning. He had taken his time in learning the city, so that not only could his small troop remain hidden until the chosen moment, but also so that they would be able, at the proper time, to make their way to the Manor without running into the street patrols that Tsanaali had anticipated, or without the need to cross any of the bridges, where he knew there could be certain difficulties.

As we look upon him now, he is sitting in an attitude of complete relaxation—indeed, his eyes are nearly closed, as if he is so unconcerned by the mission upon which is about to embark as to have difficulty remaining awake. To a degree, this was because he had the sort of cool disposition that did not, in fact, become overly concerned or agitated in such circumstances (as opposed, for example, to either Kâna or his cousin); but another reason was, undoubtedly, his understanding that the display of such an attitude could not fail to have a beneficial effect on his subordinates.

These subordinates had already begun to arrive at the small house which opened onto an alley behind Tenfingers Road in the southwestern part of the city. Each time another arrived, Tsanaali would open an eye, grunt a greeting, and then return to his apparent nap, sitting on a rickety-looking wooden chair with his feet, crossed at the ankles, up on a table.

At length, with something like the sigh or soft groan one might make upon coming from a light nap to wakefulness, he put his feet down, stood, clasped his hands together behind his back, and said, "Gentlemen, it is very nearly time, and, moreover, it seems we are all gathered here—that is, there are twenty-one of us, including myself and the signal officer who is on the roof watching for the signal, which, being four squads of four, is exactly the number we ought to have. Indeed, everything is in place, and we only await the word to go—which word we will receive from our signal officer."

"That is all very well, Lieutenant," said one of the soldiers (for they were all soldiers, although, to be sure, they were dressed, as were the others, as simple noblemen, in doublet, breeches, and tall black boots), "but, well, what is the mission?"

"Oh," said Tsanaali, "you wish to know that?"

"Well," said the other, "you perceive we have been in this city, hiding and staying out of trouble—"

"For the most part," said another.

"—for weeks now, and we have avoided all meeting at once, and have merely been waiting. But now that it is nearly time to carry out the mission for which we have been brought here, well, we will be better able to carry it out if we know what we are doing."

"That is very true," said the officer, struck by the extreme justice of the remark.

"So then?"

"Why, I will discover it to you this very instant."

"In that case," said the soldier, "you will have, I promise you, our entire attention."

"Then, gentlemen, this is it: You know that His Majesty, Kâna the First, who has won the right to the throne through conquest, is being deprived of the Orb because of a successful adventure on the part of an ambitious Phoenix."

"We know this very well," said the soldiers.

"So then, it remains for His Majesty to fight one final battle to put away all doubts in the hearts of those who believe the Orb, a powerful sorcerous artifact and symbol of the Empire, confers a sort of divinity upon its wielder—in other words, that whoever happens to have the Orb deserves the throne in spite of law and blood, merely by that fact alone."

"It is true," said one of the soldiers, "that many people believe that; I have heard such talk frequently."

"And you did not dispute it, did you?"

"No, Lieutenant. Your orders were to engage in no such disputes by word or action, in order to avoid drawing attention to ourselves. And we have obeyed your orders to the letter even when this obedience required us to listen to the most insulting conversation concerning His Majesty. The proof of can be found in my mouth."

"Your mouth?"

"Exactly. I have ground my teeth and bitten my lips sufficiently to provide irrefutable evidence that I have obeyed your orders, and I believe my comrades are in the same condition."

"And you have done right, however much your mouth may regret it. But that time is over, my friends. The battle has, even now, begun."

"This does not startle us. Have we not, on the way here, seen patrols of exactly the sort a commander would order to keep the streets free for troop movements?"

"You are good observers."

"We are soldiers."

"Well, that is true."

"So then, His Majesty is attacking?"

"Precisely. Even as we speak."

"Are we, then, to attack the enemy in the rear? If so, well, I hope there are more than twenty-one of us!"

"Not in the least. Our orders are for something entirely different."

"Well, and that is good."

"In fact, my friends, I will go further. I will say that the entire attack currently raging west of the city, is nothing more than diversion."

"A diversion? Well, a diversion for what?"

"For our mission."

The soldiers stared at each other, heads turning back and forth. At length, one of them said, "Lieutenant, do you truly say that the present battle is nothing more than a diversion for our mission?"

"I say it, and I even repeat it. So, you perceive, when we consider our mission, well, you must understand that there is no question of joking."

"But then, what is this mission?"

"I am about to answer that very question. So much so, in fact, that I would already have answered it if you gentlemen had not been positively peppering me with questions and interjections."

"Then we shall be mute as Athyra monks, General."

"And you will do right. To explain, then: Gentlemen, we are to make our way, by different paths, to Whitecrest Manor. If you look at this map, you will see your routes. The first squad follows the red line, the second squad follows the green line, the fourth squad follows the blue line, and my own squad will follow the black line."

"Very well," they said, studying the map.

"There is no surprise there," observed one of the squad leaders, "as, you perceive, you have been causing us to learn these routes for the last two weeks."

"But then," said another, "what are we to do when we get there?"

"Once there," said Tsanaali, "we are to do nothing less than take the Orb itself."

"How, the Orb?" they cried.

"Exactly. We are to take the Orb."

"But, isn't that impossible?"

"Not in the least," said Tsanaali.

"But, it has never been done."

"Well, and before Lord Tigarrae, no one had ever teleported himself, either."

"That is true, Lieutenant, and yet—"

"Moreover, we are assured that arrangements have been made that will keep the Orb sufficiently busy that, during our attack, it will have entirely lost its ability to defend either itself, or she who currently has possession of it."

"Oh, apropos—you mention this Phoenix."

"Yes?"

"What of her?"

"Well, what *of* her?"

"Do we kill her?"

The lieutenant shrugged. "As to that, it doesn't matter. If she is killed in the scuffle, there is no harm in it. If she survives without the Orb, well, that is satisfactory as well. We are not assassins, gentlemen, we are soldiers. Let us keep this in mind."

"We will not forget," they said.

At this moment, the door opened and a gentleman entered, saying, "Lieutenant—"

"Well?"

"A plume of smoke to the west."

"And then?"

"Broken off three times, so that it became three plumes."

"That is the signal, gentlemen. Let us be about it. You are all aware of your routes. My squad will see to the guards outside of the Manor, and those directly inside, which is where we will rendezvous, and all move into the chamber being used as a throne room. Now, let us go."

Taking their cue from their commander, none of the soldiers displayed the least emotion as they rose, made certain of their arms, and filed out of the house. This put them in the narrow alley behind the house, from which place they all went in their appointed directions.

Tsanaali's path, like the others, involved back streets and alleys, which avoided the patrols which were making certain the main arteries of the city remained clear. Moreover, there was nothing about these five individuals to attract attention. After some fifteen minutes of walking, Tsanaali approached the doors of Whitecrest Manor and addressed the guardsmen, saying, "I give you a good day, my friend, and I wonder why there are patrols out upon the street."

"As to that," said the guardsman, "I cannot say."

"How, you don't know?"

The guardsmen shrugged. "I only know that I am assigned to this position, so that, as a good soldier, why, I remain here. If there is anything special that is occurring to-day, well, you must know that I am not permitted to speak of it."

"And you are perfectly right not to," he said.

By the time he had completed this speech, two members of his squadron had approached the other guard as if to speak to him as Tsanaali was speaking to the first. No more speech occurred, however; instead, Tsanaali drew a poniard and, with a practiced hand, drove it into the guard's heart; in the meantime, the other guard was similarly treated.

"Quickly," said Tsanaali. "Drag their bodies behind these shrubs before we are observed."

The other two members of Tsanaali's squad appeared, and this operation was smoothly and efficiently carried out. After which the five them gathered in front of the door.

"Very well," said Tsanaali. "It is time."

They drew their swords, opened the door, and entered. The affray was short and furious—the two guardsmen within, armed with pikes, falling instantly to the five swords that charged them out of nowhere; they did not even have time to raise an alarm.

As they fell, the other squads began arriving, and with such timing that, in less than a minute, all of them were assembled in the hallway.

"Very well, gentlemen," said Tsanaali. "Down this corridor will be six or eight more guards; we must strike quickly. Beyond that is an antechamber with a single guard. Beyond that, a covered terrace where we will find Her Majesty, holding an inert Orb. Let us go."

The small troop moved down the corridor toward the Orb.

Chapter the Ninetieth

How Piro Carried Out Grassfog's Last Wishes And Learned a Little of His Family History

We must now, with some trepidation, back up just a few short hours, because, while we are not insensible to the reader's desire to know what is to become of our friends in Adrilankha, at this point our history absolutely requires that we look in on Piro, who, as the reader may recall, had been given an errand by a dying friend; and as everyone knows, few obligations are more sacred than those given by a dying friend. This conclusion, which we daresay is inarguable, brought Piro to a small village on the northern slopes of South Mountain. The village, to remind the reader, was called Six Horses, as it was founded by a lady of the House of the Tsalmoth who boasted this as her wealth. Like most mountain villages, there was little enough there: three small private cottages, a Speaker's house, a community spring house, and a sort of general merchandise store that performed double duty as the inn. Nowhere else in the area could wine or liquor be purchased, and so quite naturally this store became the community gathering place, especially on Marketday, which was the only time there was any sort of population in the village.

On this occasion, it being a Farmday, the village seemed to Piro to be all but deserted—in fact, it might be observed that the arrival of the small company that included Piro, Ibronka, Kytraan, Röaana, Iatha, Belly, Ritt, Mica, and Clari caused the population of Six Horses to effectively double. Indeed, their arrival would have created something of a sensation had there been a sufficient populace for a sensation to have anything to work with.

In the event, they stopped outside of the general store to which we have just referred, recognizing by its wide front and swinging door that it was a place of some importance. Leaving their horses in the care of Lar and Clari, the rest of them entered hoping to find wine with which to wash down the dust of traveling. They all went directly to the long shelf propped up by two barrels which served as a bar, except for Piro, who carried out an inspection of the store.

The proprietor was a Tsalmoth called Marel—indeed, the descendant of the very lady who had founded the village. Instead of horses, however, whose company he had never found agreeable, he had a store that did a brisk business on Marketdays, and provided him with sufficient wine and foodstuffs to satisfy his own needs on the other days. In addition to those items usual in such a store—milled flour from the plains below, nails and hammers from the blacksmith to the west, and wine from the local vines—there was a considerable number of furs hanging from nails along the back wall, and cloaks and coats made from this fur prominently displayed in front. The most numerous were made of the fur of the norska, but there were also fox, wolf, and even a few lyorn skins.

Piro spent a few moments studying these—both the furs, and the items that had been made from them—while Marel studied Piro. Marel's study was very precise after the manner of his class: that is, he was able to estimate to the copper penny with whom he was dealing, and, moreover, make shrewd guesses as to how best to treat with him in order to wring the most possible good—that is to say, money—out of their acquaintance. Accordingly, Marel said nothing, barely even nodding a good day, and concealed his study, waiting until the Tiassa should speak first. This was easier to do as, for some time, he was very much involved in serving Piro's friends.

Eventually Piro spoke, saying, "My dear merchant—"

"My lord," said Marel with a slight bow. He had actually considered, "My lord highwayman," as a form of address, but rejected it.

Piro continued, "These furs."

"Yes, my lord?"

"They are very fine indeed."

Marel bowed again. "This region is known for only two things, my lord. One is the quality of the fur from the norska who dwell nearby."

"Very well, I can see that. And the other?"

"The drafish from our streams. Nowhere else in the Empire, my lord, can be found—"

"I have no doubt that is true, good merchant. But at this moment, you perceive, I have no interest in fish. Whereas, in fact, considering norska fur—"

"Yes, my lord?"

"I have considerable interest."

"And you are right to be interested, my lord. In addition to the brown and white coloring, which is not unattractive, and the obvious ability of such fur to keep one warm even in the winter of the mountains, many do not realize that these furs repel water."

"How, they do?"

"Assuredly. And even more-so when they are treated with a certain oil of my own development, and upon which I have made exhaustive tests."

"Tell me, if you please, where these furs come from?"

Marel frowned. "My lord? Excuse me, but, they come from norska."

"Cha! I know that! I mean, who brings them in?"

"Ah. I beg Your Lordship's pardon. Trappers, my lord."

"Are there many such?"

"Enough, my lord, especially in this region."

"And do you know one called Tsira?"

"Tsira? Why, certainly, yes!"

"Can you tell me where to find her?"

Meral sighed. "Then Your Lordship does not care to buy furs?"

"On the contrary, my good merchant. I shall buy three of them."

The Tsalmoth brightened considerably, and said, "Pick them out, by all means."

"These three," said Piro carelessly.

"And would Your Lordship wish for any of the oil?"

"No, but I will pay you for a bottle anyway. Now then, about Tsira. I give you my word, you have no cause to fear that I am her enemy. On the contrary, I was a friend of her brother, and bring her, alas, news of his death and a small bequest for her."

"Ah, so much the worse! She often spoke of her brother. He was, then, one of your band?"

"My band, good sir? I do not understand what you do me the honor to say."

The merchant's face became quite red, and he said, "That is to say, she spoke of her brother as, well—"

"Never mind, good merchant."

"Yes, my lord."

"But then, to find her?"

"If you take the road to the west, in half a league, you will come to an elbow. Continue there as if there were no bend, and you will find a small path. When you reach a stream, follow it to the left for two leagues, and you will come to a cottage built into the side of the mountain, and that is where she lives."

"I thank you, my friend. Here is for the furs, and the oil—which you may keep—and this is for six bottles of wine to keep us warm against the chill, and this is a thanks for your help."

"Your Lordship is generous."

"Not at all," said Piro. Then, turning to his friends, who had remained silent up until this time, he said, "Come, let us go and complete this errand."

Taking their recent purchases—those, at any rate, that they

had not already consumed—they mounted their horses and, following the directions from the complaisant Tsalmoth, found themselves, two hours later, looking at a small cottage next to a brook and surrounded by siju trees, whose oblong leaves all but concealed the cottage.

"All right," said Piro, "let us now—"

"Stay exactly where you are," said someone whose words—sufficiently imperative as they were—were emphasized by a javelin which struck a tree some few inches from Piro's head, with a hollow "thunk." It remained in the tree, vibrating directly before Piro's eyes.

"Let us," suggested Piro, "remain where we are. Consider that, even if it were not for the threat implied by the sudden appearance of the weapon—a tolerably palpable threat, I think—bear in mind that we are not here for the purpose of antagonizing anyone, but, on the contrary, to perform a service for a lady who is, unless my guess is wrong, the very one who has just communicated to us in this particularly engaging way."

After these remarks, he addressed the cottage, saying, "If your name is Tsira, I would beg for two minutes of your time. And, if it is not, well, we may as well have some conversation just the same, because I give you my word, I should prefer speaking with you to exchanging javelins—the more-so as I did not bring any."

After a moment, they heard the voice again. "I beg your pardon for my greeting, but, you perceive, I rarely receive visitors here, and, when I do, well, they sometimes come in bands with the thought of larceny. And, in truth, you look not unlike larcenists yourselves."

Piro, on impulse, got down from his horse and took two steps toward the cottage. "In fact, we are what you have named us. But I give you my word, so far are we from taking anything from you, that, on the contrary, we are here to give you something without asking anything in return."

A woman then emerged from a corner of the cottage, where she had been concealed in the shadows. One glance at her was sufficient to convince Piro that this was, indeed,

Grassfog's sister—indeed, there were such considerable similarities in features and lines of the face, and even in the set of the shoulders and carriage of the head, that he might well have identified them as siblings even if he had not been, as it were, looking for the resemblance. She was dressed in norska fur in a complex arrangement such that it was difficult to identify the specific garments, with the exception of a wide leather belt, from which hung a short sword and a heavy knife, and a pair of darr-skin boots decorated with red and yellow beads. She bowed to Piro and said, "As you have said, my name is Tsira. How is it that you are looking for me? And what is your name?"

"Piro, madam," he said.

"Piro? How, the same Piro with whom my brother rides? He has mentioned your name in letters."

"That is I."

"Then, if you are here, and he is not, I fear you have brought me disagreeable news."

"Alas, madam, we are here to do exactly that, at his wishes." As he said this, handed her the pendant, accompanying this with a respectful bow and the the words "He desired you to have this."

Tsira looked at it, looked away as if to prevent her emotions from being displayed before a stranger, then, looking at Piro once more, said in a very low voice, "Did he die well?"

"Extremely well. I will relate the entire history, if you wish."

"I should like that, if you please. You perceive, my brother and I were close, so that I am interested in all that concerned his ending."

"Then I will tell you of the entire affair."

"Yes. Have your band dismount, and I will bring out a jug of the spirit we distill here, which is not dissimilar to the Eastern oushka, and will be a fitting accompaniment to the story—in the mountains, we find that our grief is at once lessened and increased by being washed in strong drink. It is something like a custom, and one of which my brother would have approved, and even expected."

"Very well," said Piro. "I should never consider encouraging you to break a custom at such a time."

This plan was agreed to at once, and while Tsira went back into her cottage and returned with several jugs, the rest of Piro's band dismounted and tied their horses to the trees. They seated themselves on the ground and began passing the jugs around, while Piro related in great detail all the circumstances of Grassfog's death. When this tale was complete, Tsira told various stories of her brother, and was repaid by more stories told by Piro and his band—some of them, told by Iatha, Belly, and Ritt, going back to his time in Wadre's band before Piro had met him.

After several hours of this, during which Tsira proved not only her memory, but her capacity for spirits (while each of the others drank more or less of it, according to his tastes, Tsira drank even more than Belly, though she showed no more effects than Piro, who hardly touched the jug to his lips), it happened that everyone except these two—that is to say, Piro and Tsira—were overcome by a combination of spirits and a long journey, and were either asleep or in the sort of daze that is the next thing to it.

"Would you like to take a walk?" said Tsira. "We can let your friends sleep, and you can see a little of the mountain."

"I should like that," said Piro.

"Very good then. This way."

"I am following."

"As we walk," continued Piro, "tell me, what is that artifact which your brother had us return to you? Is it, as I suspect, a family heirloom?"

"Oh, it is that, indeed," said Tsira. "But it is also more."

"How, more?"

"Considerably more. Shall I tell you what it is?"

"If you please," said Piro. "I confess that I am curious."

"Then I shall explain it at once," she said.

"I am listening," said Piro.

"Our family," said Tsira, "has lived in the mountains for as long as we can remember, but not always here. Indeed, it is our tradition that we once lived far in the north, and have been moving south at such a rate that, should it continue, in another ten generations we will be in the ocean-sea, which I, for one, do not think I would care for."

"Well, in fact, it does not sound like a pleasant way to live, unless by then you are able to manufacture gills, which, so far as I know, no sorcerer has yet accomplished."

"I do myself the honor of being in complete agreement. But then, going the other way—"

"That is to say, into the past."

"Yes, exactly. Going the other way, our traditions have it that we once lived in the far north of this range, in the Round Mountain."

"The Round Mountain!" cried Piro.

"I perceive you know something about it," said Tsira.

"Nearly!" said Piro.

"Well then, you know what is there."

"Deathgate Falls!"

"Exactly. And, although our family, I am told (you must understand this was many, many generations ago) lived lower on the slopes, still, it was not far, as distances go, from the Blood River and that strange place where the world ends and another world begins."

"That is true," observed Piro, "whether you are speaking literally or metaphorically."

"Well, as you may imagine, my ancestor who lived there, who was called Yngra, would, from time to time, see processions of people going past to bring the body of a loved one to the Falls, there to cast him over and send him to whatever afterlife might await."

"Yes, that is easily enough understood. But, what did your ancestor do?"

"Oh, much the same as I. He trapped, and hunted, and, in addition, sold embalming oils to those who felt the preservation of the beloved dead was waning, and incense to those who wished to make an offering at the shrine to their particular House—which shrines are located at certain intervals along both banks of the Blood River just before the Falls."

"I know," said Piro laconically.

"So my ancestor did those things. Or else," she added, reflectively, "he was a road agent."

"What, you don't know whether he was a trapper or a highwayman?"

"You must understand that everyone in our family has always done one of these or the other. Except, that is, for an occasional stray younger son who runs a tavern, thus combining both activities. Now my brother served as an apprentice to a physicker for a while, but I knew this could not last. You perceive, it is in the blood."

"I understand. Your ancestor was either a trapper or a road agent. Go on, then."

"Well, as the story has come down to us, one day a man happened to pass by the cottage—which cottage I have always imagined to be not unlike my own."

"And a splendid cabin it is, too."

"Do you think so? That is kind of you. I was born in it, you know, and so it has some tradition behind it, and, moreover, I built it with my own hands, and so it is a matter of some pride."

"I understand," said Piro. "But please go on," he added, not wishing to consider too closely what he had just been told.

"According to the tradition," continued Tsira, "one day a man came by."

"When would this have been?"

"During the Tenth Issola Reign."

"Very well, then," said Piro, who knew sufficiently little of history that this told him nothing.

"So then, one day during the Tenth Issola Reign a man came along on a pilgrimage to Deathgate, there to make certain sacrifices and prayers, and to commune with the spirits that are said to exist there."

"He was, then, an Athyra?"

"Exactly."

"Very well, then."

"It chanced that he had business with my ancestor."

"He bought incense?"

"No, he was caused to hand over his purse."

"So then, this ancestor was, in fact, a road agent?"

"Well, you must understand, those in my family who engage in robbery, also do some trapping now and then."

"It is true, your brother Grassfog did lay an occasional line of snares. And then?"

"Why, those of us who trap and hunt also work the roads during the lean times."

"That sounds to me like an excellent arrangement."

"That is kind of you to say."

"Well, and so, your ancestor, Inger—"

"Yngra."

"Yes, Yngra. And so, Yngra transacted certain business with this visitor, at the end of which, Yngra had his purse."

"Exactly."

"And then?"

"Well, the unfortunate gentleman, after the business with my brother, walked a mile further toward Deathgate, and then fell over stone dead."

"But, of what did he die?"

"As to that, I cannot say. Certainly no violence was done to him. But then, he was a very old man."

"So there is nothing remarkable in an old man dropping dead walking through the mountains."

"That is true."

"Well, but what then?"

"You must understand, my dear Piro, that Yngra had a sensitive and imaginative nature, and it made him sad that this person, with whom he had just transacted business and shared a meal—"

"A meal?"

"Yngra had the custom of sharing food with anyone he happened to rob, so at least the fellow would have a full belly to speed him on his way."

"A very complaisant robber. Being in the trade myself, I cannot but admire it."

"That is kind of you to say."

"So then, you say that this Athyra dropped dead after his business and his meal with your ancestor, Yngra."

"Yes, and Yngra felt badly about it. At first, he feared he had inadvertently poisoned his guest—which, as you know, is bad luck."

"There is little worse."

"But, as he himself felt no ill effects, and as he had eaten the same thing as his guest, he came to the conclusion that it was merely an unfortunate event."

"That seems likely. And then?"

"He nevertheless felt badly about the whole thing."

"As you say, he had a sensitive and imaginative nature."

"Exactly. And so he resolved to bring the poor fellow to Deathgate."

"How, just because he had spoken with him?"

"And shared a meal, yes, exactly."

"That was a kindly resolution."

"I have always thought so."

"Well, what next?"

"He did just as he intended: he made a sort of sled, hitched it to his horse by a combination of leather straps and tree branches, and so brought the poor fellow to the Falls. There he lit some incense in his name by the icon of the Athyra, set him in the River, and watched his body go over."

"For my part," said Piro, "I consider it a fine gesture."

"Was it not? And he was rewarded."

"How, was he?"

"That, at least, is the family tradition."

"But, what was the reward?"

"This amulet. Yngra claimed that, the next day, he found it hanging on his door handle."

"The Trey! Did he?"

"Well, at any rate, we now have it."

"Well, but does it do anything?"

"Do anything? Nearly!"

"What does it do?"

"Grassfog never told you?"

"Told me? Why, he never so much as mentioned it until he was at the point of death."

"Then, if you'd like, I will tell you what it does."

"I should like to hear; you can imagine that, after a story such as you have just told, I am more than a little curious."

"Well, when you looked at the amulet, did you observe that there are several symbols engraved on it?"

"Yes, I saw that."

"And what did you make of them?"

"Well, while I do not claim to be a sorcerer, I recognized the ancient symbols of the Serioli that are so often used in the arcane arts."

"But do you know what they mean?"

"Madam, you must perceive that if I knew what they meant, why, I should know what they do."

"That is true," admitted Tsira. "Well then," she said, taking the item out and showing it to Piro, "there are several different charms placed upon it, and, moreover, they combine in ways that are quite remarkable. That is very odd."

"What is?"

"It is glowing. Have you ever seen it do that before?"

"Never."

"Nor have I."

"Well then, let us hear about it."

"You want me to explain it?"

"I think so."

"It can be used to disrupt the workings of any sorcerous field."

"Ah! That is truly amazing!"

"Isn't it?"

"Only—"

"Well?"

"What is a sorcerous field?"

"Oh, as to that, I have not the least idea in the world, I assure you. But it was explained to me by a wizard to whom I showed it that that is what it did."

"Well, and do you know how to use it?"

"Not at all."

"Come, let us return to your cottage."

"Very well, Piro. But I still wonder what that glowing means."

"There, you see, it has stopped."

"That is true."

"And I, good Tsira, still wonder what a sorcerous field is."

"For that matter, so do I. Ah, we are back."

"Ibronka knows something of sorcery; we could ask her."

"Who is Ibronka?"

"She is the lovely Dzurlord who is snoring with her head on Röaana's stomach, her leg on Kytraan's face, and her hand on the jug."

"Ah, yes, her. Do you imagine we can wake her?"

"It seems unlikely. Nevertheless, let me try. Ibronka, my love, can you tell me what a sorcerous field is?"

Ibronka moved her leg slightly, causing Kytraan to make various snuffling sounds; then she shifted her head, clasped the jug more tightly, and sighed softly.

"Ibronka?"

"My friend," said Tsira, "I do not believe it is working."

"I'm afraid you are right."

Ibronka stopped snoring, opened her eyes, and said, "A sorcerous field refers to any area wherein the set effects of a sorcerous spell are continuous. Examples include teleport protections and alarm wards. The two advantages of a sorcerous field over a conventionally cast spell are that it may continue without monitoring for some length of time, and that additional energy may be put into the spell, increasing its effectiveness beyond what the sorcerer is normally capable of controlling. The usual way of determining if a sorcerous field is or has recently been present is the Norbrook Threepass Test." After completing this discourse, Ibronka immediately closed her eyes and began snoring again.

Piro blinked.

"I wonder," said Tsira, "if she would know how to use it."

"Perhaps," said Piro. "We can ask her."

"I am curious about something else."

"Curiosity is often a good thing."

"Perhaps it is this time, too."

"Well, let us see. What are you curious about?"

"Two things: first, why it began glowing."

"Yes, that is a good question. Next?"
"Why it stopped."
"The Horse! That is another good question. Could it have something to do with where we were?"
"Perhaps. Let us walk back westward."
"Very well."
"Ah, there, you see, my lord? It is glowing again."
"And as we continue in this direction, the glow is brighter."
"Might there be a sorcerous field nearby?"
"I cannot imagine how there could be."
"Well, but just in case, I should rather have my friends with me before going any further."
"Well, but can you wake them?"
"I do not know, but I am determined to try."
"Very well, let us do so then."
"I agree."

In fact, after some twenty or thirty minutes, they managed to get everyone in the band mounted on horseback with the exception of Lar and Ritt, who were, instead of riding, draped over the backs of their horses. There was, to be sure, a certain amount of discontent expressed at Piro's insistence, but, either because of his will, or because of their habit of obedience, they eventually managed to make their way, with the two exceptions that we have already noted.

Piro and Tsira rode in front, Tsira holding the amulet. Presently she said, "There, it is glowing again."

"Then," said Piro, "let us continue in this direction."

"What is it?" asked Ibronka from beneath drooping eyelids.

Piro explained what they knew, what they guessed, and what they wondered about, while Ibronka did her best to overcome the effects of her debauch enough to listen and try to understand what she was being told, and even think about it.

After a few hours of riding, however, our friends recovered their senses, so that by the time Tsira observed, "It is glowing even more brightly," they were all sitting upright, all acquainted with the situation, and many of them were even able to generate some mild interest in the proceedings.

"This area looks somewhat familiar," said Piro.

"I hope so," said Ibronka, looking around. "We fought something of a battle here."

"Here?"

"Here first, and then up there."

"Why, yes. I had not recognized it. Then, up ahead, there is the cave from which Zerika emerged."

"Exactly."

"I know that cave," said Tsira. "It isn't much of a cave, only fifteen feet deep. I have sheltered there occasionally during sudden rainstorms."

"Yes, that is the one."

"That is where the Empress emerged with the Orb?"

"The very place."

"How remarkable," said Tsira. "And to think it is so near my home!"

"The amulet is growing even more brightly," observed Piro.

"So it is."

"Ibronka, my love, do you think you have any idea how to make this object perform its function?"

She rode up next to Tsira and took the charm. She studied it carefully for a moment and then handed it back. "I do not believe so," she said. "It would take a more knowledgeable sorcerer than I."

"That is too bad," said Piro.

Tsira shrugged. "I wish to look at this cave."

"Very well," said Piro. "Let us dismount, hobble the horses, and investigate."

Chapter the Ninety-First

How Sethra Lavode Discovered Something of Kâna's Secret Plans

Let us now return our attention to the Battle of Adrilankha as it developed. Sethra Lavode, having seen that the battle on Lower Kieron Road was, at the moment, stable, turned to her adepts and said, "What report from Northgate Road?"

"Nothing, General. No sign of enemy activity."

"Very well. Find out what is going on at the bridges."

"The enemy is not yet there."

"The harbor?"

The adepts were silent for a moment; then one of them said, "The enemy has landed in force, and are just now organizing to move inland."

Sethra nodded. It occurred to her that, should the enemy's plan involve something other than moving in past South Adrilankha in an attempt to cross the bridges, it could be embarrassing for her. But, to the left, there was nothing to be done about it at this stage, and moreover, she was convinced that this was, indeed, the enemy's plan.

Addressing her adepts again, she said, "Very well. Inform Berigner to expect the enemy within the half hour."

"Yes, General." The adept then frowned and said, "That is odd."

"What is it?" said Sethra.

"I cannot reach Neffra."

"Well, but who is Neffra?"

"The adept on Berigner's staff with whom I have been communicating."

"Then reach another."

"Yes, General."

"Well?"

"I can reach no one."

"Well," said Sethra Lavode. "What can cause such a thing? Can you reach Sethra the Younger?"

"No, General."

"Well," said the Enchantress.

She fell silent, considering matters, then gave a rapid series of messages to messengers, and orders to subordinates, concluding with the single word "Horse!"

This remark, the reader should understand, was the command for an orderly to bring her a horse, rather than the beginning of some remarks to be addressed to the animal. Fortunately, the orderly understood, and her horse was brought to her. She mounted it directly, letting command in this area devolve on Fentor, who was acting for Morrolan, and took herself to the headquarters on the Old West Road.

"Warlord!" said Sethra the Younger. "I had not expected you."

"Well, am I any the less welcome for that?"

"Oh, not the least in the world, I assure you. I assume you wish to know the progress of the battle?"

"Yes, you have understood exactly. You perceive, I should have used one of the adepts to ask, only they appear unable to communicate."

"So I had just noticed," said her apprentice. "And, alas, it seems my ability to use sorcery is impaired. Indeed, more than impaired, I should say the ability has deserted me entirely."

"I give you my word, madam," said Sethra, "that you are not alone in this. On the contrary, it seems to be the case with every sorcerer with whom I have spoken. And, if that were not sufficient evidence, well, I find that I, myself, am unable to perform in the simplest of spells."

"That is sufficient, I believe, to prove a point, if proof is required."

"I think so."

"Well, but how can this be?"

"As to that, I have not the least idea. I have sent to the Manor to ask Her Majesty, but have not yet received word."

"So then, shall I make my report?"

"I should be very grateful if you would; and laconically, I beg."

"There is little enough to tell, madam. They press, we hold them. Indeed, we were driving them back in fine style, and I was about to do myself the honor of ordering a countercharge that could not have failed to utterly break them, when suddenly we found we were without sorcery, so that, not only was the notion of making such a charge now questionable, but, moreover, I was cut off from the officers on the line, so that I was unable to give the command."

"Ah, and have you, yourself, not been to the front line?"

Her apprentice scowled. "I have tried, three times, and on each occasion, I have been distracted by some annoying issue having to do with command—a sudden weakness over here, or change in the nature of the attacking troops over there. I give you my word, it is tolerably vexing."

"I have made this same observation on more than one occasion," said Sethra.

At this point, the Sorceress in Green approached them. She had been at the front, and been required to walk back for two reasons: the first being that, as she had anticipated teleporting, she had neglected to provide herself with a horse; in the second place, she was no horseman, and so would have been unable to ride in any event.

When she reached Morrolan and Sethra, she bowed to them both and said, "There is something amiss with the Orb."

"So we have observed," said Sethra the Younger.

"It is insupportable," said the Sorceress.

"Well," said the Warlord, "it makes it harder for us, that is all. While we do not have our sorcery, nor do we have the remarkable abilities of the Necromancer, we still have our soldiery."

"And the warlock, Brimford?" asked the Sethra the Younger.

"Alas he is, as yet, unable to produce any results. Although he insists he can still communicate with his familiars, and that they are in position should he suddenly be able to perform his magic."

"Well," said Sethra the Younger, shrugging.

The Enchantress frowned and said, "It is vexing, but I still believe that, with the Favor, the day might still be ours, especially if Lord Berigner is able to hold the bridges from South Adrilankha. To that end, I have dispatched the forces from Northgate Road to assist him."

The Sorceress shrugged. "Madam, it is not merely a question of winning or losing this battle, or even the Empire."

"How, it is not?"

"Well, you perceive, I consider these matters important—"

"I hope that you do!"

"—but it is intolerable to consider that this, this, *person* could have become so low as to open our world to the Jenoine."

Sethra stared at her. "What do you tell me?"

The Sorceress stared back. "Why, I tell you that our world has been opened to the Jenoine."

For one of very few times recorded by history, Sethra Lavode was speechless. Eventually, however, she managed to say, "Are you certain?"

"How, could you be unaware of what has happened?"

"Nearly," said Sethra.

"I am astonished."

"*You* are astonished?"

"Well—"

"Did you, in fact, mention the word 'Jenoine'?"

"Certainly I did. Twice. And now I insist upon it."

"Kâna has opened our world to the Jenoine?"

"Well, one Jenoine, in any case."

"How is this possible?"

"Why, my dear Sethra, you know as well as anyone that a skilled necromancer might create such an opening."

"Well, but then, how is it that I have not been aware of it? You perceive, Dzur Mountain is full of alarms looking for just such an occurrence."

"But my love, you are not at Dzur Mountain."

"That is true," said Sethra, struck by the extreme justice of this observation. "But how is it that you became aware of it?"

"Why, I hardly know. I simply realize—ah!"

"Well?"

The Sorceress pulled from within her blouse a small purple stone, hanging from a thin silver chain about her neck. "This," she said.

"What of it?"

"Why, my dear, you gave it to me. It is linked to the wards in Dzur Mountain. You desired me to have it, if you remember, in case Dzur Mountain were attacked, and you were sufficiently involved with the defense so as to prevent you from letting me know."

"I remember now."

"Well, it must be this that informed me, and, as it makes use of Elder Sorcery, which does not require intervention of the Orb, why, the disruption of the Orb could have no effect on it."

"I believe you are correct on all counts, good Sorceress."

"But then, what shall we do?"

"Why, I should be at Dzur Mountain. You perceive, all of my mechanisms for fighting the Jenoine are there. Moreover, these mechanisms are far too cumbersome to move."

"And, if I may ask, madam, how are you to accomplish this feat? You perceive that the Orb is not, at this moment, permitting sorcery; to ride there will take a full day, even with the post. I beg to submit that, in a day, it will be too late to do any good."

"You are right again, my dear."

"Well, and then?"

The Enchantress of Dzur Mountain frowned, and set her hand upon the hilt of the dagger that hung at her side. "I must consider the matter," she said.

"At least," observed Sethra the Younger, "we now understand why the Necromancer has been unable to use her skills, and, in addition, why the Orb is no longer functioning."

"That is true!" said the Enchantress.

The Sorceress in Green said, "Where is the Jenoine?"

"Do you know," said Sethra the Younger, "that is an excellent question."

"Do you think so?" said the Sorceress. "Then I am most gratified for having asked it."

"And you are right to be."

"Only—"

"Well?"

"What is the answer?"

"Oh, as to that, you must ask the Enchantress."

"Well, I thought I had."

"And yet, she hasn't answered."

"Well, that is because she is reflecting."

"Ah. Then, it appears, it *was* an excellent question."

"I believe I told you so."

"That is true."

"I cannot tell you exactly where it is," said Sethra Lavode, speaking very slowly, as if each word required considerable contemplation, "but I can tell you how to find it."

"Well?" said the others.

In answer, the Enchantress turned to an errand runner and said, "My compliments to the Necromancer, and I require her presence here at once."

Chapter the Ninety-Second

How Grita and Illista Made Their Plans And Discussed the Finer Points of Vengeance

As all of this was taking place, several hundreds of miles away, a conversation of no small interest was also taking place near the mouth of a deep cave. Before considering the conversation, however, we must take a moment to look, not at the mouth of the cave where the conversation is occurring, but, rather deep within it. Some twenty-five or thirty meters inside this cave—which is to say, against the place it abruptly ended in stone—there was what might at first appear to be a large, rectangular block of ice. A closer examination would reveal what appears to be a corpse encased in the ice. And yet a closer look would show that, in fact, it was not ice at all, but, rather, a sort of shimmering, transparent, and insubstantial product of the sorcerous arts.

It should come as no surprise to the reader that the apparent body held within this thaumaturgic matrix was none other than our friend Tazendra. She lay upon a sort of stone table, dressed in the black of the House of the Dzur, and covered, as we have said, with the strange spell whose appearance we have sketched. To look at her, there is not the least evidence of life to be found. Insofar as she could be seen through the wavering and shifting of the spell (or, to be precise, the most prominent visual effect of the spell) the most striking aspect of her appearance must be that her eyes are open and there is an expression on her countenance of something like astonishment.

We should add that, all around this table, there was a remarkable array of sorcerous gear: a staff stood upright, dug into the floor of the cave, and constantly vibrated. A pair of of objects rested on either side of the table, lined up with Tazendra's waist, that very much resembled the stalagmites that the reader may recall seeing in Dzur Mountain. Three head-sized crystals lay on the floor in front of her, one glowing red, another blue, and the third yellow. Upon the walls in the back of the cave were hung five bronze-colored disks, about eight centimeters in diameter, and inscribed with certain arcane symbols. And, directly over her, hung a sort of globe. We cannot say precisely how large it was, nor its color, because both its size and its hue would change rapidly as it was observed.

And in front of this globe was, perhaps, the most remarkable thing of all: an area stretching to the top of the cave—that is to say, perhaps twelve feet—and nearly the same width, that was utterly black; so black that the light from the various lamps and implements did not penetrate it. It appeared, in fact, to be a blackness with depth, and even substance. More, there appeared to be a sense of continuous motion within it, although, to look upon it, one could not say exactly how one was aware of this motion. But it carried within it a great sense of power, and threat; no one beholding it would care to come near it, much less make contact with that area of wavering darkness.

However this may be, let us turn our attention, as we indicated above, to the mouth of the cave where, as the reader might surmise, our old acquaintances Grita and Illista are holding conversation. Here the opening led out onto a ledge of reasonable size and one that, moreover, gave a good view of the surrounding region, excepting, of course, for above and behind, where the mountain itself blocked the view. It was for this reason that the first words spoken by Illista were "Have you looked above us and behind?"

"I have looked, my dear Phoenix," said Grita, "and also

used what sorcerous ability I have, which is not inconsiderable, having honed my skills during the Interregnum, and I give you my word that not only is no one behind or above us, but, moreover, there are no listening or seeing spells of any sort in operation."

"That is good, then," said Illista. "And, looking around, save for a few chipmunks, who seem busy with affairs of their own, and a few norska who are equally busy, and various birds of species I do not recognize, we are quite alone."

"I agree," said Grita. "We are alone."

"Have you inspected our Dzurlord?"

"I have just this instant completed an inspection."

"And?"

"The spell is as strong today as when we cast it. She is in a sleep like death; she feels nothing, can send or receive no communications either sorcerous or psychic, and no sorcery upon this world can find her. Her mind, you perceive, is, in effect, non-existent."

"And then, you are certain that she can be revived, in case our friends appear and desire assurances that she still lives?"

"Perfectly."

"Very good."

"And our other preparations, Illista?"

"Which ones?"

"All of them."

"Well then, let us consider them."

"Very well."

"Suppose they appear with an army."

"Unlikely. The armies are, at this instant, engaged in defending certain bridges and roads in Adrilankha."

"Well," said Illista, "but if they do?"

"Then we have our own army, graciously loaned to us by His Majesty Kâna. Small, but large enough to defend the mouth of this cave as long as is necessary. They are this moment hidden outside of the cave, prepared to spring into action upon my signal."

"Very good."

"What next?"

"Sorcery?"

"Impossible. The Orb is busy—there is no sorcery."

"That is true."

"What of necromancy? You are certain they cannot create a necromantic gate to remove the Dzur without entering?"

"So long as Tri'nagore is present in the world, even a god could not manifest within a mile of this spot."

"That is good, then."

"I think so; I am glad you agree."

"They will have no choice but to meet us, face-to-face."

"And for that, we are ready."

"Exactly, my dear Illista. More than ready, we are prepared."

"Then you are sufficiently confident of the result?"

"Oh, I am, I assure you. You know what we have prepared for anyone passing into this cave."

"I know very well."

"So," asked Grita, "you are satisfied?"

"Entirely. Only—"

"Yes?"

"Where are their friends?" asked Illista. "That is to say, why has no one appeared to rescue her? We were convinced they would be here before this. Now, all of our sorcery will not work, as the Orb is busy wrestling with the individual we have summoned."

"That is true, but, remember, if our sorcery does not work, neither does theirs. And, moreover, we are able to tap into the powers of that individual, which they are not."

"Still—I cannot imagine why no attempt has been made to rescue her. Could it be that our clue was too subtle?"

"No, my friend," said Grita. "It is not that."

"Then, could we have been wrong about them caring about her?"

"Oh, as to that, I am certain she is their friend."

"Are you? You know how irritating the Dzur can be."

"Oh, I do not question that."

"You are right not to," said Illista. "They constantly seek

quarrels, and will often dispute the simplest of arguments for no reason except that everyone else agrees. And they will hold to an unpopular opinion for no reason except that it is unpopular."

"I do not believe this is true of all Dzur, and, in particular, it is not true of this one."

"Nevertheless, if they care about her, and if our clue was as obvious as you say—"

"Neither the Lyorn nor the Tiassa is capable of missing it."

"Well then, why are they not here, unless it is because they don't care about her?"

"I said before, Illista, that that is not the reason, and I say so again."

"You are certain?"

"Entirely."

"But then, why? We expected them months ago. We had this entire mountain prepared to explode in case an army appeared, and we had sorcerous alarms to detect efforts to approach us with stealth. But yet, they have not come."

"Shall I tell you why, Illista?"

"If you know, I wish you would."

"I will explain."

"I am listening."

"They have not come, for the simple reason that they did not know she was missing."

"How, they didn't know? And yet, it has been almost a year since we took her."

"Nevertheless, it is the case. She was at Dzur Mountain, and then she went to her home, and no one had cause to attempt to reach her."

"Well, but when we set off the spell at her home?"

"There was no sorcerer nearby to detect the magic, it was daylight, so no one could see the flames, and the spell we used burned everything too quickly for there to be smoke."

Illista considered this, then nodded. "Very well, I accept that that is the reason."

"And you are right to."

"But we must find a way to inform them."

"Not in the least."

"How, we don't need to inform them?"

"No," said Grita, "because now they know."

"Oh, do they?"

"Three days ago, the Lyorn passed the doors of her castle."

"Ah, ah! So that—"

"Yes. I expect him at any moment."

"So, that is why you brought us here, now?"

"Precisely."

Illista smiled. "I must say, the timing is admirable: even as our friend Kâna is attacking, and as we have disabled any possibility of sorcerous aid for the enemy, they walk into our trap."

"I agree, we could not have planned it better."

"I do myself the honor of agreeing entirely."

"So then?"

"Then we ought to prepare for our visitor."

"Well, yes, but you should be aware that there is another problem."

"How, a problem?"

"I am convinced of it, my dear Illista."

"Well, but what is this problem?"

"The Tiassa has resumed his post."

"So then?"

"He is involved in the battle, and will not be here."

"So much the worse! But we have the others, at any rate."

"Not the Yendi, either."

"What?"

"The Tiassa has intervened on his behalf."

"So then—?"

"We can anticipate no one arriving except the Lyorn."

"Ah, that is too bad! And yet, I cannot imagine how such a thing could have happened that this Zerika has not caused the Yendi to be arrested, or at least banished."

"An unfortunate fluke."

"We must accept it, it seems."

"Well, at any rate, that will be two of them."

"That is true, Grita. At least there will be two of them now, and the others later."

"Yes. And, do you know, in a way, now that I consider, it may be better this way."

"How, better that we must delay our vengeance against the Yendi and the Tiassa?"

"Exactly."

"For what reason?"

"Shall I explain, Illista?"

"I will be grateful if you do, for you must know that I do not understand why it should be better."

"Because, my love, killing them is not the pleasure."

"It is not? And yet—"

"On the contrary, killing them ends the pleasure."

"You think so?"

"Entirely. The pleasure comes in two places: first, in the planning and preparation, and next, above all, that delicious moment when your enemy realizes that death is inevitable—that he is already dead, but is still aware of it. To extend that moment as long as possible, that is the real goal. I should like it to last a hundred years. A thousand years. I should like it to never end."

Illista frowned and considered this. "There is a great deal of truth in what you say, Grita."

"You perceive, I have spent many years considering the matter."

"And yet, we must kill them eventually."

Grita sighed. "I know. And it is difficult to get satisfactory vengeance on a Dzur in any case—even when they know they are about to die, they will not respond properly, which robs the moment of its sweetness."

"Do you know, that is true."

"Yes."

"I hate them."

"Yes."

"Well then, Illista, should we dispose of this Dzur and start over?"

The Phoenix considered this, then said, "I have no interest

in simply cutting her throat and being done with it. I want my vengeance—on her, as well as on the others."

"And yet, we have just observed how difficult it is in the case of a Dzur."

Illista frowned. "Difficult—but perhaps not impossible, my dear Grita."

"Have you an idea?"

"Nearly."

"Let us hear it then. You know that I adore your suggestions."

"You are a very complaisant conspirator, Grita."

"We are a good team."

"Oh, as to that, we shall know more when our vengeance is complete."

"That is certainly true."

"And, to that end—"

"Yes, to that end, let us hear your idea."

"Shall I tell you now?"

"At once! Can't you see I am mad to know?"

"Very well, this is it: The way to torment a Dzur is not to kill the Dzur, but rather, to kill the Dzur's friends."

"Oh!"

"While the Dzur watches!"

"Oh, oh!"

"Especially if the friend dies attempting to rescue the Dzur!"

"Illista, you are adorable!"

"So then, you like my plan?"

"It is magnificent!"

"I am glad you think so."

"And I can even improve upon it."

"Can you indeed? Well, in truth, that doesn't astonish me. Is it a good improvement?"

"You will see."

"Let us see then."

"By tormenting the Dzur, we can be all the more certain the friend—"

"That is to say, the Lyorn—"

"—charges in blindly. That is, if he sees his friend the Dzur being tortured, well, he will not hesitate."

"Perfect!"

"Then, let us make preparations to receive this Lyorn."

"And preparations as well to torture the Dzur. Apropos—"

"Well?"

"What method of torture would you recommend?"

"Well, we may as well do something practical."

"Oh, I am in favor of practicality. But, what do you mean?"

"I am referring to those others who will not be appearing yet."

"What about them?"

"Our Lyorn may not have told them where we are holding the Dzur."

"That is true! And does your idea address this issue?"

"You will see."

"What, then, is your idea?"

"I propose that we send Tazendra back to her friends."

"How, send her back?"

"Or, rather, a part of her."

"Ah! Ah!"

"Say, for example, an ear."

"Oh, yes. An ear. Dzurlords have such distinctive ears."

"Yes. And upon the packaging that contains the ear, well, we can write, in words simple enough for the meanest understanding, a description of where we are, in case our Lyorn has failed to communicate this intelligence to his friends. This will serve to also make certain that there is no possible doubt about whether they can find us."

"Grita, your ideas are brilliant. I tell you so."

Grita bowed, and said, "And, after that, if they do not appear for her—"

"Well?"

"Why, then we will send them another ear."

"You perceive that, at this rate, she will soon run out of ears."

"Well, but that is of no importance."

"It isn't?"

"Not in the least. You perceive, she has still a nose. And eyes. And, unless I am mistaken, she has, in addition, a full complement of fingers and toes."

"You are right about that."

"So then?"

"That is a total of twenty-five packages."

"I cannot fault your arithmetic."

"Oh, I have always been skilled in that field."

"I am convinced of it."

"Twenty-five should prove sufficient, I think."

"Oh, I am convinced of that, too. We will not need so many, but it cannot hurt to have spares."

"Then what do you think?"

"Of your plan?"

"Yes."

"It is a splendid idea."

"Yes. First we will awaken her, but leave the binding spell in place."

"Very well. And after?"

"After that, we will wait for our Lyorn."

"I agree. Next?"

"Once he is there, it will be time to very quickly release the binding spell."

"Yes. And once we have done that, why, we will play the part of the battlefield surgeon."

"Exactly."

"I will sharpen the knife."

"Very good."

The first thing that crossed Tazendra's mind as she awoke was the reflection that she had been asleep for a long time. Then her memory began to return—walking into her home, the sudden explosions behind her, the feeling of a spell penetrating her defenses, and the sudden dizziness. And, as her memories came back to her, she realized that she was not alone, but, on the contrary, there were two individuals standing over her. She looked from one to the other, then said, "Hello Madam Grita or Orlaan, or whatever your name is. I hope I find you well."

"Well enough," said Grita.

"And, you, madam, look familiar. You are—?"

"Illista."

"Ah yes. It comes back. So, then, the two of you are together? I trust you will forgive the insult when I tell you that I find this entirely appropriate. Indeed, it is rare that anything falls out so well."

"We are together," said Illista, bowing. "Just as you will soon be, if I may use the expression, apart."

"Indeed?" said Tazendra, yawning. "You will forgive me if I am a little weary after my long sleep. Otherwise, you may be certain, I should display more emotion."

"Oh, we don't mind," said Illista. "No doubt, you will display more emotion presently."

"No doubt. How long have I been asleep?"

"Not long. Less than a year."

"No wonder I feel so extraordinarily well rested."

"Are you prepared?" said Illista.

"For what?"

"I was speaking to my associate."

"I beg your pardon."

"I am prepared," said Grita. "As soon as we hear the chime, I will be ready to begin."

"Very well," said Illista. "But, when that happens, you must work quickly. You perceive, once I release the binding, she will be able to move."

"Oh," said Tazendra, "am I unable to move?"

"How," said Grita, "you hadn't noticed?"

"I have had no occasion to try," lied Tazendra.

"Try now, if you'd like," said Grita.

"No, madam, I have no reason not to believe you. After all, you would surely not lie; that might compromise your honor."

"Is the knife sharp?" asked Illista of Grita.

Grita held it aloft. "It is."

"Good then."

"I am ready when you are."

"What am I to lose?" asked Tazendra.

"Everything," said Grita.

"All at once?" asked Tazendra in a tone of idle curiosity.

"No, we are beginning with your left ear."

"Ah. Splendid. I have never liked that one. Indeed, I have often considered removing it myself."

"We are pleased to be able to perform this service for you."

"Well, why do you not begin?"

"Oh, we will in a moment, I assure you. We are only waiting for a guest."

"Oh, a guest. Well, I understand that you might wish to save the entertainment until your guest has arrived."

At that moment, there was a sort of chime from near the mouth of the cave.

"That must be your guest now," said Tazendra complacently.

Sliding carefully past the large black emptiness to which we referred earlier, Grita made her cautious way to the front of the cave.

"Well?" called Illista.

"It is only a Teckla, come to watch."

"To watch?"

"Well, at any rate, he has brought his own chair."

"Mica!" called Tazendra.

"Mistress? You are alive!"

"Nearly," said the Dzur.

"Who is this?" demanded Illista.

"My lackey. But, Mica, how did you find me?"

"There was a spot marked on the map in your study."

"Pah. I never make marks on maps."

"Exactly," said Mica, bowing.

"Well, and so you knew where I was. Still, how did you find the cave?"

"My lady, you may recall, I have been in this cave before, only then it was not so deep. When I came up the mountain and didn't see you, well, I thought of this cave at once."

Tazendra frowned. "But, when I saw you last, you were at Dzur Mountain!"

"The Enchantress suggested I return to Daavya to find you."

"How, she did?"

"She not only suggested it, but sent me there as well."

"But then, you have walked all the way here from Daavya?"

"Oh, I have become skilled at walking."

"That is enough of this conversation," said Grita. "You, Teckla, may watch, if you like, but do not speak. We are still awaiting another guest."

"It is true, what my lackey says," said Tazendra, addressing Illista. "You seem to have dug out this cave; it did not used to be so deep."

"And a good piece of work, was it not?" said Illista.

"Why, I must admit it was, although I cannot imagine why."

"What, you cannot guess?"

"You perceive, I have never been a good at guessing."

"I believe that," said Grita, who at this point returned holding Mica by the ear. "Put your chair there, and sit on it, and watch," she instructed the Teckla.

"I will do so, only—"

"Well?"

"It is not a chair, it is a bar-stool."

"Sit down and keep silent."

Mica shrugged and obeyed.

"To answer your question," said Grita, "for I have no objection to satisfying your curiosity, it is that we needed more space, and so we created it. It wasn't difficult."

"Well, but, if I may ask—"

"Oh, certainly," said Illista. "Ask anything you wish."

"Why make this cave bigger, instead of finding one already that large?"

"Why, because of its properties," said Grita.

"This cave has properties?"

"Certainly. You must be aware of what happened here."

"Well, we fought a skirmish here."

"Well, but what else happened?"

"After the skirmish—"

"Yes?"

"We fought a larger skirmish."

"That is true. And what else?" prompted Grita.

"Well," said Tazendra, considering, "this is where we met with Her Majesty."

"Yes, exactly. Here is where you met the charming lady with the Orb."

"So then?"

"Do you know where she had been before she emerged in the cave?"

"Why, it never crossed my mind to ask her."

"Can you not deduce it?"

"Oh, at deduction I am even worse than guessing."

"Then, shall I tell you?"

"I confess, I would like to know."

"Before being in the cave, she was in the Halls of Judgment."

"How, was she?"

"Why yes, that is where she acquired the Orb."

"It is true she had the Orb."

"So, there you have it."

Tazendra frowned. "And so—?"

"And so, that indicates this cave has certain specific and interesting properties. You must understand, it is not everywhere in the Empire from which one can appear from the Halls of Judgment."

"It is not?"

"Had you thought it was?"

"In all truth, well, I had never given it a thought."

"Believe me, there are only certain places which have that arcane pathway."

"I believe you, madam."

"So much the better, because now you understand why we used this cave."

"Perfectly, only—"

"Yes?"

"Why do you wish to go to the Halls of Judgment?"

"Oh, we don't," said Illista. "Moreover, we cannot; the connection only works in one direction. This is a place from which one can emerge from the Halls, but one can only get there from Deathgate."

"Ah, well, I comprehend. But then, if you are not going to

the Halls of Judgment, well, why did you require the properties of this cave?"

"Why else, but to provide access to a Jenoine."

"A Jenoine?"

"Certainly. His Majesty, Kâna, requires one to neutralize the powers of the Orb, and, at the same time, we required one to permit us to use these spells with which we intend to dispatch all of your friends."

"Well, but to permit a Jenoine access to our world—"

"What of it?"

"I cannot but consider it a bad idea."

"Oh, you need not fear. After you and your friends are dead, and the Orb is in our hands, well, we will banish it once more. You perceive, it is not fully here, it has only been given a certain opening, if you will, which permits some of its powers to manifest."

"Well, but what if your friends fail to take the Orb, and my friends and I slaughter you?"

"Oh, that will not happen."

"Yet, if it does?"

"Why then, being dead, you perceive that I shall not be concerned with what the Jenoine does."

"Yes," said Tazendra, "I understand that you might see it that way. And yet—"

"Well?"

"I see it rather differently."

"That is but natural," said Illista magnanimously.

At this moment, there was another chime from in front of the cave.

"Perhaps," said Grita, "that is our guest."

"Let us hope so," said Illista. "I confess, I am growing impatient."

"Bide, my dear Dzurlord," said Grita. "We must see to our visitor."

Illista moved to front of the cave and called back, "It is he!"

"Welcome, my dear Lyorn," called Grita.

"Come," said Illista. "Let us begin, then."

"Aerich!" cried Tazendra. "It is a trap!"

"Thank you, my dear," said Aerich. "But the observation is useless."

Illista walked behind the table where Tazendra lay, drew out a large, curved knife, and said, "On my word, my dear, release the spells, and I will perform the surgery we discussed."

"I am ready," said Grita, drawing a poniard.

Aerich, at this moment, stepped into the light of the lamps, dressed in his old red blouse and skirt, vambraces gleaming, wrists crossed over his chest, holding his sword in one hand, poniard in the other. He was looking, however, not at Tazendra, but at the immense, impenetrable darkness that rose directly before him.

"Aerich, don't!" said Tazendra.

"Now," said Illista coolly.

Grita released the spell.

For an instant, Tazendra was free. She started to rise, but Illista struck her hard in the chest with the butt end of the knife—Tazendra's head struck the table, and Illista quickly grasped her ear, holding it out to be removed. Tazendra coughed.

Mica stood up, picked up the bar-stool upon which he had been sitting, and struck Illista in the face.

Grita snarled and stabbed Mica in the back with such force that the point of her weapon actually emerged from his chest.

"Mica!" cried Tazendra.

The faithful Mica stood very still, an expression of surprise on his face, as blood began to trickle from his lips.

"They killed Srahi," he observed.

As this happened, Grita reached into the area of darkness with her left hand, and, with her right, she made a gesture, and immediately a sort of glow began to emerge from her skin, and, at the same time, from Illista's. Grita then gestured at Aerich, who, before he could move, was picked up and thrown against a wall of the cave.

Tazendra rolled off the table and onto her feet, stumbled, fell to her knees, and rose again even as Illista recovered from the blow struck by the brave Mica—we should add that this blow had cut her face so that she was bleeding, and was, moreover, forced to spit out two or three teeth.

Aerich shook his head and made an effort to rise, but Grita, still with one hand in the darkness, reached out at him, slowing drawing her hand into a fist. Aerich threw his head back and his mouth opened as he struggled vainly to breathe. "Do you see, Dzurlord?" cried Grita. "I am killing your friend."

Illista, who had left her knife in Mica's back, drew a sword as the Teckla, moaning softly, fell face-forward onto the ground.

And, once more, there came a chime from the front of the cave.

Grita frowned and looked toward the mouth of the cave, the spell she had been casting momentarily relaxed, and Aerich took in a great lungful of air.

"Who are you?" said Grita.

"I am the Viscount of Adrilankha," said Piro coolly. "And these are my friends. This gentleman and that lady are friends of my father. What are you doing to them?"

"Killing them," said Grita.

"I believe," said Piro, "that I will attempt to stop you."

"Good luck," said Grita. As she spoke, she made a certain gesture, and a sound not unlike that made by the striking of a large gong echoed throughout the cave. "You may now have the honor of contending with the troops I have just summoned. Should you survive them, you are welcome to do your best against us."

"May I inquire about that strange glow the two of you seem to be emitting?"

"Why? Don't you think it fetching?"

"Oh, certainly."

Grita shrugged. "Well then."

Piro turned to those behind him, and said, "Spread out. It seems we are about to be attacked."

"So much the better," said Kytraan, gripping his sword. "But I would suggest we attack first."

"An excellent notion, my friend," said Piro. "Let us do so at once."

Illista, who, we should say, was not exceptionally skilled as a fighter, swung her sword at Tazendra, who easily ducked beneath it. The Dzurlord then stepped back, reached down, and removed the poniard from Mica's back. The Teckla moaned softly. Tazendra continued her motion and, ducking under another wild swing by Illista, struck with the poniard at the Phoenix's chest with tremendous force, all of her anger adding to her own natural strength.

Rather than penetrating, however, the blade snapped off near the hilt.

Grita pointed her finger at Kytraan, who gave a strangled cry as his head, neatly severed by some invisible force, fell from his shoulders.

"I hope," observed Illista, "that this answers the question you have asked about the peculiar glow we are emitting. You can no longer harm us."

Chapter the Ninety-Third

How Tsanaali Attempted To Take the Orb

No doubt the reader is, by now, curious about what might have become of Tsanaali, whom we last saw about to enter the presence of Her Majesty in an effort to take the Orb itself. Be assured that it was not our intention to hold the reader in needless suspense, which we will prove by answering this question at once.

Khaavren had been in the covered terrace, sitting quietly in a corner having a conversation with Pel, when he suddenly heard Zerika cry out softly. Soft as it was, such a sound from the Empress at once caused the captain to come to full alert; he fairly dashed over to her. "Your Majesty, what is it?"

The Empress looked at him with an expression in which alarm mixed with confusion. "The Orb," she said.

Khaavren had been about to ask what about the Orb caused her alarm, when he realized that, instead of circling her head and glowing with some color that gave a chromatic representation of her spirits at the moment, it was a dull black, and lying in her hands.

We should explain that, in fact, the Orb was not completely inert: no one has reported, during this time, becoming aware of a disconnection to it, as thousands upon thousands reported at the moment of Adron's Disaster. Yet, it was clear at once that something was very seriously wrong with it.

"Your Majesty," said Khaavren, "what can cause such a thing?"

"I have not the least idea in the world," said the Empress, in a tone that indicated a laudable if not entirely successful attempt to remain cool.

At this moment, Pel approached them and bowed. "Your Majesty—"

"What is it?" said the Empress, a hint of desperation tinge-ing her voice.

"I do not know what is causing this, but, I wish to make two observations."

"Very well, I will listen to whatever you have to say."

"First, you know that we have been looking for the Pre-tender to strike from an unexpected direction, as he cannot possibly win a purely military action. I make no doubt that this is, at the least, part of his plan."

"Very well. Next?"

"Next, unless I am mistaken, I heard sounds in the corridor that I like not at all, wherefore I would suggest that Your Majesty take herself and the Orb into that corner, and that my friend Khaavren draw that sword which has served the Em-pire for so long, and we be prepared to do what we must."

These words were no sooner out of the Yendi's mouth than acted upon, both by the Empress and by the captain.

"They can come in by the door, or by the glass," said Khaavren. "But if they break the glass, we shall hear them."

"And so?" said Pel.

"Let us position ourselves by the door."

"Very good," said Pel. "But—"

"Yes?"

"Have you a spare sword?"

"Blood of the Horse! You haven't a sword?"

"In my apartments, but, you perceive, that will be of no help now."

"That is true. Here is my poniard. My left hand still has some weakness, so it does me no good in any case."

"Very good. I will have a sword presently."

"Of that, I have no doubt."

"Ah. Here they are."

"We can hold them for a long time at this door."

"Perhaps."

The first one through the door received the edge of Khaavren's sword across his face, the second took Pel's poniard in his stomach, at which time Pel stepped out from beside the door, took the sword from his hand, and kicked him backward into his companions.

"That's two of them," observed Khaavren.

"I wonder how many of them there are."

"Let us count them as we go."

"Very well."

"Three," said Khaavren, as he gave the next a full-extension lunge, as pretty as if it were out of a training manual, striking his enemy in her throat.

Pel spun his sword in a tight circle parallel to his body which ended scoring a long cut down the face and body of one, then cutting up at another who was attempting to squeeze to his side. "Four and five," he observed.

As it happened, the one who had sustained the long cut was not badly hurt, a fact which Khaavren pointed out by saying, "*Now* it is five, my friend," as he lowered point to run him through the thigh.

"Very well," said Pel. "I accept that."

"Apropos, how is the weapon?"

"Serviceable," said Pel laconically, after which he added, "Six," as he used an elegant move which involved a thrust that both deflected his enemy's blade and, at the same time, ran her through the shoulder.

"You must teach me that one," said Khaavren.

"I should be more than happy to, as soon as this is over."

"So much the better," said Khaavren, adding "Seven" an instant before Pel said, "Eight," as they both struck in the same manner at nearly the same time. Their blades pierced the hearts of the two soldiers in front of them so they both fell to the ground as dead masses, striking at very nearly the same instant, although one was considerably heavier than the other, introducing certain interesting questions concerning the physical properties of falling objects.

Whatever the theoretical issues involved in falling objects, the practical result of the falling of these bodies was that it interfered with those attempting to enter the room. This interference was quickly translated into an advantage for Khaavren, who held to the principle that a missed opportunity in combat was identical to giving an enemy a second chance, which, in turn, was the same as if there were a second enemy. With this principle firmly in mind, he made certain that each hesitation, stumble, or slip by an enemy was greeted by as good a thrust or cut as he could manage, with the result that, in seconds, three more of the enemy were "bit by the steel snake," as the saying is.

Pel, who was never at any time troubled about taking any advantage that might be offered in a skirmish, was even more effective: he went for his opponent's legs, and in the drawing of a breath, four more of them were on the ground, unable to rise.

At this point, however, one of the enemy, in a daring maneuver, made a leap over the wounded or dying bodies on the ground, rolled, came to his feet, and turned around, striking quickly and then recovering into good guard position.

"One of them is behind us," observed Khaavren, who was, at this moment, dueling with next soldier who, standing on the bodies of his friends, was attempting to pass the doorway.

"The observation is useless," said Pel. "He has already cut me with his stick."

"No badly, I hope."

"A sting in the left shoulder, nothing more."

"Very good."

"Apropos, he's mine," said Pel.

"If you like," said Khaavren.

Pel faced the soldier, saluted him, and said, "Hello, Lieutenant. I hope seeing me is as agreeable for you as seeing you is for me."

Tsanaali, whose blade did not move an inch as he waited for the engagement to begin, said, "Well, my dear Duke, that I had not expected to have the honor of your company only increases the pleasure with which I greet you. Is it not always so with unexpected guests?"

"Nearly," said Pel. "But come, my dear Lieutenant. Must I beg you to engage with me?"

"Not at all," said Tsanaali, who did not need to have such a compliment paid to him twice. He feinted a lunge for Pel's body, then executed a furious cut at the Yendi's head; a cut which the Yendi parried with a quick motion of his wrist, after which he replied by lunging at the lieutenant's torso with such speed that the officer was saved only by twisting his body at the last instant.

"Come," said Pel, "was that close enough?"

"Nearly," said Tsanaali, and attempted the same head-cut again, only this time dropping the point and striking for Pel's side, an attack that Pel parried easily enough by dropping the point of his own blade, and then, with a wrongwise twist of his wrist, he brought the Dragonlord's weapon out of line, after which Pel simply straightened his arm, running the point directly through Tsanaali's heart.

"That was closer," observed the Yendi.

"I believe it was close enough to kill me," said Tsanaali.

"I think you are right," said Pel, as the lieutenant, dropping his sword, fell to the ground. "Unfortunately, you have caused me to lose count."

The lieutenant, being quite dead, did not reply.

This contest, as it happened, had left Khaavren facing two of the enemy. As was his custom under such circumstances, Khaavren had given ground slowly, parrying widely and striking for the sides of his enemies in an effort to prevent them from separating. This technique was sufficiently successful as to delay them until Pel was able to rejoin him, at which point, seeing that their commander was dead, and that more than half of their number were either wounded or dying, they became demoralized, and, instead of attacking, or even defending themselves, at once turned and, in a body, fled the way they had come.

Khaavren followed them out after calling to Pel to remain behind and guard Her Majesty. In the antechamber Khaavren saw that Sergeant, the son of his old comrade, Sergeant, had been killed by a thrust through his heart before even having time to draw his sword. Khaavren reached down and gently shut the guardsman's eyes.

He continued down the corridor, observing the others who had died: Nyla, Segure, Baan, and Cendra. He refused to let himself grieve over them, however, reminding himself that he still had work to do.

He then carried out a brief but thorough inspection, finding (though he had expected it) the others of his guardsmen who had been struck down outside of the doors. This inspection assured him that the threat, at least for now, was over. Then he returned to the covered terrace. Noting that he was still holding his bloody sword, he knelt down and carefully wiped it clean on Tsanaali's body, after which he sheathed it and looked at the wounded.

Pel, after disarming the prisoners, had been coolly guarding them as they lay, some of them moaning in pain, others silent either from fortitude or weakness.

"Are you all right, Pel?"

"Scarcely a scratch, good Khaavren. And yourself?"

"Nothing at all. There should be an errand-runner or two around somewhere; do you think you can find one?"

"Assuredly."

Khaavren took over watching the prisoners while Pel left to find a runner. That his mission was successful was proven by the arrival of a runner in two minutes, who presented himself to Khaavren respectfully.

"Find the Warlord. My compliments, and inform her that there has been an attack on the Orb. All is well, Her Majesty is safe, but I wish for a company to guard the Manor, and another company to take charge of the prisoners. Do you understand?"

"Your Lordship may judge: Compliments to the Warlord, an attack on the Orb, Her Majesty is well, two companies to be sent."

"That is it. On your way now."

"Yes, my lord."

Pel returned and took over the guard duty, freeing Khaavren to address Her Majesty. He bowed to her and said,

"For the moment, we are secure. I have sent a messenger for a troop to replace my guards."

Zerika, still holding the lifeless Orb, appeared rather pale as she nodded.

"Is Your Majesty all right?" asked Khaavren.

"Yes, Captain. But I had never before been in danger when I was unable to do anything about it, but simply had to watch. I must say, I don't care for it."

"I understand, Your Majesty."

"Your guards," she said suddenly. "What of them?"

"Dead," said Khaavren. "All of those who were on duty were killed."

Zerika bowed her head. "For me," she said softly.

"For the Orb," corrected Khaavren gently.

"Well, yes, that is true."

"It was a treacherous attack," said Khaavren.

"No, it was an act of war," said the Empress. "With as much—or as little—justification as the Pretender has for engaging in this contest."

Khaavren bowed. "As Your Majesty says."

Zerika looked down at the Orb in her hands. "I wonder," she murmured.

"Your Majesty?"

"I wonder what could do this to the Orb."

"For my part," said Pel, "I wonder how much worse things will get before they get better."

"I wonder that as well," said the Empress.

"And I," said Khaavren, "wonder how long until the additional companies come for the prisoners. Because, until they do—"

"Well?"

"There is no point in getting the maid to come in here and clean the blood off my floor."

Chapter the Ninety-Fourth

How the Battle of Adrilankha Was Proceeding up to This Point

In order to understand subsequent developments, it is now necessary for the author to make a brief survey of how matters stood, over-all, in that bloody and significant military engagement that became known afterwards as the Battle of Adrilankha. We must say that, as matters now stood (it being very nearly the hour of noon in Adrilankha), the death of Tsanaali and the failure of his mission, though certainly a severe blow to Kâna, was the only notable setback he had faced hitherto.

The Warlock made continual efforts to use his abilities to summon from the jungles west of town various beasts (of which, just as to-day, there is no shortage) to fall upon the enemy, but thanks to the intervention of the god known as Tri'nagore, he could achieve no results. Yet he remained at his post, sitting behind the command tent within the fortress on the Hartre Pike, ignoring the sounds of mayhem and the feverish activity all around him, and did not falter in his attempts.

As near as we can determine, it was at this moment that the gods first became aware of the rôle played by this renegade deity, and at once launched upon a furious debate as to the best way to counter it. We shall not take up the reader's time with this debate, as, in fact, it continued for some hours or days or perhaps weeks (it is, as the reader may recall, difficult to understand the flow of time in the Halls of Judgment) past when the matter had become moot. In other words, as is so often the case with immensely powerful individuals weighed down by the sense of their own responsibility, they did nothing but confer until the time for action was well past.

On Lower Kieron Road and on the Hartre Pike, the Imperial forces, while able to hold their positions, were not having an easy time of it. We are forced to admit that both of Kâna's young generals, Brawre and Izak, were proving their abilities as tacticians: Having the initiative, both of them, but most especially Izak, used the pieces of their game with undeniable skill—sending pikemen against cavalry, cavalry against spear phalanxes, spear phalanxes against infantry, infantry regiments against javelin throwers, and javelin throwers against pikemen. Sethra the Younger, we should add, displayed no small skill herself in this game of matching regiment against regiment, but, as she was on the defensive, it was more difficult for her to break off a particular skirmish to substitute a particular unit. Indeed, on the Hartre Pike in particular, it has been asserted by several officers that, were it not for the constant and well-aimed barrage of javelins from the two forts, as well as the well-placed obstructions on the road, there would unquestionably have been a breakthrough.

Sethra the Younger's difficulties were increased by the fact that Adrilankha is not surrounded by a wall such as existed in the old Dragaera City: while those two roads were the sites of the most intense combat, nevertheless she could never forget that the enemy was capable of sending units to either side in order to come into the city from some small roadway or side-street and thus striking the defenders from the rear, or making an assault on Whitecrest Manor itself. As much as she could, she used her scarce cavalry regiments to defend against this possibility, but at times she would receive reports of such an attempt being made, find she had no cavalry to send, and so would have to quickly call up another unit to meet the threat. At times, the threat would turn out not to be real, having been either an error on the part of some scout, or a feint from one of the enemy generals (how often each of these happened is still debated by military historians), but this added to her difficulties.

Another factor that caused "the command headache" for Sethra the Younger was the corps of adepts. Although it is demonstrably untrue, in spite of the remarks of certain historians, that Sethra Lavode had counted on the adepts for all of her communication, it is nevertheless the case that, when sorcerous communication became "inoperative" (as the Sorceress in Green expressed it), a certain confusion and delay was involved in returning to the system of errand-runners—a confusion and delay that had no effect on Kâna's forces, as they had never counted on any other means of communication.

As it was, the defenders held fast through the first hour after noon, though afterwards there was no shortage of veteran soldiers to assert that it had been among the most difficult of battles in which they had ever been engaged, a report that is confirmed by not only the number of casualties, but, even more, by the number of deaths that occurred when wounded soldiers were trampled by those on both sides fighting over the same ground. In some places, it has been said, entire units fought on a carpet of bodies, their feet never actually touching the road. Whether this is literally true or an exaggeration, it nevertheless gives an idea of the intensity of the combat for the main entrances to the city. It is said that the bloodstains on the Hartre Pike, especially in the "Brutal Curve" below the fort, could still be seen half a year after the battle.

The bridges over the Adrilankha River presented a different sort of problem. While, thanks to Khaavren's explanation, the defenders had prepared themselves to hold these bridges, the plan to destroy them had to be abandoned when sorcery failed. While this was certainly to the advantage of the citizens of proud Adrilankha after the battle, at the time it was a source of considerable vexation to Berigner, who was in charge of these defenses. The problem became worse when Berigner himself was wounded by a magnificently thrown javelin, that had to fly very nearly the length of the Iron Bridge in order to find him, striking him in the upper chest and laying him out on the ground. He had to be brought to the field hospital that had been established in Round Park, and was thus out of the battle.

Command devolved on a certain Taasra, who at once sent a message to Sethra the Younger (although she thought she was sending it to Sethra Lavode) explaining the perilous situation on that bridge, as well as passing on reports she had received of heavy fighting on the Two Pennies Bridge, farther upriver. Upon receiving these messages, Sethra the Younger made the courageous decision to move the remainder of the force excepting only a token regiment away from Northgate Road (which had still not sustained an attack) to reinforce the bridges.

In the end, the defense of the bridges was successful for several reasons: First, the defense of a bridge, more than nearly any other tactical situation, gives all of the advantages to the defenders, owing to the relatively narrow space in which the combat occurs. Next, because of Beringer's skillful placement of his defending units, augmented by Taasra's continuing efforts (Taasra afterwards received a Imperial barony for her efforts).

The third factor was Daro, the Countess of Whitecrest, who left her manor in the fourteenth hour of the morning and spent the day riding from bridge to bridge. Many of the defenders of these bridges have mentioned, in letters and memoirs, seeing her and being inspired by her stern countenance, her exhortations, and her mere presence (although, to be sure, many of these refer to her as a Lyorn, there can be no question of who was meant). At one point, she herself led a countercharge of a pike regiment over the Iron Bridge against a spear phalanx (or something very like it) of determined Islanders. The reader who is unfamiliar with infantry tactics should be the more impressed as it is not in the nature of pikemen to charge; yet the Countess picked the first regiment she saw and went forward. In this attack, Daro sustained a minor wound on her left hand, but not only was the charge successful, her example did so much to inspire the defenders and depress the spirits of the attackers that for the rest of the day, that bridge was never seriously threatened.

In short, as we have had the honor to say, the bridges were held. The damage to South Adrilankha committed by the Islanders (most of it, to be sure, being done during their retreat) has never been accurately stated, but is certainly less than what would have been done had they successfully crossed the bridges and established themselves. To say the least, any questions about the loyalty of the Countess's family that might have remained after the Whitecrest Uprising were on this day put to rest for-ever.

The Warlord herself, after turning command of the battle over to Sethra the Younger, was concerned, above all, with the location of the Jenoine which she was convinced had appeared on the world. For this reason, she had called to herself the Necromancer, who, being found, reported to her promptly.

"Well?" said Sethra.

The Necromancer bowed.

"Are you aware," said Sethra, "that a Jenoine has gained access to our world?"

"Partial access," corrected the Necromancer.

"How, partial?"

"It has not fully manifested. It has an opening sufficient to attack the Orb, and is attempting, by doing so, to make an opening to manifest fully."

"Well, but where is it?"

"I have, hitherto, been unable to determine this."

"You have been trying?"

The Necromancer bowed an assent. "The forces that prevent such an entry—that is to say, the shields put in place by the gods to keep the Jenoine from coming to our world—are still in place."

"They are still in place? But then, how can it have manifested?"

"Someone has given it access by finding one of those locations where the boundaries between worlds are flawed."

Sethra frowned. "Yes. While I have not studied necromancy as you have, I have heard of such places. But, how many of them are there?"

"A few hundreds, I would think."

"A few hundreds? But then, to find this Jenoine could take days!"

"Years," corrected the Necromancer. "Each place must be first discovered, and then investigated. You perceive, these steps take considerable time."

"How many have you found hitherto?"

"Three."

"Three?"

The Necromancer signified that this was correct.

Sethra frowned and reflected. After a moment, she said, "I have never come across such a place."

"They are difficult to identify if found, even for one skilled in necromancy, and, therefore, even more difficult to find if the location is not known."

"Well then, how could our enemies have found it?"

The Necromancer shrugged. "Luck, perhaps."

The Enchantress shook her head. "You perceive, I am suspicious of anything that smells of chance when there is an elaborate conspiracy involved."

The Necromancer shrugged again.

"How else could they have found it?" demanded Sethra.

The Necromancer appeared to reflect, at last saying, "Certain demons know of such places."

"And yet, my lady, we have seen no evidence that they have summoned a demon."

"That is true."

"Well then, what of the gods?"

"Well, certainly the gods would know all, or at any rate, most of the paths from the Halls of Judgment, and these would all lead to such places."

"How, they would?"

"Without question. You perceive, any naturally occurring route from the world where the Halls are to this world would require such a point, and any such paths created by the gods would cause one to occur." We trust that the reader has at least some passing familiarity, by legend if nothing else (and, in truth, we have little enough beyond legend to work with),

with the Jenoine—those immensely powerful beings who once ruled our world, and against whom it could be said that our entire existence as a people is a struggle.

Sethra frowned, still thinking. "When Zerika emerged with the Orb after her journey to the Halls of Judgment, she must, then, have arrived at such a place."

The Necromancer bowed her agreement with this assessment.

"So that," continued Sethra, "should the enemy know, or be able to discover, where Zerika emerged into our world, they would know that this place must necessarily be a place where a Jenoine could manifest?"

"Yes," said the Necromancer laconically.

"Do you ride?" asked Sethra.

"After a fashion."

"Then let us call for a pair of horses, and, when they are delivered, mount up at once."

"Very well."

In twenty minutes, Sethra Lavode had arrived at Whitecrest Manor (some five minutes ahead of the Necromancer), and, two minutes later, she entered the covered terrace, where she observed a bloody floor as well as Khaavren and Pel and several wounded and moaning prisoners.

"What has happened?" cried Sethra.

"An attempt to take the Orb," said Khaavren.

"It was thwarted," added Pel.

Sethra looked at Her Majesty and said, "The Orb?"

"It is, as you can see, lifeless. I cannot think why."

"As to why," said Sethra, "I know well enough, and it is for that reason I am here."

Zerika nodded and held it out, as if she expected the Enchantress to take it and perform some sort of magic upon it. But Sethra shook her head, saying, "Your Majesty, it is not the Orb I require, but, rather, information."

"Whatever I know is at your disposal. But tell me, what is causing this?"

"Our enemies have managed to permit a Jenoine to manifest, and the Jenoine is attacking the Orb."

"The Gods!" cried Zerika. "Is it true?"

"I take my oath on it."

Zerika's teeth clenched and her eyes narrowed. "That they would do such a thing!"

Khaavren, in a tone of irony, murmured something under his breath about fair uses of war, but, as it was inaudible, it has not come down to us, and, moreover, Zerika either didn't hear it or ignored it. At this point, the Necromancer entered the room and placed herself next to Sethra.

"Where is this Jenoine?" demanded the Empress.

"That is what I must learn from you," said Sethra.

"Apropos," said the Necromancer.

"Well?"

"Once we learn, how are we to get there?"

"One problem at a time," said the Enchantress, grasping the hilt of the dagger at her side. Then she turned to Zerika and said, "Your Majesty, tell me, with as much precision as you can, and as laconically as possible (for you perceive we are in a hurry), where it was that you emerged from the Halls of Judgment."

"Step over to this map," said the Empress.

As they walked, Sethra said, "Once we have found the location, you will be able to create a necromantic gate, will you not?"

As if it were the matter of greatest unconcern, the Necromancer said, "So long as that god has manifested in the world, I am completely helpless."

"Now that," observed Sethra Lavode, "is unfortunate."

Chapter the Ninety-Fifth

How Morrolan Battled a God

When we last saw Morrolan, he was slowly advancing through a deserted street upon an icon of Tri'nagore. In the street were the bodies of those he had cut down, and around him were others of their band, fleeing with the sort of terror that can only be inspired by such a weapon as that wielded by Morrolan.

He did not hesitate for an instant. The thought of following those who attempted to escape did not so much as cross his mind. Instead he went directly to the icon that occupied a place of honor in the center of the village and spat upon it. Then, sheathing his sword and unbuttoning his breeches, he made certain, in a way that was as old as Eastern tradition itself, that no man or god could have the least doubt about his feelings toward Tri'nagore. While we must beg the reader's pardon for introducing this sort of crudeness, we must insist that, not only is it the case that Morrolan performed the act to which we have alluded, but, as we have indicated, this is the sort of defilement in which the crass Easterner is wont to indulge when determined to insult a god. Having stated that it occurred, however, we shall hasten on to other matters, as we would not wish to injure the reader's sensibilities by dwelling on such matters for an instant longer than is strictly required by our duty as historian.

The response was so quick that Morrolan was very nearly forced to go into battle with his breeches open. There was a shimmering in the air, similar to what might be seen upon a hot summer's day, and, as Morrolan drew his sword once more, Tri'nagore appeared next to the icon.

In appearance, that one of the Lords of Judgment whose name has come down to us as Tristangrascalaticrunagore was, indeed, sufficiently fearsome that he ought to have frightened a thousand Morrolans. In height he measured some thirteen feet, and in breadth he was little less. In spite of the way he has been depicted in certain lurid illustrated tales, he had, in fact, only two arms, and two legs, and no tail—yet what he did have for a form was sufficiently squat, ugly, and powerful (he being, in fact, covered in thick hide of an appalling orange color) that those who illustrate such tales as we have referred to may nearly be forgiven their liberties.

It was growing dark at this moment, not because it was near to the end of the day, but because there were now heavy black clouds overhead. In addition, it had become quite cold, though Morrolan was only dimly aware of these things. Moreover, there was a substantial breeze as well as a hint of thunder that may have been caused by the god's appearance, as it is known that certain of the deities announce their presence by dramatic shifts in the weather. Morrolan was unaware of this, as well.

He approached the god as he might have approached a subordinate who required to be reminded of his duty—that is, with a firm step and a fire in his eye, and, not the least hint of fear. The god himself, we should add, was in what might be considered an irate state of mind; there is a certain dignity that comes with deification, and this dignity does not take well to the defiling of one's icon—especially by a single mortal. Both the action and the implied arrogance behind it were not calculated to put this god into any sort of mood for conversation, but, rather, to fill him with the intention of grasping this lout about the middle, or perhaps by the throat, and squeezing him, slowly, so that he would have time to regret his insolence before he expired.

These plans were made, however, without first having asked Morrolan if he approved them, and, in fact, the Dragonlord did not; indeed, the notion of being touched by Tri'nagore, much less grasped, squeezed, and ultimately killed, was understandably repugnant to the Count of Southmoor, who responded by ducking under the outstretched hands and driving his sword, point first, into his enemy's stomach—a target, we ought to say, that was hard to miss. Nevertheless, his first blow did not land. Not because of any especial speed or quickness on the part of the god, but, rather, because his essential character, being at once both of the world and not of it, made it impossible for any normal weapon to touch him, and particularly difficult for even Morrolan's black wand to do so; the weapon slipped past Tri'nagore by the smallest of margins.

Whether Tri'nagore was aware of his danger even now, we cannot know; his response, however, was to make another effort to grasp Morrolan. The Dragonlord, thrown slightly off balance by his attack, very nearly fell into the god's clutches, but a twist at the last instant, so to speak, saved him. He let his momentum carry him forward, recovered his balance, raised his sword, and reflected.

"Come now," he said to himself. "It seems that this irritating—being—has a means of avoiding the point of my sword. Considering this, the prudent course might require me to break off the engagement at once, but there are some flaws in this plan. For one I do not think it will be possible, for he seems tolerably put out. And, for another, well, I have never had an especially prudent character.

"So then," he continued, "the solution must be to find a way to convince my weapon to bite, because, well, with sorcery having unaccountably failed, I have no other means of inflicting injury on him. But then, how am I to do so? It is a shame that, with sorcery ineffective, I cannot reach Arra, because it is very possible, even likely, that a little help from my Circle would be all that would be required. He may be able to suppress the Warlock's use of witchcraft, but to do so with the number of witches I have available to me, well, that would be more difficult.

"Well, and here he comes again. That was uncomfortably close for both of us—he nearly had me, and, for my part, I should have been able to slice of one of his hands if my weapon had not veered away from him. It is insupportable. My black wand, evidently, feels the same way—I can sense its annoyance. Steady there, Blackwand, I am looking for a means now to permit you to bite, and, with the Favor, I may even discover one.

"And yet, let us consider. Is sorcery strictly necessary for me to communicate with Arra? It seems to me that when I link my powers with those in the Circle, we are doing something that is closely akin to sorcerous communication, and we are certainly not using sorcery to accomplish it—at least, we were engaging in this communion not only before I had even learned that there was such a thing as sorcery, but before the return of the Orb that permits it to function.

"And so, with this in mind, might it be possible to make contact with Arra? Well, if I can manage to avoid this being again—that was close—I can think of no good reason not to make the attempt."

Having reached this conclusion, Morrolan wasted no time in putting it to the test. He thought back to those occasions, especially in the first days of his association with Arra in Blackchapel, when he had joined the psychic powers to hers, and tried to remember how it had felt. Of course, it is different when only one party, instead of both together, is attempting to forge such a chain, and, moreover, the level of connection required for actual communication is much higher than what is required for the sharing or transfer of psychic energy. The difficulty was increased, as well, by the fact that Morrolan was required constantly to dodge efforts by Tri'nagore to get Morrolan in his clutches.

Tri'nagore did not confine himself to purely physical attacks either, but, on at least two occasions, struck at the Dragonlord with enchantments which, although he never learned their precise nature, would certainly have done him no good had not Blackwand, apparently acting on its own, deflected and absorbed the forces directed at him.

In the midst of this, Morrolan realized that he was, at it were, hearing Arra's voice in the back of his head, almost as if she were behind him. He could even make out words now and then—"My lord, what is it you wish?" or something very like that.

While still concentrating on his enemy—that is, on staying out of his enemy's grasp—he managed to formulate thoughts to Arra, first asking if she could understand him, and then, when assured that she could, explaining in two words what he wished.

Arra, for her part, understood immediately that there was no question of joking, and said that she would at once gather together a Circle, leaving alone only those needed to keep Castle Black from falling, and cast a spell of finding and striking on his blade.

Twice more Morrolan had to dodge and twist to stay clear of the god, who began to show signs of annoyance and frustration, and once more the energy of some sort of deadly spell came toward him, only to be deflected by Blackwand. An instant later, Morrolan felt a peculiar sensation come over him, as if, as he later explained it, "there was a tingling running up and down my arms, my feet seemed to grow into the ground, as if I were a plant or a tree and they my roots, and, at the same time, it felt as if I were so light upon my feet that I could have leapt twenty feet in the air without effort. Also, it seemed that my vision became both sharper and more narrow."

That is, according to his own testimony, how the spell affected Morrolan. For its effects outside of his direct sensations, we can only observe that, the next time the god came at him in an effort to strike or grasp him, Morrolan stepped forward and, almost without effort, drove Blackwand deep into his vitals.

If we have given the impression that Tri'nagore's strength was, exclusively or above all, physical, we must apologize. While there is no precise record indicating which magical arts he embodied, what forces he had access to, and the nature of his existence in those regions not subject to our mundane understanding, there is no doubt that they were formidable. Yet, equally, there is no doubt that, once Morrolan's extraordinary sword had entered his corporeal body, none of these things made the least difference in the world.

It has been said that Tri'nagore's dying cry could be heard a hundred miles away. It is certainly the case that it was heard in Blackchapel, and there they wondered extremely. As far as

Morrolan was concerned, he was never able to determine if it was the astonishing blast of sound, the physical death throes of the gargantuan embodiment of the god, or some magical or psychic outpouring caused by Tri'nagore's expulsion from the world; but, for whatever reason, as the god lost for-ever his ability to manifest in our plane of existence, Morrolan fell senseless to the ground.

When he awoke again it was to the peculiar sensation of hot breath in his ear—breath that, as his wits came back, proved to be from the horse, Huzay. Morrolan patted his nose, then slowly pulled himself to his feet and looked around. On reflection, he came to the conclusion that they had made an attempt upon him while he was oblivious, and that, somehow, his sword had protected him. While there was not the least remaining trace of the god, there were, immediately around him, three bodies that he could not account for, because they had not been there while he fought the god, and he had no memory of anything that happened afterwards. Moreover, the idol he had desecrated was now, unaccountably, gone—or rather, destroyed, as he noticed what could only be pieces of it spreading out in a large circle from where it had once stood.

"Well now," he murmured. "There is something to be said for this, indeed."

He carefully cleaned the blade on the clothing of the nearest corpse, sheathed it, and patted the neck of his horse, considering what he had just been through. These reflections continued for some few moments, until, as he happened to be looking around, he found himself grimacing from the bright light high in the sky to the west.

"It is after noon!" he cried suddenly. "Why, they are giving a battle to-day, and, well, they have certainly started without me. In fact, no doubt it will all be over before I can get there.

"It is terribly vexing," he told the horse.

He frowned. "I wonder how long it will be until I can teleport again."

He patted the horse once more, and, addressing it, he added, "I wonder how you will feel about being teleported?"

Chapter the Ninety-Sixth

How Piro and His Band Attempted to Rescue Tazendra and Aerich

It was shortly after the hour of noon, on the third day of the Month of the Jhegaala in the second year of the Reign of Her Majesty Zerika the Fourth.

In Adrilankha there was battle on two of the roads and four of the bridges, where soldiers clashed, screamed, fought, and died. The Warlock, Brimford, continued attempting to make his particular brand of magic work for the glory of the Empire and the safety of the woman he loved, who happened to also be the Empress.

In Whitecrest Manor there were bodies strewn from the front gate to the covered terrace, and in that terrace the wounded lay with the dead, while Sethra Lavode fingered her dagger, which was called Iceflame, studied a map, and consulted with the Necromancer about such arcane matters as moving out of one world to another, in order to return to the first in a different place. Even as this was happening, a company of soldiers was being instructed by Khaavren on the guarding of Her Majesty, and another waited for instructions to lead away the prisoners.

Far away, in the East, Morrolan mounted his horse and waited until the Orb should begin to function again so that he could teleport himself back to Castle Black.

And in a cave on South Mountain, Mica and Kytraan lay dead, the one stabbed in the back, the other decapitated by sorcery. Tazendra held nothing in her hand but the hilt of a knife, which she quickly discarded; Aerich was slowly rising, still slightly stunned, from where he had been thrown against the wall of the cave. Piro stood at the mouth of the cave with Ibronka on one side and the trapper Tsira in the other, while behind Ibronka was Iatha, still staring at Kytraan's headless body. Röaana, Ritt, and Belly pressed forward, with Lar and Clari hesitantly bringing up the rear.

At the time it happened, the death of Kytraan did not seem real to Piro. The astonishment of seeing Tazendra and Aerich, and then the strange darkness that nearly filled the middle portion of the cave, took up nearly all of his attention, concentration, and emotion. Moreover, his training had come, first, from Khaavren, and next from the circumstances of surviving as a highwayman, and so it was instilled in him that under any circumstances, the threat must be addressed first before any emotion, whether happy or otherwise, can be permitted its expression.

He therefore turned to face his enemies, only to hear, from behind him, two unexpected sounds: the first was a sort of yell or cry from Clari, and the next was the now-familiar sound of a cast-iron cooking pan striking flush and crushing bone.

Piro did not dare take his eyes from his enemies, but he was saved from the necessity of doing so by Belly's remark, "We are attacked from behind."

Piro turned his head only slightly, in order to address the laconic order "Dispatch them" over his shoulder.

"Certainly," said Ritt, though his answer was nearly submerged in the sounds of clashing steel as he and his comrades demonstrated through action that the order, if even necessary, was entirely understood.

This segment of the battle, that is, the attack on Piro's band by the dozen or so soldiers loaned by Kâna, was, as it turned out, over almost before it began. This was thanks, first of all, to brave Lar, who, having learned from poor Mica that an attack by a Teckla is rarely expected, struck the first soldier such a blow in the head that she was not only laid stone dead on the ground, but those around her were momentarily taken aback.

And this moment was sufficient to decide the battle. Belly disarmed his man with a quick flick of his wrist, while Röaana gave hers such a slash across the face that he at once became discouraged and left the engagement. The trapper Tsira, on behalf of her brother, though too far away to engage them directly, turned and quickly threw a knife with such skill that it seemed to weave its way around her friends and strike one of the enemy, point-first in his chest, convincing him that this was not a game in which he cared to participate. Iatha and Ritt wounded four of the enemy in as many seconds, and even Clari contributed by throwing a stone that, while it did no damage to the enemies per se, certainly tended to discourage them.

In short, in less time than it takes to tell it, the attackers were put to flight, leaving the field to Piro's band, our friends safe from attacks from the rear, and Lar staring at the body of the man he had killed, wondering where he had seen him before.

Even as this was occurring, Piro and Ibronka were considering the enemies before them, that is to say, Grita and Illista.

Illista's remark, "You cannot harm us," had certainly shaken the confidence of the young Tiassa, the more-so as it had been proven true the instant before she said it. He observed the faint but unmistakable glow that appeared to either come from or surround Grita and Illista, and observed moreover that Grita had her hand so far into that strange area of darkness that, in fact, the hand was entirely invisible. He concluded that, whatever it was, it was this that accounted for their apparent invulnerability.

Unfortunately, this conclusion did not present him with any means of counteracting it.

Piro, however, had been raised in the traditions of Imperial service, and, moreover, had grown up with the stories of his father and his father's friends facing overwhelming odds as a matter of course; moreover, two of those friends were actually present. He therefore understood instinctively, as it were, that the mere fact of a task's being impossible was no reason not to attempt it. Accordingly, he at once took his sword into his right hand. With his left, he gently pushed Tsira back behind him, from a feeling that, although she had stumbled into it with them, this was not her fight.

For their part, neither Grita nor Illista had the least worries, whoever was present. Though perhaps slightly concerned that they had been invaded by a larger force than they had anticipated, and disappointed that their own forces had been defeated so easily, they were perfectly aware, first, of their invulnerability, owing to the defensive spells that they had been able to reach, if we may use the expression, from the presence or near presence of the Jenoine (from which we may conclude that Piro, in fact, had understood exactly what was occurring); and second to the offensive power at their disposal, coming from the same source. In fact, Grita in particular was not in the least concerned about survival, but, rather, how to make the suffering of her enemies last as long as possible, according to the wisdom she had earlier dispensed regarding the pleasure of revenge.

Consequently, she made a quick determination to begin by destroying Piro's band, one by one, so that Aerich, and, even more, Tazendra, could be made to suffer by observing the death of those attempting to rescue them.

The first one Grita struck was Iatha, whose throat was bloodily ripped out by some unseen force. At nearly the same instant Illista, who faced a now unarmed Tazendra, swung her weapon at the Dzurlord's legs. Tazendra slipped to the side and took a moment to look around for a weapon, even as Iatha fell lifeless to the floor of the cave. Illista advanced and struck again, this time drawing blood from the Dzurlord's left hip. She followed this cut with a thrust to Tazendra's right knee that, although it barely went home, must have caused her no little degree of pain.

"It is easier to fight," observed Illista as she stepped forward and swung her weapon once more, "when one cannot be hurt. It imparts a certain confidence, which, in turn, imparts an agreeable and effective tendency toward aggression. Don't you find it so?"

For once, however, Tazendra was in no mood for banter. We can only speculate on what she felt upon seeing her lackey, and, we must admit, her friend Mica, killed before her eyes; and feeling, as Grita and Illista had wished, the humiliation of friends dying in an attempt to rescue her. At least in this sense, the plan for vengeance was working exactly as they wished it to.

But we must add that another factor was at work: While the warriors of the House of the Dragon are justly known for the rage that often consumes them in battle, still, even the most loyal of Dragonlords will confess that, when a Dzurlord passes beyond the joy of battle, and, instead, is consumed by fury, nothing can compare—Dzurlords have been known to kill friend and foe alike in such circumstances.

And it must additionally be remembered that Tazendra was more than a warrior; she was also a wizard, and one who had been trained by Sethra Lavode, and trained during a time when there was no Orb to draw upon; and though she had no weapons nor even artifacts in hand, she was not helpless.

We cannot state for certain what powers she drew on, nor how she did it (for we confess freely that the arcane science of wizardry is as far beyond our understanding as it is beyond the comprehension of everyone who is not himself a wizard, and we have reason to believe that many of them do not understand it either). But as Illista raised her sword yet again, she gave a cry and dropped it clanging to the floor of the cave—the hilt had become, in seconds, as hot as a burning coal. Tazendra then advanced upon her, the Dzurlord's eyes glowing with such hatred that it would have checked Kieron the Conqueror himself.

While Tazendra could see as well as Piro the luminescence that appeared to radiate from Illista's skin, she could not know the properties of the spell with which the Phoenix was protected by the Jenoine any more than we can know the properties of Tazendra's magic. But, whatever it was, she was determined to test it. Driven by anger, pain, and hatred, she lifted her hands, and a terrible fury of red and amber lights flashed over Illista.

The Phoenix felt the walls of her protection spells threatened, perhaps even crumbling, and screamed "Grita!" in a piercing voice of desperation.

Grita had been, as we have said, setting about to destroy Piro's band. After killing Iatha, she attacked Belly, who fell with a horrid, gaping hole in his chest, his countenance drawn up in a expression of surprise as he pitched forward. Piro and Ibronka lunged at her together, which produced no effect except a smirk as the weapons sheared away from her. She raised her hands once more, this time toward Ibronka, but at this moment, Illista's scream reached her, and, turning, she understood at once the peril her friend faced.

She pointed her right hand, and from it, in quick succession, came three flashes like black spears, all of them striking Tazendra in the back, producing three gaping wounds, each perhaps as big around as a man's fist, with charred edges.

The Dzurlord, however, appeared not to even notice that she had been touched, much less terribly injured, so set was she upon her task. Illista gave an even greater cry than she had an instant before, and, enveloped now in a reddish haze, she appeared almost to collapse in on herself, as if the very protection afforded her by the Jenoine was crushing her. She shook her head in denial, unwilling, perhaps, to believe what was happening, her eyes wide, and, with the terrible sound of cracking bones, she collapsed onto the floor, lifeless, eyes still wide open, her body limp and distorted.

"That's better," said Tazendra coolly, speaking for the first time since Mica's death. She turned around and caught the eye of Aerich, who was even now rising from where he been thrown against the wall, and was staring at Tazendra with something like horror on his countenance. "Do you know," she observed, "I believe I have bested a Jenoine in single combat." After saying this, she smiled sweetly, dropped to her knees, gave a sort of sigh, and pitched forward onto her face.

Aerich, the cool Lyorn, the man whose nerves were as cold

as ice and as hard as iron, who had spent his life learning the discipline of the Lyorn warrior, where each action, even each thought, is predicated upon efficiency, Aerich, we say, cried out, "Tazendra!" in a high wail, and then, his face twisted in a snarl, he threw himself at Grita.

She gestured, and he was once more flung against the wall, but this time his impact was accompanied by the sickening crack of bone breaking. He slid onto the floor, and lay still, breathing shallowly, his eyes blinking, but not otherwise moving.

There was a flash of golden light, and a sound like the crackling of a fire, and Sethra Lavode appeared, followed closely by the Necromancer, Khaavren, and Pel.

Of all of them, it was Röaana who reacted quickly and efficiently. "Enchantress," she said in a voice both cool and piercing, "she is protected by some sort of spell which prevents our weapons from piercing her."

"Ah," said Sethra Lavode. "Yes, I know of such things. And yes, I can see it."

"Well, and?" said Röaana.

Sethra Lavode raised her dagger, pointing it at the darkness that concealed, contained, or, perhaps *was* the Jenoine. The darkness appeared to thicken, and, at the same moment, the glow that had seemed to come from Grita's skin abruptly vanished.

Piro reacted to this even before Grita herself was aware of what had happened: The Tiassa lunged and ran his sword through her body.

"Now, it seems, we can harm you," he observed.

Chapter the Ninety-Seventh

How Sethra Lavode, Not Without A Certain Amount of Assistance From the Necromancer, Engaged The Jenoine in Other-Worldly Battle

Grita's face screwed up in a grimace of hatred, and she uttered the single word "you" as if it were the worst sort of curse. Piro glared back into her eyes, and withdrew his blade with a cruel twist. Grita cried out, and then, blood blossoming on her shirt, her knees buckled. She fell to the ground and did not move again.

"Well struck, Viscount," said Khaavren.

Sethra Lavode, standing before the Jenoine, looked over her shoulder and said, "None of you move. This is my affair."

Between these words, delivered in a tone that assumed obedience, and the shocked dismay of all that had just happened, no one was inclined to argue, with the exception of the Necromancer, who evidently determined that these words were not meant for her. She placed herself next to the Enchantress and directly before the region of darkness that still manifested itself within the cave.

"You attack the Jenoine," said the Necromancer. "I will close the portal."

"Very well," said the Enchantress.

Sethra held out before her the dagger called Iceflame, and, as if it were a tangible enemy, struck the darkness. At the same instant, the Necromancer spread her hands wide, as if to hold a large object, then compressed them, and began to make passes before the darkness in a classic vision of the enchanter at work—indeed, her actions were so like those that are fancifully represented as the manipulations of the sorcerer, and so unlike the actual workings of the sorcerer, that one is tempted to inquire if these fancies have their origins in necromancy, or if, to the left, the demon had spent some time attending the theater, and was making motions that she understood were expected of her. In addition to these actions with her hands, she also began murmuring in a language full of vowels and devoid of stresses—a language that, like the Necromancer herself, was not of our world.

As to what exactly Sethra Lavode did here, we can know little; of what the Necromancer did we can know less. Yet we do know that, at this moment, as the Enchantress engaged directly with the Jenoine, deep in the bowels of Dzur Mountain lights rippled up and down stalagmites; walls changed their colors; sparks fired out from globes; disks, set upon slender rods, began to spin as if from their own power. Miniature lightning storms raced up and down walls, and the entire mountain seemed to move. And, in the middle of it all, sat the enigmatic figure called Tukko, turning his attention from item to artifact, from table to wall, sitting as utterly motionless amid the chaos around him as the Necromancer was animated in the stillness before her.

A great deal must necessarily have happened in a very short time; indeed, the author confesses to a certain embarrassment in being unable to devote the deserved amount of space to what must have been, in some ways, at least as great a battle as that being fought in Adrilankha. Yet, our several witnesses are able to reveal almost nothing of this contest. Sethra Lavode plunged her dagger into the darkness, the Necromancer made arcane gestures before it, and, in almost the drawing of a breath, the peculiar magical field, or pattern of energy, or emanation from another world, had collapsed on itself, dissolved, and vanished.

In that instant, what had been the greatest challenge to the Orb withered away with it. Though not as profound in its effects as the Orb's return that ended the Interregnum, the effects were more sudden.

The warlock Brimford suddenly realized that his art was having an effect as far away the god Tri'nagore was banished. Morrolan was able to teleport to Castle Black. The adepts in the army were able once more to communicate with each other, and messages began to flow one way and another with a rapidity that threatened to overwhelm Sethra the Younger with information.

In Whitecrest Manor, the Orb began to glow, and to circle Her Majesty's head once more. For a moment, she just stared at it, as if it were some strange object she'd never seen before; then a slow smile spread over her countenance.

And an instant later, as various sorcerous effects began to strike at his army, Kâna knew the first hints of despair.

All of this, all of these effects, achieved in a mere instant the result of activity that, on the face of it at least, appeared infinitesimal.

The Enchantress sighed and let her head drop, taking a single deep breath as the only indication of the effort she had expended, then sheathed her dagger; the Necromancer gave no indication that she had made any effort whatsoever.

Khaavren, who had been all but oblivious to the events transpiring only ten or twelve feet from him, knelt down next to Aerich and said, "My friend, are you all right?"

Aerich spoke in a whisper, saying only the word "Tazendra."

"I will attend her," said Pel.

Piro and his friends remained in the background. Ibronka looked at what remained of the brave Dragonlord Kytraan, whose blood was thick upon the cave floor, and at the loyal Iatha, and the steadfast Belly, and, sobbing softly, wrapped her arms around the Viscount, who, in turn, held her close—nor were Piro's eyes devoid of tears. Neither of them, at this time, seemed to find it necessary to say anything. Röaana and Ritt joined them in their silent commiseration. Tsira, who had been pushed back and away by Piro, tactfully removed herself from the cave, where she sat down on the grass outside along with Lar and Clari, looking at the strange artifact that had led them there, and wondering.

Pel spoke from the back of the cave. "Tazendra is dead," he said in a voice quavering with emotion. Khaavren bowed his head. Tears filled Aerich's eyes.

"So I had thought," he murmured.

"So is Illista," said Pel, who returned at that moment and knelt next to Aerich.

"It is past time for that one to be dead," said Khaavren.

"Yes," said Pel.

Khaavren looked over at their other enemy, and said, "I regret to say, Grita is dead as well.

"You regret it?" said Pel.

"Her death was too easy." His voice was heavy with pain and bitterness.

"Judgment," said Aerich, still whispering, "of which vengeance is a sequent, is the rightful province of the Lords of Judgment. And unless one accepts the superstitions of the Easterner, it is their only proper province, therefore it ought to be left to them."

Khaavren chuckled without humor. "I shan't begin an argument with you now, my friend."

"That is right," whispered Aerich.

Khaavren frowned. "We must find a physicker for you, Aerich," he said, "for it seems you must be badly hurt. You have not moved so much as an inch since we came through the Necromancer's gate."

"Useless," said the Lyorn with his accustomed coolness. "My neck is broken."

After an instant of stunned silence, Pel bowed his head, and Khaavren sobbed, making no effort to conceal the emotion which overwhelmed him.

Sethra Lavode knelt down next to the Lyorn and touched his face with her hand, then rose and, addressing the Necromancer, said, "Come, let us return to the city. We may teleport again, and there is still a battle to be won."

Khaavren, his face wet with tears, looked up at the Enchantress and said, "Warlord—"

"No," said the Enchantress. "Remain here with your friends. I will take upon myself the safety of Her Majesty until you return. When you are ready to leave, inform Her Majesty; I will have a teleport ready for you and your friends."

Khaavren bowed his head in silent gratitude. Sethra Lavode approached Piro and squeezed his shoulder; then she and the Necromancer vanished.

Piro disengaged himself from Ibronka, walked over to his father, and clasped his shoulder briefly. The Viscount then saluted the dying Lyorn, a salute which Aerich, as well as he was able, returned with his eyes. Then, as Pel had done to Tsanaali, Piro wiped his blade clean on Grita's clothing and sheathed his sword.

"Come, my friends," said Piro. "Let us take our dead comrades out of this cave, and leave my father and his friends in peace."

Working together, they quickly brought the bodies from the cave, Piro carrying Kytraan's head, and set them on the grass, Piro depositing his gruesome burden next to the truncated corpse that had been his friend. This done, Ibronka again came into the Viscount's arms.

"There is blood on my hands," said Piro.

"It doesn't matter," said Ibronka, softly.

He wrapped his arms around her. "The daylight is too bright," he said. "The breeze too soothing, the temperature is too mild. It is all so wrong."

"I understand," said Ibronka.

"Kytraan . . ."

"Yes."

"We went through so much, and then, to have him killed so casually, so quickly, almost as if he were nothing."

"I know," said Ibronka.

"As if he were nothing," Piro repeated.

"I know," said Ibronka.

Piro looked up suddenly. "Röaana, are you all right?"

Röaana, who wore something of a stunned expression, looked at him and nodded slowly. "Yes, my lord, I am well enough. But—Kytraan, and Iatha, and Belly, and Tazendra, and now, it seems, Aerich."

"I know."

"I am the only one left," said Ritt, suddenly, sounding surprised.

Piro frowned. "The only one?"

"Do you recall that day when we met, when Wadre was leading us?"

"I am unlikely to forget it," said Piro.

"It seems like an age ago, and yet, it has been less than two years."

"That is true."

"And of that band, I am the only one still alive."

"We have come through much together," said Piro. "All of us."

"Yes. And now what?"

Piro shook his head, his eyes coming to rest on Tsira, and on the amulet she still held in her hand, the amulet that had brought them there. He considered the strange twists and turns of fate and wondered if anyone could ever know to what his decisions would lead him. "Now? As to that, I cannot say."

Inside the cave, Khaavren said, "Are you in pain, my friend?"

"No," whispered Aerich. "I feel nothing. I regret that I cannot move, for I should like to press your hand, Khaavren, and yours, Pel."

"Yes," said Khaavren.

"I had never," said Pel, "truly believed that our friendship would ever end."

"Nothing is forever," said Aerich.

"It is one thing to know that, it is another to believe it."

"I understand," whispered the Lyorn. "For my part, well, I regret Tazendra. She had more to do."

"As did you," said Khaavren with a choked voice.

"Oh, I? I have no regrets for myself. I have had a good life, and our friendship has been the best part of it. Except for Tazendra, I have no regrets."

With effort, Khaavren suppressed his sobs, but could not keep the tears from his face.

"There is nothing in life like friendship," said Aerich. "Ours has been good. We have all been lucky."

"Yes," said Pel. "We have been lucky."

Aerich turned his eyes to Pel and he said, "I am glad you know it, my friend."

His eyes closed, and his breathing became more shallow, and for a moment Khaavren thought he was already gone, but then his eyes opened again.

"You must bring Tazendra to Deathgate," said Aerich, his voice now even more faint.

"Of course," said Pel. "And you as well, Aerich."

"Oh, I, well." Something like a smile spread over his countenance. "I had never before realized the degree to which my conversation would be hindered by an inability to shrug."

Khaavren pronounced his name, "Aerich," again, as if it were an invocation.

Aerich smiled once more, very gently, and then he closed his eyes as if to rest, and his breathing stopped. Khaavren and Pel remained by his side, unable to move.

Outside, they bid a farewell to Tsira, who, still in something of shock, returned to her home. Lar and Clari remained silent, as stunned, we should say, as any of the others, for grief and horror are no respecters of class or House.

Some few minutes later, Pel and Khaavren bore Aerich's body out, and laid it on the ground next to Iatha. Then they returned an instant later with Tazendra's.

Piro embraced his father, and said, "My lord the Count, I am sorry for your loss. I have some conception, I think—"

"Yes," said Khaavren shakily. "And I grieve for your loss as well, Viscount."

"We should see to our friends," said Piro.

Pel nodded, and, when he spoke, there was an edge to his voice, as if only by pretending to coldness could he force himself to speak. "We will return them all to the city, for now. We must get the oils on them soon if they are to be preserved for Deathgate."

"And then," said Khaavren, "it would please me immeasurably if you were to return home."

"It is kind of you to offer," said Piro. "But what of my friends?"

Khaavren glanced at them and, with an apparent effort, he managed something of a smile. "If they like, they may have positions in the Phoenix Guard. I can always set them to chasing bandits."

Piro's own smile came and went like an errant breeze on a still day. "And Ibronka?" he said.

"She is welcome," he said. "I have no more objections to make; my conscience is dead now."

Piro bowed.

"Let us return to the city," said Khaavren.

Chapter the Ninety-Eighth

How the Battle of Adrilankha Ended, And Khaavren Received an Order

After the destruction of Tri'nagore by Morrolan, and the expulsion of the Jenoine by Sethra Lavode and the Necromancer, well, it should come as no surprise to the reader that it became a different battle—if such a rout can, indeed, be called a battle at all. The fact is, history reçords few such one-sided contests as the latter stages of the Battle of Adrilankha.

When Sethra and the Necromancer returned, Sethra did not at once resume command, but, on the contrary, permitted her apprentice to continue for some time while she, that is to say, the Enchantress, made certain she understood the tactical situation.

The battle, at this time, was still continuing on three fronts: the bridges, Lower Kieron Road, and the Old West Road. We trust the reader will permit us to quickly investigate each of them.

To consider the last first, it was here that the efforts of Lord Brimford were most successful, for the simple and obvious reason that the Old West Road runs directly through heavy forests for much of its length after leaving the city. And it happened, moreover, with astonishing speed. As Brimford later expressed it, "I knew Tri'nagore was dead a minute after it happened. Two minutes later the animals in the jungle knew. Ten minutes after that, the enemy knew."

The result was that, in addition to the Imperial Army,

Kâna's forces had to contend with bears, wolves, tiassa, and, above all, greensnakes—these latter being not, in fact, so dangerous as the others, but more than making up for this in the fear they inspired. The Warlock remained in his position behind the headquarters pavilion, taking food nor drink, nor so much as opening his eyes; but General Brawre, in command of Kâna's forces there, was constantly required to bring fresh units up as old units became demoralized even before facing the enemy. And of course, the more demoralized his forces became, the more correspondingly enspirited were the Imperial forces. By the third hour after noon, Brawre was being pushed back, and in danger of being routed.

On Lower Kieron Road General Izak was, at least at first, having things more his own way; indeed, he was having considerable success in driving the Imperial forces backward, although he had not broken them. The fighting around the new-built forts was especially intense, as Sethra the Younger had decided this was as far back as she wished to be pushed, and, as Izak was young and aggressive and had no mind to be stopped, the battle had reached a fevered pitch. This situation changed abruptly at around the third hour, however—that is to say, when the Jenoine was at last banished. This change was marked by thunderclaps, flashes of light, and fires: in short, all the indications that sorcery was working once more, and the Sorceress in Green was wasting no time in using it.

The effect was not instantaneous: the sorcerers still did not entirely know how to most effectively use their abilities, and Izak's troops continued to feel that the day ought to be theirs (and it is well known that such beliefs on the part of an army create their own truths); but the effects could not be denied, and, very gradually, over the course of about half an hour, the battle turned. By the fourth hour, Izak was forced to admit that his army was in retreat, and to send Kâna a message to that effect.

The bridges, we should say, were never in danger after the moment, referred to earlier, when Daro made her famous charge. There were simply too many defenders for the attackers to break through on such a narrow path. When the additional forces from the Northgate Road arrived, Taasra sent half of them down the long stairways to the harbor, where they took small boats across the mouth of the river to come up on the Islanders from behind.

It took over an hour for this maneuver to be completed, but when it was, the results were nothing short of spectacular. In ten minutes, the battle had turned around, and by the fourth hour after noon the Islanders were utterly broken. Some of them escaped Adrilankha to the north or the east, and others managed to get back to their boats (which, because of an oversight, had not been burned), but many were forced to surrender, the condition of their release being negotiated between Her Majesty and the King of Elde over the subsequent weeks.

When Sethra finally resumed command, she at once took several regiments and sent them out under Sethra the Younger by the Northgate Road to strike Brawre's troops in the flank. This maneuver was entirely successful; in ten minutes Brawre would have had trouble finding a corporal's guard for an escort. Of course, he had no need of such a guard, as he, himself, was a prisoner, along with more than two thousand of his troops.

We should interrupt our discourse at this point by observing that it was at just about this time that Kâna turned to his cousin and said, "We have lost."

"How is that possible?"

"I do not know. They must have found a way to expel the Jenoine before Tsanaali could take the Orb."

"My dear cousin—"

"Well?"

"I, for one, am of no mind to be captured."

"With this, I agree."

"And then?"

"Let us send messages to Grita and Illista—I believe we owe them at least that courtesy."

"Now it is my turn to agree with you. And after that—?"

"I know a place not far from here where we will not be

found. The host is loyal to us, and it is well off the main road. Furthermore, the army will not reach it for at least a day. We can rest there for a few hours, and then either make our way east, or perhaps escape to Elde."

"I do not believe the King of Elde would be glad to see us."

"Greenaere?"

"That is a better idea. Come, write the messages, and I will give orders for our horses to be saddled."

"Very well."

Sethra the Younger left a reasonable guard to march the prisoners back to the city (where they were all released over the next few weeks after taking an oath of loyalty to the Orb and the Empire), after which she continued on to perform the same attack on Izak's corps. This was less successful, for the simple reason that, by the time she launched her attack, Izak was already retreating, with two cavalry regiments in pursuit.

By the fifth hour after noon, everything was, in effect, over. When Sethra the Younger returned, she bowed to the Enchantress, who returned her salute and said, "It looks as if matters are under control here."

"So it appears. Well done."

"The same applies to you, my dear. I will turn command over to General Taasra. Can you assist in arranging warehouse space for a hospital? It seems we need considerably more than we had expected here, and you have the right to claim what is needed."

"Certainly, General, I shall do what is required."

"Excellent. Then I will go speak with Her Majesty and inform her of developments."

According to orders, Sethra the Younger found Taasra and said, "My lady, I have the honor to give you command of the Imperial troops now occupying Adrilankha."

"My lady," said the other, "I accept this command, and be assured I will do my duty—the more-so," she added, "as there appears to be little enough to do beyond setting up camps to hold the prisoners."

"See they are well treated, then."

"Of course; Sethra Lavode would have it no other way."

"And may I impose upon you for your horse?"

"Certainly, I shall not need it for some hours."

"I will make certain it is returned."

"That is good of you."

Sethra Lavode returned to Whitecrest Manor and reported to Her Majesty. As we have already given the reader the substance of this report, there is no reason to repeat it now. While she was giving this report, which, we assure the reader, was tolerably pleasing to Her Majesty, Khaavren entered, and saluted them both.

"Welcome back, Captain," said Her Majesty.

"I have been back for some time, Majesty," said Khaavren. "I have been seeing to the embalming of my friends, preparing them for Deathgate."

"I'm sorry, Captain," said the Empress.

Khaavren bowed.

"Captain," said Sethra Lavode, "I have just had the honor of informing Her Majesty of the charge led, most successfully, by the Countess."

"Indeed?" said Khaavren. "That is very gratifying, and I thank you for your kindness in mentioning it."

Sethra continued her narrative, explaining what she had discovered upon arriving at the cave.

"So it was, in fact, a Jenoine," said Zerika.

"As well as certain others, one of whom was a Phoenix."

"How, a Phoenix?" cried Zerika. "I thought I was the only Phoenix!"

"Now you are," said Khaavren coolly.

"What was his name?"

"Her name was Illista," said Sethra.

"Illista? Surely not—could it be? But of course, she was exiled to Elde, and Elde has attacked us."

"You know her?" said Khaavren.

"The Orb remembers," said Zerika.

"Ah, yes," said Khaavren, then looked away, because his imaginative mind at once followed a path which led him to recall the incidents of his last association with Illista, and the adventures he had shared with Aerich and Tazendra.

Sethra, appearing to understand something of what was passing through the Tiassa's heart, made haste to continue her report to the Empress.

"The Necromancer was of great assistance. As, I should add, was the Lord Morrolan."

"Morrolan? What did he do?"

"He dispatched a god."

"A god?"

"One named Tri'nagore, who had made a pact with the Pretender, which was interfering with Brimford."

"Brimford?"

"And the Necromancer as well."

"How could he kill a god?"

"I do not know the details, Majesty. I only know he succeeded."

Sethra nodded, reflecting. "Where is he?"

"I believe he has returned to Castle Black, Majesty."

"I wish to see him."

"Instantly?"

"At his convenience."

"Yes, Majesty."

The Empress considered for a moment, then nodded to Sethra. "Splendid," she said. "So, then, the enemy is routed on every front?"

"On every front, Majesty."

"For my part," said Khaavren. "I am inclined to believe that this was the Pretender's last throw."

"Indeed," said Zerika. "We appear to have weathered the storm."

"I am glad to hear it, Majesty."

"There is, however, one thing needed to make our victory complete."

"If Your Majesty will condescend to tell me what it is, I will do my utmost of see that it is done."

"I wish this pretender to be arrested."

"Ah, yes. I am in entire agreement with Your Majesty. And his cousin?"

"Yes, she as well."

"Very well, Majesty. It will be done. But first, Majesty, I should like to inspect the guards."

"I believe the danger is past, Captain."

"No doubt Your Majesty is right, but I found six of my guards dead, and another eight wounded, just from the front doors to this room. Perhaps it was unavoidable, but Your Majesty must understand that I do not believe in the unavoidable. To me, it indicates that my defenses were inadequate, and it is only by luck that I have been spared disgrace. Your Majesty is welcome to as much courage as you please, but so long as I am Captain of the Imperial Guard, I must do as I think best in seeing to the safety of Empress and Orb."

"Well, but isn't it the case that the longer you delay, the harder the arrest will be? Consider that, even now, they must be realizing that they have been defeated, and if they are not running now, they certainly will be soon."

"Your Majesty—"

"Well?"

"I answer for the arrest of Kâna and his cousin."

"You answer for it?"

"Entirely."

The Empress looked doubtful, but she could not question Khaavren when he spoke in that fashion.

Khaavren bowed, excused himself, and carried out his inspection quickly and efficiently, after which he had his horse saddled, and he set off to the west.

By the time he reached the fortifications on Lower Kieron Road and was able to speak with Sethra the Younger, he was told that matters were well in hand.

"By well in hand, does that mean the enemy is routed?"

"Thoroughly, on all three fronts."

"Her Majesty suggested this might be the case half an hour ago."

"It was then, it is even more true now."

"So much the better. But—"

"Well?"

"Kâna must be aware of this fact."

"Undoubtedly, however slow his communication might

be." We see that, only in the course of this one battle, sorcerous communication had so spoiled Sethra the Younger that she was now contemptuous of any other form.

"Prisoners?" said Khaavren.

"What of them?"

"Have you any?"

"They are being brought in as they are secured. The enemy, as I have said, are in full retreat, so I had not deemed prisoners to be of the first importance."

"As to that, I cannot say. But there is one in particular I am looking for."

"The Pretender himself?"

"Exactly. And his cousin as well."

"If they had been caught, I should know—all of my officers are looking for them."

"Very well, then they are still at large."

"And then, you are to look for them?"

"I am to more than look for them, I am to find them. And, having found them, I am to arrest them in the name of the Empress."

"I understand, Captain. Would you care for a regiment to assist you? I have them to spare at this moment."

"Thank you, my dear General, but there is no need."

"How, you are going alone?"

"I will move faster that way."

"Not even a company?"

"I thank you, my dear, but I must be on my way."

"Then I have nothing to add except to wish you good luck, Captain."

"And the same to you, General."

Chapter the Ninety-Ninth

How Morrolan Received a Gift From the Demon Goddess and Was Uncertain if It Were Intended to Be Practical or Decorative

Morrolan was more than a little startled to discover, upon returning to Castle Black, that it was only a little past the hour of noon. He called for a guard to care for his horse, recommending especial care, as he had already become rather fond of the beast, and walked through the double-sized main door of his castle. He smiled a little as these doors opened on their own, just like the door at Dzur Mountain that he had seen.

As he passed through these doors, he was still attempting to calculate an explanation for the odd behavior of the Furnace, which he could tell (being above the Enclouding) was far higher in the sky than it ought to be.

He had only made a few steps inside when he was greeted by Lady Teldra, who bowed and welcomed him, hoping he was well.

"Why, I am perfectly well, although I confess to a certain confusion."

"Confusion? Well, if there is a way that I can assist you by helping your understanding of some issue, you have but to ask, because I believe it is best to clear up confusions in the mind as quickly as possible."

"Well, we will see."

"What, then, causes this confusion?"

"It is this: I have just been in Blackchapel."

"How, you have?"

"Yes, I just this very instant returned. And there—"

"Yes, my lord?"

"Well, it was late afternoon. And this makes me wonder if I have somehow contrived to travel backward through time, which Sethra Lavode pretends is impossible, as we all must travel forward through time at an exact rate of sixty seconds each minute. Or if I have not traveled backward through time, if, somehow, a day has gone by without my being aware of it."

"Why, my lord, I am convinced that neither of these things has happened."

"Neither? But then, what has happened?"

"My lord, today is the day upon which the Warlord reckons the battle should take place for Adrilankha. And, to judge from certain strange portents, I believe it is even happening."

"How, is it?"

"I give you my word it is, my lord."

"But then, how can it already be late afternoon in Blackchapel, and just barely noon here?"

"Well, my lord, you must remember that Blackchapel is east of us—considerably east of us. You cannot have forgotten how many leagues west we journeyed, in addition to no few leagues south."

"And so, if it is east—"

"Then dawn occurs there before it occurs here."

"The Gods! By so much?"

"Certainly."

"You cannot be mistaken?"

"My lord, this fact is well known among the Orca—that is, those Orca who sail. When they sail eastward, the day starts and ends noticeably sooner; sailing west, when wind and currents permit, why, the day becomes longer after starting later."

Morrolan shook his head. "What accounts for such a thing?"

"There are many theories, my lord, that account for it, but, so far as I know, none have been proven."

"Very well, then, it seems I must accept this. I shall have to get used to it, I suppose. Are there calculations that explain how a certain number of leagues of easting will result in day beginning so much earlier?"

"Well, yes, my lord, but traveling north and south also has some effect."

"How, does it?"

"Certainly."

"I cannot conceive of why."

"My lord, I beg you will believe me. This phenomenon has been speculated upon for many thousands of years."

"North and south you say?"

"Yes, my lord. And I even repeat it. And I have heard, although I will not swear to its veracity, that among Orca who take long voyages to the south, such as trading expeditions to Landsight, when one travels far enough south, it is just as if one were traveling north."

Morrolan spent some moments attempting to work through this in his mind, but at last he said, "It is all too confusing, Teldra; I cannot make sense of it."

"I will find the tables and charts that explain it, my lord, and I will have them put in the library so that you may look at them at your leisure."

"That will be good. Perhaps I will, too, at some future time. But for now, I declare to you that sorcery is far less complicated."

"As to that, my lord, I cannot tell."

"Well, I insist upon it."

Teldra bowed.

Morrolan frowned. "Lady Teldra," he said.

"My lord?"

"How is it that, no matter what time of the day or night I arrive, you are here?"

"Oh, as to that, well, I believe it is nothing more than chance."

"Do you think so?"

"If not, it is some instinct of which I am unaware. But then, someone must see to it that you are greeted, and that you are able to break your fast, and that any messages that may have arrived are delivered to you."

"My dear Teldra, you are turning into something that is halfway between a wife and a servant! It is hardly your place to see to those matters."

"And yet, they must be seen too."

"That is true. I require a larger staff."

"As to that, I am in complete agreement with Your Lordship. Indeed, I have mentioned this very thing two or three times."

"Have you? I beg your pardon; I must not have been attending. Well, I am convinced, and I shall certainly see to it as soon as possible."

Teldra bowed.

Morrolan took himself into the small dining room, where he was given a breakfast of sausage, klava, redberries in heavy cream, melon, and pastry stuffed with beef and mushrooms. Toward the end of this repast he was informed of a messenger, whom he directed to be sent in at once. It proved to be an errand runner from the Warlord, who informed him in tolerably laconic terms that the enemy had been defeated, and that, moreover, Her Majesty wished to see him whenever it was convenient.

"Well then," observed Morrolan after the messenger had departed, "The phrase 'whenever convenient,' which I believe I can interpret literally, is certainly gratifying, as I am not yet ready. For one thing, I must certainly be dressed properly to visit Her Majesty."

Morrolan's first use of this unexpected gift of time, however, was to drink another large glass of klava. He was therefore indulging himself in this when he was informed that another wished to see him, this being none other than his high priestess, Arra.

When she entered, Morrolan rose and bowed, saying, "My dear, come and share klava with me."

"I should like nothing better, my lord."

When Arra was seated and, having mixed the klava to her own specifications, including not only heavy cream and honey, but a drop of the extract of the vanilla bean, was sipping, Morrolan said, "I think you will be pleased to know that matters with the barbarians have been seen to."

Arra frowned. "I do not believe I understand what Your Lordship does me the honor to tell me. May I beg you to be more precise?"

"I have, last night and this morning, visited three of the hamlets where live those who raided Blackchapel."

"How, alone?"

"No, I had Blackwand with me," he said, touching the hilt of his weapon.

"I see. Well, and what was the result of this visit?"

"They will not be conducting any raids for some time, I believe, on Blackchapel or anywhere else."

"How, and the god who aids them?"

"He will no longer manifest in our world."

He said this quite calmly, while sipping his klava; Arra stared at him in silent astonishment. She wished to ask him what he meant or to beg him to explain, but, in fact, his words had been too clear for any explanation to be required.

Presently she said, "Well, perhaps I ought not to be astonished after all."

"Oh," said Morrolan, "not that I wish to congratulate myself overmuch, but, I believe a certain degree of astonishment is appropriate."

"And yet, I ought to have expected it—or, at any rate, something not too unlike it."

"But, how could you have known?"

"My dream."

"Ah, ah! You had a dream! And yet, did you not say that you have been unable to do a Seeing these last months?"

"Certainly many weeks."

"You must remember, Arra, that we are now in the Empire, where a month is only seventeen days."

"Ah, you are right; I had forgotten this circumstance. Well, months then. And yes, it is true; something has interfered with my ability to do a Seeing; but, nevertheless, I had a dream that felt very like."

"Then perhaps it was Tri'nagore who was interfering with this most exceptional and valuable ability. And, with him now gone—"

"Why, my lord, I believe you may be right! He is truly gone?"

"He is," said Morrolan, not without a certain air of complacency.

"It is astonishing."

"Well, but what was this dream?"

"Do you recall the tower you had constructed for the worship of the Demon Goddess?"

"Remember? You perceive, Arra, it is not something I am likely to forget."

"So much the better. Well, in my dream, I was standing in that tower, and I stepped through the window, and I found myself in the presence of the goddess herself, in a place all of white, with pillars and high arches. I bowed to her, and she smiled into my face, and then I was awake."

"And did it feel to you that it was a Seeing?"

"It did indeed."

"Well, that is a most remarkable dream, only—"

"Yes?"

"If you remember, I had the tower built with no windows at all, so that nothing might interfere with my ability to concentrate upon communing with the Demon Goddess."

"That is true. Only—"

"Yes?"

"I should like to look."

"You wish to climb into the tower?"

"Yes, I should like it very much. You perceive, the dream was most vivid."

"My dear Arra, you know very well that you may enter the tower whenever you desire; you need no permission."

"I am not insensitive to your kindness in this regard, my lord, only—"

"Yes?"

"Would you wish to accompany me?"

"How, you would like me to go there as well?"

"If you can spare the time, my lord, I should like it very much."

"Very well, my dear. Let me but finish the last swallow of this estimable klava, and do you finish yours, and I am with you."

"You are very kind, my lord."

"Come, then. You see that I have finished."

"As have I."

"Then let us to the tower. Your arm?"

"Here it is."

It was a considerable walk to reach the tower: a walk made more considerable by several required detours, some caused by ongoing construction, one by work to repair the small hole Morrolan had made when his sword had emitted a kind of spell on its own. Eventually, however, they reached the place where a crude metal spiral staircase wound up to a wooden trap-door. Morrolan went first, pushing open the trap-door and his head through the hole, and then stopping, crying out, "The Gods!," his voice echoing oddly down from the tower.

"What is it?" said Arra.

"Well," called down Morrolan, "I should instead say, the Goddess."

"But what is it?"

"You must see."

"My lord, I cannot; you perceive that you have not moved, and your—and you are occupying the only entrance."

"I beg your pardon, Arra. I shall move directly. There, here is my hand. Take it and come up."

"Thank you, my lord, but—the Gods!"

"Rather, the Goddess."

"Yes, as you have said."

"You dream was, indeed, a true Seeing, Arra. There is a window in my tower."

"A window? I beg your pardon, my lord, but there are many."

"How, many? I see only one, although, indeed, what it looks upon is most remarkable."

"One? You see only one window? And yet, I clearly perceive several, all around the tower. There are . . . I cannot count them. They appear to move about. It is strange. Twenty? No, not so many."

"Come, sit down, Arra. I give you my word, there is only one; I am now standing before it. And a fine, prodigious window it is, although looking through it I am growing delirious; the view keeps changing, and is, at no point, showing what ought to be below us—that is, the dawn in Southmoor, with a small stream and a bridge, and part of the walls of Castle Black."

Arra shook her head. "I cannot understand it, my lord, but I give you my word that, for my part, I am seeing many windows, each of them showing something different. This one seems to be looking out at a place that is under water—under *green* water, for all love—complete with strange fish, and the remains of a ship, or part of a ship, lying wrecked upon the bottom. This one is showing what appears to be a sort of roadway, with hundreds of strange beasts moving upon it at great speed. This one, why, this one appears to be the the same place that, in my dream, I saw as the Halls of the Demon Goddess: pure white hallways with rows of pillars, although there is what seems to be a kind of fog floating upon the ground, which fog was entirely absent in my dream."

"Yes . . . I am getting a glimpse of those same things in the one window that I perceive. But then, consider: This is a gift from the goddess. We cannot expect it to make sense, nor ought we to think to see the same things."

"Yes, yes, you are certainly right, my lord. But I think it is less a gift than—"

"Yes?"

"A token of gratitude."

"A token of gratitude?"

"Exactly."

"But, a gratitude for what?"

"Well, what did you do this morning, my lord?"

"Ah, ah!"

"I think the goddess is not displeased with the removal of this god; the Aflatus implies she never cared for him."

"You have read the Aflatus?"

"It is in your library, milord."

"I was not aware. I must read it myself, someday. But, in any case, if what you say is true then so much the better. I dare to hope the Warlord will not be displeased, either, as it seems this god had, perhaps, made a pact with our enemies here in the temporal world."

"I know nothing of that, milord, except it seems you have done something remarkable, and I honor you for it."

"You are too kind."

"Not in the least. Pray, how did you manage it?"

"Oh, as to that, you know something about it, because you assisted me."

"Yes, that I remember, only you gave me no details of whom you were battling, nor how."

"Why, after I had received the invaluable assistance of the Circle, I thrust my sword into him, and, well, he died, that is all."

"A tolerably good thrust, I believe."

Morrolan bowed and continued his contemplation of the window, at last saying, "It is a grand token of gratitude, indeed. Although—"

"Well?"

"I could wish that it were somewhere else."

"Why is that?"

"Why, so that I could have the pleasure of showing it to my guests in large numbers, instead of one at a time by bringing them up here. I wonder if it could be moved."

"My guess is that it cannot."

"You are most likely correct."

"My lord?"

"Well?"

"The windows are certainly not uninteresting to look at—"

"Indeed."

"—but I wonder."

"Yes?"

"Do you think they might have a use?"

Morrolan frowned. "A use? Do you mean such as permitting me to look upon some interesting place?"

"Yes, that, or something else."

"I had not considered that possibility. I had assumed it was, well, decorative."

"May I suggest you consider it, my lord?"

"An excellent suggestion, Arra, and one that I will endeavor to follow."

"I think that would be an excellent notion, my lord."

"Well, yes. But come, this window either requires detailed exploration, or to be ignored entirely until a later date, and I have no time now for such exploration, as I have been told Her Majesty wishes to see me."

"Yes, my lord."

"Only—"

"Well?"

"There is one thing I must attempt."

"Very well."

"There. Ah, it worked. Indeed, it was simplicity itself. Did you observe a change?"

"No, my lord."

"How peculiar."

"What did you do?"

"Well, that view of the white hallway, that you believe may be Verra's home—"

"Yes, my lord?"

"I desired the window hold that view, and, as I formulated the wish, why, so it did."

"But then, as I see a multiplicity of windows, it is but natural I would see no change."

"Oh, natural. Bah. There is no *natural* in anything that concerns our goddess!"

"Since you express it so, I must perforce agree with you, my lord."

"It may be that I can cause it to show me other things, as well as other places. No doubt some of what I am seeing are other worlds entirely. It is most remarkable."

"Indeed it is, milord."

"I should show the Necromancer; I am convinced that she would have interesting observations to make."

"For my part, I am convinced that you are right."

"Do you know, Arra, it seems to me that I could step through that window, and I should be, well, wherever that is. The goddess's home, perhaps."

"My lord, that would not astonish me. Shall you do so?"

"I am tempted."

"Well, but the Empress."

"Yes, yes. That is true. And, as we have been assured that time runs differently in the Paths of the Dead, well, I should think the same might well be true in the Halls of the Demon Goddess."

"Indeed, my lord, I believe I would very nearly expect it."

"So, then, if I do, I might be able to explore, and return with only the briefest instant having elapsed."

"That is possible."

"Or, to the left, I might step through, and step back, and find that years, or, indeed, centuries have gone by and that as a result I have entirely missed my appointment, and offended Her Majesty."

"That is also possible."

"And, then, I might step through, and be unable to return."

"I had not considered that."

"Well?"

"It is not impossible."

"Do you know, I most certainly must show this window to the Necromancer."

"You are full of wisdom, my lord."

"But, alas, I must wait until I have had my appointment; I believe empresses do not like to be kept waiting, even when they use such phrases as 'when convenient.'"

"I should not be surprised if this were true, my lord."

"Therefore, I must go and dress, and then make my way to Whitecrest Manor."

With that, he managed to tear himself away from Verra's fascinating gift. Bidding farewell to Arra, he returned to his apartment and dressed himself in the traditional black and silver costume of a Dragon warrior.

This done, he took himself once more to the courtyard and

very carefully (he was rather weary by this time, the klava notwithstanding, and so felt the need to be particularly careful in his use of potentially dangerous sorcery) caused himself to appear in Adrilankha, at the only place he was sufficiently familiar with, that being outside of Whitecrest Manor. As this was his destination, it did not, in the end, present any inconvenience.

He took himself inside to appear before the Empress, where he received her sincere congratulations on his latest accomplishment, about which she seemed remarkably well informed.

"Your Majesty is too kind," said Morrolan.

"Not in the least. In fact, I have not even begun to be kind, because, in fact, I have not yet had the opportunity for kindness. But I hope and expect to remedy this soon, wherefore I must insist that you return in a week's time."

"A week, Your Majesty? I will not fail to be here."

"Very good, my dear Count," said Zerika, and dismissed him with a thousand compliments.

As he had made the journey, he took the opportunity to fill himself in on the events of the day, which afforded him, in addition, the chance to receive the congratulations of several others, including Sethra the Younger. He learned of the attempt on the Orb, as well as the death of Aerich and Tazendra, both of whom held his esteem. He had saluted Pel while visiting Her Majesty, but had not yet seen Khaavren, for which reason he asked Sethra the Younger where the Tiassa might have gotten to.

"He is arresting the Pretender," she said.

"Ah, is he? How large a detachment did he take?"

"He went alone."

"Did he? Well, do you think he might need some help?"

Sethra the Younger considered this for a moment, then said, "It is unlikely."

Chapter the One Hundredth

How Khaavren Carried Out The Arrest of Kâna and Reported The Results of His Mission To Her Majesty

When his conversation with Sethra the Younger was concluded, Khaavren mounted once more and set out at a good speed along Lower Kieron Road. At first, he passed Imperial regiments that were involved in pursuing the remains of Kâna's army; then, after a mile or two, he began to catch up with some of those who were fleeing. At no time was he offered violence, or, indeed, anything but a few looks of fear—the Pretender's once proud army was beaten and demoralized; now divided among those who were fleeing as fast as they could, and those who, too weary and depressed to even run, had thrown themselves by the side of the road to wait for capture, or whatever else fate might have in store for them.

Those few with horses were luckier than the others, except when they were dragged from their horses by panic-stricken infantrymen who would then fight over who should get the use of the animal, until it either ran off by itself or was taken by someone and ridden a mile or two until he, in turn, would be pulled off and the process repeated. Khaavren, however, was not touched, and those who looked at his naked sword, blazing eyes, and grim countenance quickly gave him room to pass as he traveled along the road littered with swords, javelins, spears, shields, uniform cloaks, service caps, and emblems of rank.

We should add that, as fast as Khaavren traveled, and as weary as he was from a day full of battle, death, and even heartbreak, nevertheless his keen eyes missed nothing; indeed, had anyone asked, he could very nearly have given a full list of the items he passed.

In this way, Khaavren soon came to a place where, next to the side of the road, a banner lay upon thc ground—a banner upon which he recognized the arms of the Duke of Kâna. He drew rein here and considered. Looking around, he realized instantly that this was where the Pretender had set up his field headquarters.

Here he dismounted, tied up his horse, and spent some few moments making a careful study of the ground, beginning with the banner and moving in a slowly widening spiral until his sharp eyes had scanned every inch of terrain in a circle some forty yards in diameter. This done, he mounted upon his horse once more and again set off along the road, now riding, if anything, even faster.

After about an hour he made a turn, following a smaller road to the north, and he continued along this, now having left all remnants of the fleeing army behind, for a period of nearly three hours. As darkness was falling, he observed a quiet inn built of wood, and painted white. He tied his horse to a rail in front of the house and took himself to the stables, where he found a stable-boy in the process of grooming and brushing a proud black mare, with another horse, this one grey, patiently awaiting its turn.

He handed the boy a silver orb, saying, "Saddle these two horses and have them outside of the house in ten minutes."

"But my lord," said the boy, "they have only just—"

"Do as you're told," he said.

"Yes, my lord."

As the boy obeyed his orders in a fashion most military, Khaavren turned on his heel and brought himself into the house, where the host, a wizened little man, recognizing the gold half-cloak he wore, at once gave him his full attention and an obsequious bow not unmixed with a certain look of discomfort. Khaavren, with no hesitation, drew his sword and placed the point at the host's throat.

"Which room?" he said.

"My lord, I do not understand—"

Khaavren applied a little bit of pressure, the point very nearly breaking the skin.

"Which room?" he repeated coolly.

The host swallowed and, after a moment during which he must have performed a number of close calculations, he said, "All the way in the back, on the right."

"Where?"

"Through that curtain."

"Do nothing, make no sound."

"Yes, my lord."

Khaavren turned his back on the host, went through the indicated curtain, and walked all the way back until he was opposite the last door on the right. He remained still, listening until he was able to make out soft breathing from within. Then, taking a step backward, he gave the door a kick with such force that it was pulled entirely from its hinges.

Inside were two persons: a woman lying on the bed as if asleep, and a man sitting in a chair, legs stretched out in front of him, also appearing as if he were asleep—or had been asleep until rudely awakened by the door falling in.

Khaavren held his sword out in front of him with the relaxed confidence of one who knows its length and said with tolerable coolness, "Your Venerance the Duke of Kâna, and my lady the Marchioness of Habil, I have the honor to arrest you in the name of the Empress."

For an instant neither moved. Kâna made a glance at his sword, which was within his reach but not in his hand, and appeared to be considering. Khaavren said nothing, content to let the Duke make his own decision. At length, Kâna sighed and said, "Very well. Sir, I am your prisoner."

Habil said, "I am not dressed. May I beg for a moment? I will give you my parole."

"Certainly, madam. His Venerance and I will wait outside."

In two minutes, Habil joined them. Khaavren said, "Your horses are outside, saddled."

"Who are you?" said Kâna.

"A soldier."

"More than that, I think. Who betrayed us?"

"No one."

"Bah. Then how did you find us?"

"That is of no importance, Your Venerance. And now if you will be good enough to accompany me?"

Kâna sighed, nodded, and preceded Khaavren down the hall. "A soldier, you say?"

"I have that honor."

"The Imperial Guard."

"Yes, Venerance."

"The captain?"

"I am the captain, yes."

"May I have the honor of knowing your name?"

"Khaavren of Castle Rock."

"Khaavren!"

"That is my name."

"I had thought you had resigned!"

"I did, but then I was cured."

"I see."

"I must explain that, should you attempt to escape, I will kill whichever one of you is in reach, and then chase down the other."

"I understand."

"As do I."

"Then let us go."

He led them out past the host, who, in strict obedience to his orders, had made neither sound nor motion. They emerged into the night, mounted on their horses, and, without a word spoken, turned back toward Adrilankha at a sedate walk.

In the middle of the night they reached the Manor, where Khaavren instructed a guard to place them in one of the empty rooms with the understanding that they were to be watched at all times. He made a careful inspection of this room to assure himself that it contained nothing they could use to aid an escape, then remained there until he was certain the guard detachment had arrived, after which he went to report to the Empress. Upon learning that Her Majesty had gone to bed, Khaavren quickly determined to do the same.

He entered his apartment, where he was greeted by Daro, who said, "Ah, you are back!"

"Cha! You are awake, madam?"

"I wished to wait for you, though I didn't know how long you would be gone."

"I am told that you played the hero to-day, madam. Indeed, I hear you praised from no lesser quarters than Her Majesty, the Warlord, and Sethra the Younger."

"Bah, it was nothing."

"On the contrary, madam, it was a great deal. And I am delighted. But are you injured?"

"Merely a scratch on my hand. But what of you?"

"Oh, me? I had a tolerably full day."

"And yet, it seems that all is not as it should be."

"You are perspicacious, madam. But I cannot yet speak of it."

"When you need me, my lord, I will be here."

"You always are."

"I am glad you are home at last."

"Yes, I have done some riding. I had to complete an errand for Her Majesty."

"Well, and have you done so?"

"Oh, yes," said Khaavren. "It is done now."

Early the next morning, Khaavren presented himself to Her Majesty.

"You are back already, Captain," observed Her Majesty.

"I returned last night, Majesty."

"There is, then, some trouble?"

"Trouble, Your Majesty?"

"Yes. Have you returned because there is some sort of difficulty?"

"None whatsoever," said Khaavren.

"There being no trouble, then, did you require to return for additional troops?"

"Not in the least."

"Well, but then, why have you returned so soon?"

"Because the mission with which you entrusted me—"

"Yes, the mission?"

"It has been completed."

"How, completed?"

"Entirely."

"What do you tell me?"

"I have the honor to inform you that the Duke of Kâna and the Marchioness of Habil are now in an upstairs room of this manor, with guards outside of their door, and another outside of the window—which window, incidentally, I also caused to be barred, because I should have been embarrassed to have to arrest them again."

"Then they are here? Prisoners? In this house?"

Khaavren bowed.

"And you say they are under this roof?"

"Yes, Majesty, and guarded. I have even made certain this morning, before I did myself the honor to wait upon Your Majesty, that they have gone nowhere."

"So then—"

"They are here, awaiting whatever fate Your Majesty might select."

"As to their fate," said Zerika grimly, "there is no possible doubt."

"I should imagine not," observed Khaavren, shrugging to indicate that this was no concern of his.

"But, how did you find them?"

"Does Your Majesty wish me to relate the history?"

"Yes, yes! By all means!"

"In that case, I shall do myself the honor to describe the process by which I found them."

"Yes, yes. That is what I wish. And this instant, if you please."

"Very well. I concluded, in the first place, that if I were in command of an army determined to attack the city from the west, I should place my headquarters somewhere within five or ten miles of the city on Lower Kieron Road."

"Not the Hartre Pike?"

"Lower Kieron is not only wider, it is also flatter, which provides more places where a headquarters might be established."

"And therefore?"

"Therefore, I searched, and I found the headquarters at the site of Barlen's Pavilion, which Your Majesty may or may not be familiar with."

"Oh, I know it; but how did you recognize it?"

"It is not difficult, Majesty, to find a headquarters that has been abandoned in a hurry."

"How, it is not?"

"Not in the least. In the first place, there was an abandoned flag with the Duke's sigil."

"Well, yes, I understand how that would be a good indication."

Khaavren bowed. "But, even without that, there were pieces of paper scattered everywhere. One cannot have a headquarters without paper, and one cannot abandon a headquarters quickly without leaving a great deal of it behind. To be sure, much of the paper had been burned, and much had been scattered about by the winds, but there was certainly enough left to leave no doubt about what the place had been used for."

"Very well," said the Empress, "and so you found the headquarters. But they were not there, were they?"

"Oh, no. As I have had the honor to say, it was abandoned."

"So then, finding it was not of great use."

"On the contrary, Your Majesty. Finding the headquarters was so useful that, once I had found it, I knew that my quarry could not escape me."

"But, how can that be?"

"Why, all I had to do was to inspect it."

"Inspect it? But, for what?"

"Why, for indications of how they had fled, and where they were going."

"What sorts of things would tell you this?"

"Does Your Majesty wish to know this?"

"Certainly I wish to know. You perceive, I asked."

"That is true. Well then, Your Majesty will soon see."

"Very good. And so, you inspected the abandoned headquarters area?"

"I covered the ground as thoroughly as a redhound searches the grasslands for waterfowl to startle for a skilled slingman."

"Well, and what did you find?"

"In the first place, certain papers, crumbled and thrown at the fire, but not destroyed. That is to say, there were many such, but two in particular struck my eye."

"And what were these interesting papers?"

"They were both addressed to a certain Grita—someone who is of considerable importance to me, but not to Your Majesty, and someone who is, moreover, now deceased—and they both contained phrases such as, *we have lost this round*, or, *we have suffered a severe set-back*."

"Or, from our standpoint, we have won."

"Well, yes, that is true; it is all a matter of perspective."

"Yes. Go on, then."

"But each expression was slightly different, and neither of the notes were complete."

"So you concluded that these were . . . ?"

"Drafts of a message to be sent to Grita, who, in addition to being important to me, as I have said, is someone of no small importance to Kâna and Habil."

"Drafts . . ."

"The Pretender or his cousin had written these messages, and, the phrasing not being entirely correct, had abandoned the effort and, presumably, tried again, until it satisfied the writer."

"Well, but what then?"

"There were phrases on these notes that indicated thoughts such as, *we will make contact with you when we are safe*."

"Well, and then?"

"Why, this proves that they had a means of escape in mind."

"How, does it?"

"I give you my word, if they were simply running, with no destination in mind, it would have been phrased differently."

"Yes, I can see that."

"Moreover, there was suggestion that this Grita was not alone—but, rather, that there was another whom Grita was to inform of the circumstances. Of course, as it happens, I know who that other person was."

"Illista."

"How, Your Majesty knows this?"

"Never mind, Captain. Continue. You were saying that the note suggested that someone was with Grita."

"It also suggested to me something else."

"And that was?"

"That the two of them—that is to say, Kâna and Habil—were likely to be escaping alone, and together."

"I understand the together, this is implied by the *we,* but why alone?"

"Because Grita, to whom this note was addressed, was not there in their encampment, otherwise, why write a note? Moreover, I know where she was. And she was important, or why be concerned that the expression of thoughts is exactly right? In such an undertaking as this, well how many conspirators can there be who are important; that is, who cannot be abandoned when all is lost? One? Perhaps two? They wanted no one with them who would slow down the escape, or would attract the attention a large group attracts. And so, if there were one or two who were not present, who else would accompany them in their escape?"

"I believe I understand. So what did you do then?"

"Oh, I continued searching."

"And what did you find?"

"Water bottles."

"Water bottles?"

"Exactly. Water bottles."

"How many?"

"Ten."

"Is this significant?"

"Extremely."

"How so?"

"Because Kâna and Habil did not take them along when they fled."

"But, because some water bottles were left behind does not mean that other water bottles were not taken."

"Oh, certainly. But how many water bottles would there be in a headquarters area? Certainly not hundreds—they would be in a commissary area, or the supply depot, which is different, although perhaps nearby. Not hundreds, then, and probably not scores. A dozen, perhaps? Fifteen? Even twenty?"

"Well, and if there were twenty?"

"If there were twenty, and our friends only bothered to take ten, then that limits how far they expected to travel without stopping: they would not have wanted to stop on the road more than necessary. Now if it *was* twenty, that perhaps means very little; yet I was inclined to think there were not so many."

"And this meant?"

"First, that they did not plan to travel far on the first day—in other words, that they had arranged a safe place to hide in case of disaster, and that it was not far away. And permit me to add, Majesty, that from what we know of Kâna and his cousin, this didn't startle me."

"Very well. What else?"

"If they were only going a short distance, they had no need to spare their horses."

"Yes, I can see that this is useful information. But then?"

"Cha! Your Majesty, if, knowing that I was looking for two horses, riding together, and galloping as fast as they could go, I could not identify the tracks of these horses leaving the headquarters area, well, I am not the tracker I thought I was. Your Majesty must know that with stride, shoeing, size, and weight, well, it is unlikely that a close observer will be unable to identify the tracks of a particular horse."

Zerika took a moment to work out all of the negatives in the sentence, then said, "Well, I understand that. But surely you could not track them on the road, with its hard pavement, and hundreds of horses a day on it even if there were tracks to be seen!"

"I had no need to. Once I knew which horses I was looking for, and knowing that they planned to leave the road soon, I had only to look each time I came to a side road and see if those tracks were there."

"And did you find these tracks?"

"Certainly I found them; how could I not? They turned off onto a small road."

"Which you followed?"

"Exactly. Fortunately, there was still daylight, so I did not have to use a lantern, which would have slowed me down."

"Well, and then?"

"After a short time, and a few additional turnings, I found a little cabaret with the tracks of their horses leading directly to it."

"And then?"

"And then?" Khaavren shrugged. "There is little enough left to tell, Majesty. I then went to the room, acquired admission, and begged the Duke and his sister to have the goodness to accompany me back to Adrilankha. They consented, and here we are."

Khaavren finished this recital with another self-deprecating shrug.

"Captain, you astonish me."

"That is very gratifying, Your Majesty."

The next day, Zerika had a private audience with the Pretender and his cousin, the results of which have not, alas, come down to us. Later that day an executioner's star was constructed outside of Whitecrest Manor, and, after a few hours to arrange their affairs, the Marchioness of Habil and the Duke of Kâna were executed by having each limb struck off in quick succession, concluding with their heads. To their credit, it must be admitted that neither uttered a cry or a complaint, Kâna himself only observing, "I believe that I should not have made a bad Emperor, if I'd had the chance."

Chapter the One Hundred First

How the Gods Considered
The Events Which Had
Lately Occurred in the Empire

We return now, for a last time, to the realm of the gods: the Halls of Judgment. On this occasion, a judgment is in progress, but not, as is usual, the judgment of the shade of a deceased mortal, but, rather, the living embodiment of one of their own number, that being, as the reader has no doubt already deduced, the god known as Tri'nagore.

We may consider, then, that he is standing in the middle of the circle we have already described, and is, moreover, held in place, although no bonds are visible, while the Lords of Judgment consider his actions, and the appropriate punishment. Tri'nagore himself has said little while they spoke.

"Above all," observed Verra, "it was stupid."

"Stupid?" said Barlen.

"Say rather, treacherous," said Ordwynac.

"Not in the least," said Verra.

"How, it was not treacherous?"

"Not as you mean it," said Verra.

"Would you care to explain?" said Barlen.

In answer, Verra addressed Tri'nagore, saying, "Why don't you explain why it is you thought it was safe to permit a Jenoine to enter our world?"

As this word was pronounced, several of the gods made various signs and gestures.

"I did not," said Tri'nagore.

"You did not think it was safe?" said Barlen.

"I did not give Those We Do Not Name access to our world."

"He is lying," suggested Ordwynac.

"No, he isn't," said Verra.

"But then, if he is not," said Ordwynac, "how did Those We Do Not Name Except For Verra Who Does gain access?"

"I don't know," said Tri'nagore.

"I do," said Moranthë.

"How, you do?" said Barlen.

"Certainly."

"And would you care to tell us?"

"I should be glad to."

"Do so, then."

"It was necromancy."

"Necromancy?"

"Yes."

"Who was the necromancer?"

"His name is Loraan."

"But," said Ordwynac, "we have been able to determine that this Kâna made a pact with our friend here."

"Certainly," said Verra. "In order to counteract the effects of witchcraft."

"And that is all?" said Barlen.

"That is all," said Verra.

"But," asked Kelchor, speaking for the first time, "why did he help him at all, knowing that we had determined to aid Zerika?"

"As I said," remarked Verra, "he was stupid."

"That is all very well," said Barlen. "But might we prevail upon you to be more specific?"

Verra shrugged. "He was gambling that Kâna would win, that's all. If Kâna won, and he had a pact with him, well, more power for Tri'nagore. You must understand that he gets lonely with a few score of Easterners on this world, and perhaps twice as many on his own world, and a handful other places. But give him an emperor who is beholden to him, and it would be another matter."

The gods glanced back and forth, considering this remarkable chain of reasoning, and, at the same time, curious about whether their associates found it plausible.

At length, Kéurana said, "That's stupid."

"So I have explained, sister," said Verra.

Tri'nagore stood silent, indifferent, as if this conversation had nothing to do with him.

"For my part," said Kelchor, "I am inclined to believe it."

"As am I," said Moranthë.

The gods studied Tri'nagore with various expressions of puzzlement, disbelief, annoyance, and disgust.

"Well," said Barlen, "what do we do with him?"

"Nothing," said Trout.

"How, nothing?" said Barlen.

"He is no longer able to manifest on that world," said Trout. "That is sufficient."

"And this council?" said Nyssa.

"I suspect," said Moranthë, "that no inducement could convince him to manifest here for a hundred millennia."

Barlen chuckled. "As for that, I suspect you are right."

The others of the gods nodded their agreement.

"You may go," said Barlen.

Tri'nagore vanished without a word.

"So then," said Ordwynac to Verra. "It worked as you wished it to."

"Nearly," said Verra.

"The pact with the Dragonlord certainly proved fruitful," said Kelchor.

"It is kind of you to say so. But what is most important is that, once more, we have kept the world safe, and now the Orb is back, and the Empire is well on its way to returning."

"I do not disagree," said Ordwynac. "I freely confess that you were right. In a hundred years, the Empire will be as it has always been."

"Twenty years," suggested Kelchor.

"I wish to observe," said Verra, "that certain parties will be appearing before us for judgment soon—parties who have played no small rôle in these events."

"Well, what of it?"

"There are certain of them that I should like to reward appropriately."

"You know very well," said Barlen, "that we neither reward nor punish, but, rather, make judgments for the common good."

"I know very well," said Verra, "that you have always insisted that this was the case, in spite of overwhelming evidence to the contrary." Barlen appeared about to argue, but Verra said, "Come, can I not claim this as a boon?"

Barlen sighed. "Very well. For my part, I have no objection. You may judge them as you will. You may consider it a reward for your victory."

"I would prefer to think that it has been a victory for all of us," said Verra.

"That is a good opinion to hold," said Ordwynac.

Chapter the One Hundred Second

How the Empress Showed Her Gratitude and Khaavren Obtained a Leave of Absence

The celebration for the victory of the Battle of Adrilankha lasted an entire week. During this week, the only merchants who were open were those selling comestibles and potables, and they did such a brisk business that their capacity was strained to fill the orders. Few of these orders, be it understood, were for the official celebration; but there is nothing like an official celebration to spawn and encourage scores of unofficial ones.

The streets were chaos, littered with broken bottles, cracked paving stones, pieces of door, bits of paper, occasional residue of fires both sorcerous and mundane, exhausted city guards, and other signs of celebration. There was one organized procession, on the second day after the victory (that is to say, the day after the executions), in which Her Majesty rode through the streets escorted by the army, to the cheers of a people who were by this time delighted to be celebrating as much as for the actual cause. It wove its way around the city, even crossing over the Iron Bridge into South Adrilankha and making its way up the River Road before returning on the Two Pennies Bridge, by which time, darkness having fallen, it became a procession by torchlight, which is always a moving experience.

In addition to this procession, there were dozens of spontaneous parades, smaller, often begun by squadrons of the army and requiring Khaavren to act as a police-man to bring them under control and put them into one of the stockades that had been hastily thrown up to house the prisoners taken in the battle.

On the third day of the celebration Sethra Lavode gave the orders to move the army out of the capital, which helped a little.

Morrolan was often seen at Whitecrest Manor during this week, visiting with Her Majesty or with Khaavren.

On the fifth and last day of the celebration, Zerika summoned all of those most concerned in the victory to the manor. The covered terrace being too small for such a gathering, the Countess of Whitecrest volunteered the ball-room, which was tastefully decorated for the occasion by a single Imperial sigal, a banner with the Phoenix, another banner with Zerika's arms (gold crossed with red, an Orb, a scepter), and the finest chairs that could be procured. There were gathered the Council of Princes, and other representatives of the Great Houses, as well as those Peers who were able to be there. Sethra Lavode and several of her officers occupied one side. Pel remained quietly in the background. Khaavren occupied a position by Her Majesty's left hand, his eye running over those assembled carefully, though more from habit than from any need.

Daro, Piro, Ibronka, and Röaana were as near Khaavren as could be contrived. Ibronka and Piro, out of respect for Khaavren's sensibilities, avoided any physical contact with each other. Ritt stood next to Röaana, looking as if he would have preferred to not attend.

Brudik, Lord of the Chimes, announced the arrival of Her Majesty. Everyone would have stood for her entrance, save that there was no room for chairs, and so everyone was already standing.

When the room had quieted and Her Majesty had seated herself, Zerika distributed distinctions as follows:

The Sorceress in Green was appointed to be Court Wizard and special counselor to Her Majesty.

Sethra the Younger was made Warlord, the Enchantress

having informed Her Majesty that, the crisis now being over, she wished to retire to Dzur Mountain. Sethra the Younger could not keep the delight from her countenance, and bowed repeatedly, murmuring thanks in which her words could not be distinguished.

Sethra Lavode, for her part, was given nothing, but the ban upon her presence at court was lifted, and an official apology was tendered both from the Empire, and from the House of the Phoenix. While it was impossible to be certain how pleased the Enchantress was at this honor (for to have a dishonor removed can be construed as an honor), she made a deep courtesy in response, and those who knew her best—that being the Sorceress in Green and Sethra the Younger—believed that, for one of the few times in her life, she was truly moved.

For Morrolan, the county of Southmoor was raised to a duchy, to include all of his other counties and baronies as part of it.

This generosity on the part of Her Majesty astonished and delighted him far more than, in fact, he would have expected, although his principal reaction was to observe to himself that Lady Teldra would be delighted to be seneschal to a Duke. He bowed very low to Her Majesty and expressed the desire that he would have the opportunity to die in her defense as soon as possible.

The Viscount of Adrilankha, Ibronka, Röaana, and Ritt were granted an Imperial pardon, although Her Majesty neglected to specify the crimes for which they were being pardoned. Nevertheless, this did afford Piro, Ibronka, and the others a certain peace of mind.

Next, Her Majesty summoned his Discretion the Duke of Galstan, who came forward, dressed in the modest costume of his office, and bowed deeply.

"My dear Galstan, I wish to acknowledge here, before the court and all present, that, some days ago, I did you a monstrous injustice."

Pel bowed, saying, "Your Majesty need make no such declaration; it is sufficient to me that I have been of service to the Empire."

"You have been of great service, Duke, and, moreover, your loyalty has been proven by the blood you spilled upon the floor of this very room." We must observe in passing that Her Majesty had written this speech thinking that the ceremony was to be held in the covered terrace, and had neglected to change it. At the time, no one noticed the error, but we feel obligated to mention it to avoid introducing unnecessary confusion.

"Your Majesty is too kind," said Pel.

"And yet," said the Empress, "the fact remains that, for a while, trust was broken between Empress and Imperial Discreet. However much I might regret it, such a breach can never be entirely healed. For this reason, I have no choice but to remove you from your post."

Pel bowed, keeping his disappointment entirely from his features. This he was able to do for two reasons: The first was that he had, all of his life, trained himself to prevent his emotions from being visible upon his countenance. The second was that, although he did not know what Her Majesty might have in mind, he knew that, after all that had happened, she would not thus publicly disrate him without having some compensating reward in mind, and so he waited patiently.

He did not have to wait long; she continued at once saying, "You have proven your courage, my friend, and your wisdom, and you have shown by all of your actions that the interest of the Empire itself is dear to your heart. I can imagine no better use for your skills than to be my Prime Minister, and so help me with your counsel and your skills to aid in the rebuilding of the state that has been so battered and torn. Will you accept? If not, I shall have to find something else for you, because I tell you frankly that I will not permit talent such as yours to be wasted, nor loyalty such as yours to be unrewarded."

However much he might have expected, and however much he might have hoped, the ambitious Yendi had never dreamed that he might rise so high—or, at least, so high so soon. Khaavren observed, with a certain pleasure, that not only was Pel trembling, but he was, for once, unable to keep his ecstatic gratification from showing in his eyes.

At length, Pel spoke in a creditably strong voice, saying, "Your Majesty, I only hope that I can prove myself worthy of the honor you have given me, and I give you my word, I shall, every day, try my utmost to insure that Your Majesty never for an instant regrets having shown me this trust."

"That is all I can ask," said Her Majesty.

As Pel at last backed away with trembling knees, the Empress said, "And last, let me see my Captain of the Guards, Khaavren of Castle Rock, Count of Whitecrest."

Khaavren came forward and bowed humbly to Her Majesty, who in the first place deeded him the small but fertile valley for which he was named, and so the title of Marquis, with which Aerich had addressed him so long ago, was now his in a most official sense; his pleasure in this title was real, yet it was not unmixed with sorrow, as he could not help but regret that he would not be able to jest upon this subject with Aerich.

Zerika, however, had not finished the granting of titles to our brave Tiassa. "Lord Khaavren, or, should I say, Marquis, is it not the fact that, alas, your father passed away during the Interregnum?"

"It is true, Your Majesty, I had that misfortune."

"And your mother did not even live so long?"

"Your Majesty, my poor mother was taken to Deathgate before I first entered the Imperial service."

"And is it not also the case that, a thousand years before he died, your father was forced to sell the county of Shallowbanks back to the Empire?"

"Alas, Your Majesty, my family has never been wealthy."

"Well, I shall not make you wealthy, my friend, but at least you shall have, once more, the name to which you are, by tradition, entitled; and the county of Shallowbanks, as well as the marquisate of Khaavren, are now restored to you."

"Your Majesty!" cried Khaavren, dropping to his knee and bowing his head.

"You are pleased, my dear Captain?"

"Oh, Your Majesty!" said Khaavren, and when he looked up at her, tears could be seen glistening in the old soldier's eyes, and it is only just to add that, on this occasion, not all of these tears were of sorrow.

"Well, well," said Zerika, for her part delighted to no end, for it is well known that there is little in life that brings us greater pleasure than to give joy to someone about whom we care deeply.

This concluded both the awarding of distinctions, and the celebration of the victory, but, as the reader no doubt must assume, it only began the repercussions of the battle.

In the next two months, all of the Houses sent representatives to Adrilankha to swear fealty to Zerika, concluding with the House of the Lyorn, whose representative, the Count of Flowerpot Hill and Environs, without withdrawing any of his earlier remarks, confessed that, with all of the other Houses having officially confirmed Her Majesty's position, it would be inappropriate for his House to take a position so clearly contrary to fact. The Count then, still without any allusions to the charge he had made before, told Her Majesty that, if she wished, he would withdraw as Heir so that someone could be found who "would be better suited to this important honor."

Zerika smiled benevolently, declined, and said that she could imagine no one else who would better represent the interests of the House of the Lyorn, and that she looked forward to the opportunity to work closely both with him and with his House in the upcoming Meeting of the Principalities. It is only just to add that this action was suggested to her by the ingenious Yendi, who had also counseled the Lyorn to tender his resignation, and that this method of proceeding acquired for the Empire a strong and very important ally for the upcoming meeting, as well as securing for the Count his position as Heir, which had been somewhat tentative of late.

The following day, Khaavren begged for an audience with Her Majesty, who was, once again, busying herself with the plans, drawings, and models for the new Imperial Palace, as well as for the Great Houses to be erected around it (a task that involved much consultation with Daro, we should add, as no small area of the city of Adrilankha and the county of Whitecrest needed to be demolished as part of this construction). In addition, there was the meeting to which we have referred above, which occupied no few hours in Her Majesty's day. Nevertheless, she was more than willing to take two minutes to attend to the brave Tiassa when he presented himself before her.

"Come in, Captain," said Zerika. "Is there some way in which I might be of service to you?"

"There is, Your Majesty, and a great service it would be."

"Name it, then, my friend; you know that I have no small affection for you."

"I am not insensitive to this, and I think Your Majesty knows how grateful I am for the honor you do me."

"Well, what is it, then?"

"Your Majesty, you know that I lost some friends in the late battle."

"Alas, Captain, I know it well."

"And now that the battle is over, and something of normalcy is returning—"

"You wish to bring them to Deathgate?"

"Yes, Majesty. I would wish a leave of absence, in order to complete this errand, which is of no small concern to me. The bodies have been anointed, and preserving spells have been cast on them, but, nevertheless—"

"Yes, Captain. I understand. How long will your errand require?"

"I do not know, Your Majesty. Perhaps as much as a year, as we have chosen, in honor of Aerich in particular, who would have preferred it, to bring him the long way, rather than using teleportation."

"I quite understand, Captain. Very well. I grant you, and your friend the Prime Minister, leaves of absence for two years from to-morrow."

"Your Majesty is most gracious."

"And then it only leaves me to wish you the very best of fortune."

Khaavren bowed and took his leave, going at once to the terrace, where he found Daro, Piro, and Ibronka all engaged in conversation. He tenderly kissed Daro's hand, embraced

Piro, and nodded cordially to Ibronka. "Come," he said, "what is the subject under discussion? Tell me, and perhaps I will have something to say on it."

"Perhaps you will, my lord," said Daro tenderly. "Look, then."

She pointed out toward the sea. Khaavren, looking in the indicated direction, at once saw what he identified as the masts of a ship.

He turned to the Countess and smiled, no words being necessary.

Epilogue

How They Returned To Deathsgate Falls

It was on a mid-summer's day in the third year of the Reign of the Empress Zerika the Fourth that Khaavren, Pel, Piro, Ibronka, Röaana, Ritt, Lar, and Clari came to the place where the Blood River begins to flow fast and straight, picking up speed for its plunge over Deathgate Falls. The air was sharp and cold, and there was a trace of snow upon the ground as they made their way along the bank.

Ritt and Lar each drove the wagons, as they were the only ones who could handle a two-in-hand; the others rode horses. The giant jhereg circled high overhead, but, because of the size of the party, were content merely to observe.

They stopped just past the icon of the Chreotha. Lar and Clari managed to pick up Mica's body, wrapped in its black blanket, carry it across the water, which here came only to mid-thigh, and bring it to the icon of the Teckla. They each lit a stick of incense, and Clari left an offering of wheat and tears. Then they dragged him out into the water, removed the blanket, and watched him drift away. Lar set in the water his bar-stool, which drifted off behind the body. Khaavren, Pel, and the others watched in silence until it had vanished behind a gentle curve.

They returned to the west bank, mounted their horses once more, and continued.

They did not stop at the icon of the Tiassa, although Piro,

Röaana, and Khaavren all solemnly saluted it. Khaavren said, "Viscount, when my time comes—"

"Of course, Father."

Pel, who was riding behind them, said, "I suppose that, if there is a time to be morbid, well, this is it."

Khaavren turned around and gave him a look that is impossible to describe.

When they reached the icon of the Dragon, they drew rein, and the wagons creaked to a halt.

Piro lit incense at the icon and left an orange as an offering (though we have not mentioned it before, Kytraan was especially partial to this fruit). Then Piro, Ibronka, Röaana, and Ritt picked up the white blanket holding Kytraan's body (his head had been sewed in place before the embalming oils and preservation lotions had been applied, as was customary under such circumstances), and, wading out into the river, they set him down, held on to the blanket, and let the current carry him away.

They continued a little farther; then it was time to pick up Tazendra's body and bring it across the river, wading through water over their knees, to the icon of the Dzur. Pel lit the incense, and Khaavren left an offering of dogwood. Pel and Khaavren, by themselves, then carried her body back into the water, set it in the current, and removed the blanket. Tazendra drifted away toward the Falls while Khaavren and Piro stood in the middle of the stream, watching her.

"She seems to be smiling," said Pel. "Was that deliberate, when she was embalmed, or was it actually her expression?"

"I'll leave you to wonder about that," said the Tiassa.

An offering of bread was left at the icon of the Tsalmoth for Iatha, and one of sugar was left at the icon of the Iorich for Belly. Ritt performed both of these rituals, and helped to bring their bodies into the river.

They returned to the west bank, and continued past the icon of the Hawk until they reached the Lyorn, just before the sculpture of Kieron the Conqueror, which in turn was just before the wide area leading to the lip of the Falls.

"That is where the fight was," observed Piro.

Khaavren looked around and nodded, his sharp eyes and lively imagination re-creating the battle in his mind. "And she leapt from there," he said.

"Yes."

"I can nearly see it."

Piro nodded.

"I honor her for it," said Khaavren as he dismounted. "It was one of those moments that define a person. You have the choice between the desperate but necessary, and the possible but useless. Not many can make the right choice there."

"And for others," said Pel, glancing at the black blanket in the wagon that contained the remains of Aerich, "it is easy."

Khaavren nodded. "There were, indeed, things that were easy for him that would have been difficult or impossible for anyone else."

Pel knelt by the icon of the Lyorn and lit a stick of incense. Khaavren laid a topaz there.

"Do you think he enjoyed life?" said Pel.

"Of course," said Khaavren with no hesitation.

"How, you really think so?"

"Certainly. When you are making your plans and schemes, and watching them come together piece by piece, or when you have discovered a way to cross a street by manipulating a sorcerer into teleporting a crate there, after manipulating a warehouseman into concealing you within the crate, then you are enjoying life."

Pel chuckled. "I do not deny what you say. And then?"

"And when Tazendra was in a battle, the odds overwhelmingly against her, she was enjoying life."

"You are right again. And Aerich?"

"For Aerich, well, he was one of those who took pleasure in merely the passing of the days, and the growing of his grapes, and the knowledge that he had done his duty."

"There are not many like him," said Pel. "Even among the Lyorn."

"That is true."

"And what of you?" said Pel.

"Me?" asked Khaavren.

"Yes. When are you happy?"

"Come, help me with his body."

They brought him into the stream and released his body into the river, watching as it went over the lip of Deathgate Falls and disappeared in the swirling mist.

Conclusion

How the Author, At Last, Closes His History

In the sixth year of Zerika's Reign the Palace was deemed, if not finished, then at least ready to occupy, and so Khaavren and Daro had their home to themselves once more. For some years Piro and Ibronka shared this home with them, but, in the long run, the strain of living with Khaavren's grudging approval began to irritate Ibronka, and so she and Piro acquired an apartment in the city—an apartment which they continue to occupy, for which reason it would be indiscreet to reveal here its precise location; and discretion, while not the most stern duty of the historian, must nevertheless be considered.

It was also the case that, every morning, Khaavren was required, instead of going down stairways and through corridors, to instead mount his horse and ride three-quarters of an hour to the Palace in order to arrive at his post. More than this, there was always a delay, more or less prolonged, while he made arrangements for the stabling of his horse in whatever was being used that day for temporary stables. Remembering the old Palace, where horses were not permitted to be stabled within a certain distance of the Imperial Wing, Khaavren did not see fit to complain of this. Another effect of Zerika's occupation of the Palace was that Khaavren no longer saw Pel quite as often, as the Prime Minister believed he could do his work the better the less visible he was.

If the reader is confused about our reference to Her Majesty occupying the Palace in the sixth year of her reign, while the reader recalls very well the procession and celebration accompanying her entry into the Palace at the beginning of the eleventh year, we should observe that when Her Majesty officially announced the Palace as ready to occupy, she had already been unofficially conducting Imperial business there for some years.

There is no reason to imagine that there is any truth to the stories of artisans working on the Palace and messengers running errands there becoming lost among construction and amid the constantly altered temporary passageways, so that they were never found, wandering still to this day within closed-off sections. As we say, we have no reason to believe such tales, but the nature of the construction then occurring was certainly such as to give these stories a certain veracity.

Piro and Ibronka continued to see Khaavren and Daro socially, which was better for all concerned. In addition, they also saw Zerika, and Shant and Lewchin (the latter two of whom eventually became more friendly with Khaavren, in spite of the Dzurlord's innate stubbornness). Röaana and Ibronka were officially accepted into the Society of the Porker Poker, though the Society never did actually meet as such during the remainder of Zerika's Reign. Zerika claimed it would begin meeting once more when she stepped down from the throne. There are rumors that it still gathers once every decade; whether this is true we cannot say.

Morrolan's entertainments at Castle Black continued to be legendary, as did his sword, which became especially famous at the Wall of Barrit's Tomb years later. Sethra the Younger and the Sorceress in Green were often to be seen at these affairs, along with less savory characters, and the Enchantress of Dzur Mountain herself was an occasional visitor, as was the Necromancer, who continued to live at Dzur Mountain, and, so far as we know, never returned to her own world.

Ritt joined the Imperial Guard, where, in the year eighty-five, he received a promotion to ensign, which post he continues to occupy at this writing.

Her Highness Sennya died in Adrilankha in the ninetieth

year of Zerika's Reign. It is known that Ibronka was at her deathbed, although we do not know of what their last conversation consisted; nor would we be inclined to divulge it if we did, because there are some matters that should, perhaps, remain beyond the scope of history.

To the reader who has, we hope, a certain sympathy for the brave Khaavren, and wishes to know how he lived out the remainder of his days, we cannot answer this question, for the simple reason that, as we write these pages during the glorious reign of Her Majesty Norathar, he is still alive, and at his post, and, perhaps, making more of the history we have endeavored to tell. While we do not anticipate continuing to chronicle his actions (at some point, after all, the historian must give way to the purveyor of *news* even though these two categories of the reporting of facts are often interchangeable and sometimes very nearly identical), we shall pretend to place a terminus on a road that continues to open before us.

Yet, the reader may wonder, as Pel did: Is Khaavren happy?

This question, in addition to being intrusive when considering a man who yet lives, breathes, and perhaps even reads these words, is more complex than it may appear. The Khaavren we first met—that is, the bright, talkative enthusiast who arrived one day at a hostel in the village of Newmarket—is dead. He died once when betrayed by Illista, again when His Majesty Tortaalik was killed, yet again when he became estranged from his son, and again at the death of Tazendra and Aerich, who were, in essence, a part of him.

Yet there is a man who wears his boots (and his sword), and who speaks with his mouth, and feels with his heart. This man is, as far as we can know, happy in the continued affection of his son, and the love of his wife, and the performance of his duty—that is, the continued feeling of being useful in a cause in which one fervently believes. Is this happiness? Insofar as the duties of an historian require an answer to this question, permit us to suggest that it will do.

While we know, then, how Khaavren lives, it is less certain with regard to he for whom this history is named, that is, the Viscount of Adrilankha.

There are stories, here and there, of occasional appearances by the Blue Fox. These take the forms of popular songs, folktales, rumors, and poorly established reports to local constabularies. In these stories he is most often found rescuing a noble but helpless widow, orphan, or Teckla. It is possible that these stories have some substance in truth, but then, the author is certain that these stories would occur whether or not this dashing and romantic figure ever donned his azure cloak again—he had become a legend, which removes him from the realm of history, and thus from the concerns of this author, whose only concern with legend must be to the extent that the belief in these legends has an influence on the actual course of history.

And yet, it must be admitted that such an influence can be considerable. When man acts upon a belief, the truth or spuriousness of the belief does not alter the action that has been taken, and the actions of men are based upon beliefs, whether the prosaic and obvious belief that, perhaps, one is more efficient after a night's rest, or the more daring and intriguing belief that one can convince another to take a particular action by reasoned argument, or the courageous and idealistic belief that one knows how to make the world a better place. It is always man's ideas which drive his actions. This has, at times, resulted in great evil; but as we look around us, we cannot doubt that it has resulted in greater good.

History and legend, as well as the individual's own experience (of which the knowledge of history and the sensibility of legend are a part), help to form the beliefs that determine action, and here is where the telling of history finds its intent. In giving the reader an understanding of even a small part of the truth, and thus helping him to understand his world, and perhaps even helping him to understand something of the consequences of choice, we have, to paraphrase Master Hunter, made a contribution to keeping at bay the evils of despair that follow from a false vision of inevitability.

Seeing our own rôle, then, as the introduction of comprehension and hue where there was confusion and sallowness, we hope, as we conclude as best we can the history of our friends, that the reader may take away from this journey something that will help him to follow—or create—his own path through the myriad of choices and actions that, together, form the complex tapestry that we call history, or life.

Afterword

ENCOUNTERS WITH PAARFI AND THE GODS

A Series of Biographical Vignettes Incorporating a Mythographic Account that May, Through Juxtaposition, Prove Informative

By Ivan Sekély, Witch-Antiquary of the North

This is not a preface, and ought not be used as one, though it should be admitted that no actual harm will be done thereby; the fish does not care if is served before the cheese, though the diner may, if he is mindful of the ginger.

Doubtless many, if not most, of you are wondering who on earth is this individual chosen to grace (if that is the proper word) the concluding volume of this series, why he among all the living was chosen, and what ought to be expected. To answer these questions in reverse order:

I have not the faintest idea.

I was requested to perform the service by Paarfi of Roundwood himself, with whom, as the persistent will discover, I have a long and rather varied acquaintance.

My formal office is generally held to be mythographic, sometimes mythopoeic, and occasionally literary; in general, I might be described as one who dwells in the upper attics of the House of the Athyra, in the hope that the other bats will teach him to fly.

When I first encountered Paarfi of Roundwood, it was in the distant town of Cenotaph. This place draws its name from an ancient monument to what was probably a battle, though the sources disagree. I was present to research representations of Ordwynac on ceremonial lanterns, when I discovered that Paarfi would be visiting to meet his reading public; I took one of his books and went to the dealer's stall where the event was to take place.

As I arrived, however, Paarfi was gathering to depart in what seemed a great hurry, to the confusion of other waiting book-buyers and against the background of some kind of commotion at the nearby inn. I held the book out as he passed, and reminded him of a meeting some years earlier at the University, whereupon he smiled somewhat tensely, scribbled a message on the flyleaf, and was gone in the next moment.

After allowing the ink time to dry, I read:

Three Aces of Swords
is at least one too many to be caught holding.
Yours in haste, P.

The reader, whose attentiveness we must always presume, will have noticed that I have used the phrase, "the first time I met Paarfi," yet spoke of a prior meeting. Understand that my use thereof does not indicate our absolutely initial encounter, but our first meeting under a particular circumstance of time and place, or condition of the man himself. I have seen objections, in the voluminous academic criticism of his recent work, to multiple iterations of, let us say, "Khaavren crossed such and such a river," as if it were the same river each time, which any mythographer can tell you is a patent impossibility. I would not fill your time and precious memory with repeated occasions of identical meetings; the first time scholars agree that the bean soup at the University refectory bears small sign of beans, and less of soup, being much like the fiftieth such.

* * *

When I first met Paarfi of Roundwood, we were both at the University, I as a visiting scholar-without-portfolio, he still as an undergraduate. Precociously as usual, he had attained that state of aggrieved anomie that, while it attends only a few of the student population, is a grave affliction to that number.

"Have you noticed," he said, over hot klava and a cold pear pie, "a particular condition amongst the distinguished graduates of this academy?"

"I can think of several such."

"It is only one I have under consideration."

"Well," said I, "discarding such minor matters as wearing the University colors or carrying a sword marked with the sigil of the University combat team—"

"Particularly among those who were not members thereof."

"—yes, particularly so—there is the frequency with which they are found at the Inn of the Phoenix and Infant, or as it is known so well locally, the Roast and Rugrat."

"A fact indeed, which marks you as an astute observer of your surroundings. But not the one I think upon."

"Perhaps, then, it is the habit, which is fairly universal these days, of dressing as very old men while at lecture, regardless of actual age or sex."

"We are glad to be reminded of this affectation," said Paarfi with approval, and an early appearance of his. "You will agree, I venture to say, and understand that I am not diverging from your subject, that men and women are more alike than they are different, and in this I do not refer to my immediately prior observation."

"Well. And well."

"Then, young scholar, if we are to make of this a drinking game, we shall both be insensible long before a victory is determined, and while this might be pleasurable in the short term, it might also prove expensive, given what I have observed to be your tastes and despite my volume. So, as the huckleberries are in season, as it were, allow me then to purchase you a drink, and we shall nigh instantly be at the object of our duello."

"Well," Paarfi then said, acknowledging that no disingenuity was intended by ordering a good but modest wine, rather than the sweet essential which I had otherwise imagined would be his gift to us both.

Once we were served, he continued, "As you know the way to a student's heart, I shall call it first blood and concession. My predicate, then, is that these emeriti are all *still here,* excepting only those misfortunate or careless enough to be dead. Now, sir, what other institution is so retentive of its output? Healers go off to their practices, soldiers join a company, or likely several in series, even the Court sees some rotation, with the Cycle if not more hastily and violently. To take it to extremes, even the village midden gives up fertilizer to the general, and the occasional piece of furniture and oddment to the more, or shall we say less, particular. Only here is Time caught in an impasse."

"It must be said that no other such institution has the eminence and respect of this one."

"Well; and yet, ought this not encourage some diffusion, knowing that one's talents would only shine the brighter, away from so much brilliance?"

"Perhaps if we may venture so far—"

"'We'?"

"Yes, esteemed scholar, you and I as well."

"Ah. Well. Proceed."

"Let us syllogize then. I pretend that they are here to be in one another's company. You pretend that they are here not to be in the company of others. They pretend they are here because they have chosen not to be someplace else. Is this good?"

"This is good," Paarfi said, and simultaneously raised his glass, and as he knew that I knew that he knew, all was well.

Now, I ought speak of my ancillary purpose today, which is to recount a tale of the gods that may, let us hope, have some relevance to the principal matter of Paarfi of Roundwood His Life Work and Character, as the letter I have received from his publishing house defines it and them.

It will be understood by the manuscript-fatigued mythologian, but perhaps requires amplification for those who have spent more time in other galleries of the great Library of the World, that attributions in tales of the gods are problematic, and in some few instances wildly divisive, as the healers of any center of learning will attest. When, in the course of the tale, it is said that "Verra said such," or "Barlen played thus," I describe an action definite to the story, but only my interpretation, arrived at through research and comparative study, of which of the gods indeed performed it. It might seem absurd, not to say blasphemous, to suggest that the mythographer cannot distinguish Verra from Moranthë, leave aside Barlen from Ordwynac; yet this is, as many examples affirm, entirely the case.

As an illustration familiar to the general, Arriskalo's *Kéarena and Kelchor Walk the Streets of Dragaera by Night in Search of the True Steel* has been, there can be no possible doubt, derived from the same ur-text as e'Zisya's *Trout and Tri'nagore Wander Dragaera by Night in Pursuit of a Decent Cup of Klava,* so much so that itinerant theatrical troupes routinely maintain one scenario for both, ascertaining through the casual enquiries of an advance-man which story the next town most favors, and cutting the cloth to suit.

When I first met Paarfi of Roundwood, he was attempting to teach a colorfully plumed Eastern bird to recite an equally colorful phrase, and simultaneously to hold the attention of a handsome young woman, who was also dressed in bright colors, though with fewer feathers involved. Which action had his primary attention I could not tell, though the woman, of course, already knew how to speak.

There is a small but vocal group of theologians that maintains it to be a rank impossibility (small but vocal groups of theologians not being given to denouncing the merely improbable) that the gods should play games of chance. The larger audience, however, and a vast number of stories of "the gods at play," hold an opposite view; indeed, most people insist that the gods gamble, and would, at least in terms of their representation in stories such as Paarfi's, think less of them if they did not.

In this matter, I can do no better than to quote from the aforementioned *Trout and Tri'nagore Wander Dragaera by Night:*

> Tri'nagore turned an orb over in his fingers. Though he and his companion still wore human form, there was a clicking as the coin revolved, as if it scraped against scales.
>
> "They may exchange these for food, clothing, a safe or at least somewhat comfortable place to sleep, the services of a healer, or a temporary companion."
>
> "So they do," said Trout.
>
> "Yet you must admit that for food and shelter we have no requirement. Of healing I will not speak, and our lovers must be otherwise attracted."
>
> "It would be absurd to disagree."
>
> "So why, then, do we play at hazard in just such a fashion as they do, when our hazards are of such a different character?"

Now, most of the world must know how Trout replied. For those who may be young, or provincial, I shall return to the point in good time, be assured. But for now let us resume our former narrative.

Two words must now be said concerning the games the gods play. It will be recalled that they hold converse on the meaning and purpose of such activities, and indeed what are gods, whose actions *are* meaning, *are* purpose, to do other than so discuss? Whether these interchanges reach the level of argument (that is to say, in the common sense of acute disagreement, not the scholar's sense of brooking no disagreement) is a matter of mythopoeic interpretation, as some writers will have the deities quarreling almost incessantly, while others have them differ only to show many sides of a single thought.

But for all this, Tri'nagore's observation is true: while the idea of risk is by no means unknown to the gods—Adron's Disaster, we may assume, was accounted a mischance—they do not wager in terms of the price of dinner or even the price of blood. Honor, however, is a concept they know, and how many times have we heard such mortal declarations as, "On this I stake my sacred honor," followed by a sequence of statements that, in the gambler's argot, hedge the bet?

And, too, the gods have a concept of place and prominence, and if they are never wrong, then still one may be more right than another (the reader is referred to the old Court entertainment *Fishes in Their Season* for a most entertaining illustration thereof).

When I first met Paarfi of Roundwood, he was at work on a retelling of the Eastern legend of the Fenarian gulyás—nosferati, whose immunity to the hostile effects of garlic lends them a distinctly tragic grandeur. This work would have occupied several volumes of text and at least two more detailing the recipes sampled by the characters during their long quest. We discussed this over our dinner (a quiet affair of some few courses—fried pork and cabbage rolls, a fish stew, a small duck, cold soup of wild cherries; the rest escape my recall), and, to my everlasting regret, I suggested that perhaps the searching out of these dishes was more Paarfi's motivation than the ancient tale of the hungry undead. Paarfi replied that such thoughts had occurred to him as well, as might be indicated by his proposed title for the work, *Blood and Paprika*.

My regrets are due to the fact that this work seems to have been set aside, if not abandoned, and while I would for nothing be without the books we have and have promised, still the selfish promise of assisting in the historical research seems a lost thing, and all the more romantic therefore.

I could go on, but as the pressmen have been advised that *The Viscount of Adrilankha* is to be published in three volumes, so I am instructed that it is not to become four.

And now, worthy patrons, to our story. It is one generically known to mythographers as *The Gods Play at Eidolons,* and it is unusual in that it involves the entire pantheon, and shows them playing not the common games of Orbs or Bones, but a variant on the contest of symbols known in our gambling houses as Seven-Clawed Jhereg.

As the play begins, the gods settle themselves into their circle within the Halls of Judgment—this step is always mentioned, sometimes with considerable detail of the taking of positions—and each deity receives a secret allocation of two eidolons—images of a particular type and value. Most often the types match those found in the gaming cards of this world—Swords, Orbs, Dzurs, Maidens, and suchlike. Other times they are exotic: Storms, Wounds, Songs. In a few tales the symbolism is obscured from us, though it may somewhat weaken the story to have Verra, let us say, holding the Threes of the Nameless, the Endless, and the Timeless.

It is often asked how the gods, who are given to know all things, at least in the immediate present and the majority of the past, can not know what eidolons their companions have drawn forth. Some maintain that the gods, as part of the system of balance that must exist among such powers, can keep secrets from one another; another view, much favored by the common population, is that the gods could know if they so wished, but they politely do not ask.

When the players pronounce themselves satisfied with the distribution of the eidolons—and in this no one questions that it is not an issue of possible error but solely of courteous assent—they examine their secret holdings, and decide whether or not to enter a wager and join the play, or withdraw.

In the instance to hand, Barlen found himself with the Ace and Seven of Swords. He decided that the strong card and suitedness were worth the risk, and entered his wager.

Verra saw the King and Heir of Orbs, a very strong draw. She no doubt debated whether to match Barlen's wager or advance upon it; seeing the number of players yet to speak, she only matched.

Moranthë saw the Three of Orbs and Heir of Cups, and quietly withdrew.

Kéarana saw the Eight of Orbs and Heir of Dzurs, and, after a long moment of hesitation, likewise left the play.

Ordwynac held the Four of Cups and Five of Swords. He entered his matching wager as if the process bored him.

Nyssa held the Six and Eight of Cups, and matched.

Kelchor saw the Nine of Orbs and King of Dzurs, and remained.

Trout held the Eight of Dzurs and Heir of Swords, and being a wise god departed the hand.

Tri'nagore held the Two of Swords and Ten of Cups, and stayed.

In the next phase of play, three more eidolons appear before all the assembly (those who have abandoned play generally still watch, and often comment sharply). These new images are the common property of all, because, as will surely be apparent on reflection, while each deity has his or her own aspect and power, the greater substance of the Universe is held in common among them. These three additions are known as "the Fall," in token of the great shift from the prior world of gods and their dreams alone, to the establishment of the mortal, material plane.

Our Fall was the Seven of Orbs, Seven again of Cups, and Three of Dzurs.

Barlen now had three Sevens, and wagered again.

Verra saw three Orbs, but no real improvement, and of course the prospect of the remaining two eidolons being suited was small. She withdrew.

Ordwynac needed a Six to make a straight. He wagered and advanced.

Nyssa matched this wager, for what reasons we cannot guess.

Kelchor and then Tri'nagore saw no prospects and dropped out.

Now another jointly held eidolon is added, this one known as "The Four Ways," both because it is the fourth such symbol and representing the paths of the compass, the winds, even a mundane crossroad. In our case, this was the Five of Cups.

Barlen still held his three Sevens, and wagered once more.

Ordwynac now had two pairs, though one was in common (and that the higher in value). Perhaps only from his oft-remarked inertia, he matched wagers.

Nyssa now had four cards in line for a straight, and a straight flush as well. Some tell this story with a touch of precognition on her part, though no gambler would so descend. She raised the wager. The others matched.

Finally one last joint eidolon is shown, this one known as "The River of Dreams." (In certain mortal games, I have heard it called "The Paths of the Dead," but this jest has not yet entered the mythic literature.) All those who remain in competition after the wagering then select five eidolons from the seven available to them, in an attempt to create the most powerful combination.

In our instance, the Four of Orbs appeared.

Now, anyone who held a Six would have a straight. Barlen still held only his three Sevens. He gave what we might call (in mythographic terms) a sigh, and withdrew.

Ordwynac had the choice of three pairs, but of course could choose only two, and another high card, for his final pattern. He wagered and advanced.

The non-gambler may wonder at this, and even the amateur player might ask how deities could hope to bluff one another into withdrawing with superior holdings. The simple answer (and there are complex ones) is the same as that of the wager at all: while one does not wish to walk away, one also does not wish to lose more greatly than necessary, particularly when the option to walk away was there.

Nyssa matched the wager.

Ordwynac said, "Show."

Nyssa's nothingness rippled faintly. "Your pardon?" she said, but revealed her straight.

"Well," Ordwynac said. "And they say *I* am a gambler."

* * *

When I first encountered Paarfi of Roundwood, he had just gone through a distressful round with his former publishers and suffered the storms of academic criticism (though, as has been observed, it was a storm that brought down a great many trees no one heard fall), and I asked him, over a dish of "outlaw's soup" and a spectacular Soproni wine, why he had chosen the (then) rare and difficult task of recasting history in this particular narrative fashion, given its uncertain prospects, footloose manner of life, and highly variable reputation.

He answered me as the wise Trout answered Tri'nagore: "Because it is the only game in town."